Capital Encounters

Love, Loyalty, Freedom, Flings

Dawn Wright

This novel's story and characters are fictitious. While the businesses, locations, and some organizations are real, they are used in a way that's purely fictional. The opinions expressed are those of the characters and should not be confused with the author's.

ISBN: 978-0-9980787-0-0

Dedication

This book is dedicated to my late brother, Ryan. You would want my dreams to live on. May you continue your Wushu kicks in Heaven among the bright blue skies. XOXO till infinity.

table of contents

1: the move and the green-eyed monster

Summer

At twenty-seven years old, I'd finally earned a salary that made it possible for me to move out on my own. I'd soon become a DC resident and no longer one of Arlington, Virginia. Exhausted, I attempted to keep my gray sweatpants from inching down by resting my hands on my very slender hips. I pursed my mouth to one side of my face, taking inventory of the boxes I had stored in our postage stamp-sized living room. Even though I had sworn to people my unwavering enthusiasm about venturing to live on my own for the first time, some part of me felt indifferent, and I didn't know why. The voice of my anal-retentive roommate interrupted my thoughts.

"Summer." Our eyes met. I cracked a nervous smile. "The movers just called regarding the moving date. I confirmed it for you."

One thing I wouldn't miss? My roommate's bland expressions, or her stoic demeanor. I reasoned that my financial crutch made it possible for me to have tolerated her for a year and a half.

"Okay. Thanks, Lora." I sighed and managed to fit into the narrow space on the couch between the arm and a box resting on the cushion. It didn't take a rocket scientist to figure out that she wanted her condo to look like a home again.

I noticed Lora's lingering presence. "Are you nervous?" she asked.

Swiping my hands up and down my thighs, I replied, "You could say that." I looked at her expression. She appeared to be genuinely curious and maybe even concerned.

"You will be fine, Summer. Living alone may take some getting used to, but you will adjust." With bright eyes, she smiled with what appeared to be pride, before heading to her room with her red ponytail bopping behind her.

We were both ready to move on from this living arrangement, since we'd both received raises with our promotions. I was slowly climbing that career ladder, from a receptionist at a staffing firm to one of their junior recruiters. Lora no longer needed a roommate, and I no longer needed a residential subsidizer. Besides, we lived in Ballston, an upscale section of Arlington. Not a place for penny pinchers. Although one day, I knew I'd make it to Northwest, but for now, I could only afford to relocate to Southwest DC; and, anything beats living with a roommate. Luckily for Lora, her parents owned the condo but decided to rent it out to her once they relocated back to New York City.

Talk about having handouts. Well, I didn't have any handouts. As an adult who grew up in a single-parent home, I had to do everything on my own. Having a moment to think, I realized that this promotion vindicated all my post-Delaware moves. The guilt of leaving my mom behind years ago for college had almost devoured my already tiny body. I never gained back the fifteen pounds I'd lost in college. I could only hope that maybe this promotion made it all worth it.

Yesterday finalized my move into my apartment. I'd already anticipated walking the overcrowded strip in Georgetown on a Saturday morning. But before joining the foray of anxious shoppers, I decided to stop for a quick breakfast. Despite the crowded eatery at La Madeleine, I chose to pay and stay, because the food tasted great and it'd been a while since I'd dined there. The place was so packed that I feared having no place to sit. I grabbed a tray anyway and proceeded with my order once the line moved.

After paying the cashier, my eyes did a quick dance to locate a place to sit. I couldn't help but feel like a new girl in the middle of the high school cafeteria looking for the friendliest face with whom to eat. I spotted a woman in a trench coat with her nose and eyes buried in light paperwork, comparing one document to another. I took a chance because all other options were closed.

"Is—is this seat taken?" Her hazel eyes shot up as the hand clutching the pen froze. "I . . . I mean, there is no other place to sit and I—"

A smile broke through her tight lips, exposing perfect white teeth. "No, no." She waved a hand. "Some company would be great." I watched her scoot her papers into one hand and into a briefcase as I took my seat. Her long ponytail swung with each hurried motion. "I'm just grading papers here."

I gave her a grateful smile and ironed my skirt with my hand under my butt to keep from wrinkling the material. I swore I heard a slight accent with that semi-raspy voice. She hesitated and offered a hand. "Emily. Emily Gray."

I accepted her hand and replied, "Summer Stevenson."

"I know, it can be so crowded here." With a light laugh she added, "It's the food." Her big, pretty eyes sparkled. "The food is great."

"That it is. You're a teacher?" I asked as I spooned oatmeal into my mouth.

She nodded. "Mm-hmm. Yes. Third grade, in fact."

Yes, an accent. I knew I'd heard it as I barely masticated my oatmeal. "Really? Which school?"

"Here in DC—Northeast. Dana Key Elementary? Heard of it?"

I squinted my eyes and tilted my head. Why did I pretend to think when I knew I hadn't heard of it? "Uhh, I don't believe I have."

Emily gave me a half-grin. She almost giggled. "Most people haven't. But yeah, that's where you'll find me. And you?"

"I'm a junior recruiter. Well, actually, I just got the position."

"Well, congrats." Her eyes popped as she sipped her water.

"Thank you." I felt shy, and I knew my smile reflected it.

"Where do you work?"

"Oh, I doubt you've heard of it. It's a mid-size agency. DuBois Staffing?" With narrowed eyes and a spoonful of oatmeal in front of my lips, I waited to see if she could recall the name.

"I think I've seen the building. You're in a building with other businesses. Right?"

I nodded, "Yes, yes. We're in Ballston."

"Yup." She shook her index finger at me. "I entered that building a time or two to do my taxes on the second floor."

I couldn't help but chuckle. "That's us, but on the seventh floor."

Emily absently watched her fingers play with the edges of her napkin. She sighed.

Taking a bite of my eggs, I asked, "Where's your food?"

She looked confused before smiling again. "Oh, right. I'm meeting someone."

My fork rested in my mouth, and then I snatched it out. "Oh, no. I didn't . . ." Clearly, I was imposing and started to shift my tray with both hands. I couldn't move fast enough.

"Huh? No, no, oh, gosh no, please." Emily shook her head at me. "Sit down, Summer. You're fine, you're fine." Ushering me with her hands, she assured me to stay seated. "Once she comes, I'll go up and get my food, too." Her eyes became animated before I had a chance to respond. "Oh, there she is."

I turned around to see who she was talking about. My mouth dropped, revealing chewed egg, but I couldn't help it. She looked stunning.

The confident woman sashayed toward us. The brown hair that swept the top of her arms almost matched her medium skin tone. Her pouty mouth puckered slightly as she held back a cocky grin. Her opened anorak jacket, revealed a cropped lime sweater that allowed the bottom row of her six-pack abs to say 'hello' to the world. She marched in her black pumps like no one's business and froze when her waist greeted my face. I instantly felt small in her presence.

She rapidly spanked her clutch against her outer thigh. "Who is this?" Her chin pointed at me before taking her eyes off mine to meet Emily's.

A chipper Emily answered, "Oh, this is Summer. Summer Sssssss . . ." Emily's eyes asked me to help her memory.

I stood up promptly with a chip on my shoulder and offered the broad my hand. "Stevenson. Summer Stevenson."

Her tongue poked her cheek, and I supposed she might've had an attitude. It surprised me that she accepted my handshake. "Brooke Brazile."

I smirked until her grip almost broke my hand. I tried not to cry out, so I grimaced instead. I didn't know why, but I couldn't tell if I liked or hated her. Maybe in this little bit of time she came off too strong. "Nice to meet you," I replied with little conviction as I sat back down to eat.

"It's a pleasure to meet you, too, Summer." Brooke arched a perfectly waxed brow at me and took her place in the third chair. She studied me through her beautiful brown eyes as she reached in her clutch to pull out a business card. "If you ever need a wedding planner," she said as she slid her card across the table. "Here."

She squinted in confusion as I almost choked on my water. I placed a hand across my heart. "Oh, honey, thanks. But I assure you, you are feeding hay to a cat when it comes to me and marriage."

Brooke's eyes widened before she broke into laughter. "Not a response I'm used to hearing, but okay. I get it." Emily and I sniggered. Lora's words rang in my head. You will be fine, Summer. Looking at the faces of these two girls, I instantly felt better about my move.

After breakfast, I gave my phone number to Brooke and Emily before heading back to my new home. As I stepped into the elevator, I realized that I'd officially made it on my own. Not bad for a poor girl from Delaware. My old neighborhood crossed my mind and how my mom should be begging for new scenery, but not her. She loved her neighbors and the familiar stores and streets. The idea of moving elsewhere didn't appeal to her too much.

The elevator stopped on the fifth floor and I stepped off and pulled out the key to open the door to 5F. The smell of fresh paint greeted my nostrils as I locked up and maneuvered through the boxes, following the pathway that I'd made through them. It felt strange to be in my own home. It wasn't much, but for now, I could call it my own one bedroom, one bathroom apartment.

Grateful that I'd paid one of the movers an extra twenty to set up the television and cable box in my bedroom, I stripped down to my underwear and replaced my top with a sleeveless t-shirt and draped it over my bare breasts and stomach. I called my mom before flicking on the Style channel.

I fell asleep with the remote control on my belly and awoke at night. My body felt whipped. Saturday had slipped through my fingers, but the night was still mine to capture. I rolled over and grabbed my cell phone and called Max. I'd met Max in a coffee shop on my first day of work at DuBois Staffing. He'd interrupted me just as I'd prepared to inhale my sesame bagel. I didn't know how to resist a guy with a nice smile and gentle brown eyes.

We dated enough to qualify as boyfriend and girlfriend. But broken dates and schedule conflicts strained our infant relationship. So, we settled on being friends with benefits, which suited me just fine. In the long run, I could do without marriage, since I grew up as a loner with few friends. Besides, having a great career topped my list.

He picked up with a cough. "Hello?"

I smiled. "You know who this is. I'm programmed into your phone."

Max chuckled. "Okay, Summer. You got me."

"You sound tired."

"Work. What can I say?" He moaned and yawned.

"I wouldn't recognize you if you weren't a workaholic."

"It's been a while since I last spoke with you." I heard a sudden spurt of energy in his voice. "So, what made you call?" Max and I broke up four months after I'd joined DuBois Staffing.

I hesitated. "Well, I moved to DC and wanted to know if you wanted to catch up. You know, come over and check out my new digs?" Silence took over. My stomach locked in mid-breath as I waited for a response. Maybe I'd come off too forward, especially since it'd been a while since we'd last talked.

"Sure," he replied. I exhaled with relief. I didn't want to make a fool out of myself.

"Good." After texting him my new address, I got up to take a shower. Once out, I went through a box containing my clothes. I fished through some dresses and stopped when one caught my eye. My boss attached a bonus of two thousand dollars to my promotion, so I treated myself to a few new clothes and used the rest to afford the move. I rested a blue dress against my body and walked over to the bathroom since the boxes hid my full-length mirror.

A tiny-framed woman stared back at me with small breast and a head full of wavy, brownish-blonde hair, which complemented my golden complexion—the result of having a White mom and a Black father. The father I barely knew. He died in a scaffolding accident while working on a building when I was just four. Thanks to the photos that my mom had hanging around the house, I could see Dad's resemblance as my stare locked into my own reflection.

I shook myself until the somber thoughts rolled away. Max. I needed to focus on him. I threw the dress over my head and shook into it until it hugged my frame. Pleased with the way it fit, I attempted to do something with my hair. An hour later, a knock at my door drew me away from the mirror. Satisfied, I yanked the door opened to find a familiar man wearing a leather jacket and loose-fitting blue jeans. Max smiled at me longingly instead of stepping through my wide-opened door.

"Well, ya' just gonna stand there, man?" I teased with a friendly smile.

"Maybe," he replied through his grin.

I yanked him by his jacket. "Get in here."

Emily

Lost in her thoughts, Emily absently walked around her living room. She stopped to trace the slight build-up of dust on her window ledge. Just a piano, a bookshelf and expensive paintings served as décor in that part of her five-bedroom row house. She sat on the piano stool positioned next to the window. Sitting, she raised the blinds to peer out the window to watch the children play in the backyard next to hers. She and her ex-husband intended to build a wooden fence, but their divorce nipped that plan in the bud.

Crestfallen, Emily decided to take a walk to the neighborhood playground. Tightening the belt of her trench coat, she felt the wind gently push against her body as soon as she opened the front door. Upon her arrival, she sat in the swing and absently kicked her shoes into the mulch, swaying her body with each kick. The woe-is-me attitude seemed a bit healthy from time to time, so she welcomed it. In fact, Emily embraced it, because the Lord knew she'd grown tired of the strong front she had to uphold at work when co-workers went overboard with the pity glances.

Just when she felt the tears greet the rims of her eyes, Emily noticed a brown shoe beside her boot. Daring to look up, her eyes met the gaze of a man with friendly, blue eyes. Feeling bashful, she offered a reluctant smile and slowly lowered her eyes to the ground. But on the way down, she noticed hands stuffed in pockets on either side of a generous package below a flat midsection.

A very masculine voice said, "It's good to see that adults still appreciate the solitude a playground can offer. Well, when kids are not around." He snickered.

Biting her lower lip with reservation and nervousness, Emily looked up and offered a weary grin. Barely above a whisper, she said, "Hi."

The handsome man extended a hand. "Zach."

Emily gave his hand a weak shake and settled her hands on her lap. "Hi."

Zach's eyes squinted with humor. "Two hellos. Do you have a name?" Before she could respond, he flipped his hands up into the air. "Oh, wait, don't tell me. Linda?"

Seeing Emily's confounded expression hastened his explanation. "It means—"

"Pretty. In Spanish," Emily completed. "I know. I'm Puerto Rican."

Intrigued, he took a step back, putting his hands back into in his pockets. "And I just heard a hint of a sexy accent."

"So, you're observant," she retorted standing. She just wanted to be alone with some peace and quiet. "My name is Emily . . . though my dad wanted to name me Anita." She didn't even know why she told him so much. She scolded herself for it.

"Glad he didn't," he said with a hint of a snide tone.

"Later." Put off, Emily proceeded to leave the handsome man.

Summer

The hot Chinese dishes hit the placemats in front of us. The steam carried tasty aromas to our noses. "Mmmm." I giggled. I opened my eyes to see Max with a fork, ready to devour his food.

"I'm starved. Haven't eaten since, uhhh, yesterday?" He stabbed his fork into the pile of rice and commenced eating his beef-fried rice.

Chewing a mouth full of rice and swallowing, I replied, "You really should do something about your awful work schedule." I smiled. "I mean, come on. It's been how long since we've dated officially and you're still spending ninety percent of your time at work?" I shook my head and slid my fork into my next bite.

Max gave a shoulder shrug with a smile. "I have to be able to do things like this, Summer." He waved his fork between us. "You know, treat us to meals."

I shifted my body under my bent leg. "Oh, honey, I'm not your responsibility. The jig was up a long time ago. We threw in the committed towel, and now, you can save for one."

His expression turned serious. "You—you don't want to try this again in the future?"

I placed a hand on my hip, puckered my lips and looked heavenward. "Max, I can do a relationship here and there, but for the long run," I shook my head with regret, "I just don't think it's in the cards for me." I placed my hand on his fork-holding hand. "You understand, right?"

The relaxed atmosphere disappeared. "Summer." He cleared his throat with eyes full of despair. "Summer, you're the most beautiful and unique woman I know. You're comfortable in your own skin . . ."

I began to tune him out and almost choked on my rice. Me? Confident? Yeah right. Once I tuned back into his prattling, I picked up at the part where he said, "I didn't think you'd take that break-up as our seal of fate."

I stuffed a fork full of rice in my mouth until my cheek protruded. Then I shoved a big piece of broccoli into the other side. I didn't want to answer this sad sap. I didn't like offering explanations. In fact, tonight I just wanted the benefit part of our friendship as the dessert to this meal. Sure, I wanted to catch up because it'd been a while. Well, a few months since we'd enjoyed a sit-down moment. But the contents of this conversation seemed so out of the blue. I couldn't watch as Max peered at me with expectations, so I stared down at the checkered tablecloth. Maybe he would tire of my long chewing and resume eating. I choked down the last swallow and met his eyes above the rim of the glass of water as I sipped. No such luck. He patiently waited for an answer. I placed the glass down and ran my tongue against my bottom gums, searching for leftover food. I sighed.

"Max, I don't . . ." my already raspy voice sounded strident. "I don't know what to tell you. Look, if I gave you any indication in the past that I wanted us to develop into something more in the future, then I'm genuinely sorry."

Swiping the cloth napkin across my lips, I added, "I'm not too convinced that I'm one of those people who has to be married with children just to fulfill the prodigal dreams of a big house, lofty furniture, daycare expenses . . ." I hung my head low and placed a saluted hand on my forehead, staring down into the wrinkles patterned on my blue dress.

"Summer." Max sighed, and I looked up to meet his gaze. "We don't have to do . . . the whole nine yards, you know. It doesn't—your 'prodigal dream,'—doesn't even have to manifest right away. We can start off, just me and you, a year or two for now. After a real commitment, we could see how we feel about everything." My lungs tightened and perhaps were on the verge of collapsing. I felt as confined as an elephant in a Smart car.

My fork dropped, my hands waved with caution. "Wait a minute, wait a minute, Max." I cried as tears welled up. "This is not what I came to talk about. You have *completely* caught me off-guard." I stopped talking when I noticed other diners looking back at me. They turned back around one-by-one after they identified the face with the voice of confined hysteria.

"Could you lower your voice?" he begged. "Sheesh."

And he had the nerve to look irritated. I wanted a smoke, and I didn't even smoke. I'd seen my co-workers do it in a moment of stress or when work began to feel insurmountable. "Sorry," I mumbled irritably. This back-and-forth started to feel like a lifetime, so when I saw our waitress, I couldn't let her get away. I held up my hand. "Check," I mouthed with a furrowed brow.

Max panicked. "S-so what? You're leaving?"

"Uh, *yeah*."

He angrily swiped the cloth against his mouth and hammered a light fist on the table. "Well this is just great, Summer. You've managed to not only embarrass yourself, but me as well."

If I had to take some blame, that was fine. But I also didn't ask to be confronted with questions of my unforeseen lifetime resume. I capitulated. "Fine, fine, blame it all on me. I just need to get out of here, Max. I don't mean to be—"

"Rude?" He stood and slapped a generous meal-and-tip-covering bill on the table before the check arrived.

My angry ex paused and peered down at me, shaking his head before marching out of the restaurant. I appreciated our seat in the front, because I couldn't bear the embarrassment of passing various facial expressions reading, "What happened?" as I left.

I grabbed my sweater and raced out the door to follow him, thinking I could catch up to Max on foot, as he approached the subway. It was too late. I saw him being lowered with each second by an escalator into the Metro station. So, I stopped. A family-oriented guy like Max didn't deserve to get caught up with a loner like me.

I didn't have a car since I worked close to my prior residence. I relied on my toned legs and the Metro system. It only seemed right to take a walk along the sidewalks with the crowds of people to clear my head from his dramatic exit. Ambling the sidewalk, I mumbled under my breath, "Asshole," as I kept my eyes downward. Just when the night couldn't get any weirder, I heard a voice say my name as a question.

"Summer?" I couldn't quite figure out the voice before turning completely around. When I saw her staring at me with a smirk and two hands on the same hip, I let out a mental sigh and gave my best fake smile. "Oh, hi."

Emily

Emily tried to walk away, but she spun around and stared impatiently into Zach's eyes when he said, "Hey." He threw his hands up in the air. "Okay, I can be a jerk. But

I've never liked that name. An Anita with choppy, black hair bullied me in the second grade."

Emily giggled with softened eyes. "Were you really bullied by a girl?" she asked with doubt.

He tucked his lips inward until they were concealed and smiled with a nod. "Yes. She used to greet me every day with a punch in the stomach. My father raised me to be a gentleman, but to be a tough guy. And my mom encouraged me to solve friendship issues on my own. I couldn't tell anyone I was getting beat up by a girl. Besides, I told my teacher once, and she really didn't believe me. So, I grew up hating girls with that hairstyle or name. Silly, huh?"

Pursing her lips to one side of her mouth as she listened, Emily sought to assure him. "No, no. That's not silly at all. You were being a gentleman."

He appeared shy for the first time as he smiled. "Would you like to come inside for some hot chocolate?"

Emily looked at him suspiciously and smirked. "I don't know if I should do something like that." Sternly, she added, "I literally just met you."

"Come on. I live right there." He pointed to a house just a few doors down from hers, but across the street. "I'm new to the neighborhood. I'm cold and I can use some hot chocolate."

"Ohh, right. I saw you move in a few weeks ago. Well, welcome to the neighborhood." Zach nodded a "thank you." "With whom do you live?"

"My eight-year-old son. He's out with the babysitter getting ice cream. He should be back any moment. I just came back from the hardware store and noticed you. Decided to come say hello."

"Where is his mom?" Emily felt guarded.

"She lives across town—Maryland to be exact—but we were never married. I let him finish a few weeks more there at his old school while I unpack and set up the house."

She supposed she took an interest in Zach's single life since her marriage didn't work. "Why didn't you marry her?"

Zach laughed. "That's a conversation I'm willing to share, but in the warmth of my house."

Still reserved, Emily removed her coat at the door, clutching and twisting her hands, questioning her judgment.

He motioned a hand to his sofa. "Please, sit. I'll be back." He hit the remote to light the fire before leaving her alone in his living room.

With her coat slung over one of her folded arms, she made her way to his sofa. Sitting with her legs crossed in her tight blue jeans, she observed his living room through uneasy eyes, taking in the visual of plastic rolled up beside a wall with a can of paint nearby. Minutes later, Zach passed a mug of hot chocolate into her hands and took a place on the arm of the sofa with his drink cradled in one hand. The fireplace blazed, casting a romantic orange glow inside the room.

"Well, Emily, to answer your question posed back there—"

She held up a hand, stopping him. "Oh. No, you don't have to Zach. I got caught up in the moment." She was just grateful for a change of scenery. Much to her surprise, being in the company of someone new and of the opposite gender offered some sort of relief.

"Oh, no." He took a sip. "I don't mind. Don't mind at all." He raced a thoughtful hand up and down his thigh and sighed. "Enzo's mom, Heather, was a liar. She was also a serial cheater."

Not knowing what to say, Emily just took a sip of her chocolate. "Well, that's horrible. Why do you think she did all of that?" she finally asked.

Zach chuckled half-heartedly as he pondered her question. "Not sure. I think she always felt like she had to prove her self-worth by the amount of men she bedded. When I found out she lied about her dad's death as well as not having a degree, I lost it. That's when I realized that it didn't make sense anymore trying to make sense out of her."

They sipped and chatted about the neighborhood, as she explained how she fell in love with the field of education. He became animated when he told her stories about designing houses. About half an hour later, Zach set his mug down on the fireplace mantel and stood in front of her with an outstretched hand. Emily's eye's danced with nervousness. What did he want? What did he expect?

"I see your mug is almost empty. Do you want more?"

Emily exhaled anxiously and laughed inside, but turned red on the outside. She took one last sip and handed it over with a smile. "No. I'm good, thanks."

Zach placed her mug with his. "Tell me, which school do you teach at?"

"Dana Key Elementary."

His face lit up. "Get out of town. My son will be enrolling there."

Emily smiled. "Yeah?"

"You said you teach third grade, so you may be getting him. Heather wanted to handle all of that. That's why I'm not sure who his teacher is."

"Well we'll know soon, huh?" Emily stood with intentions of leaving. Even though she enjoyed meeting a new male face, she didn't want to overstay her welcome on the first visit.

"I suppose so. Wow."

"Maybe I should go."

Alarmed, Zach asked, "Why? I would like to know more about you. It's only fair," he teased.

She smiled. "Okay," she relented. "Well, I live alone and . . ."

Zach placed an index finger on his chin as he listened. "You live in a big ole house. These houses may not be the newest, but they're definitely not the cheapest. So why are you in a big house by yourself? The old lady next door who gossips about everyone said that a man used to live with you. Am I overstepping?"

Emily froze in consternation. "Good ole Mauzy always running her 82-year-old mouth." She didn't want to talk about it. "Y-yes. I was married," she replied as she played with her fingers nervously, "but not anymore."

"Okay," he caught on. "We can leave it at that. I hope I didn't upset you." Zach wore a regretful expression.

Emily couldn't quite lock her eyes with his. Finally, she lifted her lids and said, "Well, it's just one of those things that you'd rather, you know—"

"I can't imagine a sexy woman like you being alone," he blurted.

It'd been so long since she'd even tried to connect with a man. Emily cracked a crooked smile and blinked. "Thank you," she whispered.

Zach waved a hand at her. "Let me show you something." He wrestled one of his big hands into a pocket of his jeans. "Here's a picture . . ." Emily stood shoulder-to-shoulder with him, watching him straighten his cell phone into his hand. He slid the bar on his screen to unlock the phone. A chime went off. "Oh, a message from Heather?" Zach explained, "She likes to send me pictures of our son, so let's see what she sends since that's all I wanted to show you anyway."

Emily said, "Oh. This should be nice," with hope in her eyes. She didn't move as she watched him open the sent data.

"A video I suppose. Not too good with these smartphones. I prefer the flip ones myself."
Emily chuckled. "But who would go back to those now?"

"Right?" He raised the phone to allow her to access a better view. "Here we go." The frozen screen showed a fireplace, but once Zach's finger pressed the play button, Emily gasped when she saw what the video revealed. That moment made her want to go back to a flip phone.

Summer

She stood there, beautiful as before. If I could ooze green, I would, and envy would be its name.

"What are you doing on this side of the district, Summer? What brings you by?" Her smile was of subtle sass, as if waiting to judge my answer as the truth.

"Well, Brooke, I had a date. Didn't go all that well." I wanted to shoot myself for telling her that much information. I bet she had no trouble at all finding love or keeping it. Now she knew she was better than me in another department. Let's see: looks, check; confidence, check; love and attention of men, probably a check; successful career with a local reputation, and check.

Brooke walked toward me slowly, with one foot in front of the other. Catwalks must've been her thing. *Man.* I had another opportunity to greet her abs again. She stared straight into my eyes. "You wanna join me?" This was the first time I'd ever seen her show a sincere expression in the whole day I'd known her.

"Sure, okay. Where?" Why did I feel honored that she wanted to spend time with me? Oh, yeah, because of the checklist.

"Let's hail a cab and head to Georgetown. My treat."

Fifteen minutes after agreeing to her idea and sitting through red traffic lights, we arrived at a very crowded and dim pub filled with smoke, young people and loud music. Seated at a table all the way in the back, Brooke removed her coat and I my sweater after we ordered our drinks. It was hot in here. We had to crank up our voices just to hear one another.

I told her about my background, and I was very curious and excited to hear about hers. So far, I only knew of her career path and that she was twenty-seven like me.

"Yeah, so I've been here all of my life. I moved away to California to attend Pepperdine University before returning."

"Why didn't you stay there?" I asked with genuine interest.

"Well," she frowned. She took a sip of her Long Island Iced Tea. "It's not because of my warm, fuzzy family. I grew up as an only child to a mother colder than a freezer who would've rather seen men after work than me. When she saw how it affected me, she'd tell me to get over it. She'd tell me that children grow up and go, but men are meant to stay." Her face turned bitter. She poked her ice with her straw. Obviously, the Long Island had settled in.

"And your dad?" I pressed.

She shrugged. "I don't even know who he is. All I know is that he's a man named Greg Brazile. I don't remember him at all. She said he left when I was a baby. I don't wanna be anything like her. I left California, because it never felt like home. Plus, it was too big to conquer, and I'm here to conquer." Her demeanor changed with every sip, and I became less jealous as I became more aware of her more-than-lackluster past. "So, why don't you wanna be married to Max?"

Now it was my turn to take a long sip from my margarita. "I don't know. He wants too much, and I can't give that to him. I find it scary that he suggested marriage over a date when we couldn't even make a relationship work." I shivered. "I don't want that kind of life—marriage and all that." My tongue traced the top of my teeth as I continued. "I'm a rookie at living by myself, I'm just learning who I really am, and now I'm supposed to be ready to take on another person? And you know what the sad thing is?"

"Hmm?" Brooke tried to focus with blank eyes. She took more sips as she listened while bopping her head to the music.

"Had we never broken up initially, I may have warped into one of those women who become bridezillas. We'd be shopping at Ikea and Pier 1 Imports on the weekends." Speaking it out loud made my head hurt even more. I took another long sip. Brooke flagged the waiter down for water.

She must've read my confused expression. "Chiiiile. Never go over one glass. Always gotta keep control. Besides, how do you think I stay beautiful?"

To my dismay, she wasn't teasing. Her looks reflected her beliefs though. I smiled and decided to stop as well then told the waiter that I would also like a bottle of water. Brooke blurted, "Well, hey, I would love to be married with children somewhere down the line. I want the whole shebang. So, if you and Max have no future, send him my way."

I couldn't determine yet how much I hated her, or if I simply admired her for always coming across as brash. But she was crazy to think I would "send him" her way. I had no intentions of handing over my benefits package regardless of how he and I separated. The nerve. I watched her miserably poke her straw at the cubes in her glass again before shoving it to the center of the table. We bopped to the music and took in the scenery as we waited for our water. Brooke reached inside her clutch to place a twenty and a ten on the table. We grabbed our water bottles as I thanked her for the drinks.

"Let's go outside," she suggested. Before I could reply, she'd already jumped up and grabbed her clutch. Obviously, she was used to calling the shots in her life. So outside we headed.

We squeezed through a crowd of smokers to welcome the fresh, crisp air that greeted our noses, bringing relief from the body odors and cologne that plagued the pub. Brooke looked at me with those one-of-a-kind wide eyes. "Hail a cab?"

I nodded. "Sure." It didn't take too long for a driver to notice us. We eased into the cab, Brooke first.

"Penn Quarter, please."

My head jerked from the cab driver to her in shock. "You live there?" My inquiry sounded more like a demand than a question.

She gave me a half-scornful look. "Problem?" Her eyes locked into mine with patience, as she waited for an answer. Almost salivating, Brooke waited for a chance to be challenged. Maybe I came off weird, so I dialed back my jealousy.

"No." But I couldn't play it off and I'm sure that didn't go above her head. "I was just surprised, that's all." And add that to the checklist: residence, check.

"Why?" Her eyes stared at me in amusement with a smile. Yup. If I didn't know if I liked, admired, or hated her earlier, I knew now. I loathed her, and with no good reason other than jealousy.

"You're so young, you're single and you live in Penn Quarter. Lucky, you." I placed the cheesiest smile on my face.

She replied casually, "I'm on top of my game." Brooke's expression turned serious as she nestled in the corner between the seat and the door. "I studied magazines when I was a child. I grew up in a very raggedy house. I'm talking wood panel walls and old green carpet. I wanted a nicer home. I didn't dream of a Prince Charming to swoop me up. I think my mom wanted that. I tapped into my passion to change my life." She turned to face the window. "I'm writing my own life."

And I respected her. If nothing else, I respected her. Brooke knew where she'd been, where she was going, why and how. She and I had the same amount of time on this earth, but one of us had more focus. Suddenly, I felt ashamed and behind in life. Brooke shot me a quick glance before looking out of the window again.

"Anyway . . ."

"No, no, Brooke. I . . . I get it."

Brooke threw me a piercing look. "Do you?" She readjusted her bottom to point her knees in my direction. "I think you need to walk in my childhood shoes to really get it."

We rode in silence the rest of the way. I thought about my mom and me. Thought about how life had rewarded Brooke after such misery. One would look at women like Brooke and presume them to be beautiful, lucky and slightly entitled. Women who seemed to have it all usually came from nothing. I wondered if being stripped at birth equipped people with a better drive.

Emily

Horrified, a wide-eyed Emily covered her mouth with a hand. She looked away from the phone and at Zach. "That's you? That's you doing that in the video."

Zach turned as red as the butt cheeks on a ten-year-old boy who'd gotten a spanking from his dad for vandalizing commercial property with friends. He quickly pushed the phone back into the pocket from which it came.

"Oh, man. I don't know what to say." His hands washed over his face in true humiliation. "You gotta believe me, Emily. I would never show this to you on purpose. This was an accident."

Emily stepped back with realization that ultimately, this man was a stranger. Her hands frantically flew up to the sides of her head. "So, why would Heather send this video of you with your pants down whipping your penis back and forth," she pointed at his midsection, "with-with-with your little hips making it move, if you two are over?"

Zach became hysterical, apparently trying to make sense of things himself. "Sh-sh-she's stupid and loose. She's never sent anything like this before. She recorded this when we were together."

Emily gave a sarcastic smile with folded arms. "Great. So, it's nice to know that that's what you like to do on your time with the ladies." She spun around. "Where's my coat? I'm out of here." She didn't know him well enough to judge him, but she couldn't help it. It spoke volumes about his character, and in her healing stage, she needed to back away from unnecessary insanity.

"Oh, please, come on, Emily. I was drunk there on Christmas with her a few years back."

Emily donned the coat quickly. "Mmm, hm."

Zach's pleading expression inched closer to her face with desperate hands flailing. "You got to believe me. This—this is not me. It was a moment. A bad one."

"I can't say that it was nice meeting you." She lowered her eyes to his wooden floor as her shoulder pushed past his. "Excuse me."

Emily trudged through his wild lawn and across the street, berating herself for being so trusting of a stranger. Emily couldn't believe that she would see him any given day. *Never mess with a neighbor*, she scolded herself. She wanted to smack herself for exercising poor judgment, but the wind did a better job at it than she ever could.

Summer

We arrived at Penn Quarter. Brooke paid the driver once we pulled up in front of a tall, tan building. Following her inside, the people at the front desk greeted her as she marched with a true sense of belonging. I never knew I could learn so much from someone the same age as me. I followed close behind until we reached the cluster of elevators. As we waited, Brooke gripped her clutch tighter and offered me a faint smile before looking at the floor.

"Why did you invite me here? You barely know me." We stepped inside the first elevator that chimed. She pressed button number six before looking at me.

"Well, you're certainly not my type, so you don't have to worry about anything happening." She slid her neck from right to left at me with a smirk." Besides, it's the weekend." My mouth dropped open.

"I didn't mean it like that, Brooke." Taking a shot back at her I said, "I may be desperate for some action, but I still prefer dick."

She shrugged. "Whatever makes you happy, Summer."

We stepped off onto the sixth floor. A smell of newness overtook my sense of smell. New carpet, fresh paint.

"How long has this building been here?"

"Not even a year. I just moved here myself." I got the feeling that she just wanted to show me how she lived. I was already jealous of her, and just when I found a reason to relinquish the ugly green monster, she surprised me with something new to make the monster come back. I got that feeling in my gut which told me to prepare myself to be jealous all over again. Brooke was about to show me just how much no amount of excuses could pardon failure.

I waited with anticipation as she turned the key to the final lock. The emotion I felt was like the feeling you get when you're about to see something repulsive. You know you shouldn't look, but you can't look away. You knew that it would be on your mind when it was time to sleep, and you could only fall asleep after obsessing about it to death. I didn't know what made me feel so inadequate since the moment I saw this woman. However, once she turned the key, I was quickly reminded.

When she opened her door, I knew that I had to accept what lay before me. My feet steadied on shiny, cherry oak hardwood floors. Her condo stretched like a map of success. A very pleasant and fresh smell of vanilla hit my nostrils. The well-lit condo stood new, spacious, and updated, with plenty of windows. Modern and chic. Brooke decorated with gray and turquoise as the primary colors and splashes of red popped up tastefully. Everything matched. This was more than what anyone should have in their twenties.

Creeping around from one room to another, I couldn't hide my reaction nor did I care. My mouth dragged on the floor as I tiptoed. I entered a bathroom and flicked on a switch.

Brooke chuckled. "I'll leave you to tour. Want anything to drink?" she asked as she walked away.

Aloof, I replied, "Uh-huh."

I suddenly realized that though we shared the same age, this lady didn't share a roommate when I'd had one. On a scale of one to ten, my hatred for this girl easily soared past ten. I turned off the light and went to the final bedroom. Brooke decorated her bedroom with Moroccan style and colors. Stylishly placed in front of a sheer drape, her bed sat as the focal point, centered in the middle of the room. I made my way to her small but generous-sized patio. Even one square foot would impress me. I decided against opening it and slid the door back, because I got the point. Brooke couldn't only wake up and see the view, but she could smell it as well.

"Hey." I looked up to see Brooke holding two glasses. "Sparkling blueberry cider."

I walked the distance to meet her at the door. "Thanks," I said as I accepted my glass.

"You're welcome. Come back to the living room, please."

"Sure." With that, Brooke spun on one foot and led us to her living room. She sat on the rug and I on the couch.

With her calves peeled against her thigh, she advised, "Relax," before sipping, steadying her weight with a hand on the floor. She peered at me over the rim of her glass. "Take your shoes off. Get comfy."

After seeing someone so beautiful and young have all of this, I needed a real drink. I think I wouldn't have been bothered so much if she were a guy. I'd never been one to compare myself to guys. In fact, I'd always expected guys to get ahead easily because of their gender. However, to see a woman slay at an early age made me realize that maybe I should be happy that it was possible as a woman, especially one who shared my skin color. So, I did just that. I kicked off my shoes to bend my knees so I could rest my feet beside my bottom.

Her face softened. "What did you expect? Did my place live up to your expectations?" She rested her drink on her thigh.

Her question humored me. I figured that to surmount my jealousy, I should confront it. "Sooner than later, I would love to have what you have," I admitted reluctantly. As a grown woman, admitting real feelings, ugly or not, defined maturity, not so much ownership of fine possessions.

Brooke pressed her lips together and nodded, looking away. Then she explained, "Summer. This was hard, very hard. I started off real small while in college. Each earning went toward my tuition. I put my reputation on the line. In California, my reputation was embarrassing. I started off rocky and got my tail whipped." She snickered before taking another sip.

"It takes a lot of guts, Brooke."

"I can tell you so many stories of disaster that helped shape me into the independent tornado I am today. I saved my pennies to pay back my loans while I was in school. I've never owned a car just so I could save extra money."

"I simply couldn't afford one. Still can't."

She shrugged. "If you're serious, you'll get there." We sat in silence for a few seconds before she continued. She placed her glass on the coffee table and said, "When I came back to DC, I was polished. Not a pro, but polished. I became a pro here." Brooke eyed her feet as she started to rub one. "I don't allow myself to come home until the sun goes down. Yeah," she added as she looked around, "this took fire-in-the-belly work."

I nodded absently. "Well, I admire you, Brooke. I really do," I said in a faint voice.

I tried so hard to beat the green monster away on my own, when all I had to do was confront the enemy. Now that I had, the monster ran away on his own with his tail between his legs. Now that I kicked presumption to the curb and learned to befriend the act of true communication, my jealousy of Brooke slightly waned. In fact, I didn't even hate her. I smiled at her genuinely for the first time, because now, I respected her. I raised my glass and she returned my smile as she accepted the toast. That night, I stayed and laughed with Brooke until midnight before she kicked me out. "A true diva needs proper rest," she explained. And now that I knew her background, I understood.

2: rich encounters

Emily

"I'm here to look at the piano that you have listed online." The words came out sounding more like a question than a statement. The thin, African American woman with the New York accent looked back at Emily through almond-shaped eyes, waiting for a confirmation that she had the right place.

Emily stepped back to allow her in. "Oh, right. Come on in." She smiled and shut the door behind the woman. Emily ambled her way back to the room with the piano as she explained herself. "Yeah, I don't need it here. It belonged to my ex." She stopped before pointing to the piano. "I'm sorry. I didn't catch your name."

The woman offered a quick apology and extended a formal hand. "Amber Hamilton. I'm so sorry for being all up in ya' house without tellin' you who I am."

They shared a giggle. "No worries," Emily replied. "Yeah, so it's fairly new, no scratches and it's barely been played."

Amber scratched her button nose. "Just eight thousand dollars for your parlor grand?"

Emily nodded, "And, like the ad said, it's a Steinway. It needs to go."

"I see that." She studied it without a touch. "Shhhheeesh." Silence fell between them. Amber told her, "But, you know, you can't go wrong with a Steinway. Besides, in the store, I'd have to cough up more than this. So, it's okay." She placed her hands in the front pockets of her narrow trousers. She examined the piano, tracing her finger along the lid, "Does look like new," then on a key. "Well tuned, too." Sticking her hands back into her pockets, Amber told Emily, "Okay. I got an envelope full of cash."

"So, you play?" Emily placed a brunette strand behind an ear.

"I do." She smiled with pride. "I actually offer lessons in my home over in Southwest. Well, I just moved from Southeast a few months back, but it's how I make my money to survive. I grew up with a gift, so I also perform to makes ends meet. You know what I'm sayin'?"

Emily inhaled as she tried to take in all the information. "I see."

"I ain't tryna' step on your shoes—I mean toes—but why you sellin' such a nice piece anyway?" Amber looked at her with subtle disapproval. "I mean, even if you don't play . . ."

Emily exhaled between praying hands. "My husband—well, my ex-husband now . . ." She peered down in deep thought as the black pool of misery slowly sucked her back in. "He used to play it, and, in fact, that's how he won my heart. I would go to his house, and he would play me a tune." She clasped her hands in front of her, tugging nervously at her fingers looking downward. "I fell wide open into love. No reservations. I had never fallen in love before. Threw caution to the wind. I wanted to be like my parents . . . in love, but I had friends who tried and got hurt." She peered at Amber and shrugged matter-of-factly. "And now I'm one of them."

"Sorry, girl." Amber wore a sympathetic expression. "Can I ask what happened?"

Emily raised an eyebrow at her with disbelief that she might be dumping all of this on a stranger. On the other hand, she also didn't mind talking about it since she hadn't discussed him in detail in a while. "He left me. He . . ." Tears welled again at the bottom rims of her eyes.

Amber took a step forward. "Oh, honey, I'm sorry, uh—"

"Emily."

Amber gave a quick nod. "Right, we don't have to talk about it, Emily. I don't want to upset you like this."

"It's okay, you know." She giggled anxiously. "I should be the one apologizing since you just came here to buy a piano, and instead you got a stranger dumping a sad-sap story on you." Emily exhaled a deep sigh and placed a palm over her midsection.

Joking, Amber replied, "Are you kiddin' me? Strangers are the best company." Emily broke into a broad smile. "No, really. It's good to have an ear, even if it belongs to a stuffed animal."

Emily laughed and waved a hand at her. "Well, to tell you the truth, last year, he just woke up and decided that marriage was not for him. We were only together for a few months. He said that it was a big mistake and that he would resent me forever for urging the idea. But I didn't, his parents did. True, I talked about it a lot, but what woman doesn't?"

Amber raised a slow hand. "Me?" They chortled. "I'm in it for fun, nothing else. Girl, if they ain't rich, then we ain't got nothing to talk about. He can have a little dick, but if he got money, a trip to Neiman Marcus will make up for that. Okay?"

They burst into laughter. It felt good to talk about this with someone who could make her laugh at it all. She couldn't do it with Brooke, because Brooke just didn't get it. And Brooke certainly couldn't make Emily laugh about it. Maybe Amber was right. Sometimes all you need is a good stranger.

"Well, I can tell you from firsthand knowledge that having a rich man isn't everything that it's cracked up to be."

Amber shrugged. "I can appreciate that. But I'm really sorry that that joker did this to you. You seem cool so far." Amber shook her head with disapproval.

Feeling touched, Emily replied, "Thank you, Amber. And you know I'm thinking of selling this place, too. One day. I just can't bear another minute in a big space with massive memories. I need a roomy apartment where the walls won't feel so big."

"Do you keep in touch with Andrew?" Amber asked.

Emily smirked with confusion. "Umm, that wasn't his name."

Amber shrugged. "Well, I had to give him a name since you didn't."

Emily chuckled. "Funny. His name is Eric. And no, he avoids me like the plague. He cannot even bear the sight of me." Amber stood there with a pouty frown to let Emily know that she sympathized.

"Well enough about me and my sad tale. What about you? Who is this lady buying my piano?" she teased.

Amber perked up with a grin from ear to ear. "I'm from New York originally. Haven't even been down here for a year. You know, a friend of mine lent me her couch and then I saved enough to get my own place in Southwest at the Waterfront."

"Ohhh, okay. That area has come a *long* way over the past five years. Where in New York are you from? I could tell by the accent." Emily smiled. "I love it."

"Thank you. I grew up in Harlem. Whew. I'm aliiive," she said jokingly with both hands up. Emily chuckled, but then Amber admitted, "I wouldn't have it any other way, but you know I just had to get outta there. I needed space, air, a different scene, a slower place. It's exhausting."

"You ever think you'd go back?" Emily tilted her head as she listened.

Amber thought about it. She folded her arms. "You know, it's too early to tell . . ." her eyes drifted to the floor, "too early to tell. But hey," she gazed at her with animated eyes, "I heard an accent, where you from?"

"What you hear is a Puerto Rican from Pittsburgh. Yup. I went to Penn State but got my master's degree in education here at George Mason."

Amber pointed at her. "I heard of that school. I'm not the college type though. Too lazy. I love music way too much. Honey, I knew I was done after high school." Emily smiled. "You, my friend, sound like you could use a break from the monotony." Amber pointed two gun-shaped gestures at her with an open mouth as she waited for a response. "I don't have many friends here so what do you say?"

Emily folded her arms. "What did you have in mind?"

"Well, I'm going out tonight. My friend—my rich friend, Osha—is having a party at her mansion."

"Ooooh, I don't know." Emily began pacing with folded arms. "I don't think I'm up for partying."

"Think about it. You seem like you can use a change of scenery, meet some new people, and perhaps you can find a new guy. So, what do you say?" Emily could feel Amber studying her. "Come on. I can use a new face. Osha will be too busy to stay around with me, so what do you say?"

Emily stopped in her tracks and raised an eyebrow. "Where's this party located?"

"In McLean. You interested?" she teased as she circled around Emily.

"Well, can I bring two other friends? You'd really like them. Well, I just met one of them but she seems cool. I'd like to know her better."

Amber's eyebrows raised in curiosity. "Oh, yeah? It's gon' be lit. You won't regret it."

Summer

"We cannot use a person like that at our agency, so don't bother calling her to see what happened this morning. She should've shown up for the job this morning, and now we look bad. I don't want to lose this client because of her." I shook my head in disapproval as Angie, the senior recruiter, stood over my desk as I sat behind it. "And why was it so hard to locate the files of other candidates this morning? Did Lora not show this to you? This is why you knowing the digital format is so important. We need to fix that, because this cannot happen again the next time an employee decides to stand us up. We always have a back-up solution in hand. Fran will have all our heads. Let's clean this up quickly."

I felt overwhelmed. I nodded, pressing the files against my chest. "Yes, I agree. I'm sorry and I'll figure out the database immediately."

"It's not all your fault. We all have to share some responsibility." Angie's black hair whipped while she shook her head as if to clear it. "Anyway, thank you for your diligence today. I'll meet up with Lora to see what she did with you," she said blandly as she left my office.

I exhaled a huge sigh. Hopefully Lora wouldn't lose her promotion to senior recruiter. Happy to have my office to myself so I could pack up my desk, I began to clear out for the day. Outside, darkness started to fall as cabs filled the street while cars honked every few seconds. Then my phone rang.

I wanted to say, "Good afternoon, we're closed." But what I really said was, "DuBois Staffing, Summer speaking."

"So, your business card comes in handy." The voice on the other end of the line had a slightly recognizable accent. It was my new girl, Emily.

"Emily Gray?"

"Just Emily will do. Listen, I have an invite and Brooke said she's going. I was invited to a party in McLean by a woman who bought my parlor piano. I can't believe I'm going, but would you like to come? Being in this house is driving me nuts. It's home and work, work and home."

"You know what? After the day I've had, all I can say is, where's the *party at*?"

A Yellow Cab pulled up at the curb in front of me. I waited for Brooke in my short, burgundy dress. I just couldn't wait to see what the diva would be wearing. Not out of jealousy this time, but for sheer amusement. No doubt, she would go all out. I enjoyed the anticipation. It felt like waiting for a real-life Barbie to reveal her red-carpet attire. Besides, Emily told us to dress up, but not ballroom style. I heard a voice in the background say, "More like cocktail." So, what did the Diva Barbie choose? Funny, I already had so many names for this girl because she really was a firecracker.

She stepped out with one turquoise stiletto hitting the ground first. I saw a bare, brown leg and then the other leg and voila. Brooke rose in her black, cap-sleeved dress with both hands on her hips. She looked hella sexy. Black and turquoise never looked so good.

We hugged.

"Hey, girl," Brooke said in excitement. "Look at you." With one hand in mine, she spun me around. I felt like going back inside to change.

"Well, hey. If I were still envying you, tonight would be the right moment. My sweater dress may not cut the mustard after all. I'm afraid you've put me out of business."

We shared a laugh and it felt great to be rid of awkward feelings. She didn't know that I couldn't afford to buy something extravagant, nor did I own anything on that level. I could've worn the same blue dress that I wore on my date with Max, but parties always called for something new and she already saw me in that, too.

Brooke told me, "I think someone will come home with you tonight."

"Let's hope so. I've been horny ever since Max tapped out on me last weekend."

Brooke looked around and grabbed my hand. "So where's our ride? How long are we expected to wait in front of the Wharf?"

"Well if they stand us up, we can at least chow down on some yummy seafood," I replied.

"Yuck. I hate seafood," Brooke frowned. Then her eyes brightened with a smile as she pointed. "Look, I see Emily's truck."

Yup, Emily sat behind the wheel of the Sequoia at the red light. I saw the other woman on the passenger side. "Does Emily know that they can make a right on red?" I shook my head in confusion.

Brooke's forehead wrinkled. "Yeah, don't know why she won't turn."

The tan Sequoia finally drove through the entrance and stopped at our feet. Emily rolled down her window to wave an inviting hand. "Get in," she called. Brooke and I giggled with excitement like two teenagers and crawled in the second row. Emily's head swung around and so did the mocha-colored woman. "Guys, meet Amber. I sold my piano to her and she invited us out tonight." Emily appeared so perky with her big grin.

Flashing her teeth, she said, "Hey, ladies." Amber had a very pretty face. Not a goddess's like Brooke's, but just as pretty as Emily's. Women would kill for her almond-shaped eyes. She wore a stylish haircut that stopped at her ears and accentuated her oval-shaped face. When she waved, I noticed a musical clef tattooed on the inside of her wrist.

Brooke shook her hand. "Hello, there. I'm Brooke." She smiled and then gingerly pulled the safety belt across her chest.

I shook her hand as well. "How's it going, Amber? I'm Summer. Nice to meet you." I eased back into the seat and secured myself with the safety belt.

"Hey. Did Emily ever get around to tell you guys that it's a masquerade party?"

Brooke and I turned to one another with the same confused expression. I didn't know how to reply. "I . . . I . . . I—"

Emily's head swung around quickly to say, "Sorry, guys. Amber forgot to tell me when I was on the phone with you guys. But we already stopped by The Party Store to pick some up."

Brooke and I exhaled relief. "Cool. What'd we get?" I asked.

Amber yanked a bag up from the floor. "Take a look." She tossed the bag to me, and I chose a black sparkly mask. I flipped it around as I studied it. "Never done this before."

"Hand it to me," said Brooke. When she took hold of the bag, she fished around and picked out a red mask with yellow lines. "Do we have to?"

Amber's brows pinched. "You don't like it?"

"I don't."

"Well, some people take them off anyway as the party wears on. So, no, you don't."

"Don't you think it'll be fun?" Emily asked.

"No," Brooke replied without hesitation and handed it back to Amber along with the bag.

I shrugged. "Well, I do. I'm keeping mine."

"High five." Amber held a hand in the air until I met it with a laugh.

"You guys are nuts," Brooke said chuckling.

Amber replied with, "Are you guys ready to paaaaar-taaaaaaay? Wooooooooohoo." Brooke and I looked at each other and laughed.

"Yes," we all screamed back at the wild child.

Amber announced, "Then McLean, here we come."

I didn't know what the night held. I did know that the time had come for me to let my hair down, come out of my shell and to live life to the fullest as a woman living independently.

We arrived at the mansion in total disbelief. Well, except Amber. She'd been here before. Following the brick walkway that led us inside, we stepped into a social gathering of rich people sipping on champagne and wine. I had to assume that they were all rich, even though my group wasn't. No one cared or noted our entrance. They just continued with their conversations. The number of visitors filled more than one room. Live music of soft violins played in some rooms, and pianos in the other. Servers walked around with trays of drinks and appetizers. Buffet tables lined some walls with food. My eyes studied the crown and trim moldings above our heads. I glanced down at the marble tile under my boots. Boy, I hadn't a clue what these people did for a living to afford a home like this.

Brooke whispered to us, "Where are the people who look like us? Are we really welcomed here, Amber?"

"There are some people of color up in here. You just gotta keep walking. Chill guys. These people are cool." She slid the green mask over her eyes.

Already studying the crowd behind my mask, I snickered as Brooke rolled her eyes. I whispered to Brooke, "I'm sure we're welcomed here. Let's just keep going in like she said." Brooke shot me a doubtful expression and proceeded. Emily bit her lower lip, suppressing a chuckle.

"Osha," Amber called to a tall blonde with high cheek bones who made her way toward us. A huge smile spread across her face when she saw Amber. The hostess lowered her mask with the stick as she squinted at the woman who called her name. Amber told us very little about this friend of hers. Osha was a woman from Russia married to Leonard Bardwire, a fat founder of a chain of hotels, whom Amber told us had to be about twenty years Osha's senior. Amber said that we could call him Leo, should we meet him.

She had a strong accent. "Hello, darling." Osha and Amber air kissed one another on either cheek. "Mwah. Mwah."

I turned to Brooke and Emily with a raised brow. Emily pinched her lips to the side of her face. Brooke rolled her eyes and leaned toward me to say, "So fake." I snickered.

Osha turned around to ask, "And who are these lovely ladies?" Her dark blue eyes smiled at me as she extended a hand to each of us one by one.

"Summer Stevenson." The other two followed suit. "Thanks for having us here. You have a stunning home." She thanked me with a hand over her heart.

"Well, ladies, drink up and mingle." Osha rubbed Amber's shoulder. "I'll see you later." Amber waved as Osha turned to walk away to point a server in our direction. We each took a glass from the tray and sipped as we watched Amber interact close by.

Amber gave a few hugs to men—who were no doubt affluent—and air kisses to their wives, whom she knew by association. When Amber had a moment to take a breather from being ambushed at random, she turned to us to say, "Once you know one rich person, you go from there. Usually, the rich hang with the rich like the poor hang with the poor."

I couldn't help myself. I had to throw a joke her way. "So, what are you?" I asked with a sideways glance and a smirk before sipping the finest champagne.

We all chuckled, including Amber. I loved her sense of humor. "Uh, smart. You see, my law is work for the wealthy and you become wealthy."

"Now does this include sex services?" I teased.

She shrugged casually. "Hey, if a wealthy man needs a quick blow, I'd do it and take his money with pride and get perks. Otherwise, you're just stuck with a poor man who will just treat you to a cheap meal. Instead of a perk on the side, you get a pain in your side."

Emily stared up at her new, taller acquaintance behind a blue mask covered in pink glitter. "So you should consider collecting a letter of recognition from each man. You blow one, get a good grade and get a recommendation. You know, raise the bar in pay."

"Pay for performance? Dear Patrick Squire the Second," I started, pretending to write in the air. "Madame Amber deserves all accolades of tea bagging for approximate suction and pressure." I could barely finish as Emily and Brooke almost fell over in hysteria while a less amused Amber watched with her hand on her hip. Perhaps the champagne contributed to the uproar, or being hidden behind a mask, because I barely knew this woman and offending her didn't concern me at the moment. Her tongue caressed the corner of her lips as she tried not to laugh.

"We highly recommend you consider her strong skill set and abilities," I continued.

She just raised her Louis Vuitton handbag. "Well, laugh all you want, you crack heads, but how do you think I afforded this?"

"Tea baggin'?" Brooke chimed. And we broke out into another gale of laughter.

"Do you know how many extra piano lessons I would have to teach just to pay for this after rent? No. So, I can thank Leo's friend, Rob, for this. Old White men with money," she clicked her tongue against the roof of her mouth. "Don't leave a party without one. Ta-ta crack heads. Mingle around." She blew a kiss and walked away. We stood close to an unlit fireplace in a crowded room of guests, servers and a pianist.

I looked at Brooke and shrugged. "Well, I guess she serves as a prime example of why women would rather work around the clock than to wait at the rich-man bus stop to be picked up just to afford the finer things in life."

"Exactly," Brooke replied.

"Oh, come on guys. Be nice. Amber just has a different way to her hustle. Brooke, you work very hard and get paid generously. Amber just . . ."

"Opens up and says, 'Ah'?" I couldn't help it. Emily playfully smacked my wrist and smiled. "Well, doesn't this just make her a prostitute?" They stared off and shrugged. "I mean, the typical person just expects an orgasm and a verbal confirmation of excellence, but she wants to be paid afterwards. So, doesn't this make her a legit prostitute?"

Brooke said, "I'd have to concur."

"Enough, guys. Come on. Let's go see what this party has to offer." Emily pulled our wrists as she stood in the middle while we began our search.

"Well, I can certainly mix some business with this pleasure," Brooke said. "Can't help but think of the potential clients some networking could bring."

The possibility of bringing someone home for the night excited me. It'd been a long time. Since Max didn't come through for me that night, he'd set me back tremendously. I decided to take advantage of the men in heat tonight.

The search to see who would be available proved to be quite easy. My wandering eyes made the women in relationships paranoid, and grabbing the arms of their men told me that. Others weren't so subtle. Some went as far as stealing quick kisses. Good grief. So, I decided to look for men with a glass of champagne and a hand in a pocket, chatting with other men or simply standing alone. Because of my lack of confidence, I had to think of a way to grab a hot guy's attention once had mine.

By now I'd broken away from the others. I wasn't aware how or when I lost my pack, but somehow, I stood alone. If they needed me, I had my cell set on vibrate, since I knew I wouldn't hear the ring.

My glass rested against my lips as I scoped the room. So much beige everywhere—the walls, the furniture, and even the guests' clothing. I felt confident that I wouldn't be hard to miss in my burgundy dress. My eyes scanned and lingered, scanned and lingered. I could never be so bold to do this alone without a mask. When I saw a hot single guy, some random chick would happen to sense my radar from another room and, low and behold, his arm would be jerked into hers. At this point, I could do nothing but roll my eyes. Were all girlfriends this annoying?

But then I spotted a gentleman in a corner wearing tan slacks. The handsome man seemed to be alone. I studied his build. Not bad. With broad shoulders and a bulge in the right place, it appeared he stood over six feet. And despite his buzz-cut hairdo, I could see that he had dark hair to match his olive skin. Searching for his hands, I found them anchored in both pockets. Fighting my turtle-like nature, I furtively studied his stare behind his silver mask. I wanted to know what held his attention, because unfortunately, it wasn't me. His first gaze led me to the champagne and glasses on a server's tray. I didn't miss him bouncing on the tips of his toes; he seemed bored. I wrestled with the idea of talking to him. No, no, I couldn't. Instead, I took the cowardly way out and decided to skate toward the server to get in the hot man's view.

Dare I look up to see if he notices me now? Nice going Goldilocks. You didn't pick a dress with a good cleavage shot. A quick idea ran through my head, suggesting that I use my legs, but I was convinced that it would take more than knees to get his blood pumping. Hmmm. I had to hurry while in his sight. *Okay, Summer. Think. Think.* Leaning against the fireplace with an elbow on the mantle, I decided to perch my butt out. Gee, how many fireplaces did these guys have? Since the guy still ogled the server's tray, I decided to top off my glass of champagne.

I popped a slender hip out and said, "Excuse me, sir?" He spun around, about to leave. "May I have another glass?"

"Sure. Cristal or—"

"Yes." Those rappers didn't brag about this stuff for no reason. As a first-time drinker of Cristal, I rated it beyond good. I bet Amber's had it more times than I've been laid in the last year.

I took a sip and kept up the pose. Deciding to look up once more as I lowered the glass from my lips, I noticed that he'd disappeared. I didn't know where. Before I could panic, once two girls moved, I noticed that he'd started my way. I barely escaped a minor choke as the Cristal slid down my throat. Too late. It appeared I could be getting what I'd asked for. The hot guy inched closer to me with a mischievous smile. What to do? I turned to search the room frantically for a friend. Even Amber, but no cigar. Like a plane, he'd landed.

Of course, his full-lipped smirk turned out to be quite sexy. "You alone?"

I immediately melted under his accent. This man made my stomach flip. In the circles of the mask, I managed to see some of his dark, bushy eyebrows above his light brown eyes. They pierced my green eyes effortlessly, as he stood so slack with his hands still hidden. I couldn't help but wonder if he had any hands? He could be a pirate with two hooks. And if he didn't have hands, I wondered what size his hooks were.

My shaky hand coyly stroked a strand of hair from my face. "Hello." I struggled to dial back my awkwardness, obviously, a failure, given my quick wave and a throat clearing. "Umm, no I'm here with friends. You?"

"Alone. I'm a co-worker of Leo's." He bit his lower lip.

Don't do that to me, don't do that to me.

Cohesive words didn't come easy. "Why is that? Why are you alone?"

He shrugged. "I've been to these parties before." His eyes looked toward the ceiling before falling back into mine. "Nothing new. Besides, I already mingled. But I do know one thing." He raised an eyebrow.

Determined to kick my nerves to the side, I leaned in closer and playfully raised an eyebrow back. "What's that?"

"I'm bored. I'm lonely, too. Everybody has someone, but you and me. So, I figured you would appreciate some company. Am I wrong?" He grinned and winked. I loved the tone of his voice.

Hmm. What was he trying to say? He had to stop being so effortlessly sexy. It was beginning to wreak havoc on my lower half. Already at the mercy of my vagina because of my unintentional extended stay on Celibate Island, I couldn't afford to be teased.

"Soooo, did I win your attention by default?" I flirted back by biting my lower lip, too. I flung my Amazonian hair over my shoulder with a hand.

He chuckled. "No, not really. But if you were ugly, I wouldn't be here."

I shrugged and gave him a corner smile. "Can a girl get a name?"

"Ruben. And you?"

"Summer." I gave him my hand to shake. He removed one of those elusive hands to reveal a big manly tool. Yes. I could see them on my thighs right now. I had to get out of here. "Well Ruben, I'm bored stiff here. Should I tell my girls—?"

"Tell them that a nice guy is going to drive you home tonight after we chat in my convertible."

Oh, yeah, just chatting. Liar. I smirked with sheer cynicism. I couldn't be mad at him, because I wanted what he wanted. Regardless, tonight would be a night of firsts. I'd never been in a convertible before, and I definitely didn't go places alone with strange men. More and more, I was beginning to see a method to Amber's madness. Well, at least the part where she partied with rich people. "Sure, let me call one of them." He nodded once and smiled. So suave.

I got through to Brooke and she warned me to be safe and wished me well. I felt like running out. The mansion offered a great experience, because again, I'd never been in one. On the other hand, I'd never gotten lost with a rich guy. An adventure awaited, but I didn't know what kind. He disarmed a black, convertible BMW. Never been in one of those before either. I knew one thing: no matter what happened tonight, I had an experience of seeing how the rich lived, up close and personal. Television showed it, but seeing it, being a part of it, that was another story. Ruben opened the passenger door and lowered me into his car by my hand. When he joined me inside, he cranked up the ferocious motor and took off toward the opposite direction from which the girls and I'd entered. Would I become wind chimes tonight or one sexually satisfied woman? This would either be the end of me or the ride of my life.

Emily

In the kitchen, feeling nervous about being in a home with a crowd of people, none of whom she knew, except for her entourage, minus one, Emily leaned over the kitchen island and popped a strawberry in her mouth. Brooke had gone to use the ladies' room, and Amber was somewhere over the rainbow. Out of nowhere, a sudden touch that swiped Emily's side made her jump. No one had touched her there since Eric.

Spinning to see who it was, Emily froze in consternation as she processed the familiar blue eyes that stared her into stone behind a black mask. He removed it quickly, narrowing his eyes at her. Emily reluctantly removed her mask.

Eric.

The same tight peach skin with short salt and pepper hair, clean shaven face and new crow's feet told her that it was indeed Eric as he peered down at her. Was this really happening? What was he doing here?

"Emily?" he whispered, still squinting his eyes in disbelief. "What are you doing here?"

Shoot. I'm in his world. Amber set me up.

Emily had a few seconds under pressure to reason. Eric made at least a million a year, and always hung with the affluent. He worked in Tyson's Corner, which neighbored McLean. His being there made perfect sense to Emily now.

Tears tried to flood her eyes, but she willed them away—at least for the duration of being face to face with Eric. Like any woman with pride and dignity, she held her head up high when facing the man who shattered her heart.

"I'm here with my friends."

Eric dug his hands in his pockets and poked his sharp chin in the air. "Oh, you have friends now?" he asked portentously, looking down at her from his nose bridge.

Emily shifted on one foot. She didn't know how to handle him. In her head, she heard the comments that she'd endured when growing up: *What's the matter with you, girl? You need to get yourself together. Come on, Emily, you are a strong, Puerto Rican woman.* Her sisters couldn't fathom her passiveness. They had that attitude that she didn't seem to possess.

Regardless, nothing worked. Instead, she found comfort in twisting her lips in embarrassment. How could this be the same man who'd caressed her at night? The same man who'd toasted with her when she'd received her masters and the teaching job? The same man who'd made love to her? The same man who'd slow danced with her and told her that she was the most beautiful woman to ever hit this planet? Was he still in there somewhere, or did he never really exist?

Amber

One of Leo's friends, fifty-five-year-old George Butler, had a love for younger women, despite his marital status. His wife didn't frequent parties for a lack of interest. In a room with very few people, Amber made sure that her intentional moves didn't go unnoticed by George. She considered it a perk to be in a home with many rooms. People couldn't talk about what they couldn't see.

The New Yorker presumed that he couldn't be caught stepping out on his wife, even though he didn't do a good job at hiding his lust. He didn't even bother to wear a mask. She bent at the waist to pick up hor d'oeuvres from the layout on the table to give him something to think about. When she chose the one she wanted, she put on a show. Straightening at the waist, Amber offered him a profile view of her as she gingerly placed the hor d'oeuvre in her mouth. No doubt a generic move, but Amber felt certain that that would suffice. And she was right.

George increasingly became worked up, shifting his tie and twisting his lips. The time to go in for the kill couldn't be more perfect. She poked her tongue out as far as possible and placed the last bite on it before retracting it back into her mouth. Like a bee to a flower, he approached her.

George cleared his throat and stuck out a firm hand. "George Butler. You?"

She accepted his hand after the last trace of hor d'oeuvre passed down her throat. Ignoring his request for her name, she replied, "You know I can do to you what I did to this hor d'oeuvre."

George looked around suspiciously. They were in a room with two other guests. He leaned in to say, "Meet me upstairs. I'll be waiting for you in the hall."

Amber nodded with a grin. She waited for a few minutes to pass before she located two dark staircases, one of which, led directly to the desperate, old man. She felt confident that they had gone undetected by the partygoers. In the darkness, she could only see the silhouette of the old, horny man waiting in the hallway. Considering his history with Leo, Amber didn't question his permission to access that level. He found a room for them to enter, and without wasting time, Amber knew how to handle her business.

"George." Amber cupped him gently at the crotch and massaged. "My name is Amber. And tomorrow my rent is due." Amber already had her rent covered, but he didn't have to know that. She wanted him to understand where she was coming from before too much time escaped.

"Done," he said weakly. He stroked her hair and gave her a gentle push downward to indicate his expectations. He quickly unfastened his pants and slid everything down south to bare it all.

When Amber descended, she imagined dollar signs on his pink and wrinkled genitals in order to give her best performance. Holding his genital with her mouth, Amber heard a short squeak two minutes into fellatio. She wanted to doubt the funny sound, but the smell confirmed her suspicion. With some of him in her mouth, she looked up and asked, "You gon' really fart while you gettin' head?"

Not only did he look extremely embarrassed, but his apologetic expression told Amber what she had to do next. She rested her bottom on her heels as she straightened. Her eyes looked upward to meet his.

Snatching off her mask with little patience to spare, she said, "Mutha' fu . . ." Amber didn't want to offend him, so she shook her head and rolled her eyes with a sigh to show her disapproval. Irritated, she informed him, "I'm gonna have to charge you extra." Amber wanted to throw up at the smell of something rancid.

His expression became concerned. "How much more?"

Even though she already knew the answer, she smiled and asked, "George, are you married?" while she massaged him. He closed his eyes and with an opened mouth, he tried to breathe.

"Yu-yes."

"Well, George. Does she do what I'm doing?" Her smile turned naughty. It seemed blatant that she wouldn't be there if his wife exercised a tenth of Amber's skill, but she didn't see the harm in reminding him of that at this crucial moment. Frankly, that was Amber's appeal to older men, especially the married ones. The older ones relied on money to snag younger women. The older, married men found that sex dwindled, and they longed for sexual excitement. However, when they were old, rich, and bored, the combination benefitted her the most. Amber waited for an answer, but George could barely speak.

With his head still cocked back, he barely answered with a, "Nah."

"When's the next time you're gonna get this?"

"How much, Amber? How much to keep you tonight and maybe more nights?"

Since the stench passed, Amber resumed her initial job. Just when she knew George was going to descend into an orgasmic abyss, she relinquished her hold and sat back on her heels. "Two thousand now and a grand per night." Amber targeted him with the knowledge of his worth. A thousand per night meant nothing to a man with old money and no children.

His head snapped down in desperation. "Get back to work and you'll get what you need. Just don't tell my wife. She could clean me out." George didn't wait for Amber. He pushed her back into her pool of talents and she got enough cash for "rent."

Summer

We made it to the top of an abandoned hill—a great place to park. However, cops could easily hide out here. Ruben cut the car engine as we stared at the dark trees. Luckily, a street light a few yards away illuminated the area. I wondered what he had in mind as we sat in his convertible.

Deprived of stimulation, the idea of being here with him excited me. My adventurous days involved work and watching television. The routine sickened me. In that moment of silence, I wondered the whereabouts of the other ladies. How different my life had become from just a week ago. Who knew that Lora's words of wisdom would be an understatement to life on my own? It frightened me to live alone, but at least I didn't feel lonely. My friendships with the girls looked promising, and thanks to Amber, I was learning how people of a whole different social class lived. Parties at mansions? Riding in convertibles? Wearing nice clothes to real events? My life consisted of going to cafes and coffee shops to meet a few people here and there. I rode the Metro or bus of course, not convertibles. And my clothes were for dining at hole-in-the-wall restaurants. Tonight, seemed unrecognizable. Even though tonight didn't change my personal life for good, the visuals showed me the life to which I could aspire.

He lifted his mask, revealing a handsome face that briefly stole a beat of my heart. Ruben reached for mine, leaving me with my teeth anxiously piercing my bottom lip. His lips cracked with pleasure. "Beautiful." Relieved, I giggled like a schoolgirl passing a love note to a boy in class.

I couldn't help but pass my happy mood onto Ruben with my nineties photo-booth smile.

"What do you do for a living?" I asked.

"I'm a right-hand man." He smiled without teeth, meaning: *We're not facing trees away from a party for nothing.*

"Oh, impressive. Well I'm a junior recruiter. Just in case . . ." I started to give up as I turned my head slowly to take in the scenery to my right. That man didn't come here to talk about our careers. Again, I wasn't mad at all. One of us had to be forward, and of course, it couldn't be me.

"I love your skin," he blurted as he traced my shoulder with his index finger.

Turning to him, I replied, "Thank you." He made me smile again.

The hot man unbuckled my seatbelt and then his own so he could lean in close. Ruben lifted my chin with two fingers. "I didn't come up here to talk. I don't think you did. Did you?"

I had to listen closely to understand him, since his sexy accent coated his words. I didn't mind it at all. In fact, all women should have to do this at least once before they die.

I shook my head. My heart knocked against my chest like an angry fist on a door. This man was old-school handsome with charm and confidence. I loved his classic dark hair and bushy eyebrows. Ruben was manly, in a world of men wearing skinny jeans.

"You were the only one wearing a dress quite like that. I saw your curves before you got that second drink. I was just . . . studying you."

Embarrassed, I laughed into the clawed hand covering my face. I removed my hand as my eyes gleamed into his. "Me, too. I was scheming."

Ruben smiled. "I know. So now that we've both accomplished our missions, come with me." He hopped out of the car and rushed to the hood.

Aye, aye captain. I followed him. The minute he placed those large hands on my waist, a rod of fire struck through my midsection. Yikes. They backed me up until my bottom touched his hood. He towered over me while closing the gap between us inch by inch. I loved first kisses. Either they sparked something or repelled the attraction. The question of whether he could kiss remained.

I kept my eyes open until I could feel his full lips. But I didn't immediately get what I wanted. Instead, he seductively withheld his kiss with lips hovering close to mine. Those manly hands caressed my back, played with the hem of my dress, then finally moved to the back of my thigh while resting the other on my hip. His lips still hovered over mine like a helicopter above a building, waiting to land. I could feel his breath against my lips, warming them with his flavor.

When Ruben's hands found a home on my butt, he softly rubbed each cheek in circles, squeezing them more. The cold air exhaled against my skin once my dress gathered above my butt. That rod of fire steamed into a rocket, ready to explode in a place that'd been asleep for way too long. It felt exotic to be sexually explorative outside in the dark with this man. I was seventeen years old the last time I behaved mildly wild outside. It paled in comparison to this liberating moment. I trusted him to take care of us outside in the dark if danger were to present itself. The naughty side of me wanted to be seen, watched, and lusted after. I kind of wanted an audience. A show with this much chemistry deserved that and popcorn. The fact that we hadn't kissed made it even better. He'd yet to place his lips on my skin, not even on my neck. I didn't doubt the time would come, but when?

"I wanna suck your skin until my mouth goes numb," he mumbled.

My vagina flipped. I didn't know what was stopping him. He removed my dress, and I didn't care. I didn't care about the cold, a wild coyote, a lusting pervert, or the cops. I cared about the fact that this man and I had passion that needed exploring. Was this his style, or did he want to make it last with me? I decided on the former since we'd just met at a party. I refused to define anything or pump my ego. I made up my mind to shut up and enjoy. Max couldn't evoke within me what Ruben had managed even without the intercourse: the longing, the adventure, the heat. What Max and I had amounted to sex, which couldn't sustain a marriage. Ruben had already convinced me that he could deliver. I wouldn't need to hear from Max again.

My dress sat on the car hood, stretched out as a barrier between my skin and the car's hood. A hotel room would've been nice, but the outdoors ironically made the experience feel more personal. A hotel mirrored a cliché. Outdoors on top of a hill broke all the rules.

I sat on the hood as Ruben undid his belt, button and zipper. He unhooked my bra, setting my breasts free. The cold air hit my nipples and enhanced the realness of the experience. I loved and reveled in my physical exposure. Ruben lay on top of me, gently, as he positioned his lips above mine once more. I felt the evidence of his excitement and mine, too. I never understood public screwing, but I did now. It took longing and sensations to a new level, especially with a stranger. Not knowing what he was all about or what would happen aroused me. I could do this again and again. Mama wouldn't want to hear about her daughter doing this. Classy women and ladies didn't do this. But did unorthodox always have to mean trashy in the world of sex?

He removed himself from being on top and pulled out his wallet to pull out a condom. Good. Classy women did unorthodox acts while protecting themselves. Clearly, unorthodox didn't always mean trashy. Well, not in my book.

Ruben lowered his pants just enough. I saw everything that proved his manhood. If he caught my wide-eyed stare, he could read my satisfaction. Now, the next step would be to see his performance. I had to see if he bought a high-performance car to make up for his lacking in other areas.

The knuckles on his big hands scraped down the sides of my thighs as he removed my thong. It. Was. Show time. Once again, Ruben lowered himself as he entered and inched his mouth toward mine. He froze when he gazed into my eyes after he had no more left to give. We looked each other over once more before finally connecting with our mouths. It was all romantic. They were soft cushions, and he worked them very slowly. As he became more invested in the kiss, so did his thrusts, with his length skating against the walls of my core, nice and slow. I wanted to feel his skin, unwrapped and raw. But as a one night stand, I had to take it the safe way. I closed my eyes and settled on my back, taking it all in, literally and figuratively. After being on my back for minutes, I couldn't take it anymore. I wanted more. I wanted to hurt him, rip him into passionate little shreds. Suddenly, I sat up and gripped him by the shoulders like a mama bear with wild claws.

He gripped my chin, pressing his fingers into my skin and said, "*Quiero que cada parte de ti.*"

I didn't know what the hell he said, but the intensity wasn't lost in his irises. Everything I needed to know I found in his expression. And it drove me crazy. Whipping my arms around him, I pushed my body into his chest, wanting to leave the car behind. Gripping onto him, I'd become his koala bear; his body was my tree. Moving my body back and forth, I grinded the life out this man, never taking my eyes off his. Ruben needed me just as badly, and somehow, he got us to the closest tree and eased me up against it. The slight discomfort on my back from the bark and the sweet indulgence from his thrust concocted the best pull between pain and pleasure. I swung my arms behind me, holding onto the tree as Ruben banged into me harder, and I cried out in happy pain like the irritating girls from porn videos. Dying inside, I couldn't help but thank Amber repeatedly in my head. I locked my ankle boots together and imprisoned Ruben for the duration of this passionate moment. And I realized, that this man could have it anytime, anyplace.

Emily

Figuring she had nothing to lose, it was time to stand her ground, even if she was shaking on the inside. "Why wouldn't I have friends, Eric?" Emily crossed her arms and waited for a response.

"Are you still using my last name?" His glower told her that he'd hit the peak of annoyance.

Emily decided that it would be pathetic for him to remember her like a bird with a broken wing. She placed a thoughtful finger over her lip. "Hmm. Actually, gray is one of my favorite colors." Emily then poked a quick finger on his chest. "So, yes. I'm still using 'Gray.'"

Emily spun to leave, but Eric grabbed her by the arm and turned her to see him. "Well, why don't you go back to Rosado? Hmm?" Eric made it sound more like a threat than a friendly suggestion.

"Because gray is how I'm feeling most days," she replied through gritted teeth.

Emily snatched her arm from his; he hissed at her in frustration. She walked away with the sashay that she'd seen Brooke do since the day she'd met her. Eric may have broken Emily, but her pride wouldn't allow him to see that. Ironically, he may have also been the one to put her back together again.

Brooke

Brooke toured the mansion, mingled with people, landed a few new clients, but didn't find a man worth dating. Once again, this night ended up being beneficial to her career more so than her love life. Despite having nothing else new for Brooke to prove, evident by her independence and the fact that she'd made a name for herself, she still wanted a foot massage at the end of the day. Because she felt good about being single for some years, she couldn't deny now that loneliness had started to eat away at her. Brooke had to admit that sometimes you just shouldn't have to do it all alone. But that didn't mean that she would snatch up the first man with interest just to be released from the cuffs of loneliness. So, for the time being, she had to make it work.

Brooke reminded herself that patient women didn't kiss frogs. No, a woman like Brooke only wanted to place a king in her castle once. Consequently, the patience required to climb the ladder of her career happened to be the same amount needed to find the right man. Glad that she didn't settle, Brooke went home alone a happy camper.

3: the bucket of pooh

Emily

Emily woke up at 5:30 Friday morning, yawning as she lay in bed wearing an oversized t-shirt. Still not able to fathom that she'd finally come face to face with Eric Gray after four months of calling him to no avail, she swung her legs out of bed and put on her slippers. Their cozy warmth embraced her feet as she stood and made her way to the shower.

Allowing the warm water to hit her face, she closed her eyes and embraced the memory of last night. Eric's face occupied most her thoughts: his sexy black and gray hair, tight skin and piercing eyes full of condemnation. Why did Eric see her as such a nuisance? Emily had felt like a possum at "his" party, wishing that she could've comforted herself by noting a negative observation about his looks, but she couldn't. At least her ex-husband didn't have a hot lady hanging all over his shoulder, especially after he glared at her with such contempt. Other than that, there wasn't much that she could say about him, except that he looked better than before. Maybe Eric had cosmetic work done. Or perhaps her absence in his life offered less stress and benefited his looks.

Summer

Moaning as I woke up with my limbs sweeping the bed and a smile as wide as a crater on the moon, I couldn't believe that Ruben had hit the spot that no other man had. Way to go. Before he left, Ruben had asked me to call him this weekend. A great lay was just a phone call away. How nice. I also remembered being in Emily's truck on the way to the party and the girls talking about meeting up at La Madeleine this Saturday. But I was tempted by Ruben's invite to call. I wondered if doing it again this weekend would be too much too soon. However, the time had come to get up, get ready and join the rest of the population in the hustle and bustle.

After a shower, I settled on a black pencil skirt with a white, ruffled-lapel blouse under a red blazer with a brand-new pair of red, suede stilettos. Locking up my apartment, I felt in charge and ready for the day. Boy, a promotion with a bonus to finance a wardrobe reboot was tantamount to a first day of school with new rags. What an awesome feeling.

I strutted down the hallway once I stepped off the elevator and grabbed the glass door to enter the agency. Jessica, our receptionist, flashed me the biggest Friday smile.

"Happy Friday, Summer."

"Yes, Jessica," I replied as I kept my strut. "You, too." I returned the expression as I remembered that it was payday. *Oh, yeah, payday*, I celebrated with a song. Cha-ching. How could I forget about that? I logged on with my phone to check my bank account balance: fifteen hundred dollars. Not bad considering how just a few weeks ago, I brought home less than a thousand per check.

I entered my office and placed my bag and coffee cup down on my desk before a familiar voice said, "Knock, knock," on the open door behind me.

I spun around to see my small-framed boss and agency owner, Fran Dubois, enter in her signature hairstyle: a French roll—either that or a ponytail. With a complexion, slightly darker than olive, my Iranian and French boss spoke with a dainty accent which showcased her combined ethnicity. Forty-seven and married without children, she lived in a lovely home in Alexandria, Virginia.

Fran barely smiled, but despite her serious demeanor, overall, she seemed nice. I used to be very intimidated by her. When I figured out that an employee's competence held the key to her heart, my fear of her erased and respect took its place. Everything had to be perfect in her world, so it surprised me that my performance impressed her. I didn't see it coming. She'd pulled me into her office one day and told me straight and to the point, *"If you want it, come Monday, you will be a junior recruiter."*

Fran returned last night from her vacation to France. I would've stayed in bed and come in on Monday. But I guess that's the difference between us.

I greeted her with a smile. "Good morning, Fran."

"Good morning, Summer." Without a smile, she asked, "How do you like your position so far?"

"Loving it. Thank you again for giving me the opportunity to perform at this level."

She waved a frail hand at me. "Don't thank me. I did what was natural. You performed, I promoted. It's in the unspoken contract of great management," she teased. "But I came by for two things."

Curious, I crossed my arms. "Oh?"

"Number one: You need to meet with one of the senior recruiters to help you conduct a better phone interview with candidates." I felt a slight sting in my stomach. The criticism took me by surprise. "Kent said that you lacked a sense of confidence."

"Sure," I replied with a strong attempt to appear like a trooper. "Anything to improve."

"Excellent, and point number two: I would like to invite you out to dinner with me and my handsome husband this Saturday night. At some point, when my employees do well, I like to learn more about them, so I can hang on to great talent."

Dread suddenly washed over me like water from a shower head. Well, I couldn't say no to the boss. "That's sounds great," I lied, hoping that my semi-stiff smile didn't give it away.

A weak smile brushed her face, so I read it as relief. "Great. I'll give you the details before you go, so be sure to stop by my office on your way out. Let me coordinate this with my husband." On her way out, Fran spun around at the last minute. "Summer? Do you have someone you can bring, a date perhaps?"

I pinched my throat as I tried to process this moment, wishing she were still in France. I shook my head nervously. "No, not really."

"Too bad. But, uhh, date or no date, see you on Saturday." With that, she turned on her heels and left my office.

"Great," I mumbled as I held my head.

Brooke

Alone at Starbucks, Brooke stirred her coffee while gazing out of the café window to observe the people as they strolled by. She watched and wondered about a man sifting through the trash, until she spotted a young mom pop her preschool-aged daughter on her butt, and then she noticed a man stop in the middle of the street while talking on his cell. Not surprised, Brooke shook her head in mock disbelief as she blew into her coffee before sipping.

"Yuck," she mumbled, before heading to the coffee station to jazz up her drink with some nutmeg and honey. Pleased with the taste, she made her way back to her table and sat. Crossing her legs in her knee-length skirt, Brooke pulled out a portfolio of a client who needed to pay her seven grand for her services.

Brooke had to buckle down on her client list for the month. She had three small but lucrative weddings, which, combined, stood to pay her at least eighteen thousand dollars. Months like these made or broke her—she normally limited herself to working with only two brides per month, if possible. Otherwise, if she kept up at this rate, unfortunately she would need to expand and create a team.

Brooke loved working independently since working with others made her head hurt and impeded her idea of total control. Sadly, she was one wedding away from an ulcer with the amount of pressure she faced just to live up to her name. Each day her appointment book filled up. Each bride-to-be needed her for some decision or another. Now, she had to juggle her schedule among three demanding brides in the same month. Regardless, she had to find a way to always make each bride feel the most important. However, Brooke wouldn't have her clients any other way. Her attention turned back to the world outside the window until she heard a nice and deep voice.

"Excuse me." Brooke turned her head reluctantly to an incredibly handsome Black man towering over her. She took a moment to study his features. Under his long wool coat, she could see a built frame with signs of sinew dying to pop from under his dress shirt. Brooke loved a man in business attire, especially one with close-shaven hair like his.

Brooke eyed him, squeezed her crossed legs once and bit her bottom lip. "Hi," was all she could muster in reply. She wanted him right then and there, in the middle of the Starbuck's floor. But then she considered all the dirt and decided that two combined tables might be better.

A smile escaped his full lips. "Can I sit here?" Since the coffee house was slow now, she instinctively almost asked why. But, instead, she just nodded, and he sat down. "There's a new law in DC that states you can't drink coffee alone."

Brooke surprised herself by laughing—something she didn't do too frequently. "Horrible joke. Cute," she threw a hand against her chest, "but horrible."

The sexy businessman shrugged with a grin. "It revealed that beautiful smile though." He removed a hand from his pocket to introduce himself. "I think you wanna know my name." He raised a playful brow. "My name is Jackson Sloan."

She rolled the tip of her tongue to the roof of her mouth before deciding to give up her name. Wedding planner, she reminded herself. Oh, yes, reputation. Her hand flew out quickly. "Brooke Brazile."

"Hmm. Love it." They smiled at each other. "So, Ms. Brazile, tell me—"

She interrupted him. "No, no. Just Brooke. I'm not married, and I'm not your teacher. Please."

He peered at her with crossed arms as he scratched the goatee on his peanut butter-colored skin. "Okay," he said with a laugh, "Brooke." He repositioned himself in his chair. "Why don't you tell me why you're drinking alone?" His brown eyes brushed her up and down, causing Brooke's loins to clench involuntarily. Not able to do anything about it, her pleasure suffered at the hand of some pain.

Brooke noticed his empty hands, and with a friendly smile, asked, "Well, where's your coffee?" She leaned back in her chair, lifted her coffee to her lips and blew gently into the cup, all the while offering him a flirtatious, playful stare. She didn't feel the need to immediately inform him of her relationship status, despite spilling the beans that she wasn't married.

"I just finished it." Hunching over his spread legs, he shifted his tie and wet his lips with a quick flick of his tongue.

Brooke grew increasingly hot, no thanks to the coffee. Boy, she wanted to take him home, but that wasn't her style. However, for him, she would be willing to reconsider. "Then you broke the new law in DC, huh?" Brooke smacked a hand to her mouth to shield her laughter.

Jackson pointed a finger at her. "So, you like my joke, huh?" His lips spread into a wide grin. "Can I be honest with you?"

"Well no one likes a liar," a composed Brooke teased. The more he talked, the more she figured he must've been slightly nervous, to say the least.

"I came over because I couldn't let you get away." She silently relished his words. "I watched you order your coffee, I watched you fix it again. I watched you stare out the window." Jackson peered down at his hands as he peeked back up at her. She supposed he was trying to see if he'd said too much.

Never one to give too much away, Brooke placed her coffee cup on the table. "Aren't stalkers supposed to be, I don't know—secretive?" Then her straight lips gave way to a curve at one corner.

Jackson chuckled. "Not a stalker. I just haven't seen someone as beautiful as you in a while." He sat upright again.

"Okay." They exchanged a brief, intense stare in silence, although, their deep attraction made the moment feel like an eternity. With broken nerves, Brooke cracked under pressure and lowered her stare to her coffee. Since he took a leap of faith by putting his pride on the line, Brooke decided to level with him. Her long lashes swept the air with a lift of her eyelids. "Well, I'm DC's finest wedding planner, and I live over here on this side of town. Anything else?" With legs still crossed, her foot tapped the air as she tried to calm her inner nerves. Not too many men made her nervous, but his hotness and bluntness killed her. Not a normal reaction for Brooke.

"Is that it?" he asked.

"Well, what do you want me to say? You really haven't asked me a question." Brooke uncrossed her legs and brushed a piece of hair off her face. "What do you do?"

"If my background impresses you, will you ease up?"

"Give it a shot," she halfway teased with a smirk.

"Okay," he clapped his hands together. "I work for the government. I'm an IT specialist for the Department of Energy, and I live at the National Harbor."

Brooke wanted to fall out of her chair, but her open mouth would have to suffice. "It's so beautiful over there." Located on the shores of the Potomac River in Maryland, the National Harbor sat south of Washington, DC with an impressive marina and upscale real estate, high-scale restaurants and unique shops. With a great job and residency, Brooke couldn't deny that Jackson looked good on paper as well as in person.

"I can't lie, Jackson. I'm impressed. But I don't know who you are as a person, so I'm still stuck with nothing." Amused by their exchange, she licked the corner of her mouth and folded her arms.

Jackson smirked at her. "Well, are you asking me to ask you out?"

Normally reserved, something told her that taking a risk with a man like Jackson would be worth it. "Okay. You can." She rubbed her lips together and gave him a flirtatious grin.

"Well, are you available this Saturday night? I would love to take you out to a seafood restaurant near my house."

Brooke crunched her nose. "Um, anything else would be fine. I don't do seafood. That ocean taste thing . . . sorry."

Jackson shook his head. "Hey, don't worry about it. Look. It's your night. What time?"

My night. She liked that.

"Eight?"

He flashed his hands in capitulation. "Eight it is." They both reached for business cards at the same time—he from inside his jacket and she from her purse—and they both chuckled at their simultaneous actions. It had already appeared as though they had something in common. Jackson stood to pass her the card pressed between his index and middle finger. When she reached for it, he lowered his neck to kiss her lifted hand.

Releasing her hand gently with a serious face, he told her, "I can't wait." They locked stares. With parted lips, Brooke struggled to process the way he made her feel as she watched him walk away. Inexplicably, Brooke felt the sincerity from his gesture, even though she considered the possibility that she only sensed what she wanted to. Only time would reveal his true intentions. Brooke contended that something had to be wrong with him. A single, good-looking man with a nice job? She decided that the future would answer all her questions and that a date would be the best way to find out.

Amber

Amber smiled as she placed her hands on top of the eighteen-year-old girl's hand. "There," Amber told her. "Like that."

"Okay." The girl stroked a dirty blonde piece of hair behind her ear. "You really know what you're doing. We have to keep seeing each other."

"Yes, because if you don't, you'll never get better. Practice your perfect fifths over the weekend and I'll see you on Tuesday, okay?" They both stood up from the bench as the student agreed. "You gettin' better, Samantha . . . gettin' better." Amber exhaled and made her way to the door to show her out.

Behind the closed door, Amber made her way to her cell phone to make a call. "George, what's goin' on? You looking for me to squeeze your balls or what?" George told Amber that he had big plans for her on Saturday, since his wife would be out of town with her sisters. Then, as soon as they hung up, Amber's phone rang. It was her only family: her sister.

"Mara, how's it going? I miss you."

"I miss Dad. I hate campus life. Living with strangers is hard. I feel like a reclusive freak."

Amber and Mara had lost their dad to a sudden heart attack right before she left NYC. Now, Mara had just started college as a freshman at Columbia University. It saddened her when she left her sister behind in New York to move in with an old friend in Southeast DC. She tried to convince Mara to leave New York and all those memories behind, but she had a scholarship and couldn't pass up such a great education. Amber didn't believe in college and the concept of delayed gratification. Instead, she preferred to gamble, work, hustle, or do anything necessary to earn money as soon as possible.

She had to be the mother figure of the household after they lost their mother to crime when Amber was in middle school. While New York would always be home, her departure served more as an escape. On the other hand, she felt bad for her sister. Her scholarship and college plans were concrete before their dad's death. Currently, college was the only way Mara had to escape from the streets of poverty.

A sudden flashback of living in New York reminded Amber that she didn't come from much and how scared she was of being without. In New York, she'd lost many years hanging out in the streets with men who couldn't rub two pennies together. If they could, she knew it was dirty money from hustling drugs. She could recall the men in the streets building her up to feel special only to blindside her with lies. Fed up with it all, Amber ran the moment her friend called her from DC with the opportunity to move in and take over her home piano lessons. Now, here she was in DC, ignoring men her age in favor of the older ones with money. She knew she couldn't possibly fall in love with men over a certain age, so she wasn't scared of getting hurt, but of only being unpaid.

"Sweetie, I don't know what to tell you." She could barely hear her own voice. "You just have to hang in there and stay outta trouble. Things will get better, I promise."

"Okay, but are *you* staying out of trouble?" Mara challenged.

Amber hated that her estranged friend in New York squealed about her sexual life to her sister. She didn't want to expose her sister to that side of her. The thought made her heart ache.

When Mara heard silence, she said, "Come on, Amber. You know dad would be worried about you."

"I'm fine. Please, Mara, I'm happy. I'm the older sister, so you let me do the worrying. I'm worried that you're not handling Dad's death too well." Amber took a seat on the couch.

"It's just that I'm lonely and I wish I had you, that's all."

"Can you try a little harder to make friends? I mean, I can fly you out here for a visit on a weekend that works best for us. I refuse to see New York anytime soon, and I got these lessons. You know what I'm sayin'?" She bit her fingernail.

"Yeah. I mean . . . I suppose I can try harder, but you should really lay off being so tough on New York. It was the men, not the place."

"Yeah, well. After dealin' with the men up there, the men down here seem harmless. I don't need them to love me, we can just do what we do and move on. In New York, I had no-good men in my ear all the time, Mara. It was a distraction. You know this." Ready to change the subject, Amber said, "Hey listen, since Dad didn't even have a life insurance policy for us, I'll send you money every week, no matter how much, just as long as you have somethin'."

"Thanks, Sis. Listen, umm, are you still mad at Dad for not leaving us anything?" Amber detected Mara's reluctance to scratch the surface of that topic.

Amber scratched her head and rubbed her cheek with her free hand. "Mara, I just don't get that part. Am I mad? I guess a lil bit. There ain't really no excuse why he didn't have that part in order. He woke up every single mornin' just to work and keep us afloat when we were children. He saw the struggle. I just don't understand why Dad didn't do that one part to protect his girls. I'm an adult, I know I have to handle my own affairs. But you were still a dependent. I mean, for once, I just want to see a man in my life do everything right." Amber held her forehead. She really didn't want to go there with her sister today, but that's what happened these days when they spoke for more than five minutes.

"Amber, I know how you feel. But I guess our dad had the immortal syndrome. You know, thinking he had all the time in the world. Who knows? I mean I guess at this point, we'll never know, right?"

"You got that right. Look, I gotta run, but do me a favor."

"Hmm?"

"Mara, find at least one friend, someone you can trust, not just anybody. Like—study hard and have safe fun. That's it. I'll do more lessons if I have to, but I'll send you money. Dad failed you financially, but I'm not going to. All right? I love you."

"I love you, too, Amber. Please, be careful down there. You're all I have left." Mara's voice was fragile but serious.

"And you, too. Talk to you later?"

"Of course. Goodbye." And she hung up.

"Bye," Amber said in a hoarse voice, but she was too late.

Amber stared at the phone before resting an elbow on her thigh as she placed her chin in her palm. In New York, she had to be concerned with making it day-by-day, because of the fast-paced life. In DC, she hadn't a clue what the future held now that she had time to sit and think. Sure, life seemed easier. There were no more filthy men, just filthy rich men.

But were they really any cleaner? They were men who paid for sex and most of them had wives on whom they cheated. Then Amber had a thought. Did the fact that they had money make it all look more sanitary?

Emily

With her class gone to lunch, Emily sat at her desk alone in her classroom. A pencil eraser poked her cheek as she took a break from grading. Her brain kept running off while she tried to grade. "Ms. Gray?" The immediate sound of a fragile voice startled her.

Emily jumped and turned to her door. A very lean mature woman stood at the door with a child. She'd never seen his cute little face before. Catching her brain and coming back to Earth, she answered, "Yes?"

"This is Enzo Lerner." Emily's brows crinkled. Of course, he's here. The penis whipper's child is here. The gray-headed administrator's voice went from pleasant to stern. "Ms. Gray, I need you to wake up and come take your student, and walk him to lunch or let him stay here for today. Either way, I have mounds of paperwork that needs attention."

Emily pushed herself upright. "Oh, oh right, right." As she walked toward Enzo, she mumbled, *"Por qué yo no recuerdo?"*

"Pardon?" the administrator asked.

"Oh, nothing. Just talking to myself." She cringed inside and thought, how crazy am I today? It all had to be Eric's fault. She gently took her student by a shoulder. "Thank you." The lady just nodded once and turned on her heel to leave.

"Enzo, I thought you were going to be here this morning. You can put your backpack every day right there in that empty cubby next to the fishbowl." Emily pointed as his eyes followed her finger. He nodded and began releasing his arms from the straps as he made his way to his new cubby.

"Well, I was supposed to come this morning, but my dad said we had to wait for Mama first before I could leave."

"Wait for your mom? What do you mean?" With her back turned to the boy, Emily started erasing her notes from the board since the class would be back in fifteen minutes. She took a quick glance at Enzo as he removed his lunch bag from his backpack and located the desk with his name. Enzo flung his bangs from his face as he sat and began to speak while he unloaded each food item from the bag.

"Well, since today is my first day, and I don't do well with change, my dad thought it would be nice for my mom to help send me off. So, she had to drive to our house, because she lives across town. She lives in Bethesda. They drove me here . . ."

Out of all the schools. Out of all the teachers. Out of all the children. It came down to Emily Gray and Enzo Lerner. She couldn't believe it even though she was prepared for it. Why did she go to Zach's house that night? Why?

"Well, okay, honey. Thanks. Eat up." Her tight smile stretched like a rubber band. "Well, go ahead and eat," she managed to say. "You need to be done by the time your peers return."

He nodded. Oblivious to his impact on Emily, he was just happy to peel the layers off his cheese stick.

Summer

Stirring my spaghetti in the kitchen, I spooned graham cracker ice cream into my mouth. The phone rang.

"Emily," my raspy voice answered. I was pleased that she called.

"You won't believe the day I had today."

"What happened?"

"Remember the penis whipper?"

"Yeah," I replied with open jaws as my mouth froze from the cold cream.

"Yeah, well, his son is officially in my class. Can you believe that?"

I almost choked on ice cream with laughter. "Are you serious, Emily? This is too rich." I had to place my carton on the counter.

"Ha, ha, Summer. Glad I could amuse you with my pathetic life."

"Well, I mean, come on. How likely is it that you would be the teacher to a kid whose daddy accidentally flashed you his junk?"

"I just see his dad's penis when I see this kid's face. How fair is this? FML."

"Ohhhhh. I'm so sorry." I couldn't suppress my laughter enough to handle humor while eating ice cream.

Unconvinced she replied with, "No, you're not."

Leaning my backside against the counter, I placed a socked foot on top of the other. "Well don't feel too bad. Tomorrow night, my boss wants me to have dinner with her and her husband. The thing is, it was not a request but an order." I spun around to turn off my noodles and pour out the boiling water.

"Yeah, but that is one night of torture. I have a whole year with this kid. Arghhh."

"Well, try not to take it out on the kid."

"Okay, I'll call you tomorrow. I'm standing here naked and getting cold."

Confused, I asked, "What?" as I located the sauce from the cabinet.

"Oh, well, I'm standing here naked. About to get in the shower."

"Don't let me stop you. My dinner is ready anyway. Later."

"Later."

"I just think that he thinks I'm exotic because I'm black." On Saturday morning, the girls and I met up at La Madeleine for breakfast. We listened to a lively Amber in a reddish-blonde wig prattle on about George.

"Or, it could just be because you haven't suffered yet from varicose veins and your butt isn't frowning yet." Brooke offered a very monotone but humorous opinion.

Amber rebutted Brooke's opinion with, "No, no, I think he likes chocolate. I really do."

"George is an old fart who is happy to eat fresh apple pie . . . nothing more, nothing less," I said.

"O*kay*?" Brooke said. We gave each other a dull high-five.

Amber pouted and sipped her tea. I added, "Now, if he tells you to pretend to pick cotton then . . ." We all fell over laughing.

"Where's our food?" Emily whined.

"Hey, hey. Listen," Brooke started. "I met this fine, fine man at Starbucks." She filled us in on a handsome man named Jackson, while she fanned herself with her hand.

"Whooooo," we teased.

"We have a date tonight, you know." Brooke beamed. "And he has a government job and a home at the National Harbor. Fine, employed, and residentially tasteful." She batted her lashes as she gushed heavenward.

"Aw, hell," Amber said. "Let me know when something's wrong with bruh."

"Oh, please," Brooke replied, snapping back from mushy world. "There doesn't have to be anything wrong with him."

"Yeah. Okay. Too perfect. Watch."

Brooke's eyes hit the ceiling. "Whatever, Amber. Only *you* think something has to be wrong with people."

Amber said, "Well I—"

"That's awesome." I lightly smacked her hand, attempting to change the subject. "You gotta be really happy."

"I am, I am, I am."

Emily shared her story about being Enzo's teacher, at which they cackled before pitying her, and I told them about my date tonight with the big, bad boss.

"Are you sure you're not going to be auditioning for a threesome?" joked Brooke.

"A-ha. A-ha, ha ha." I replied dryly.

Amber asked, "How was that night with that dude from the party?"

"If you could only see me blush." Embarrassed, I fanned fan myself as my stomach did a flip. They were all in my face.

"Oh, my, gosh. Look at her," they gushed.

"It was . . ." I bit my lower lip and looked down. When I lifted my eyes toward them, they were staring at me with mouths gaped, waiting to hear more. "I have never, *never*, felt so pleased. He hit the G-spot, the Y-spot, the X-spot, and every spot on the alphabet." They made so much noise that some people looked at us, despite the existing noise in the eatery.

I continued. "I mean, something about doing it outside like two trashy teenagers with no place to go. It was strange being a grown woman with my tits hanging out and letting this strange man just devour me in public." I lifted my hands and stared at them. "He had these really big manly hands, and I heard him mumble something in Spanish, too. It was too hot." I turned to Amber, who stared at me like a deer in headlights, only with a spoon hanging in her mouth. I placed my hand on her shoulder. "Thank you. Thank you, sweetie, for buying Emily's piano and for inviting her to your party." Emily sat diagonally across from me. I reached for her hand. "And thank you, missy, for inviting me." I placed my clasped hands against my chin.

Brooke shook her head with a longing expression. "Man, what I wouldn't do for some dick tonight." We all gasped at *her* language. Shrugging, she replied with, "What? When you hit my stage of celibacy, you don't want no penis you want dick. I'm way past being polite about it."

"You got that right," I mumbled. "Ruben didn't just share his penis. He gave me *dick*. There is a difference," I pointed out matter of factly. We all high fived one another as we hooted in agreement.

Amber placed a gentle hand on Brooke's arm. "Honey. I'm afraid my short presence in your life has rubbed off on you already. Welcome."

After we cracked up, Brooke told Amber, "Honey, that's a stretch." She told all of us, "But I just can't sleep with a man after knowing him for such a short time."

"Then I guess you better jerk off first." Amber shrugged and sipped her tea.

"Ladies don't jerk, you nasty whore," Brooke replied and threw a balled-up napkin at her with a smile.

Emily added, "Hey. You all have prospects. I'm afraid my vagina is like an ornament for my body at this point. Looks pretty, no use for it though."

We pouted but Amber suggested, "You can start a vagina catalogue." When we all furrowed our brows and wrinkled our noses, she explained, "Grow some hair, braid it, snap a pic. Then add—"

I smacked the table playfully, fighting the urge to giggle. "Stop it, Amber. Don't tease."

It was too late. Even Emily covered her face with her palms as her shoulders rocked in humor. Giving up, we let it out as the plates slid in front of us. We ate, chatted and listened to Brooke enthuse about tonight. I was so happy for her. I should've been telling them that I had a date with

Ruben tonight and not with my boss. Determined to suck it up and be present in the moment with friends, I tossed my disappointment to the side like Brussel sprouts on a dinner plate.

Brooke

Brooke laid out five outfits on her bed and finally decided on one. She chose a sleeveless, spice orange dress that stopped mid-thigh. Loving the plunge neckline, she felt sexy and irresistible. She wanted to tease Jackson, but not to the point where his expectations would ruin the night.

Brooke left her apartment for the cab that the front desk notified her of. Before too long, the view of the Potomac River came into view. Brooke had already called Jackson with a heads-up that she was nearby. When the cab turned the final corner, she saw a tall figure waiting. Yup, that was him.

Brooke's stomach flipped as the cab came to a halt. She began fumbling in her purse when a knock on the driver's window made her jump. The driver rolled down his window and she heard Jackson say, "Excuse me, sir. I'm paying for this lovely lady." He looked toward the back seat and opened her door. "Come on out, Brooke." She hopped out of the cab.

Brooke greeted him, hoping that the symposium of butterflies in her stomach would settle down. "Hi."

Jackson smiled. "Hi, there." He studied her, waiting for his change. He clinched his jaw and gritted his teeth. "My, my. You look gorgeous, Brooke, like a true beauty."

She laughed. "Thank you. Look at you." Sizing him up in his black jeans and matching sweater she added, "You're as handsome as I remember."

After the transaction, they talked and ambled toward his apartment door. She thanked him for paying for her cab ride.

He told her, "There's no way I would let you pay to see me."

"Well, it was very kind of you, nonetheless."

Jackson shrugged. "I made a nice dinner for you. Hopefully it'll meet your expectations." They walked down the hallway of the fifteenth floor and stopped at apartment 1502.

"I'm flattered." Her hand lay across her chest.

He smiled down at her as he unlocked his door. "Surprise."

Once in, Brooke saw a very modern and clean apartment, which met her standards. Immediately, her nose sniffed out something pleasant cooking. The dining room table stood visible from the foyer, and she immediately got the sense that he'd worked hard for this moment. Brooke's mouth opened in amazement.

"You really cooked this nice meal for me?" Candles lit the table around carved turkey, gravy, California mixed vegetables, mashed potatoes, and asparagus. A bottle of champagne in an ice bucket waited on the side. Impressed, Brooke grinned. This man. The fireplace crackled in the distance to set the romantic tone while lounge music played low.

"So, you do like it?" he asked with a grin.

"I do, Jackson. Thank you." She felt as special as a schoolchild with a trick to show the class.

"Let's take a seat." He ushered her to the table with his hand on the small of her back. That one touch made her want more as his innocent touch made her stomach flip like a dolphin in the ocean. Jackson pulled out her chair and pushed her in. He served her the foods that she chose and did the same for himself.

"Hmm, who taught you how to cook?" Brooke asked before biting into her asparagus.

"I went to culinary school before college. I learned a lil' something." He forked a piece of turkey into his mouth.

"Hm. But now you're in the government?" Brooke couldn't hide her curiosity. "I mean, from cooking to computers . . . what a leap." Knowing that she may have been overstepping, she still found it difficult to control her expression of doubt.

Releasing his fork, Jackson smirked with one hand on his lap and the other curled on top of the table. Reluctantly, he answered, "Yes, it is." His mouth briefly tightened and his eyes dropped to his plate.

Brooke didn't want to let up. "So, I want to know more about you."

Once he finished chewing, he followed up with a swig of champagne before replying. "Fine. I was born in North Carolina to two young parents. They were eighteen, and having two children cramped them financially. So, they moved back to Chicago and moved in with my dad's parents. Eventually, they got on their feet. Even though I went to Illinois Tech, I moved here for job opportunities and a scenic change."

"Oh, so you're from the Windy City. I don't meet too many people from Chicago. And I've never been there before."

A little bit of sunshine beamed back into her date when he smiled. "Maybe I can take you there one weekend."

"Jackson, I would love that." Her smile revealed a dimple. "But you didn't explain to me why you didn't make cooking—"

"Please. Stop." Jackson held a polite hand in the air and shifted in his chair until his posture straightened.

"But this tastes so good. It's wonderful," Brooke blurted. When his eyes whipped into hers, she got it. "I'm sorry. I'm so sorry, Jackson."

He scoffed. "Really, Brooke?" Eyeing her with doubt and then with a grin, he said, "Maybe one day, baby, but not today."

Learning her lesson, Brooke nodded. "Okay," she told him very lightly as she lowered her ashamed eyes onto her plate of food. The last thing she wanted to do was lose a great man on the first date all because she couldn't keep her mouth shut.

They finished their dinner and traded light information, sharing their favorite colors, college stories, and other talents. Afterwards, Jackson moved them to the living room to get more comfortable.

Pleased with their chemistry, Brooke decided to share her past. However, she kept it simple to avoid scaring him off too soon by simply telling Jackson that she and her mother weren't close. She offered him a quick explanation to her success, with it being attributed to hard work, strong networking, and passion.

Brooke sat with her knees to her chest, revealing a generous portion of her thigh. She saw his furtive glances, so she decided to straighten her legs and cross them at the ankles.

"So, Jackson, what do you look for in a woman?"

He sighed and raised an eyebrow at her, and she started laughing. He said, "Nah, I'm just messing with you." Brooke laughed more with him than with anyone else. "I look for beauty and grace. Without that, you're kidding yourself. I need to be strongly attracted to her. That's what keeps me passionate."

"But what if the woman gains weight or—?"

"No, Brooke, it's not like that. Personality is part of a woman's beauty. Because I would be screwed if she got into a car accident and messed her face up."

Inside, Brooke let out a sigh of relief. Even though people made a big deal about her looks throughout her whole life, she didn't need a superficial man. She was looking for a genuine stand-up man, so she continued to listen.

"I like women who take care of themselves. I want to know that my woman took a little extra time to make herself feel good regardless of a man. You seem to have mastered that."

Pleased, she said, "Well, thank you."

He asked, "More champagne?" Brooke nodded. Jackson stood up and reached for the glasses and bottle. He poured her a glass and handed it to her. She thanked him. "Excuse me."

Jackson left the room abruptly. She stood with interest in the paintings on his wall. One painting in particular, caught her attention. Brooke absently raised her glass at ear level as her other hand propped her elbow while she studied the artwork.

"I also like a woman who knows what she wants out of life." Startled, Brooke jumped, and the raised glass spilled on Jackson's white shirt. Brooke noticed that he'd removed his sweater. He jumped with outstretched arms.

"Oh, no." She covered her mouth with a hand. "Let me help you, please."

Before she could head to the kitchen for a towel, Jackson said, "No, you good, Brooke. Girl, you good." He chuckled and added, "I ain't gonna die. I went to hang up my sweater, because I got too warm. I didn't mean to sneak up on you." As she apologized profusely, Jackson lifted the dress shirt at the hem to wipe down his damp skin with his hand.

"No big deal, baby." He peeked up to see her smirking.

Brooke realized that he caught her eyes staring at his stomach and not his eyes. A taste of his tight, glistening, lower abdominal stole her complete attention. He unbuttoned his shirt and gave her a full view.

He teased, "Oh, great, Brooke. Now I've got to change." He tried to study her, but Brooke bit her lower lip as she avoided his stare.

Facing away, she told him, "Maybe I should go, Jackson." Concerned, he stepped closer to her and gently turned her face to meet her eyes. Brooke's lips separated.

"Hey. Did I do something wrong, Brooke?" His eyes squinted in confusion.

"No, no, Jackson." Her knuckles rested against her lips. "It's just that I think we should continue our date on another night, that's all."

"Well, this ain't the only shirt I own." His joking didn't work.

His sexy eyes seduced her, stealing her ability to stand without buckling, and her heartbeat picked up. No man had ever made her feel more than an initial attraction. She'd never been in love. But with Jackson, she felt like a magnet inside of him attracted a magnet somewhere inside of her.

"What's up? Talk to me." He'd almost become a blur to her. She could hear him, but she wasn't listening.

My pussy is on fire. I want to rip his clothes off and screw him senseless on his own floor? I want to drop to this floor and own his penis.

"Brooke?" His voice sounded like an echo of meaningless noise.

Brooke contemplated taking advantage of the possibilities, while considering the idea of resisting and waiting it out. What if touching Jackson felt right at this moment, but wrong later? He wasn't a pair of shoes that she could try on and return later, and that horrified her.

Amber

That same night, Amber was the hare and Brooke the tortoise in the sex department. She'd already arrived at George's home. In fact, she sat cozy in his mini mansion while his wife enjoyed a cruise ship adventure with her sisters. George and Amber stretched out on his bed to watch random cable channels while feeding each other strawberries and whipped cream.

"This is the life, Amber, my young, chocolate bunny." Amber hated when he chewed and talked, but she grinned and bore it. Instead of seeing white cream on the corners of his mouth when he talked, she replaced them with miniature dollar signs.

Amber rubbed his gray, hairy chest with her palm and raised a bare thigh over his legs. "Darling," she started as she traced her fingers over his face. "You did remember to change the sheets before I came, right?"

He peeked at her from the corner of his eyes. As he shook his head, the lose skin on his throat shook too. "No, I didn't, but my housekeeper did."

"Good enough for me, George." Amber smiled and straddled him.

"Whoopsie," George called out as he struggled to balance her. "I see you're ready to get into action." He slapped one of her thighs.

She placed a finger over his thin lips. "Shhh. Not yet." Amber rocked back and forth on his groin. "What do you think your housekeeper will say if she catches us or sees me here?"

George closed his eyes in pleasure. "I . . . I don't know, my chocolate bunny. Why?"

"George, will she tell on us? Huh, George?" Amber had fun teasing. She bit her bottom lip.

His head bent so far back that she could only see nostrils and cavity fillings. "Who's gonna tell her?"

Amber knew she had him in a weak position, literally and figuratively. She chuckled. "George, I was thinking about buying a new piano. I want to be able to play a great piece for you, but in the buff." Amber stopped rocking.

George's chin hit his chest. "You know Amber, I'm beginning to think that you think that you can throw any figure at me and I'll shell out."

Instead of panicking, she stated the truth. "Well, I'm beginning to think you think that you can find this," she pointed up and down at her body, "package anywhere." Pouting, she crossed her arms over her chest and dismounted from on top of him. She landed on her back, but then turned it to him.

"Sugar." He tapped her on the shoulder. Amber refused to face him unless she heard something good. "Look, uhh, I know I'm not in my prime, and that I'm no looker. You think I don't know that what we do is wrong to my wife and that you can be giving up your treats to someone else?" His heavy breathing was louder than normal, and Amber hated it at normal.

"Sweetheart, you're killing me here. You just got paid. What do you do with the money? You should invest it so, you know. You don't have to do this just to get by. How about you buy that piano with all the money I gave you?"

George stopped talking, but at this point, Amber fumed with annoyance. This was no longer a game to her, so she flipped on her side as fast as a fish out of water and peered at him. "Invest? Invest? Do you think I care about the stock market, or having a square hold onto my cash as he sees fit? I'm earning this money that I get from you. You're right. You're married, and that will never change and I really don't care. You're right. I could be with a man way more handsome than you. Therefore, when I sleep with you, George, I feel like I should name my figure, because this is not a joyride. So, yes, the least you can do is stop being cheap. Or, you can always go back to relying on your wife to make you feel a fraction as good as I make you." Amber heaved under a boulder of anger, but somewhere, she suspected that she went a little too far. George confirmed her suspicions. Speechless, they couldn't look at each other until he spoke.

"Well. Amber, I think you're beautiful, and we could've had fun together. I may be old and ugly, but I do have money sense and a small fortune. I may be married, but my wife has always been there for me and is never condescending. And now that I say that and now that I see a young, beautiful woman sitting here in her spot on our bed, the more I realize that I'd rather take a class with her to learn rocky road sex, than to have it with a woman whom I must pay and who has no clue about what it all means or amounts to in the end. So, Amber, you are not going to get another single cent from me. I won't even pay you to keep your mouth shut. I've gambled before, and I can do it again."

Flabbergasted, she placed a hand on her chest. "So, you want me to leave?"

"Promptly."

Embarrassed, all she could do was suck her teeth and offer an apology. "Look, I'm sorry." Tears came to her eyes. The thought of being wrong all along when her sister tried to warn her rubbed her the wrong way. "George, please," she tried under a strained voice while wiping her unstoppable tears. "George, I didn't mean any of it. I know I came off nasty, b-but it's not like what you think, or, like it came out. You have to reconsider."

George stayed seated on his bed. "For who, Amber?"

"Didn't you want to role play with me? R-remember that?"

He shook his head vehemently. "Not like this, Amber. I'm not willing to go broke for you."

Amber stood, peering downward at him from beneath her eyelashes. "You said the night I met you that you'd pay me a certain amount, and when I stated my rate, you agreed."

He shrugged like a little boy. "You were tickling my balls, what did you think? You coulda' asked if I ate a donkey sandwich for dinner, and I woulda' said yes. I mean, I paid up that night, but you want a down payment for a car every time I see you. I can stroke myself for free if worse comes to worse, Amber." George threw his hands up in disbelief.

Quickly composing herself, Amber decided to go all out. She figured that his little bruised ego could be iced with a visual. She looped her fingers into her underwear band and tugged them down as she alternated her hips up and down until they revealed her groin. Luckily, she'd waxed. That never failed to excite any man.

George's eyes nearly bulged from his head as he gripped his sheets for mercy. "Didn't I tell you to go?"

Determined to push away her emotions, Amber twirled her panties around her index finger. She smirked. "Okay, fine." She slipped her feet into her high heels and walked toward the bedroom door as she continued to twirl her panties. Amber sashayed her bare butt to let him see what he was kicking to the curb. It was a bold move, walking away with just a bra on, but she'd gambled before and won on the slots. A man wasn't any more difficult to Amber. She figured she should try one more special touch. Amber dropped her panties and reached down slowly to pick them up. She heard the bed sheets ruffle like a cat scratching crazy claws all over the fabric.

Before Amber knew it, her back had been slammed against the cold door. George had moved so quickly that she didn't remember him turning her around to face him. With one arm pinned against the door beside her, George asked, "How about we negotiate?" His eyes grew intense and his breathing sounded like he was fighting a racing heart explosion.

Amber peered down furtively at his manhood. His friend was wide awake and it told her that the ball was totally in her court. "Four thousand tonight and you will never see me again?"

"You are so lucky that my attraction to my wife is as strong as a baby's punch."

With an accomplished smile, Amber smiled. "Good."

"Wait, not so fast." His eyes burned holes into her soul, and it kind of turned her on. "I'm the boss. It's going down my way."

"Ok," Amber whispered.

"Pretend you were caught trying to escape from your master."

Summer

I sat at the table of a seafood restaurant in Arlington across from my boss, as we waited for her husband. I tried to go light on the appetizer by tearing the smallest pieces of bread from my dinner roll. Nothing else could say 'loser' any more, than sitting here on a great Saturday with none other than your boss. Nothing.

Fran checked her watch. "I cannot understand what could be keeping my husband like this."

I decided to crack a joke to ease my own mind. "Is he always on time like this?" Or maybe that was just rude.

Surprisingly, Fran kind of ditched the conservative act and let her guard down. "Honey, if it were sex he would have been eight months early." We shared our first laugh. Her version of a laugh was a smirk and mine was, well, a laugh.

I popped another piece of bread into my mouth and asked, "So how long have you been with Mr. Punctual?"

"*Married*, Summer, we're married," she corrected.

"Oh, yes, married. Right." And just like that, Fran reappeared. Note to self: Don't get too comfortable.

"We've been married for seven years. We met at an antique auction."

Yawn. I tried to sound intrigued. I raised my eyebrows at her. "Really? What'd you buy?" Man. I should've been an actress, because she really thought I cared.

Right when she almost responded, she pointed above my head and said, "Well, there he is."

Okay. Where was this fatty old man? I turned behind to my right, but to no avail. Fran stood and said, "Gee, honey. You really kept us waiting."

So, I checked my left. I came face to face with her husband's thigh.

"Summer, this is my husband." As my gaze raised to follow the towering body, it appeared to be happening in slow motion. When my eyes reached the face, I just about died.

Brooke

"W-we can't." Brooke stared her temptation right in the eyes.

Puzzled, he asked, "You mean I can't kiss you?"

What should I do? What should I do? Would the kiss would lead to something more? She just couldn't handle that. But what if she did sleep with him and liked it? Then what? She felt like she was on a game show where at any time Jackson would say, 'Brooke, I need an answer' before all bets were off.

"I . . . I . . . I," but it was too late. Jackson decided for her. Suddenly, she felt the softness of those full lips covering hers. Despite the coldness of his lips, they made her feel so warm. He held back his tongue and just allowed her to feel his mouth resting on hers.

Since she didn't back away, Jackson took the liberty of going further. He squeezed both of his lips around the top of Brooke's. Unable to resist, she allowed herself to taste his, involuntarily devouring what she had in her mouth.

Jackson's intensity increased, grabbing the back of her head with a handful of hair. His other hand caressed the nape of her neck. Brooke wanted to see his passion, and she found herself staring at a man with shrugged shoulders, engulfed in the moment. And she loved it.

She took her hands and held Jackson timidly by the waist, afraid of what would happen next if she decided to let go. It wasn't her. Women like her waited. Besides, what would the girls think?

Emily

Emily removed the TV dinner from the microwave. "Pathetic," she mumbled. She couldn't believe that it came down to a TV dinner at her age. She could've at least ordered take-out.

Making her way to the sofa of the family room, Emily kicked her feet up on the coffee table and turned on the television with the remote.

She stopped flicking to watch an episode of a crime investigation series. Remembering that she lived alone, she decided against it and changed the channel. Bravo always had amusing entertainment, so she stopped on a dramatic scene between two women. A few bites into her meal, she heard a knock at her door. Immediately, her heart raced as she froze. No one ever knocked at her door at this time before. *No* one. Placing her prison dinner onto the coffee table, she stood up and tiptoed to the window beside the door.

Puzzled, she checked her watch and read the time. "Nine-fifty? Who would be at my door?" she mumbled as she shook her head in slight annoyance and panic. She slid against the wall to avoid being seen. Peeking over her shoulder, she lifted the curtain just enough to peek at the porch. Nothing.

Cussing under her breath, Emily crouched and slid past the window without producing a shadow and quietly checked through the peep hole and sighed. Wow. Out of all the men it had to be him. However, she felt relief that there wasn't any funny business and willed her heart to stop racing.

Emily disarmed the locks and snatched the door wide open. "Really, are you trying to give me a heart attack?"

Zach could barely look at her. "I'm sorry?"

"It's 2016. Nobody has random visitors anymore." Obviously, Zach didn't know what to say. "I live alone, Zach, and it's dark."

When it all dawned on him he said, "Oh! Oh! My apologies. I wasn't thinking. It's just that Heather just picked up the boy so I could finally step away. May I come in?" he asked with a tip of his cowboy hat.

Emily squinted in suspicion and peeked out of the door to spot any potential witnesses. She didn't want to be caught talking to a pervert. "What do you want?" she asked with a hint of irritation.

Zach pressed his lips together. "To apologize, little lady."

Emily hissed, "Oh, stop it. We're not in the South."

"Emily." He held up a hand. "May I come in?"

She folded her arms and studied him. "Why? What are you going to show me this time? You got a video of you opening your butt cheeks to the camera?"

He grimaced. "Please, Emily, nothing of that nature. I said I was sorry and I am." She realized that Zach did seem apologetic. "So, may I?"

Emily relented and yanked her door open to accommodate his shoulders. "You got two minutes." She held up two fingers. "Two." She closed the door behind him and crossed her arms.

"Emily," he said as he clutched the rim of his hat against his chest. "I understand that you are Enzo's teacher."

She sighed. "Yeah. I got him." She dropped her defensive arms as her expression softened.

"I'm sorry, Emily. What you saw on that video just didn't represent me. It was drunk, holiday fun. I really thought nothing of it at the time, and I certainly don't know why she sent that."

Emily's jaw dropped. "So, flagging your," she motioned her hand at his lower half, "genitals is fun? You're a handsome man. You don't have to resort to such lewd behavior."

Zach nodded in agreement. "You're right. With Heather, my life was crazy, so I got out. But I just don't want you to feel some kind of way against my boy."

Emily's tone softened at the thought of mistreating a child. "Zach, I would never do anything to make a child feel wronged. Please believe, you can trust that your child will receive equal treatment as though I never saw your phone." Emily began to feel appreciative that Zach came over to share his concerns. "And I know you were just letting your hair down with someone you trusted. It feels good. I didn't mean to berate you so much."

"Thank you so, so much Emily." Finally at ease, Zach gave her a genuine smile of gratuity.

Even though he'd apologized, she was curious about one thing. "Since your two minutes are pretty much up, I do have one question to ask." He raised his eyebrows to show he was listening. "Well, if he was not in my class—"

Zach cut her off. "Of course, I was going to apologize. I couldn't leave things that way."

They smiled at one another. "Well, thank you, Zach. It really means a lot to me that you stopped by."

He placed the hat back on his head. "Well, I should be on my way." A hungry Emily nodded as he opened her door to show himself out. He paused before exiting.

"Thank you again, Emily, for being a kind enough woman to hear me out. You didn't have to. So, thanks."

Emily nodded again with a faint smile and with that, he proceeded to leave. Even though Emily no longer harbored bad thoughts about the penis whipper—and had decided to respect his actual name for future reference—she didn't understand why his visit made her feel a little subdued.

She sat on the staircase and cupped her face in balled fists. "Oh, Eric," she whimpered.

The irony of it all. She saw decency in the least-expected person. The same man who committed a lewd act on a phone was the same man who made her think about love. No matter how hard Emily tried to shake Eric, it wasn't working. Some days were better than others. The moment of spending two lousy minutes with Zach made her realize that, if she could, she would still take Eric back—in a heartbeat.

Brooke

"Stop." Just like that, Jackson backed off. Brooke's hand rested on his stomach, rising and falling with his every breath.

Out of breath, he could barely manage an, "Okay," with surrendering palms. "I understand, Brooke. I'm heavily attracted to you, and it's too much, too soon. I get it. I should've controlled myself better."

Brooke's breathing trembled and he managed to regulate his. She looked at him with eyes in a trance-like state. "It's not a blame game, it's attraction." Brooke touched her overworked lips and felt like dropping to her knees in capitulation, even though she'd be putting way too much on the line too soon. Next thing she knew, she'd be pacing in her condo, waiting by the phone and obsessing over him with friends. She saw it way too much and never wanted to be like those women. So, she figured it would be better to leave now while she still had control than to stay and let the sexual deed happen and give up her soul.

Jackson turned his back to her and placed his hands at his waist. He gave her a profile view. "Brooke, I didn't mean to uhh, to umm, you know."

She wanted him to face her. She stepped forward and reached out to place a hand on his broad shoulder. "Look at me, please."

Jackson did and he looked disappointed. "Brooke, I'm not used to this."

"What do you mean?" she asked.

"I want you badly. But clearly you want to take things slow, and for the first time, I don't mind." He could barely look up at her. He started to rake his fingers across his lips in thought. "I haven't brought a girl to my house so fast in years now. Some end up attached way too fast and begin acting crazy."

Brooke nodded. The fact that he'd made an exception for her left her speechless, but she wanted to assure him. "Well, that's not me."

He smiled without showing teeth. "I know." Jackson held his hand out. Without hesitation, she slid her hand into his. It felt right. "Let me get my car and take you home." Brooke didn't know what she was doing until she did it. She lurched forward and placed a soft but lasting kiss on his mouth. As she stepped back, she bit her lower lip, staring innocently into his eyes.

Jackson's head jerked back in confusion as he chuckled. "What was that for?"

She shrugged. "Just because I think I've found a gentleman."

Jackson cruised past the crowd at the Verizon Center and turned left to access her neighborhood. He was lucky enough to find parking right in front of her building. The growling of his Challenger stopped when he cut off his engine. They sat in the dark car, waiting to see who would break the silence first.

Jackson turned to face her. "Tonight was one-of-a-kind, don't you think?"

Brooke smiled. For the first time in a long time, something else other than work made her happy. "Jackson, if nothing mattered, then I wouldn't have stopped you—or us."

"I know, Brooke."

"Well, you say that, but this could be our last date. I don't want to hold you back from what you need."

Jackson stroked the back of her hair. "Hold me back? Nah. Sex comes and goes, and I can find that anywhere. But if I was upset, then I woulda' called you a cab, right?"

She shrugged. "I suppose so."

"I wanna see you again," he said quickly.

Brooke could feel her heart flutter a few beats. "When?"

"You'll be doing me a favor, so you tell me when." She loved the sound of his husky voice as they sat in his cherry-colored car.

"If that's true, then you call me this week to follow up," she told him in the softest tone as she unbuckled her seat belt. She kissed him on the cheek, "Bye," and hopped out abruptly.

It wasn't even two seconds after strutting away when she heard his door pop and shut. "Hey, Brooke," he called as he got closer. When he caught up he said, "Hold on, girl." In front of the revolving doors, Brooke stopped and faced him with a smile.

Jackson stood in front of her. "Whoa. Did you have to leave so suddenly?"

"Yes. If you want more time with me, I told you to make the next step." She kissed him on the right cheek. "Thank you for paying my cab fare." Then she kissed his left cheek. "Thank you for cooking an awesome dinner." She pecked him on the lips. "Thank you for driving me here like a real man would." Brooke placed a gentle hand on his cheek, stroked it and let it coast down his chest before removing it. "Good night, Jackson."

His expression told her that he wanted more from her, whether it was time or physically related. "Okay, sweetheart." Jackson nodded, "Good night." Brooke waved with wiggling fingers and went through the revolving doors. She felt accomplished, even though the date tested her discipline. But at least she knew she left him wanting more.

Summer

My heart almost somersaulted into my stomach. Was her husband really Ruben? *Ruben*? But in that short time, I knew I had to collect myself before Fran, my boss, would toss me to the wolves. I had a home to maintain. God knows that searching for a new job with the stiff competition was not at the top of my Want-To-Do list. Even if I could contain myself, the million-dollar question was, could he?

I stood as best as I could, considering that my legs were as strong as noodles. When I had flashes of my junk on the curb, and all my new clothes getting ambushed by strangers, I knew I had to pull it together. If I convinced myself that I was an actress earlier, well now would be the time to prove it. Otherwise, I'd have to marry thirsty Max just to get by. That is, unless he'd already moved on.

I tried my best to study Ruben in the short time I had. He mirrored my pathetic expression. Fran had too many years on this planet not to catch stupidity. Oh Lord, I'm going to be homeless. His eyes froze as he registered my face. I could tell his stomach had catapulted into his heart. Now either he was way older than he looked, or he was young and she was a cougar. Either way, I accepted his big hand to shake it. Wow. Was I really going to be punished with memories of a car hood and freezing nipples? Clearly.

Ruben's firm hand shake reminded me of his performance: strong. He fared a forced and strained smile.

"Hello, there, umm, Summer. How—how are you?" He used his other free hand to cup our gripped hands. Ruben nodded once and released my hand before sitting next to his wife.

Calmly, or so I hoped, as I sat down, I said, "It's really nice to see—I mean—meet you, Mr. uhh—"

"Sotolongo," he finished. I loved the way his name rolled right off his tongue.

"Right." My smile was so fragile, and I was so nervous. I prayed Fran couldn't tell.

My boss peered at me with pure sincerity. "Are you okay?"

I took a quick swallow of water. "Umm hmm." I nodded, but even I wasn't fooling myself.

Fran waved a playful hand at me. "Oh, it's okay. Ruben always has this effect on women." How ironic. When she finally decided to flash a smile with teeth, I didn't find anything funny at all.

Luckily, she peered back at her menu and failed to notice my lack of enthusiasm for her joke. The server came back. As I held the menu at nose height, I took the opportunity to steal furtive glances at Ruben. I could only imagine that he felt like dying, too.

Ruben completely hid behind his menu. I decided on steak and mashed potatoes, even though I doubted any of that would stay down tonight. I couldn't believe my boss' husband screwed my brains out a few days ago. No, not possible.

Once we all placed our orders, Fran dismissed herself to use the ladies' room. I was so grateful to have this moment with him. I wanted to ring his neck.

Ruben looked so guilty. "Umm, excuse me, Mr. Sotogotologo?"

He squinted at me and tilted his head to the left. In a dull tone, he said, "It's Sotolongo."

"Whatever. Why didn't you tell me you have a wife?" The irritation made my nostrils flare.

"Please, look, Summer." He flashed his palm to stop me. "My, uh, wife likes to pretend that we're not fighting a separation. Why do you think I'm here? She's desperate to look like we're a solid couple to other people. Look, it makes her feel good to drag me along to things like this. But I want out, and she's resisting."

I quickly peeked behind me to make sure she wasn't near. "Ruben, why not be honest and divorce her?" I began to feel like I slighted her chance at improving her marriage. "Why cheat on her?"

Ruben appeared remorseful as he placed a finger over his top lip with an elbow propped on the table. "It's not as easy as you think, Summer."

"I never pegged you for the older kind, Ruben." I couldn't believe that he tricked me with his naked ring finger that night. However, he had it on tonight. "When we met, she was different. She wasn't so uptight like she is now. Once she reeled me in for the long haul, she slowly became a nagger. Nothing I do is right anymore." Ruben threw his hands up. "I'm bored and tired, Summer. It's as simple as that."

"Gee, Ruben, when I said I wanted dinner with you, I didn't mean with your wife." I gave him a final evil eye as I swiped a strand of hair from my face.

"Okay, what did I miss?" Fran's perky voice snuck up behind me as she reclaimed her place at the table.

As the night went on, Ruben and I did the best acting of our lives. As far as I knew, she didn't even pick up on our facial shenanigans. I did see a more relaxed side of Fran, but nothing that screamed, 'This is why he married me'. I was beginning to wonder if there was more to this story than what Ruben told me. I guess I would never know.

Fran did intrigue me with a story of how they went to Florida so she could meet his Cuban family. She didn't give any inkling that they couldn't endure the long haul. My biggest beef was trying to imagine her hanging from the rafters with a sexually competent husband like hers. I could only imagine Fran nagging about the bed sheets. *Oh, dear. Try not to stain our new Egyptian cotton, 500-thread-count sheets. Oh, dear. Oh, dear. Oh, dear. Eek.* I hated women like that. I smirked and chuckled, but I knew she thought it was because of her story.

Later on that night, Fran asked me what I liked, as she endeavored to discover my key motivators to a great and consistent performance. I wanted to tell her that it would be Ruben and that letting me roll in the hay with him would be a great reward to guarantee my best performance. But as the night went on, I found myself wanting to ring her neck for being able to go home with that hot Cubano.

Fran picked up the check as she refused to let Ruben do it. He couldn't hide his subtle disappointment. Fran appeared oblivious to his looking away as she signed her name on the tab. Apparently, this wasn't the first time Ruben had been denied to show up as the man in their marriage. Irritated, he tapped the table with a finger as he waited.

Without looking up and while adding the totals, Fran complained blandly, "Ruben, please." He exhaled and leaned back into their bench cushion. When she was done, she looked up at me with an actual smile on her face. "There." Fran dropped the pen on the table.

I placed my hands together and then intertwined my fingers. "Thank you so much, Fran. This was a lovely dinner, and I had a blast hearing about your vacation stories and meeting your husband."

"Well, please, Summer. Don't even mention it. Maybe we can do this again. Besides, out of all the people I've treated, you have been the most delightful."

I placed my hand over my heart. "Awww, thank you." *Even though you have no clue I know what your husband looks and feels like. Thank you.*

"My dear, how are you getting home?"

I'd thought nothing of it. "Oh, uh, the Metro." Fran's eyebrows furrowed. "Or, I can just hail a cab."

"Well, Ruben and I took separate vehicles here, so—"

Ruben swooped in like a crow on a carcass. "Where do you live?" he asked casually.

"At the Waterfront." He knew exactly where I lived. What was he up to anyway?

With his hands in his pockets, he said, "Honey, I really don't feel good about you tripping to DC this late. I have to drop off some basketball tickets to Alan anyway. Would you like me to drop her off?"

I had to play along. "But, Mr. Sotolongo, isn't that an imposition?"

Fran tapped her fingertips together while she contemplated. "Well, I guess that does make more sense. But you have to be okay with this, Summer. Whatever's best."

"Well, I really feel bad for having my boss drive from Arlington to DC and then to Alexandria so late." The truth was, I would rather be stuck in a car with her snake-of-a husband than to be bombarded with more family stories or questions about my boring life.

"Well, I would feel even worse having my employee in harm's way after a date on which I insisted, because I let her take public transportation this late at night." Fran winked. Okay, she was a little charming.

After a few more minutes of verbal exchanges, we left. Fran drove herself home and Rubin walked us underground into the garage to take me home in his all-too-familiar convertible.

At first, we didn't say a word after climbing in. After we strapped on our seat belts, we sat still as he ran the engine for a minute. Suddenly, he turned to look at me.

"Summer, I swear to you that I was actually drawn to you the night we were intimate."

I spun my head to look at his pleading face. "Okay, but that is the least of my concerns. Your naked ring finger had me in front of my boss and her husband with whom I had sex. Just take me home."

"Okay," he agreed reluctantly. We drove in silence for the first five minutes. Then he said, "I really can't stop thinking about you. I haven't been able to."

I felt my karma had come for messing up Max's head and heart. I considered calling him to see how he was doing.

"Just drive," I replied.

We arrived at my home in about fifteen minutes. When he started parallel parking, I realized how unnecessary it would all be.

"Wait. What are you doing? I'm tired and ready for some sleep." I really wanted him in my bed, just one more time. I felt like an addict.

"Gentlemen walk their dates to the door."

"Now you wanna be a gentleman? Gentlemen don't cheat or lie. And besides, we weren't on a date. And if we were, it was by default." I felt like he wasn't buying my attempt at being mean or firm.

"Well, how about I show you tonight that I can be one?"

I couldn't respond fast enough. He had already hopped out and come to my side to let me out. My door opened and his large hand awaited. Ohhhh, nooo. Not that hand again. I slipped mine into his and that was all she wrote.

The electricity and the memories of that night flooded me like a hangover. He didn't let go as we approached my building. I didn't fight it either. I couldn't explain feeling the adrenaline rush chancing it with my boss' husband.

I didn't have a doorman like a friend of mine or a front desk with staff members to greet me. We just marched to the elevator like a couple. I had completely forgotten about Fran. Maybe I just didn't care to remember or consider her. Still in silence, Ruben followed me to my door. When we arrived, I stopped and turned at him, drawn to his chest. "Okay, this is my joint, buddy." I slapped his arm and pulled out my key.

"Yeah, but I had a few glasses of wine. I could really use your bathroom."

Such a liar. "Fine." *And you are so easy, Summer.* Ruben took one step in with me, and when I turned to secure the door behind him, one large hand slid on the side of my waist, then the other. He held me close with his nose against the tip of mine.

I found it hard to look into his smoky eyes, so I settled for the bridge of his nose. "R-Ruben. What about your wife?"

"Summer, have you ever heard of the line, 'So wrong, it feels so right?'" We breathed into each other as I gripped the opening of his button-down shirt. I played with his collar and traced my hands down his chest. I thrust my tiny hips until my groin pressed into his. I swallowed hard, and so did he.

Ruben tugged at my long hair. His lips came swooning down and they barely touched my ear lobe. His breath caressed my ear. I panted. I felt his lips against my neck. He kissed my neck all over. A married man was kissing my neck all over.

Someone, make him stop. I pleaded, but no one could hear me, and I didn't want them to. What about work on Monday morning? I felt my leg slide up against his thigh. What about the discomfort that I was going to feel the next time I had to interact with Fran? Was it my fault that this man seduced me in my home? Why did being so weak turn me on? I guess as long as I could blame it on being weak, I felt like I could escape prosecution here.

The first time it was hot because we were strangers going at it outside. This time, it was hot because he was married to my boss. That made the intensity worse. I jumped onto his body and swung my other leg around him. I locked him in position like on the first night. Luckily, I wore an ankle-length skirt.

My stomach reacted to the conductor playing around in there. As I hugged him with my legs, Ruben walked us against the wall outside of my bedroom. He removed my shirt and threw it out of sight. I worked his buttons, but not fast enough. Ruben took over and revealed that familiar sinewy chest as he tossed his shirt somewhere into oblivion.

I could hear the rain outside starting to fall. What a perfect melody to a great moment. With my back pressed against the wall, I felt like my position mocked my real-life situation. I knew this was so wrong, but every time he breathed on me, or placed his lips on my neck or lips, I was down for the count.

"Baby," he hissed through strained breath.

"Ruben," I moaned as he ripped my panties off in the dark. My legs dropped so that he could remove my skirt down my hips, as I his pants. I would die if he ripped my seventy-two-dollar skirt.

I saw his shadow, but then the street light from outside emanated enough light to reach inside my room between the blinds. For a moment, I could see the passion and torture of lust on his face. He held up my panties and smelled them. "Mmm," he inhaled with closed eyes. Hitting me with a dead stare, he lowered them above his mouth, circling his tongue around the material.

I succumbed to dying painfully at the hands of horniness. "Take me to bed," I whispered. He swept me up and led me to my room then placed me down on my bed. I sat up and freed my breasts from the constraints of my bra. I threw it somewhere to the side in the dark.

I was completely naked and ready as he pulled out another condom. Every moment absent from his touch almost drew me back to reality. Almost. I had a couple of last thoughts of my boss and one final mean thought. I wanted to justify my actions by telling myself that if she couldn't take care of her husband, then maybe I should have the right to. Yes, that would be my excuse until Ruben and I were done. I knew he would need an excuse as to why he hadn't come back home in an hour from now, but I couldn't worry about that. I was more than happy at that moment to be the cause.

As Ruben lowered himself onto me, I wanted to explode as I fantasized about the pleasure that I would have with him. Our lips locked and so did something else. Mmm. That was it. That was what I longed for. Our bodies rolled around on my bed as our forbidden experience made my arousal peak.

Ooh, so bad. The whole thing was explosive. I saddled him like a horse and let it all go. We were in sync. How could Fran not take care of this? I shrugged it off. I lowered my chest onto his chest and kept up the rhythm. Then

Ruben threw me over and unleashed his furry from behind, the weight of his body smashing mine. I buried my face into my pillow and reveled in each thrust. Just when I neared completion, he withdrew and flipped me back over to assume the top position.

"Summerrrrrr. Ooh. *Tu cuerpo . . . te necesito, mi amor*." Of course, I didn't understand what he said, but the only language I needed to understand was pleasure.
And that was all it took. A few mumbo jumbo words and I'd reached my limit. After calling out each other's names, he collapsed on top of me, along with the weight of guilt and realization of the consequences.

Imagine how crushed my body felt.

4: decision, decisions, decisions

Summer

*I*t was Monday morning.

It was Monday morning.

It was Monday morning.

The thought kept burning into my head, and I didn't know what to do with it. I usually washed my sheets on Sunday, but the smell of Ruben's cologne resided in the thread, and I wasn't mad. I couldn't let myself wash him away. Something was happening to me. I felt comfortable putting too much on the line for a man.

I rolled over and placed a chunk of hair under my nostrils and locked it with my pushed-up lips to help resist smelling my linen. Anything but the familiar smell of him. Anything. I'd better be careful. One whiff of me without another shower and hair wash and Fran would smell her husband on me. I jumped out of bed and rectified that with a shower.

Brooke

Brooke expected to wake up from the sound of her alarm clock, but instead, she awoke to the sound of her cell phone ringer. "Who is this?" she asked in a raspy voice as she rolled over to pick up her phone. She smiled at the programmed name and number as she answered it. "Jackson."

She could hear his smirk. "I couldn't call you Sunday because that may have been too fast for you. Didn't wanna scare you away."

Brooke's heart began to race. He was the morning cup of coffee that she needed, filling her up with immediate energy. "No, no. That's silly to think that way." She tossed the covers off her legs and stood up beside her bed to get a better view outside of her window. "I would've welcomed that call."

She liked his manly chuckles. "Did I wake you?"

"Don't worry about that. Where are you?" Brooke squinted against the sun.

"At my cubicle . . . talking to you . . . pretending to read the files on my desk."

Brooke wrapped an arm around her waist. "Oh, naughty boy," she replied with a monotone tease. "You better earn that salary." Secretly, it flattered her.

"Do you want to teach me about work ethics after work today?" he asked. She sensed the pleasure in his voice at the idea of seeing her.

Concerned, she started with, "Jackson?"

He laughed. "Brooke? What's with the urgency behind my name?"

"I reconsidered the next time we should see each other again. I have three major weddings coming up, and I don't really know when we can have a real date again."

She heard silence and panicked. Her stomach knotted with tension. *Great, I pissed him off.*

"No, no. I get it. You're busy and so am I. But because I want to see you, like, as soon as possible, I have no problem making a fit for you. Look, sweetie, you just met me. You didn't know you would meet such an awesome guy who wanted your time. Do your thing this month. I don't want to be the reason your check is short. But next month, I expect you to pencil me in. Oh, and at the top of the month. Deal?"

Brooke couldn't help but feel giddy at the thought of a man being so understanding. "Wait. Not a deal, Jackson. I didn't mean to push you off for a month. That's a little steep, don't you think?" She didn't know that she had her index nail between her teeth.

"I don't know, sweetheart, you tell me. It's your schedule, your life. I'll wait for you in every sense, Brooke. But you just have to remember my existence."

"Jackson. Why are you so patient? I'm flattered, not complaining." She let out a hesitant, nervous laugh.

"I think you're worth it. Don't you?"

Jackson caught Brooke completely off-guard. "What? Uh, of course. No, I was just saying that—well, you know. I'm impressed by your patience, that's all."

"Look, I don't wanna get in the way of your work. You did your thing before me, so I expect you to keep on, as will I. I'm still gonna make time for you. Besides, I can't get in a way of a woman in charge of her life. I respect that too much."

"I—"

"I could talk to you all day, Brooke, but I gotta make these coins. Go ahead and hit me up later, all right?"

"Yeah?" She plopped back on her bed.

"You have a blessed day, baby. You'll be on my mind. All right, queen." She heard a click.

Queen? Queen? Brooke felt like a queen before meeting him. But any man giving a woman such a lofty title in this early stage made her feel suspicious. Was he a smooth operator, or a sincere man? Brooke rested the cell phone against her chest, as she lamented the fact that she couldn't call a decent mother to receive advice. But she knew three decent girls whom she could turn to for advice.

Emily

Emily had her sling briefcase and purse on her shoulder as she descended her staircase carefully in her heels. She'd been in a funk the whole weekend. Landing at the foyer, she remembered at the last minute to grab her gradebook from the kitchen island before officially heading out. As she slid the gradebook into the briefcase, she heard a jiggling noise at the front door that startled her. It was bad enough that she overslept and had to notify the school so they could find her a sub. In all her tenure, that'd never happened.

Who could be at my door?

Emily ran out of time to react as the door creaked open. "Who—who's there?" Emily demanded. Her eyes darted nervously as she waited for someone to approach. A knife. Would she resort to that?

"Relax, relax, Emily." She exhaled in relief at the sound of the familiar voice.

The familiar man with salt-and-pepper hair came into view, and her heart stopped. "Eric?" Her voice cracked as she placed a hand on her stomach to catch her breath. She held onto the island for support as her knees turned to jelly. "My God, Eric! You scared me to death. You couldn't call first?"

Eric had a smug look on his face. "Why aren't you at work? That seems to be the more important question. You know I have to get my last few boxes from the spare room. I came now hoping to spare you. But here you are. I didn't bother looking for your car. Figured you'd be gone."

Emily thought she'd recover, but then she saw a tall woman emerge from behind the wall. She had a long, blonde ponytail secured tightly at the top of her head. A trench coat covered her thin frame. Emily felt like she was looking at a White, taller version of herself. Wow. She ran into him alone at a dinner party, but in her house, he had company. How bizarre. That was it. She wanted to die, right there and then. She wanted to die.

With his hands still in his pockets, Eric pointed a wool-covered hand toward the woman. "Emily, this is Kyele, Kyele, Emily." Eric gave Emily a toothless, smug smile that read, "Take that, bitch."

Kyele simpered with a lousy, "Hi," and looked away. *Oh, he's going to get it,* Emily promised. *This bastard is going to get it.* She didn't know how, but trying to twist the knife in her stomach at every encounter had past the point of unnecessary. He'd made her the enemy, because he was too weak to reject the idea of marriage at his parents' insistence. Emily knew she didn't do anything wrong but accept.

Even though she initially wanted to die, anger consumed her now. Emily didn't leave him in the poor house after the divorce. She only kept the house. That was it. Eric was just happy to be free, but now he resented her and she didn't know why.

Emily took another look at his uncomfortable "Kyele." She couldn't seem to muster enough guts to face Emily. She absently dragged her heel across the wooden floor, avoiding Emily's piercing glare. Emily turned her hazel eyes back to Eric. He just stood there with a matter-of-fact expression.

"So, we're done here." Eric spread a large hand in the air. Emily hated her ex's smug mentality. She appreciated her cut ties with a pompous man of his caliber. Emily wasn't sure if he'd always been this disgusting and she was too in love to notice, or if he'd elevated his snobbish side because of Kyele.

Eric turned on his heel and grabbed the mute girl's hand and led her upstairs. With arms crossed and an angered but shattered heart, Emily saw her past fade around the corner with his future in tow.

Summer

I sat at my computer, reading our clients' job openings and hoping to find matching employees through our agency, but the list meant nothing to me. I couldn't stop smiling to myself as I kept on replaying the images of my bed romp with Ruben.

After our climax, Saturday night, a deep kiss with the hot Cubano led to one more round. We promised each other that we had to stay away from each other. Unfortunately, I deemed him the perfect lover.

I wasn't interested in marriage, and he couldn't give it to me. My attraction to him stemmed from the realm of intensity due to circumstances on top of his looks. He was married. That was forbidden, but that made the attraction fun and enticing. Then he was the husband of my boss. She didn't know what to do with him, obviously, and it drove me crazy. It was like owning a Ferrari that you couldn't drive, because it was a manual. It wasn't right. Just sell it. I hadn't seen Fran all morning, but she normally came on her own schedule. It gave me time to think about the situation. What could I do with Ruben? What were the stakes? Would I find him enticing and the fling sensational if he were to become suddenly single?

He was hot, and I was addicted to the idea of another sexual encounter before I found out who he was. But the stakes were raised and things grew hotter when I found out the truth. If he were just married to any other woman, how resistible would I find him then? But knowing that he was my boss' husband made it fun to move close to the fire. I just couldn't figure out why I seemed okay with the risk of getting burned. All this assessing, and I still couldn't quantify anything.

I needed to call a friend. Should it be Emily or Brooke? If I wanted to know how to use or burn Ruben, I would call Amber. But I wanted to know how to make sense of my situation.

Emily reminded me of a delicate flower. She'd been married and my dilemma could possibly offend her. Brooke had never been married, but she planned marriages. Oh, great. Maybe Amber would be the best bet. I sighed and hopelessly placed my chin on my palm.

Well, at least I had options. With three friends to choose from, maybe I didn't need to select. I could possibly face all three. I called Brooke first.

"Hello?" her confident voice answered.

"Brooke," I replied with urgency. "I need you."

"Great, because I need you, too. When and where?"

Oh, it felt so good to be so needed at the right time. "Lunch? Can you do it today?"

"I can do dinner. My schedule is tight. I'm running low on sleep so I have to request that you come to my part of town."

"At this point, I'd go to India. How's seven at Founding Farmers? I can go for a hamburger."

"See you then." Too busy to say goodbye, she hung up. In the meantime, I could concentrate. If Ruben could keep his mouth shut—and that would be a big if—maybe facing Fran would be a cakewalk.

"Summer. What a pleasure. How was your weekend?" I looked up to see Fran's toothy smile. It was nice to see them, and not because they were dazzling white. This woman never smiled. Suddenly, she was buddy-buddy with me. Or so it seemed.

"Oh, Fran. I had a lovely weekend. I had a nice time over dinner with you. I really did." Even though I slept with your husband. I felt like a pig, and if I were any lighter, I would have blushed a high shade of rose. Seeing her face offered me the answer that I struggled to arrive at minutes earlier. It was very wrong to sleep with another woman's husband. Now, that didn't mean that I desired him any less.

"That's great, Summer. Did Ruben bore you during the car ride? He likes to get on a kick about sports."

"Oh, no." I waved a hand at her. "He didn't bore me with sports."

Fran looked a little puzzled, but not suspicious. She held an envelope in her hand and absently swiped her fingers across the top crease. "No? Well, that's weird. He never misses a chance to bring sports up with people. Well, what did you guys talk about?"

Caught off-guard, I stumbled to think of something. "Oh, uh, well gee. I don't really remember. I was out of it by the time we had finished dinner. I was stuffed like a turkey, and I usually tune out the world by that point." I released a nervous giggle. Man, I hoped that she bought it.

"You wore full well. And I must say that out of all my dinner invites, you were one of my favorites." Fran smiled genuinely. I liked it. It was warm and charming, and I could start to see how Ruben may have been drawn to her. I also thought I couldn't feel any worse, but I did. I let her man bang me out twice in one week. The first-time offense was unbeknownst to me, but the second time was just irresponsible and my fault. I'd better not get married or else my karma would be heavy.

I didn't know how to handle this conversation any longer. I only wished that it would end. "Thank you, Fran. It was nice to get to know you, you know, aside from the business standpoint. Oh, and did my ride home from Ruben inconvenience you guys?"

"I was asleep when he came home. I conked out fifteen minutes after arriving home. He mentioned tickets to a game during breakfast and that he escorted you to your door and that was all. What a gentleman. So, enough of that. We have an emergency staff meeting at two. Two employees are not returning."

I grimaced to show sympathy and to subtly urge her to tell me more.

"Kathy and Emmanuel," she whispered. "Between you and me, they didn't follow the cyclic steps of the recruiting process, and it bit us in the tail. He thought he could share a shortcut, she tried it, it backfired, and now they are both out of jobs and we need to replace two spots. See you at two." Fran turned and left. She left me feeling at odds with myself.

I'd sent a text message to Emily to meet us at Founding Farmers once Brooke told me that she'd invited Amber. She confirmed that she would and that she had a juicy story. Emily and juicy just didn't seem to go in the same sentence to me.

However, here the three of us were, sitting at the table, waiting for Emily to show up. We'd already placed our orders, including Emily, who gave us permission to order anything for her that we wanted. In the meantime, we listened to Amber as she told us how ecstatic Mara was that she'd mailed her an envelope of cash and a plane ticket to DC.

Minutes later, Emily joined our table in a hurry. "So sorry, guys, for being fifteen minutes late."

"It's okay," we all said in unison.

"I mean, really, I was late for everything today." She must've been upset, because she rambled something in Spanish before continuing as she unwrapped the scarf from around her neck. "Can you believe my butthole ex-husband had the nerve to let himself in with his mute, dumb woman, Kyele? I mean, it's like her parents wanted a son to name Kyle, but ended up with a girl, and spun it to Kyele. I sound like a Southern belle when I say that name. Ridiculous.

I spun an impatient hand at her. "So, what happened?"

"Oh. Right." Emily explained the whole morning to us. Our mouths dropped as we eased in to hear intensely." Yes, so he looked at me like he had won a prize and like, I was this stupid woman alone in a big house that needed cats to complete the pathetic ending to my life. I don't know. I don't know. He was talking down to me as his mute lover looked like she was thinking, *I didn't sign up for this part*. So how I'm going to get him back?"

I pointed a finger at Amber. "Consult her."

Amber turned to her with a smile as she placed a hand over her heart. "Me?" Emily raised her eyebrows at her, waiting for advice. "Okay, well, what does he treasure most?"

Emily looked genuinely lost. "I . . . I don't know."

"Well, think. You sit here and think. Meanwhile, I'll tell you guys about my slave-and-master date with George."

"Shut up," Brooke replied. We fell over laughing in disbelief as Amber confirmed the night's events.

"I know. I was blown, too. Y'all, I'm talking red, old, sagging balls all up in my face. I was almost hoping he would die when he was slappin' my butt as punishment for 'trying to escape.' But then I realized I wouldn't have gotten paid."

Brooke looked like she had eaten something sour as she listened.

"He told me my punishment was to be spanked, and then he smashed his nuts and big, ugly bolt in my face to arouse himself even more."

"Ewwwwwwww," we all replied.

"The spanking wasn't enough to turn him on?" I asked.

Amber shrugged. "I guess not. But I told myself: shoes, handbags, your sister, blah, blah, and blah. Some thousands of dollars made it worth it."

Brooke sat quietly as she stared at the table. We fell silent and took note of her withdrawal. Without a trace of humor, she slowly raised her eyes and shook her head slowly. "I just don't know how you do it."

"Do what?" Amber challenged. Pursing her lips to the side, Emily looked elsewhere, sensing the shift in comfort.

"I don't understand how you can do that for a living." Brooke didn't bite her tongue, and neither did our New Yorker. One was classy with her blunt tongue, and the other one didn't have a filter.

"Well, I don't understand how you deal with those stuffy clients of yours. You have to probably run around town kissing a lot of tail, but that's you. This is me. We get paid the same amount from clients."

Brooke stared at the table as she carefully contemplated what to say to keep things cordial as possible. "Amber, no offense, but I can make almost twenty grand with one client, and I'm not kissing tail. I believe that is, literally, your job."

I couldn't help but burst into laughter because it was true. "Well, if you have balls in your face, there is a chance you had a big, droopy butt in your face, too."

"Shut up, Summer," Amber snarled back. Her head jerked back with a lowered chin and raised brows. With a suspicious tone, she asked Brooke, "Bih, you tryna throw shade?"

"Don't be calling me a bitch. Watch it. And it's not shade." She smiled. "It's truth."

"She didn't say the whole word," I shrugged, "if that helps." They ignored me.

Amber replied, "Okay, well, Brooke. I share my stories with you, but I don't have to explain my actions to anyone."

"But, Amber," Brooke tried calmly and borderline emotionless. "What do you do with your money? Do you invest it?"

Amber flipped her hand in the air every time she said, "Invest? Invest?" as she looked to the ceiling. "What is with you and George? Do I look like a Wall Street head to you?"

"You don't have to be that type, Amber. I just think that there is a smart way to maximize your profit, that's all. Eventually your knees will get tired and you will thank me for pointing out a way to make your money make you more money. That's all."

Amber shook her head and rolled her eyes. "Moving on. Next."

Brooke spoke up with a more aggressive tone. "Did you like playing a slave? Did that not make you feel devalued as a person? A White man wanted to play that power role on you in 2016 and you're a Black woman?"

Amber snapped and defended herself in a high whisper, "Brooke. That man turned over six thousand dollars in one week, *one week*, on one, not two, but one piece of pussy. Do you think that really sounds like someone with real power? He was so weak, all I had to do was put up with him for a few hours and I got paid more in one day what more than most women earn working a nine to five for five days, and let us not forget that I do make an honest living offering piano lessons in my home. Sleeping with men for money is not my only hustle." Brooke shrugged as a sign of giving up.

Emily turned her head in different directions and said, "Guys, shhh. Keep your voices down."

Brooke said, "Too late."

"Ladies," I said, wanting to change the subject to salvage any hope of peace. "Listen, remember the guy I slept with at the party, Ruben?" They nodded, "He's the husband of my boss."

Emily choked on her soda. Amber snapped her attention to Emily and placed a hand on her back. "Are you okay, honey?" Her eyes were wide with fear as she watched Emily nod frantically. She coughed to clear her throat.

Brooke tried to come to terms with what she heard. "Soooo, wait." She pointed a low finger at Amber. "You're getting paid to sleep with another woman's husband," and then she aimed at me, "and you're sleeping with a married man willingly, and on top of that, he's the husband of your boss."

I nodded frantically. My eyes filled with horror. "Yeah." It sounded awful coming from another person, and worse coming from Brooke.

"Wow." Brooke looked traumatized as she stared downward. She shook her head as she contemplated my words.

"Emily, you're awfully quiet," Amber chimed in.

We all looked at her.

Emily said, "I don't envy you two. I mean, on one hand, you have old, ashy, balls in your face, and on the other hand, you have a heffa stealing the man of her *jefa*."

"What?" we all asked.

"*Jefa*. It's Spanish for a female boss."

We'd all succumbed to laughter. The cases sounded pathetic.

Amber looked at me with wide eyes. "What are you gonna do?" she asked. She and I'd crossed the same line, except I crossed my boss' line, and she earned commission on her bad karma.

I smirked at her before saying, "Uhh, that's why I called my buddies." I leveled my hand in front of each of them to accept any offerings.

Brooked chimed in. "Gee. My little issue pales in comparison to all of yours. I feel blessed today."

My curiosity piqued. "Yeah? What did you need to see us for?"

"Well, at the end of our conversation, Jackson called me 'queen.' During the conversation, he offered to stay low for a month until my clientele needs died down. I just need help reading his sincerity." She caught a glimpse at our dull gazes that read, "That's it?"

Amber decided to shoot back. "Skunk, you have high school problems compared to us. We got real women problems. Even Emily's got you beat. You wanted to make a fuss over you just to hear us pipe Jackson up as the man of the century. Get outta here with that."

"What's wrong with wanting to fuss over my life? And yes, remind me that I've met Mr. Right." Brooke wasn't diffident about admitting the fact that she enjoyed being indulged at times.

"All right, to the ladies' room I go." Amber stood up and walked away.

The server came back to pass out our food. We smelled our dishes and checked out each other's plates before ripping into our food.

Brooke took the time to further discuss her concerns when Amber left the table to retrieve our order. "So why would she not think to do something meaningful with her money?" She poked into her chicken salad to get her first bite going. "I can't even begin to fathom bringing home that much money, especially on a regular basis, and not save it for a house or marriage. I mean . . . *something*."

I nodded as Emily sat there with a blank expression, trying to stay neutral. "I know," I chimed. "I love fun and shopping, too, as much as the next person. But, when you rake in as much as Amber does when she can, it's time to reconsider old habits."

Emily chewed on her lobster mac and cheese, cleared her throat and looked at me. "Speaking of old habits," she said as she straightened her posture. She had our attention. "What are you going to do about sleeping with a married man?"

I had to admit that she got me. Here I was offering my two cents on Amber and her finances when I couldn't even manage an affair. I pointed a finger at her plate and crinkled my brows with mock concern. "How tasty is that lobster mac? Did we do good by you?"

Emily slightly cocked her head and wrinkled her lower lip. "Oh, stop it, Summer. You were the one who brought it up, and now I feel that we should really talk about it. I was married once, and I think that what you are doing can have devastating effects."

I conceded. It was time to really talk about it. "I don't know. That's why I'm here." I truly felt hopeless.

Brooke placed a hand on mine. That little gesture really felt good. In fact, I really could've used a hug at that moment. I didn't know what I was doing with Ruben and why. More importantly, I didn't know what to do about him in the future.

"I don't want to leave him alone," I said. "I feel drawn to him. Maybe it's the way we did it, maybe it's who he's connected to, maybe it's the thrill of getting caught. But I can say that he's one great lover." I couldn't help but smirk.

When Amber resumed her place at the table, Emily turned to Amber to say, "We're discussing Summer and that married man."

Amber picked up her cheeseburger and said, "Well, if he's a great lover like you say, then keep him. Being that I've had my fair share of lovers, finding one who can make you grin in the middle of the day ain't easy to come by." She winked before clamping her teeth into the burger.

I could only fidget with the edges of my napkin.

Emily bit her lower lip and shook her head in distress. Clearly something weighed on her mind. "But he's married Amber. Mar-ried. Doesn't that mean something?" She rolled her eyes.

With a cheek full of burger, Amber replied, "Yeah," with an expression that read, 'duh.' "He ain't getting what he needs at home, so he's looking elsewhere."

"Why is he off the hook?" Brooke asked after swallowing her food. "Why can't it be that his wife is trying to meet his needs, but he's just greedy? It's not really any person's job to fix a marriage if she or he isn't in it." She took a long sip of her water.

I began to feel like a guest on a talk show. I was the topic of interest as my audience discussed my situation. I didn't want this much attention, and at this point, changing the subject seemed like a great idea.

"Hey, guys. Can we just, I don't know, talk about something else?"

Amber of course, ignored my request. "I'm not saying that someone is guilty or innocent. I'm just saying that when my clients pay me to sleep with them, they typically complain that the women in their lives are boring or not fulfilling. In fact, my men are usually married."

In disbelief, Emily asked, "But don't you feel guilty?"

More and more, Emily and Brooke's opinion toward Amber began to feel like they could apply to me as well. I could feel my chest drop into my stomach, because I'd evidently become That Girl. I came across as a THOT who couldn't care less as long as she got her orgasm with exotic fun in the process. Brooke and Emily were too nice to tell me that I was behaving disgustingly, so they told Amber because she resisted the idea of her being the problem.

Amber froze for a second and replied, "No," and resumed eating one fry after another.

Emily looked disturbed. "I just, I don't know. Maybe seeing you get paid generously for your services makes it so real for me. Before, I just thought it was fun and games and here and there, but you actively get clients to do what their wives can't or won't do."

"Emily, I'm a girl from New York who had a rough life. This is me, and I do what I have to do. My parents are gone and I have a sister who depends on me. I chose not to go to college, and this lifestyle works for me. Your responses, disapprovals, and beliefs will not make me wake up and 'see the light.' Okay?" She took a sip of her soda. "So, for the sake of all of us, just give it a rest. I didn't break up your marriage. So, please do not blame me. However, these men that I sleep with are makin' a decision to cheat and if I'm the one who will make that happen, so be it. If it ain't me, then it's another woman. If they were so happy, I wouldn't get paid. Therefore, if a man is willin' to pay, he already prepared for that moment, and he's well past miserable. I offer tricks, skills, and want no commitments, just money. Now what miserable man wouldn't want that?"

Brooke smiled. "Gee, Amber. Can you write my business overview?" She chuckled all in good fun. I couldn't help but find the humor in that, too.

Amber shook her head and smiled. "You guys are sick." As she chewed, she looked at Emily and asked, "So, did you figure out something he treasures?"

Emily looked confused until she remembered that Amber was referring to Eric. She fanned a hand in the air. "Oh. Oh, no it's okay. I was just mad at the time. But if I do decide, I'll consult you." Truthfully, I think Emily feared the help that Amber had to offer.

Amber shrugged. "Okay." She continued to eat.

Brooke cleared her throat reluctantly. "Well, I know my problems are juvenile compared to you nuts, but you guys never did tell me what you think about Jackson's intentions."

I took advantage of the opportunity to shift the attention to Brooke. "Well, we kind of did. I see no red flags where Jackson is concerned. I say enjoy, queen." I chuckled and Brooke playfully squinted at me.

"I agree," Emily said seriously.

Amber took a quick break from inhaling her food to say, "Let's just say that I don't think he'll be the type to request my services."

Brooke's mouth fell open, but we all shared a good guffaw. Amber may've been good at creating tension, but she was also great at breaking it.

"This food is to die for," Emily said, rolling her eyes with pleasure.

"Mmm, hmmm," Amber agreed.

Roasted pork chop and good friends? Nothing else could wash stress down better.

5: the juggling act

Brooke

Brooke lay in her bed with Jackson on her mind. Her eyes chased the reflection of headlights that moved across the ceiling as cars from the street drove by. She struggled to get to sleep. No man had ever invaded her mind and sense of independence before.

A smile washed over her face as she imagined what it would be like to have Jackson lying next to her, on her bed. So far, he had seemed to be everything that she wanted in a man: tall, educated, thoughtful, and into her. But it scared Brooke to think that she may lose his interest just because of her work schedule. It really shouldn't be that hard to make time for him since she made time for the girls, right?

Brooke fluffed her pillow one more time, determined to call Jackson the next day to set a date for the weekend. With that last thought, she fell fast asleep.

Brooke woke up at midnight to a sound at her door. No, a knock. Startled, she shuffled out from beneath the sheets and comforter to see who could be so rude. She felt too upset to be scared. Besides, she had security, so the person couldn't be too much of a threat. And why didn't they notify her prior to the person's arrival?

Standing on the tip of her toes, Brooke checked the peephole to make sure that she knew the person. Upon seeing the face, her heartbeat sped so rapidly that she worried her heart would literally burst. Not because the person was bad or posed a threat, but because it was Jackson.

Brooke used the mirror on the wall next to the front door to give herself a rapid once-over. Luckily her hair had managed to fairly stay in place. Jackson knocked again before she had a chance to snatch it open after unlatching three locks.

There he stood with a big grin and a bouquet of cosmos. "May I come in?"

Brooke couldn't be mad despite the time. "Certainly."

She did a mock curtsey as she let him through. Closing the door behind her, he spun to face her. His outstretched arm placed the cosmos to her face, hiding his.

"These are for you."

Brooke grabbed and smelled them, before heading for her kitchen to find a vase for them. She placed water inside and placed them on the bar countertop. "Jackson. These are lovely." She covered her heart with a hand. Her eyes glowed with a genuine smile. "Thank you. Thank you so much for these."

"Well, I had to bring them to you. I couldn't wait. Someone as beautiful as you should have them delivered personally by the person who thinks highly of you."

Brooke couldn't help it. She met him in her dining room to offer him a hug, but he stepped back. She froze, hurt and confused.

"No, sweetheart. It's okay. You don't owe me a thing. This is me showing gratitude. I have to go, but please," he started to back up with a smile on his face, "call me when you can." He nodded and marched for the door.

Almost frantic, Brooke requested, "No. No, wait, Jackson." This man meant it. He only wanted verbal gratitude and the thrill of knowing that he delivered the cosmos personally. He stopped in his tracks.

Puzzled, he asked, "Is everything okay?"

Brooke could only frown and shake her head as she twisted her fingers. "No, it's not. No." She quickly closed the distance between them, pressing her body against his. "Stay. Please stay." She chanted it as a soft but desperate hand ran up his arm, and until he lowered his face to hers. "Jackson, stay."

His hand cupped her face. Brooke closed her eyes and enjoyed the touch with a tilt of her head into one of his hands. When his breath caressed her lips, Brooke decided to go for it. She moved her head up slightly, just so she could meet his mouth full on; his lips parted. Once their tongues touched, both of her arms wrapped around his neck, owning more space. Bending at the knees, he swooped her into his arms. A strong hand rested on the crease of her buttocks and upper thigh. They moaned and grunted in each other's arms as Jackson tried to figure out the location of her bedroom. At the mercy of not wanting to give up his full lips, Brooke pointed her snapping fingers in the right direction.

In her bedroom, Jackson placed her down gently on her bed. "Take off your clothes," she quietly demanded.

Standing above her, he tossed his coat onto the floor and then started on his sweater. It rolled above his defined abdomen and over his head. He reached for his buckle.

"No," Brooke interrupted as she rolled onto her knees, "let me." She always wanted to be just like those women in movie scenes who took the initiative to undress their men. Now it was her turn.

Jackson placed his hands in the air signaling his surrender to her request. Brooke bit her lower lip and pushed down on the sides of his jeans to reveal black boxer briefs. He raised his feet from underneath the stacked denim that pooled at his ankles.

"Now, it's your turn." Jackson stood above her, expectantly, as she steadied herself on her knees.

She placed her fingers at the hem of her thigh-length nightgown. Brooke thought she would be scared, but she wasn't. It had been a long time since she'd had sex, and surprisingly, the anticipated anxious nerves weren't there tonight. More than ready and very confident in her body, she wanted Jackson to see that.

Pulling the spaghetti-strapped gown above her head, she revealed two very ample breasts and a tight stomach above a pink thong. She wanted Jackson to have fun removing those. Brooke smiled when she saw him swallow and grow hard at the sight of her bare chest. Generously endowed, she noted. Taking his hands, she placed his fingers on the lacy band of her underwear, and he took it from there. Brooke lay down to help facilitate his undressing endeavors. She moved her hips up, and he removed them from her hips, one side at a time.

Finally nude, Brooke felt his body heat as he lowered himself on top of her. She opened her legs and wrapped herself around his fit body. She'd found her home and was happy to be intimate with a man for the first time in—well, she'd lost count. Patience paid off.

"Put your sword in my cave. Put your sword in my cave," she chanted.

When he did, it hurt at first, but he took his time and her desire made it quite easy to accept it. He stared into her eyes and whispered, "Oh, Brooke. You were certainly worth the wait."

That sent Brooke over the edge. She kissed him with more passion than before, and they rolled around on the bed. They couldn't stop in time, and she knew it was coming, like falling over a cliff. It was doubtful that Jackson could swap places with her in time. Oh, no! Oh, no! *Thump*! Brooke inhaled one deep, loud breath frantically and sat upright immediately. She panted as sweat glistened on her chest and drenched her neck. She patted her forehead and saw a swipe of sweat on the back of her hand.

Jackson. Where did he go? In her bed alone, the sun had started to rise. "Nooooo," she whined in a low tone as she smacked her palms against her face. "A dream? Seriously, Brooke?" she whispered. "You loser."

Wait. Did . . . did I really . . . have a response to that dream? Spreading her legs, she plucked the trim of her underwear out from against her bikini line and peeked at the crotch.

Wet? Yes. "Wow," she said quietly. "A wet dream? I actually had a wet dream?" Brooke crossed her legs and fell on her back. She shook her head disapprovingly at the ceiling. "Pathetic." The sudden ring of her cell phone made Brooke sit up. She couldn't help but snicker at his awful timing. She knew before seeing the screen that it would be Jackson.

"Jackson," she whispered. The dream made her feel a little more daring, frisky even. The dream reminded her that there will come a time that she'd have to reveal her secret to Jackson. The secret that no one else knew but her.

He snickered. "Good morning, beautiful. Did you sleep well?"

She bit her bottom lip as she giggled. "That's an understatement."

"Why?" he asked.

"Pleasant thoughts."

"Oh, yeah? I've been having rough nights sleeping. Maybe you can tell me your secret so I can sleep like a baby, too."

"Oh, I'm not sleeping like a baby," she blurted. She grimaced and smacked a hand against her forehead. Too much, she realized.

"But I thought—"

"Oh, well, yeah, I mean—you know, you think good things and you fall asleep faster."

"Hmm. Then I'll think of you and that may help."

Well, he could return the favor. Though amused, she decided to change the subject. "Hey, I thought you should know that I have decided to throw caution to the wind and see you this weekend. What do you think? You busy?"

"See. I knew you could live dangerously. And I think I can pencil you in."

"Funny. When and where?"

"Your house at eight?"

Oh, great. Her dream could come true. Possibly playing with fire, she agreed anyway. "Okay. Eight o'clock, baby."

"Now that I'm your baby maybe I should get you some roses for that."

Brooke couldn't help but crack up, and she found it difficult to stop.

Jackson chuckled. "Brooke? You okay over there? Did I miss something?"

"Oh . . ." She fanned at her teary eyes. "Inside joke, that's all. Inside joke . . ."

Maybe one day she could tell him all about it.

Emily

Sometimes a lunch break could mean a lot to a teacher at certain times than others. Finally, alone, Emily decided to give Eric a call to see if he was willing to meet up for lunch.

"Hello?"

"Hi, Eric."

"Emily, what can I do for you?" he asked impatiently.

"Look, I'll make this quick." He grunted.

Emily paced near her desk as she rubbed the temples of her head with her free hand. "Look, I would just like to know if I can go into detail about what I have to discuss with you, but over lunch."

"You would like to eat lunch with me to discuss something that is on your mind, you mean?"

"Yes. Absolutely. That is what I was trying to say. So much for speaking concisely as a teacher." That was kind of a joke for her. "So, what do you say?"

There was a pause. "Look, Emily. If you're trying to get back with me—"

"What?" Emily let out a short, nervous giggle. "No, no. It's nothing like that." She took a seat in her chair. "It will be quick and pleasant, but I just want to speak in person. It's too much to say over the phone, but pleasant enough to be discussed in person."

"I get it. Well, it can't be until the weekend or maybe early next week, Ems." Emily couldn't believe that he called her by the nickname he gave to her after he confessed his love for her. Her eyes became glassy.

"Not a problem, Eric. I just think we need to have this conversation, but I can wait to see what your schedule looks like. If you can make it sooner than later, though—"

"Yeah. I'm actually out of town, visiting those old friends of mine, so that's why I can't accommodate your request at this moment. But yes, Emily, I can do it promptly upon my return."

"Gambling, huh?" Emily covered her mouth; she really didn't mean to say too much. He didn't have to confirm. When they were a couple, he would occasionally go out of town to visit friends in West Virginia and gamble with them at the nearest casino.

"That's not your business," he scoffed.

"No, no. I'm so sorry, you're right. Forget I said that."

"Yeah."

Getting back to the reason she called, Emily told him, "I really appreciate it, Eric. It means a lot." She bit her upper lip in thought as she stared at the back of the classroom, too numb to wipe the tear from her eye.

"Yup." Eric hung up. She hated when he yupped people when they were married, but he never yupped her. Now, she was just like everyone else in his world—a commoner who would be yupped.

This made Emily consider the fact that perhaps she should consider dating someone else. Because, even though he called her Ems for the first time since the divorce, he'd turned right around and given her the 'yup' response. And that made her feel like yuck.

Summer

Across town in Southwest, Amber had parked her rental car outside her apartment building. She made up her mind. She was going to Charles Town, West Virginia to play the slots. She didn't know how to play the table games, but she was okay with trying. After begging me to join her, I decided to leave work early to go and do just that. I told Fran that I had a splitting headache and, without question, she replied, "Why not? Go home, Summer. When do you ever take off anyway?" She smiled that genuine smile, and I thought about Saturday night with Ruben and, suddenly, my decision to gamble with Amber felt like the best idea. I shut down and was out of there before I knew it.

We were in a rented Ford Taurus, and Amber had already plugged the address into the navigation system.

I was surprised. "Aren't you a regular there, Amber?"

"Ehh, I mean, I frequent this casino, but usually someone else drives. I'm also taking this alternate route that someone took me through the last time. I'll let the GPS do the work, because I don't want to take any chances." She fastened her seatbelt and looked at me. "You do want to make it back here before it's too late, right?"

I smiled. "That would be nice."

"Okay, then let's not take any chances on getting lost." She reversed the car, pulled out of the parallel space and headed toward the casino.

We talked about high school experiences and then men in general all the way to the point of the mountains. The drive felt long and beautiful with cattle and horses decorating the sides of the two-lane highway. We discussed childhood memories and our mothers. I missed mine because she lived in another state, and Amber missed hers because she had passed on.

"So, what brought you to DC?" I asked as I swiped back my hair.

"My childhood friend used to live in New York but moved to DC a few years ago. She got in a car accident. It screwed up her hands."

I crinkled my brows. "That's terrible . . ."

"Tell me about it. It broke my heart when I saw them." Amber shrugged. "Well, she taught piano lessons in her home. You know, she had a great amount of clients. One night, we were on the phone and I was complaining and almost in tears over my life in New York. It was like a light bulb went off in her head or—or like God intervened to get me out of a hopeless situation. She didn't want to leave her clients hanging; she loved them. She asked if I would come and take over, you know, to help offer normalcy to them and to get me out of a jam. She had to know that they were in good hands." Amber took a quick peek at me. One stare at her quivering mouth let me know that she was trying to keep from cracking up. I released my bout of humor. "No pun intended," she claimed while allowing herself to enjoy the joke. She swore one hand in the air. "Honestly. I realized it only after I said it."

I pointed a finger at her as I collected myself. "You are so wrong, Amber. So wrong." I shook my head.

"Hey, but you're cutting up, too."

"Couldn't help it." Composed, I asked, "So do you visit her?"

"I should, but I've been so busy. At least I call her. I guess I should visit her before too long though." I liked having learned more about Amber. If we were going to spend so much time on the road together and in our personal time, then I should endeavor to learn where she came from and what she was all about. Inevitably, we'd move on to the topic of Emily.

"Why do you think she wants to be with Eric so badly?" Amber asked.

I shrugged. "Because she loves him."

"Do you believe in love?"

Without hesitating, I answered, "I try not to," without turning away from my window. "Don't care for that kind of stuff."

"Hm." I believe I caught her off-guard. "Well, look at you. I really wouldn't have peeped you as that kind."

Turning to her with a smile, I waited for her to answer me. "Why not?"

Amber shrugged. "Just not used to many women feeling like that. You kind of seem like a little innocent woman. Maybe I'm stereotyping. I'm used to women in the street feeling that kind of way. You seem like you would have no trouble findin' any man about something. I'm a little thrown off. But cool." She kept her eyes straight. I nodded and turned my attention toward the winding road ahead.

"Yeah. It's just not on the top of my list. I prefer a great career and my freedom."

"I hear you. At last, someone who sees things my way."

I chuckled and decided to deflect to Emily. "Clearly, love never makes sense, but I get that when you look at the way Eric treats Emily, she should be very over him. But I think she knows taking him back would be stupid if it were an option. They really haven't been divorced that long. She just needs time."

"Summer, not to upset you, but do you know how you would feel if you were the cause of the divorce between your boss and her husband?" Wow. Effort to deflect failed. I could feel her eyes on me as she steered the car.

I sighed. "Well, even though Ruben tells me that they are already on the brink and she's holding onto him, yes, I would at least still feel like the catalyst." I hung my head low and rubbed the back of my neck.

"You know, I met Emily first, but I like you the most." I looked up to see her smiling at me. I grinned back at her.

"Thanks. I think you are wild and fun, too."

"I like Brooke. I really do. But I feel like she needs everything to be in order and I just don't roll like that. I cannot be that girl who thinks every single thing through. I like to have fun. No, I *love* to have fun. I like the fact that you and I don't need the same man day in and day out to be happy. You and I, we enjoy life."

I giggled.

"I mean, think about Ruben. He gives you what you need. Why should you feel bad about that? If a married couple cannot communicate their shortcomings, then they get exactly what they deserve."

I pouted my lips and tilted my head in thought. "Yes, they should be able to communicate shortcomings, but . . ."

"But nothing. A marriage is but a piece of paper if the two who are in it are no longer bound by love but merely by the paper."

I shrugged and took in the scenery. "I feel that you are right, because I don't quite believe in the institution. I just feel that people should respect it. I know I sound like a hypocrite, but if I had my way, if I knew Ruben was married when I met him, I woulda' honestly walked away. Now, I'm attracted to the mess of it all."

"So, then bow out, or own what you are doing."

I turned my gaze at her. "*I am, Amber.*" I'd become upset and my voice showed it. I didn't care. "I'm owning what I'm doing. Why do you think I'm bothered by this?" Amber always thought she knew what she was talking about.

But she wasn't fazed. "Ummmm, Summer, if you totally owned it, you would be like me, doing your thing and not looking back with regret. You are very inconsistent. You did it twice, so you are likely to do it again. Own that possibility, accept it and do it. Then, just forget about it because your regret doesn't take it back. You think being regretful will change what you did? Do you think your boss would care that you regret your affair after doing it on purpose after finding out he was married? No."

I sighed and rested an elbow against the window pane of the door as I held the side of my head.

Amber softened her approach, because she could see that I'd become upset. Unfortunately, she was correct. I was lying to myself, thinking that I could blame it on intentions, whether they were good or bad, instead of admitting that it was what it was.

"Look, Summer. I bring this up because I see that you are going to be caught in the middle instead of on the right or left side. Either you leave it alone, or enjoy the affair and make no apologies. It doesn't matter if you know the wife or not. Ruben has cheated, is cheating, and the other woman is irrelevant. It could be a horse. Whoever it is or whatever, it's not her. It's not Fran. She's not married to you. You're not her sister. Ruben allowed this to happen. She needs to be mad at him. If she hates it that much, she will either work out their marital shortcomings with him, or call it quits. They are not happily married, so . . ."

Amber's reasoning for coming between a married couple made sense in the sickest way, but it lacked merit. A marriage was a marriage, for good or bad, and I had contributed to the bad. The question was: Would I continue to contribute to the bad or leave them alone so that they may become good?

Once we arrived at the casino on this weekday night, the smell of smoke seeped into my nostrils and the sound of the constant chimes and animations from the slots resounded in my ears. I found the constant noise annoying. My expression must've given it away, because Amber stopped walking to show a big grin on her face as she stared at me.

"Don't worry, the more you come, the more you'll get used to it."

I wasn't sure there would be a next time, but I didn't tell Amber that. Instead, I responded with a disingenuous grin and furrowed eyebrows as I followed her to the game of her choice.

After walking for what felt like an eternity, she chose a slot and plopped in the chair in front of it. She pulled out her cigarettes, lit one, slid a twenty from her wallet and inserted it into the machine. "Here," she handed me a Benjamin. I stared at her with a blank expression. She nodded. "Take it. This is the least I can do since I invited you, and you were cool enough to come. Either this or you'll get bored."

I reluctantly took it. "Thanks, Amber. I'll spend wisely." Or, pocket it for a new pair of shoes. Instead, I figured, "Why not? I should play something."

Amber shook her head at me in disbelief as she tapped the button, keeping her eyes on the screen. "Please do, because I cannot stand one more uptight broad."

She was right. It was her money, I was there, and watching her the whole time would grow old fast. I decided to try my luck on Lucky Sevens, so I took the machine next to her and sat. "Come on, punk, come on you piece of . . ." I heard her gripe at the machine.

I scratched the side of my head in confusion. I really didn't know what all the numbers on the buttons meant. Amber snickered at my dilemma before explaining how to bet. So far, my experience didn't match the slot's name. Minutes later, Amber stood up as she waited for her ticket to spit out. "Look, don't take it personally. I like to move around frequently when I gamble. You're not scared to be alone, are you?"

"I got you Amber, no worries."

"Excellent," she replied. "Then I'll put my phone on vibrate and how about you do the same. We won't be able to hear our phones in here. Keep it close to your body, though. Okay, mama?"

"Right." I did it before I would forget.

"If you need me, please call ASAP." I nodded at her and she walked away. No surprise that we wouldn't be doing this together for long. I was kind of looking forward to being with her as we gambled, just for thrill's sake. But it didn't shock me, because that woman usually pulled many rabbits out of her hat.

Amber

Amber circled around the game table, happy that she wore white jeans in the middle of fall and had gone braless in a see-through lace camisole. She lived to tease men and needed to find a high roller in West Virginia on a weekday at a Black Jack table. That was the only table game she could play at with minimal skill, but sometimes, it interested her enough to watch and distract the men. Amber pulled out a lollipop and twirled it around the inside of her mouth. She used no skill at all to grab the attention of a man sitting a few chairs away from her at the same table.

Every now and then their eyes would meet but never lock. She decided to go in for the kill, by locking eyes as she twirled the lollipop in her mouth with mastery. The dealer tried to act neutral, but she didn't care. She needed a client and she loved playing the game of reeling men in.

Amber pouted and pretended to be disappointed when she lost. Wanting to see how the gentleman took it, she looked up at him and didn't avoid his intense stare. It was the most intense stare ever. It almost made her tap out first, but she couldn't live with herself if she did that.

The man looked quite handsome thanks to his chiseled jaw line and peachy complexion. He didn't appear to be a day over forty, but it could've been great genes, although, he did have a generous amount of gray in his black hair. Even before standing, his long legs snitched on his height. In just a few steps, the handsome man stood next to Amber.

Amber twisted her chair just enough to face him. She smiled, feeling accomplished at her work. It worked on this handsome player.

"Rough game?" His lips gave way to a slight smile, his eyes scrolled from her legs to her face. "You do look a little rough around the edges in the skills department. Still, I like to see a woman play cards among men."

Amber giggled and stood up. She offered her hand. "My name is Amber. You?"

He smirked before he accepted her hand. "Eric. Are you from around here, Amber?"

"No, I live in DC. I came up here with my girlfriend."

Eric elevated a brow. "Really. I'm from that area, too. You know, so many of us gamblers come up here to play."

"Yeah." Amber paused a moment, thinking about Emily. Emily's Eric? "Where's your wife, Eric?" She had to get some answers immediately.

Thrown off, he placed a hand on his chest and replied, "Me? Oh, no, no, no. I've never been married."

With instant relief, Amber felt happy and bit her bottom lip. "Good."

"I'm here visiting friends. Just decided to catch some alone time before seeing them tonight."

"However, maybe I shouldn't keep you then, since you have friends here."

"No, I could use the company. Sometimes it's good to be with a fresh face. I'm staying at the hotel right next door. I could use some champagne and good cable right about now. The night is kind of dead here."

Amber decided to cut to the chase. "Are you telling me you want to get out of here?" she teased as she rocked up and down on her tippy toes.

He chuckled. "I don't believe in dancing around the point. I'm about to leave. I'm not having such a good time as I had expected and quite frankly, wearing business clothes beyond the clock is a drag. I guess, Amber, I would like to spend the rest of the night with a beautiful lady like you. What do you say?"

"Okay, as much as I would love to make this possible, I do have my girlfriend here. I would have to check with her. Also, I would need to know how to get home. If I let her take herself home tonight, I need a way back tomorrow. Any suggestions?"

Eric seemed a little put off. "I don't know what to tell you, but I can't wait forever, darling. I can tell you that there is a shuttle that goes from here to DC. You can stay with me until it returns tomorrow. Or I could pay for your own room after whatever happens tonight. Your choice."

Amber needed to let this man know what she was all about. Apparently, he had money. A little test that she performed on men would give her further insight. "Let me see your time, please?"

Eric shook his wrist from under his sleeve. "Here you go."

Amber pretended not to notice the impressive Victorinox watch as she read the time. This man has money. Everything about him read cocky, high-profile business man. Usually, Amber would target older men, but she felt that this young man might be able to afford her price. However, her older men usually pined on the inside for a young, one-night steamy stand. This guy could clearly get any woman on his own, with or without the money. Besides she would never ditch Summer, or let herself get stranded in West Virginia, unless this man knew the truth. Putting everything on the line later made no sense if it would cost her.

"Thank you." Eric took his arm back. "Eric." She gave him the come hither with her index finger and he leaned in to hear her. "I can make this the best night of your life. I assure you, you never knew you had a cock until you've had a night with me."

Eric seemed intrigued, but he was smart. He straightened back to his normal posture. "Are you leading to a proposition, Amber, one involving something in return?"

"Honey, I'm so worth it. I guarantee, you will never see another woman the same. So, are you in?"

"How much, Amber? Get to the point."

This would be tricky, since he didn't ooze a bit of desperation by no means, so she had to try something else. "Have you ever tasted chocolate before?"

Thrown off, he smirked with a crinkle in his forehead. "Uh-uh. You would be my first. It crossed my mind a few times, but that's about it."

"Why, Eric?" Amber had fun purring at him like a kitten.

"No real reason."

She cleared her throat. "One thousand dollars and I'll make you feel more alive than any other woman has. Guaranteed."

Eric swiped his gaped mouth with his hand as she raised an eyebrow at him. "I don't know if I should find a woman to slap you or just find a corner and hoot. However, your constant guarantees make me want to find out why you would rate yourself so high. Secondly, you are very lucky that a grand doesn't mean much to me when I want something. And right now, I want you." He gazed into her eyes so hard Amber swore he could see her soul. "Don't make me regret it, Amber. If you screw this up, I ain't paying."

"If I wasn't sure I could prove you wrong, I would jab you in the lip for your pompous attitude. But since I know I'll have you screaming like a little bitch, let's do this."

Eric held out his hand for Amber to shake, "You talk a good game. Never close a deal without a shake. Deal?"

"Deal." Amber accepted it. "Stay put right quick. I need to find my friend to tell her what's up." The truth was, Amber wanted a young client for a change. She'd had enough of droopy scrotums and old penises.

Summer

Amber located me easily, especially since I hadn't left the vicinity since her departure. I did manage to play the other surrounding machines. As she approached me, her white pants and big grin came into view.

"So, how's your luck, honey?"

I waved. "Umm, I'm doing okay. I still have fifty dollars." I took a break from playing to see what she had to say.

"Summer? I have a huge favor to ask of you."

She made me dread her words when she placed her warnings before the next sentence. "What now, Amber?"

"I . . . I uh, I met this guy and he wants me to stay the night with him, and he will be my client, you could say. Do you mind taking the rental back to your place, and I can catch the train to your job for the keys or whatever? I'll give you another Franklin for the inconvenience." She twisted her fingers anxiously, waiting for my answer.

I sighed and avoided her eyes. Yeah, I could use some alone time to think without anyone's opinions. "Your GPS will give accurate instructions, right?"

"You are the best, Summer. I mean it, girl." She hugged me tight and when she drew back with her hands on my shoulders she said, "Now just watch out for the deer, okay?"

I rolled my eyes playfully. "Gee, now you tell me." But then her safety and what we were about to do really hit me. "Are you going to be okay? You don't know this man, right?"

With her hands still on my shoulders, she replied, "Summer, we will be staying at the hotel right next door. I'll call or text you the name of it in a second. Tonight, my message will say 'Hamilton,' and that will be the exclusive code word for 'I'm okay.'"

"Why not just put, 'I'm okay?'"

"Uhhh, it's too basic and broad. Besides, if he's crazy, and uses my phone to pose as me, you will know I gave you a safety word. Gotta go. Love ya'." Amber placed the keys and Franklin in my hands and kissed me on the cheek.

"Whatever, girl. Love you, too." I decided that the wise thing to do would be to get out of dodge as soon as possible, since I would be skating down a mountain watching for deer and driving on unfamiliar back roads.

I located the car, which took me about ten minutes since I got a little lost after forgetting the parking level number on which we parked. I didn't know I wouldn't have Amber helping me out. This week had taught me so much about her. She may have been fun, but this lady had minimum boundaries. I keyed my address into the GPS and with 66 miles to go, I headed toward the exit. I managed to find my way to the right street in the dark, turned left at the light, and headed home.

Amber

Amber and Eric walked toward his maroon Mercedes. The black leather seats accepted the contour of her body with grace when they hopped into his two-seater. The engine purred upon starting.

"Nice car." She smiled at him as she stroked the back of her short hair.

"Well, it has to match the man."

"Gee, Eric, are you always this serious?" She watched him fidget with his radio buttons.

"Seatbelt," he ordered, pointing to her side without looking at her.

"Well?" Amber insisted as she followed his orders.

Pulling off, he answered, "You really don't know anything about my personality."

Reading that she needed to back off, she relented with, "Okay, I can respect that."

The forty-five second ride was quiet. Eric parked the car and they headed to the lobby, into the elevators, and to the top floor. They entered his generous-sized room that came with a mounted flat-screen television and a sitting room beyond his sleeping area.

"I'm going to take a shower, Amber. Wait for me here?" He removed his coat and started to unbuckle his pants but left them on and pulled off everything on top to tease Amber.

She wanted to melt at the sight of his defined abdomen and chiseled arms. Wow. She forgot what it was like to sleep with a man around her age as opposed to some old man.

"Oh, absolutely." She replied as she stared at his chest. He had her licking her upper lip, but she didn't care. Honestly, she could have sex with him for free, so she figured she had nothing to lose.

"Good," he replied with a quick toothless smile. He headed for the shower, leaving Amber standing still and full of lust.

Summer

I drove down the snaky, dark back roads of West Virginia, keeping an extra eye out for deer. I didn't realize how creepy this ride would be in the dark. I could almost ring my own neck for allowing Amber to talk me into this ride back home alone.

I began to feel better when I entered Ashburn, Virginia. I was no longer in no-man's land, but rather in civilization as I knew it. Still about a good hour from DC and wide awake, I felt comfortable. At this point, I could say that I was enjoying my drive home.

It felt incredible to let my mental hair down before reflecting on Ruben and Fran. If I were to think about this clearly, I could reason that since I didn't want anything more from Ruben, I could dispose of this affair and move on. On the other hand, I had to be honest. This may have been the best sex I had ever had. Therefore, if I were to kiss Ruben and this affair goodbye, then I would start a quest to find the next best lover. The quest sounded like a reality show. My lips eased into a smirk. Yes, imagine me, Summer, looking for love on a reality show. I shook my head, giggling with the back of my hand pressed against my mouth. Didn't want the drivers at the traffic light to see me cutting up alone.

Now I had to consider nixing the reality show in favor of carrying on with the affair. The consequences of this included getting caught by Fran and then fired and losing the possibility of references. What recruiter didn't want to say that they worked for Fran? Her agency ranked at the top in this area. If she didn't find out and Ruben and I continued to carry on, then I would be the bad girl in the middle. In this society, I would be classified as a slut and homewrecker. No one liked a homewrecker. I could never call my mom and say, "No, I'm not dating, I'm not in a relationship, I'm not exactly sexually inactive, I'm not engaged and certainly not married. In fact, Mother, I'm the other woman. I'm . . . a homewrecker."

And I had to ask myself . . . could I live with that?

Amber

Amber had stripped down into her black lace underwear. On her back, she posed on the bed with one leg draped across the other, showing off a fleshy thigh. The water cut and in seconds, Eric emerged from the bathroom with a towel around his waist. His tight chest glistened with water droplets. Amber shivered with pleasure as Eric approached her.

"Hot chocolate," he said with a naughty grin.

"Tasty vanilla," Amber replied.

The towel hit the floor when he released the knot. Amber sized him up. It wasn't the biggest, but certainly not the smallest. She felt like Goldilocks because it was just right.

Eric lowered himself onto the bed, flattening his body onto hers. A big hand caressed her thigh before he separated her legs. Amber embraced him as her hands ran up and down his back. As she began to kiss his shoulder, she noticed a sizable black tattoo on his right shoulder blade. "What's that?" she asked.

He nibbled on her ear. "What's what?" he asked breathily.

"That tattoo?"

"An eagle. Shhh, Amber. Let's not talk."

Amber smiled and whispered in his ear, "You got it." She pushed him off and ordered, "On your back. Now."

Grinning, he said, "Yes ma'am."

With one hand, she traced a finger from his chest down to the trimmed hair surrounding his genitals. "Lemme grope this rope." He smirked. She ran her hand up and down his shaft and threw a finger at him. "You're gonna wanna tip me, too. Watch." She arched her back to place her mouth over his tip.

"I don't know about th*aaaaa*—ah ah aaaat."

Amber knew she was getting that tip, and not just the one in her mouth. After she made him go, "Whuh-wooo," she told him, "Get some chocolate in your mouth."

Eric didn't hesitate or ask any questions. He did as he was told, and his performance was good enough to make Amber think that she should be tipping him.

It was a wild ride, but Amber enjoyed sex with a young man for the first time since New York. She gripped his salt and pepper hair and called out his name. He could almost make her forget her current life as she knew it—almost. Remembering life with Eric stopped after tonight, she decided to enjoy it, because the future held nothing but old, flabby men and droopy scrotums.

Brooke

Brooke stared at her reflection in the mirror. October's harsh cold would never allow her to go outside in her sleeveless halter dress, but an indoor date would. She wiggled a foot to admire her Sergio Rossi pumps. Half a grand never looked so nice on a foot. She had been waiting for the best time to wear them.

Brooke followed the aroma of food drifting in from the dining room. Before getting dressed, she had already ordered a generous amount of food from a Thai restaurant. To beat a prompt man like Jackson, Brooke figured she only had about twenty minutes to set up before his arrival.

She couldn't be more pleased with the setup. The variety of small-portioned food spread from one side of the table to the other. Aromatic candles burned as Italian jazz played softly in the background in the dimly lit dining room. Peering into her kitchen, the clock read seven fifty-nine on her microwave. Then she heard a knock at her door. She playfully rolled her eyes with a smirk. Of course, Jackson wouldn't leave her with one extra minute to spare. Approaching the door, she stole one last look at herself in the mirror closest to her door.

She verified his presence through the peep hole. Exhaling, she snatched the door open and greeted him with a huge smile and a hug.

"Mmm, Brooke. You smell so good." Jackson filled his nostrils with her light perfume before letting go. Brooke silently cheered herself for choosing the right fragrance. Fragrances . . . they were either a hit or miss.

When she drew back and closed the door behind him, she said, "You look good, as usual." Then she bit her lip, feeling that she might've said too much. But it was the truth. Brooke watched Jackson wiggle out of his leather coat to reveal a V-neck sweater over a button-down shirt accessorized with a tie. Handsome, handsome, handsome.

Her sexual dream encroached her thinking, so she quietly thanked her lucky stars for having a forgiving complexion that could withstand the test of blushing. However, she couldn't hide her blank stare and slightly tilted head from the man who was hanging his coat on the rack. He noticed that she left the planet.

Jackson smiled. "Brooke." He waved a hand at her. "Are you there?"

Startled, she jumped. Brooke swallowed and poked her tongue into her cheek. "Yup." She turned on her heel. "Follow me."

"Hey, there."

Brooke turned around to see Jackson step closer to her. He reached for her hands and pulled them up to his lips, giving tender kisses as he gazed into her bright, brown eyes.

"Gorgeous. What kind of man would I be if I didn't acknowledge how beautiful you look right now? Seeing you in this pink dress is something that not just any woman can pull off."

Brooke's heart raced like a horse out of the gate and her dream came back to her with the memory of unfastening his pants. She lowered her eyes to his belt buckle and stared at his narrow hips. With heavy eyelids, she stared into his eyes.

"N-not a very good one?"

"Brooke . . ." No one said her name like him. Being drawn to another human being like this seemed abnormal. He made her body respond in ways that no other man could achieve. Rice, spring rolls, chicken, soup . . . everything was on the menu at Brooke's home tonight but sex. Maybe that menu needed revising.

Brooke felt an ache between her legs that she doubted she would feel again as he continued to draw his body close to her, placing kisses on the back of her hands, the inside of her hands, the side, her wrists, while never looking away. Their eyes died into each other's, and it felt scary and sexy all at the same time while the Italian jazz played softly in the background. The scent of fresh Thai made the moment more delectable.

She finally managed to whisper a quick, "Yes, Jackson?"

But who needed words when their bodies communicated in private places? His hand rested above her bottom as he traced it up and down her back but without crossing the line. It showed Brooke just what she would be missing if she didn't give him permission to proceed.

They rocked gently from side to side with the music, a slow dance in her foyer. His other hand nestled in the cave of her tilted neck, her forehead relaxed on his shoulder. His husky breathing warmed her skin . . . inviting her to his mouth . . . testing her restraint.

"Do I make you feel good?" Jackson struggled to speak. Brooke's other hand remained on his side.

"I think so." Brooke didn't know if she sounded unsure or factual. "Of course . . . do I?"

"I would rather show you how you make me feel. Words are a waste at this point."

"O-okay. How?"

With their faces hidden from one another, they continued to dance around what they truly wanted. Brooke wanted him to make all the first moves, because without them, she made herself believe that she no longer acted in accordance of a lady. Maybe Jackson would appreciate it if she did more, because then he wouldn't feel like he needed permission.

"Tell me, it's okay."

"Okay, for what?"

"To kiss your neck."

"You . . . you can do that." *The games we play.*

Behind closed eyes she waited for his first move. Then his cold lips hit her warm skin. "Again," she directed.

Jackson did what he was told with one continuous kiss after another in the same spot, never taking his hand away from her neck. She toyed with the idea of returning the favor.

"Jackson." He didn't stop but grunted in response. "I want to know if I can make you feel good, too."

He grunted a yes. Standing on the tip of her toes, she gained enough height to flick the lobe of his ear with her tongue. She traced kisses from his ear down to his neck and stopped at the collar of his dress shirt.

"Naughty girl, you. You didn't get my permission to do more," he teased. She giggled as their faces remained hidden from one other. He grabbed her hand from his shoulder and lowered it to their sides as he intertwined his fingers with hers.

Without any hint of humor, Jackson pulled back just enough to face her as he swallowed. "Brooke. I'm almost at my limit with you."

She didn't know what to say. If she didn't put an end to this tension, she would lose control way too quickly. Trying to conceal her panic, she led him to the table by the wrist. "Sit anywhere," she offered.

Positioned across from one another at the table, they each selected dishes to make up the meal on their plates. The silence between them was louder than the clacking of the silverware. Jackson decided to break the ice.

"So, what were you like as a child?"

"That was random," Brooke replied with a grin.

"I'm curious. You speak, I eat."

"Ha. You pig," she joked. He winked at her. Brooke wanted to suggest the bedroom after his eye gesture. "Well. I was quiet, focused and obedient but lonely. My mother and I were a twosome, but we weren't close. I had very few friends. On the other hand, I was too caught up in a fantasy world to really care about reality. Reality hurt, so fantasy was a good escape." A sigh followed her brief silence. "And you? Popular, I suppose."

"I'm sorry to hear about your childhood, Brooke." He gazed at her as he swallowed a spoonful of rice. Brooke could read the sincerity behind his intense stare. She waved dismissively at him.

"Oh, it's okay, Jackson. It's in the past and it's the reason why I'm a determined soul today. Why don't you tell me more about your family?"

"You're right." He seemed reluctant to confirm what she suspected. "I was popular. I grew up in a great family."

He shrugged casually before chewing the rest of his spring roll. "I mean, it was my parents and my sister—twin, actually. We were happy-go-lucky. My parents loved each other, they still have each other to this day, and my sister is my world." He crossed his fingers. "We grew up very close. She lives in Virginia, and works as a financial analyst. My parents are in Chicago, like I told you the last time."

"I didn't know your sibling was a twin sister."

"Yup."

"Wow. How cool."

Grinning, he stopped eating, staring thoughtfully at the table with his smile fading. He said, "I think I can tell you why I don't cook professionally."

"Oh." Brooke wiped her mouth with a napkin and waited for him to continue.

"It was a passion of mine that just didn't like me back."

"What do you mean, baby?" She reached out to place a concerned hand on his.

"I was losing almost two years of my life with cooking, and I gave up. Threw in the towel and went to a traditional college to become someone. And I look at you, a woman into her calling, and look what you've become. A superstar."

"Because I didn't give up. You wanna make it happen? Let's do it. It ain't too late, Jackson."

"Maybe." He smirked. "Thank you. Thank you, baby. But I got bills to pay. I can't slip up now. I cook on my own and that has to suffice for now." He rubbed her hand. "Besides, I like tech."

"Okay."

They shared some high school stories and decided to take their glasses of wine to the sofa after dinner. Brooke sat on the couch and Jackson took the opposite end. He smacked his lap.

"Give me your feet, lady."

Confused, she asked, "What?"

"Your feet. Every woman loves a good foot rub."

"Well . . . I won't argue so here." Brooke felt shy, but she wiggled down into the sofa as she turned her body to allow her feet to rest on his legs.

Jackson peered at her with a grin as he examined her shoes. "These look hot on you."

Brooke whispered, "Thank you, Jackson," with a sexy smile.

Jackson slid her shoes off one by one, and examined her well-manicured feet embellished with pink nail polish. "Brooke, as busy as you are, how do you manage to be so on point? I get the feeling you're like this even when you ain't got no man. Am I right?"

She nodded once with a dopey smile on her face. "Yes, you are." The wine and the foot massage were getting to her.

"I'm impressed. When a woman shows off for a man, it takes no time for the real her to show. There are always some inconsistencies or something that gives it away. But you got a clean home, nice clothes, you look well-presented and you're successful." Nodding with pride and a big grin, he told her, "I think I hit the lottery."

Jackson and Brooke refused to look away from one another. Her tongue caressed her lower lip as she enjoyed his firm but gentle foot rub. His massages slowed, as he became lost in the moment. He took her by the calves and yanked her closer, so that her buttocks were on his side and her knees arched over his legs.

Brooke released a nervous giggle. "Jackson, what are you doing?"

"I want you here and not over," he pointed to the other side of the sofa, "there."

"Why?" She really didn't think that the obtuse act would work given her position on the sofa.

"Why do you ask so many questions when the answers are usually obvious?"

"Maybe it isn't right now," she challenged in a flirtatious tone.

Jackson rested his hands on her knees and licked his lips; his face told her that he wanted more. Brooke melted again in the place that he couldn't see. "Well, Brooke. How can I make it obvious to you?"

Almost rid of all nerves, horniness ruled her now. "Make the answer clear."

He twisted to the side and closed the space between their faces. When his nose touched hers, she began to tremble at the knees and grow short of breath. Jackson peered into her light brown eyes like a quest to read everything about her. Her long lashes flicked with a slow blinked. He reached out to move hair from her eyes. Brooke swallowed a bubble of fear as Jackson's jaw tighten. His head tilted slightly, and he placed a slow kiss on her lips. He drew back an inch to examine her expression.

"More," she said.

Jackson came in again, motivating Brooke to raise a hand to rub the back of his neck. There were no breaks this time as Brooke decided to taste Jackson. Jackson invaded her mouth with urgency, clearly disregarding any notion to take things slow. Brooke moaned as their breathing became shallow and rapid.

She eased back, relinquishing her grip on his neck to look into his eyes to say in a light whisper, "Jackson, I need you. Make me yours."

Jackson's forehead furrowed. "Brooke, I wanna screw your brains out."

"Get me out of this stupid dress," she quickly replied in a hushed tone.

Brooke didn't want to play it safe. She was tired of being reserved, especially for a man like this. If this relationship moved forward and then collapsed, at least she would know that it wasn't because she held back at any point. She wanted a husband, dammit. And if Jackson were to make the final checkmark of husband material, then he'd certainly have to pass. That particular checkmark would have to be fulfilled. At the end of the day, Brooke knew herself—a woman who got what she wanted because of standards, and no person, man or thing could ever compromise that. Negotiating her bottom line of wants wasn't going to fly. So, Jackson would either be all in or all out. Tonight, would determine that.

Jackson pressed his forehead against hers. "Baby, baby, wait. Are you sure you—"

"Why do you ask so many questions when the answer is so clear?"

Jackson grinned. "Touché, baby."

Brooke wriggled out of his lap and stood up. She gave him her back and waited to feel his hands. When she spun to face him, she said, "Do it now, or don't call me again."

He stood up with a mission. "You don't have to ask me twice."

Jackson grabbed her close to him, pressing her backside against his groin. Brooke looked up at the oversized mirror on the wall. She smiled at herself, watching him kiss her shoulder, while she felt his knuckles brush against her skin as he began to untie the knot on the back of her neck. His other hand worked between her thighs, pinching the insides below her womanhood. Brooke had an arm raised backward to cradle his neck with her face turned to kiss him.

Aggressively, Jackson lowered the top of her mini dress to reveal one large breast. She spun around and grabbed the hem of his sweater to help remove it. They worked as a team to destroy the threats of fabric that slowed them down from connecting with one another. As he unfastened the buttons, she pulled at the knot of his tie. The final reward of his bare chest prompted the memory of her dream.

Brooke lowered her head to focus on his buckle and pants button. She stopped as he chose to peel off his dress socks. Jackson looked at her and asked with very little breath, "Why are you still wearing too many clothes?"

Boldly, Brooke challenged, "If you don't like it, then do something about it." She raised an eyebrow at him and shot him a menacing smile.

Jackson yanked the dress to her ankles in one sweep, revealing her black underwear. He spun her away from him and began placing kisses from her nape then down her back. When he reached her butt, he peeled her underwear off slowly, placing kisses on the bare skin of her cheeks. He quickly pulled them down to her ankles, and she stepped out of the them. As he kissed her cheeks, he licked them and then softly bit into her skin. He couldn't see Brooke grinning, biting her lower lip in pleasure.

He stood up, panting softly. "Nice ass."

Brooke did some observing to see how he compared to her dream when she noticed the rise in his pants. "Nice package."

Jackson pulled her naked body close and looked down at her. "I see that you live up to your last name."

"Jack*son*. *Stop*," she giggled. "You're embarrassing me." He smacked her butt. Reacting as if it hurt, she said, "Ow. My Brazilians hurt more than that."

"I'm gonna turn that booty red, since you got a smart mouth."

"I'm not scared anymore. I feel completely safe with you," she whispered.

After a moment of silence, he replied, "The moment I saw you Brazile, I wanted to do something to you. Every night when I go home, I picture this moment repeatedly, and I just want it to be perfect."

"It's perfect, Sloan." Brooke wrapped her arms around Jackson's neck tightly and closed the distance between their lips. Brooke moaned and raised her thigh against his. He bent slightly at the knees to pick her up.

The reality surpassed her dream. She remembered him getting lost in her dream before taking them to her bedroom. Reluctantly, she sacrificed the comfort of his lips long enough to say, "My bedroom is down that way, Jackson. It's the last door at the end."

He nodded and when they made it there, Brooke had to decide if she wanted everything to play out like her dream. In no time, she decided, no. She wanted something more, something different. Jackson did the obvious thing and lowered her onto her bed in the dark. *This is perfect.* He stripped away his pants. She sat up as she waited for him to fit on top of her. Towering over her, she saw his manhood at attention and saw his six-pack close to her face, so she reached out and felt it. Hard, just like she imagined. Her hands didn't stop there. They lowered to his penis and she heard him release a grunt in reaction to his arousal.

Jackson lost control. Before Brooke knew it, he'd pulled her by the thighs to straighten her body so he could access her with ease. Brooke called out in pain, clenching her teeth together. Pressed against her body, Jackson grabbed her back and the nape of her head to roll her over so she landed on top as they kissed. Brooke really wasn't in the mood for hot and slow, but more for hot and heavy. She wanted to enjoy it, but she couldn't hold out by taking it slow. She wanted Jackson just as much as he'd wanted her. It also wasn't easy for her to hold off on things that she'd been dying to try.

"Spank me."

He stopped, with little breath to spare. "What? Really? On our first night?" He had perplexity written all over his face.

"Come on, Jackson, spank me." Throwing an arm forward, she told him, "Let's just do it all tonight."

Without hearing her request a third time, Jackson sat up and threw Brooke over his lap and whacked her butt hard.

"You like that, don't you?"

Even though she cried out in pain with her fingers digging into the sheets, she said, "Mmm hmmm." He spanked her a few more times and she cried out with each strike. "Yes! Oh!" She felt the sensation carry down to her vagina and realized that she had enough. "Stop, Jackson." Immediately, he stopped and helped her up. Straddling him, she said, "I'm sore," with a pout, as her fingers toyed with his silver necklace.

His hands kneaded her butt. He mocked her pout. "Daddy's gonna nurse you back to health."

Brooke shifted on his lap. "Yeah, daddy. Hurt me with your cock."

"Ahhhh, you're a little freak, huh?"

Brooke grinned from one corner of her mouth. She traced her fingers around his lips while his eyes told her that he liked it. Stuffing two fingers into his mouth, she told him, "I'm your freak and you're gonna like it."

On top, again, he unleashed her updo and grabbed fists full of hair on each side of her head. It didn't hurt Brooke, because she anticipated the pleasure. She moved to Jackson's pace, but it felt as though they couldn't move as fast as their desires. She could feel Jackson, but she wanted more and all of him. Her legs caressed his lower half as he kissed her all over her nipples before biting them. Brooke called out in pain, battling the intensity. Jackson thrust into her with a deep force that sent waves of great sensation in all the places she forgot she owned. Brooke could feel herself nearing her peak. She had so much desire stored inside and an undying craving for Jackson, that it didn't surprise her when she felt like a volcano ready to erupt.

"Brooke," he groaned through gritted teeth. "Baby, you feel so good, so tight." He heard and felt Brooke collapse beneath him with a loud cry.

Jackson's deep, dark moan caught in his throat. His head fell into her shoulder before he rolled over. With the initial sexual encounter behind them, they indulged in slow and passionate repeats as the night wore on. Exhausted and elated afterwards, sprawled on the bed, Brooke and Jackson stared at the ceiling. It felt like love. It felt like Brooke just met her best friend.

"Hey, Brazile?"

"Sloan?" The new nickname warmed her as much as the body heat between them.

He rolled over to tell her straight to her face, "I don't want to see other women."

Brooke wanted to stand up on her bed and jump like a child. It seemed impossible to believe that she would no longer be single when people inquired about her love life. The girls would have a friend in a committed, healthy relationship. She wasn't being paid to be with him, seeing a married man or encountering an angry ex. The time had come for her to be with a man who wanted her and only her. A great, quality man with intentions of taking her off the market. And with that thought, she replied, "I don't want you, too, either."

Without hesitation, he said, "Done."

Toning down her excitement and playing it cool, she replied, "Done." Without a word, they held hands and made it official.

6: in a pickle

Summer

$\mathcal{I}$t had been days since my trip to the casino with Amber. I hadn't seen Ruben, as his wife happened to mention that he went out of town. How sad that she didn't know that she'd informed "the other woman" of his whereabouts.

I stared at my computer, not able to concentrate on the posted resumes before me. I was not in the mood to talk with anyone. Last night, I'd decided to hit the bar with a happy Brooke who'd told me about her official relationship with Jackson. She'd pushed the envelope and enjoyed two drinks, while I'd decided to go for five. Brooke had warned me that I had to go to work the following morning, but the alcohol made it hard to reason.

It was already Friday, and I'd begun to wonder why I just couldn't have waited until tonight to get hammered. A sudden superficial knock sounded at my door frame. I looked up to see my smiling boss.

"Summer. Tomorrow, I need to see you at—oh, are you okay, Summer? You look quite pale." Fran squinted at me, and as much as I appreciated her more relaxed treatment of me, I was in no mood to indulge or entertain her.

"Yes, Fran. I'm fine." I couldn't smile, so I decided to tell the truth. "I just had a little too much fun last night, if you catch my drift."

"Oh, dear. Well I hope it passes because you will probably enjoy my champagne tomorrow night at my house." She had a mysterious smile on her face.

Really, Fran? Really? You are killing me. I couldn't begin to fake happy. "T-tomorrow?" I straightened my shoulders, becoming quickly alert.

"Well, tomorrow, I could really use your presence. Bring a friend. Ruben's coming back tomorrow and—" I almost choked on my saliva as I tuned her out at the mention of

Ruben's name. Was this lady determined to kill me by the New Year? *You wanna make it to the top, Summer. You wanna make it to the top.*

"S-so I can bring a friend?"

Fran's smile widened. "You make my life so easy around here, Summer. Yes. Bring a friend, tomorrow at nine." Once Fran turned, my head frantically turned every which way until I spotted my phone under a stack of papers on my desk.

Amber, you owe me, girl. I couldn't get my cell in my hand fast enough.

"Hello?"

"Tomorrow night at nine, you belong to me."

"Ohh, Summer, tomorrow—"

"No, I need you, no excuses, you owe me."

Amber relented. "Oh. Fine. Well what I gotta wear?"

"Good question. It's a dinner date, no slut or tight attire. Conservative at the least. Got it?"

"Okay. Relax. What you think, I'd come out with my left tittie hanging all out?"

"Yes."

"Whatever. Will you be picking me up or meeting me?"

"Shoot. We're going into Virginia. A car's in order. Oh wait, we can take the Metro and cab it the rest of the way."

"Your boss? Is she at it again?"

"You are one smart cookie." Knowing that my girl was going to come through for me immediately lessened the burden.

"Well, all I can say is wow, and I cannot wait to meet her and her hot husband. I got to see what the Ruben rave is all about."

I almost repeated her words as I laughed, but I didn't want my boss to overhear me saying "Ruben rave," especially since she had a habit of coming to my door at random. "This means a lot to me, Amber. I cannot bear it alone anymore. I've certainly dug a grave that I can't seem to get out of."

"Say no more, I'm glad to help."

"Right. Later." I hung up and exhaled. This should be fun.

Emily

Emily checked her watch as she waited for Eric in a Bethesda, Maryland restaurant. Nervousness ate at her stomach like 10 fat men at a buffet. Finally, she saw a tall, handsome man with the distinct salt and pepper hair color and chiseled jawline secured in his business coat. As usual, his smartphone was glued to his face. The server walked him to Emily's table, and he ended his call.

Eric sat and managed a smile that seemed to slightly ruffle his soul. He could barely look into her eyes for the duration of his greeting. He pushed the menu to the side and linked his long fingers into one another. "So, what's this about?" he asked, as if Emily were a business client. Even the business clients would've received a friendlier greeting than this. He perched his posture forward and stared square into her eyes without blinking. Emily pushed back the vortex of memories that attempted to suck her in if she stared long enough.

She had to collect her scrambled heart before speaking. "Oh, uh, right. Thank you for coming."

"Sure."

Emily exhaled as she tried to collect her nerves. "I just wanted to know Eric, what happened?"

"I don't follow, Emily." He took a sip of water.

"I'm trying to explain," Emily quickly replied. "I just can't stop wondering . . . I . . . I could have sworn that we were okay, Eric, when we were married. Did I do something to you to make you hate me now? I just can't take this broken bond between us. It's like hatred has taken over." Emily's voice started to crack and her eyes welled with tears.

He set the water down and sighed. His eyes moved back and forth thoughtfully from the table to her. He nodded, but he never chimed in. Emily guessed he was letting it all sink in.

"I'm sorry, Eric, if I did something to make you turn away from me. I just wish that you had told me so I coulda' stopped doing whatever it was that offended you."

"No, stop, Emily. I don't hate you." He sat back against the chair, rubbing his hands on his legs. He crossed his arms and sighed deeply. "Emily. I never hated you. And please stop apologizing. You should be the last person to do that."

"Then why didn't we work out, Eric? I can't move on. All you did was tell me that you couldn't and you were gone. I received divorced papers, because you told me you felt pressure to marry me, and then all of the sudden, I became the enemy." Emily's brows pinched in frustration. "Eric. You gotta help me here. I can't move on, because I still feel married. You didn't give me a chance to beg, plea, punch or question you or nothing. You were as cold as ice." He reached out, barely patting her hand before pulling back. Even though he seemed uncomfortable, he also didn't seem comfortable being distant any more.

"You saw me at the party and gave me such attitude that I couldn't wrap that moment in my mind to make it make sense. Do you understand what I'm saying?"

Eric nodded and sighed. He licked his fall-kissed lips as he rubbed his hands together. "I can't believe that I'm going to do this but I suppose it's time." Her forehead crinkled so he continued. "Emily, I was cruel to you because I . . . I didn't want to get married—not at that time anyway. It's just that my mom urged me into doing it sooner and my dad fooled me."

Emily's forehead wrinkled. "Fooled you? What do you mean fooled you? Your dad got sick and—"

Scoffing, he said, "My dad. About that fool . . ." With eyes darting around to ensure their privacy, he leaned forward again.

Internally, Emily struggled to compose herself by calming her emotions. "What?" she asked, feeling both nervous and suspicious. She wasn't sure she wanted to hear it.

"I was too embarrassed to tell you everything. My dad lied about being sick. He did that to get me married. He kept telling me that he was scared that he wouldn't see his only child get married. I felt guilty and even though I was in love with you, marriage was far from my mind." He exhaled and ran a hand through his wavy hair. "Look Ems, I thought I was giving him what he wanted. Getting married at that particular moment wasn't exactly about you as it was for him."

Emily felt disgusted, like she was breathing insipid oxygen from within. "Excuse you? M-maybe you're lying now. You know, you're the sick one, Eric. Don't blame your poor parents—"

Eric tried to pacify her by swiping his hands. "Emily, look please, hear me out. My dad did do this. I overheard him talking to my mom after we got married. There was so much heated anger, they didn't hear me come through the door. My mom was yelling at him and I heard her say, 'You better tell Eric the truth when he gets here.' I made them confess on the spot. He wouldn't say anything out of fear, so my mom did."

Emily's breathing turned shallow. Her wild hands flagged him to stop. "Eric, please. Why would your dad do something so rotten? This story sounds so silly. Why would he think of hurting your mother?" *Couldn't Eric just own the fact that he'd busted up our marriage on his own?*

"Because, my dad is used to getting everything his way. My parents aren't wealthy because my dad is some passive business man. He couldn't stand having his only child not married with no children. To him I wasn't bringing anything to the table. His defense was, 'What are you waiting for, Eric? I may be dead and gone before you get the ball rolling.' His friends had him beat by a milestone in that area. I was disgracing him, coming across as a loose bachelor—a playgirl or something. That's unacceptable in his inner Potomac circle, especially at my age. Also, he figured you would get pregnant soon afterwards." He let out a bitter laugh. "They are not the perfect couple you think they are. My dad had his affairs and has treated my mom like a dog and has taken her for granted. I think he's learned his lesson and he's admitted he's gone too far. Still. I'm not really talking to him now."

Struggling to take it all in, Emily started to feel like a child whose parents told her that she was conceived by accident. She felt like a bigger fool than she could've ever imagined. "And you walk out on me? You could've told me this."

"Emily, honey, think about it. I'm supposed to tell you that I married you to satisfy a dying wish? I'd already felt like scum."

The blaze of heat in Emily's chest burned her enough to want to vomit. Struggling to compose herself, her eyes steamed with tears that hesitated to fall as she crossed her arms in anger. Her hand circled the air. "You know what this tells me?" He nodded with shame. "That you never felt close enough to me to be honest. You let me figure this out on my own for months, in agony. All you had to do was get over yourself and let me hurt with decency, not by sparing me as you hide and go figure this all out. How nice of you to take *your* time needed to get it together, meanwhile, I go to bed every night, staring at the ceiling feeling like I was too thirsty for you or something." She pointed a finger at him and through gritted teeth told him, "You should feel like scum."

Eric slammed his back against the chair with a thoughtful sideways stare. He closed his eyes, as almost to hide from her ugly words. With a closed mouth, he froze and sighed before opening them again when he told her, "I did and I do. I'd figured that my mom was right. She pulled me to the side before I decided to propose to you and said that I should consider marriage and that I would grow to love it. She was trying to make her husband's dying wish come true and she loved the idea of me getting married. So, they were both egging me on, but one of them did it from a place of deceit. You should've seen it, Emily. My mom was distraught and my dad milked the sick role. I felt so much pressure. I had visions of my father in a coffin with his dying wish unfulfilled. When a child has to fight to get approval from a parent, wanting it becomes an obsession, even when that child isn't close to the parent. I figured marrying you would right every wrong between my father and me. But the issues between us was because of him.

"I just couldn't tell you flat out that his condition propelled the proposal. They were no perfect example, Emily. That is why I also didn't want to marry you at that moment. I felt I would destroy something great. I didn't think I was husband material. I needed more time to let it come naturally. When I learned the truth, I panicked. I divorced you because I didn't want our lives to model theirs. I loved you too much Emily to become a rotten husband. If I tried to break it off easily, you wouldn't have let me because you're so kind and optimistic. You woulda' insisted that we try. I mean, what were we supposed to do, go back to dating? That's backward. And starting marriage off on the wrong foot with lies is a recipe for failure. I figured that I had wasted enough of your life and that you should be far from me, and the only way to do that was to make you hate me. I tainted us, I tainted what coulda' been. I couldn't wake up every morning and look into your pretty hazel eyes knowing that my dad had robbed us and that I allowed myself to marry you out of guilt. I wanted you far from me. And it worked."

Eric froze as he tried to read her soul through her eyes. She closed them tight as a tear fell onto the table. The burning in her chest had dissipated and turned into sorrow. Sorrow for two young people who could've had it all. When she opened them, she found his palms up and open, waiting for her hands to accept his.

Even on their pseudo wedding day, she didn't see the look in his eyes that she saw now. Filled with nothing but sincerity and ache, he told her, "From the bottom of my messed-up heart, I am sorry, Emily. I am very sorry. I could've handled this better but I didn't know how. And for that, I'm sorry. I . . ." Looking at the floor, he inhaled sharply as he tried to find his words. "Mm—I wasn't man enough to deal with this."

Relieved that he could admit his shortcomings, her hands eased into the place that used to be home for her. Making contact like that for the first time since their divorce felt strange and wonderful, all at the same time.

After a few seconds of letting it all marinate, she eased them back to wipe her tears. "Well. Thank you for that."

He nodded. "Meant every word."

She felt calm again. "Wow," she said in a shaky voice. "Imagine where we could've been by now without any inference."

"Yeah," he realized.

Feeling overwhelmed, Emily asked, "So how long did he think he could keep up the sick act?"

Eric's eyes fell dull, zoned out. "My mom never did go into how she found out exactly. Think she put it all together or something. Doubt he woulda' confessed to my mom on his own. I really think he would've told us both that he was "cured." He didn't care. All he cared about was getting what he wanted."

Emily was speechless. "How could he do that to you?"

Out of his trance-like state, he motioned a finger between them as he blurted, "How could he do that to us? My father has been a poor father figure. I was always closer to my mom, because we were both victims of his madness. I can't tell you I'll be devastated when he dies. I'd be sad because he's my father and my mom once loved him deeply, and we do have memories. But for my sake?" He thought about it for a moment. "Nah."

The server came with their salads. Confused, he told the server, "I didn't—"

"I did," Emily told him. "I took the liberty when you were on your way. It's your favorite, Salad Niçoise.

"Oh, I see. You're right." He looked at the server. "Thank you."

This was the Eric that she knew and fell in love with: a kind man with manners and feelings. "Eric. I'm glad that we had this talk. You don't know how rough it's been."

"No, I do." He gave her the sincerest smile since their divorce as he held a fork in his hand. "I've been wrestling with these emotions, too. Pretending like we've never happened ain't working."

Emily raised a finger in the air. "Just one question?"

"Mm?" Eric replied as he chewed.

"When were you planning to tell me the truth?" Staring at him, she couldn't eat, even with her rumbling tummy.

Eric chewed with a thoughtful expression. "I was still embarrassed. I was embarrassed of it all. My actions, my dad's . . . so I don't know, but it was eating me alive. I loved you more than I have any other woman. Some of my irritation was genuine, Emily, because seeing you made me wrestle with the fact that I should tell you when I wasn't ready to face it. I don't know, Ems. I think I was waiting for me to get over feeling robbed first. In a way, my dad robbed me, too. He manipulated me and I felt like hell. I'm disappointed that my mom stood by his madness these years." Eric shrugged. "Oh well." He lifted some tuna with his fork. "What can you do? Just wished I handled it better for your sake."

For the first time since their divorce, Emily finally realized that she and Eric had been on the same roller coaster of emotions while riding in different cars. The lunch date of honesty was like the stopping point, where they could both finally jump out and stretch for the first time. She didn't doubt that he felt just as haggard from the ride as she did. And even though it was tempting to keep the bitterness with her for making her endure an unnecessary year of loops, falls and twists, she knew she had to let it go. It was time to let it go. Appreciative that their feet stood on new grounds in their relationship, apparently, she was still dizzy because, Emily still couldn't tell where that left them. So instead, she focused on digesting her reestablished relationship with a side of salad.

Amber

Sheet music covered Amber's chest as she lay on her couch in her Southwest apartment. It rose with each breath she took. Maybe she was trying to take a nap, or maybe she just needed actual solitude to think. The last few weeks had been wild. The contrast between George and Eric humored her, but somehow the encounters rang with regret.

She couldn't care less that George had a wife, or that she accepted his money in exchange for her giving up her goods. Amber couldn't believe that she had to put up with old, out-of-shape men when there were young and lean men like Eric. Did Emily's Eric rank as hot as hers? She bet Emily's Eric stood short with a flabby stomach. As cautious and proper as Emily was, Amber just couldn't see her with a man as powerful and wild as the Eric with the eagle tattoo. If he did have a tattoo, she guessed it would be of a library book.

Amber began to chuckle silently, and then she let it out. The tension of keeping up with her clients escaped her at the hands of her humor. She cracked herself up sometimes. That moment had become long overdue, and it felt good to her. Composing herself, it occurred to her that if it wasn't money on her mind, then it had to be men. It seemed like piano had taken a backseat while she tried to find sexual clients. Her survival depended on clients. They were either paying her for piano lessons or for sexual gratification.

Amber's laughter ceased as she pondered that for a moment. She wasn't exactly surprised at who she'd become, considering her hatred for rules. They gave a sense of living in a box of standards made by society. Who were these people who tried to dictate how other people should live? What made them right and her so wrong?

Done with worrying about it, she shrugged as she sat up. Maybe her mind had kicked into high gear, because she questioned how long she wanted this life of hustling old men. If Amber faced her situation with honesty, she found the thought of Eric wanting something serious arousing. At that moment, Amber could admit the truth. Being tangled with old, unattractive men for sex kept her in control, because she knew she would never become attached by lust or fantasies beyond the call of duty. When it was over, it was over. But with someone like Eric, regardless of cash and him being a client, the cut-off may not be so simple. Amber found herself thinking about that night at random moments: chopping onions for dinner somehow led to thoughts of that eagle tattoo, his tight stomach, or his handsome face; taking a bubble bath alone made it more fun when she could reminisce about that night, especially when sex toys sat around the bathtub; or impeding thoughts of white, rustled hotel sheets ruined her chances of playing a song on the piano to completion. What if she only slept with Eric-types from now on? She'd become a sex bucket and soon find herself calling Eric-types for fun sex, with the option to forgo the pay, just to have "one more night."

Shaking her head, Amber concluded that she had to stay with older clients. They were more desperate, lonely, and loaded. They had issues, and she could play on them. All her older men had complaints and had grown bored of their old ladies and were having limited bedroom action. When Amber surfaced, she always came like a breath of fresh air— a young, attractive woman promising to give them an experience like no other. They would fall for it. She knew which ones would take the bait and which ones to leave alone. Her reputation must've grown, because old women at parties would squeeze their men's arms tighter as she passed. Unfortunately, the wives had no clue that they sent red flags that their marriages were in trouble. When they let their guards down and left the room, Amber would find their husbands and in five minutes or less, she would sweep them away like a thief in the night.

Amber reasoned that she was probably thinking about Eric more than she'd anticipated, because he was a change of pace. Once she slept with another old man, Eric would be yesterday's news. Yes, a friend of Osha had sent an invitation for a party tomorrow night, and she knew just the right person to take.

Summer

Saturday night. My stomach sat at my feet. I couldn't believe that I had to encounter this man again with his wife, especially in their home. Although, I had to admit that I missed his voice. I couldn't help but hug my stomach with a mushy smile. I stood in front of my floor-length mirror wearing a tiered, chiffon dress, that stopped a few inches above my knees. Even though I had taken the time to blow dry my hair straight, I decided to pull it into a low ponytail.

The truth was, I couldn't wait to see him look at me the way he did. However, I didn't want it like this, and certainly not in his and Fran's home. I should rebel with a call and tell her that I've caught the bug. I knew that I wouldn't so I decided to suck it up and deal with it. But then a disturbing thought crossed my mind: What if Fran knew about her husband and me and decided to keep pulling these stunts until one of us collapsed from stress and confessed? I calmed down and reasoned with myself. She wouldn't do that. What wife would sit around and watch her husband cheat with the same woman whom she employed?

Okay, so Fran didn't know and it was up to us to make sure that she didn't. I think tonight would be the best time to cut ties. I'll tell Ruben if he drives me back home today. Drives me back home—I'd forgotten about that possibility. Oh, no. He'd take Amber home and then me. Then he would walk me to my door. I would try to resist him with a push but it wouldn't work. Maybe I should call Max to pick us up. Maybe Amber and I'll be stuck in Virginia waiting for a bus to take us to a Metro station. Ruben would never drive us to the Metro station and come straight back home and Fran wouldn't allow it. We could take a taxi after dinner again. That would work. If we tell Fran that we took a car, she would be the one to peek out of her window to see.

So, yes, we will call a cab upon arriving to the closet Metro station to Fran's house, and call one after dinner. Okay, okay, I can do this. Ruben, can do this. He won't even be into me this time around. Certainly, he'd used this time away to come to his senses, as had I.

Amber puffed on her cigarette as we waited for a taxi at the King Street Metro. I didn't know why I cared so much about what Fran thought, but I didn't want her to smell smoke on us. Or maybe I worried that Ruben would, so I wanted to put the blame on Fran instead.

"Amber, maybe you should hold off on the smoking until we leave their home. I don't think Fran would want—"

Amber sucked her teeth, rolled her eyes and said, "Oh, please. That ole bitch ain't sittin' in this cold. Is she?"

I shot her a mommy disapproval look. Amber tilted her head at me and inhaled one last long, strong puff, before throwing it on the ground and mashing it with her pointy-toe patent leather heals.

"Thank you, Amber." I smiled just to stick it to her.

"I'm mad at cha," she shot back in a dull voice that told me not to push it.

"Where is the next cab?" I shivered in my blue wool coat.

"You know this lady got some issues. Why she want some hot, young woman to be flaunted all over her husband's radar?" I shrugged. "Boy," she continued, "if you and Ruben didn't know each other before, she sure woulda' made this affair possible all on her own."

"Oh, Amber." I saw a yellow cab approaching. "Here we go." I flagged it and on cue, it stopped in front of us. I told the driver the address and he reset the meter as we headed toward Fran's house.

We arrived in front of a big, single-family home. Her house appeared to have been around for a while, but I could tell it was easily worth over one million dollars. Amber froze to study Fran's brick house as I paid the fare. The cab drove off, but I wanted to tell the driver to wait like a limo driver out of fear that Fran would suggest that Ruben take us home.

Amber never blinked. "Look at this broad. He's with her for the money, huh?"

"Not everyone does everything for money, Amber."

She lifted a challenging brow at me. "You sure about that?"

I gently tugged her sleeve. "Come on. Time to roll. Pray for me, Amber. I need it."

"Why? God didn't tell you to sleep with a married man."

I playfully slapped her arm, but I didn't smile. "Now don't go getting self-righteous on me." We walked leisurely toward the not-so-humble palace.

"Don't worry, I totally believe that Fran is giving her husband away. Hey, maybe I should sleep with him for a buck." We both fell over laughing.

"Hey," I yanked her sleeve again. "I beat you to the punch, but I'm giving him what he needs for free."

"Well then I suggest you start charging so if you lose your job for this fool, you'll have some coins to fall back on."

We shared a huge laugh but caution washed over me. "Shhh. And I ain't charging, Amber." I put a shaky finger to my lips. "She may hear us. She could be near a window or something."

"Right." Amber nodded with composure.

"Here goes." I knocked. Fran must've been nearby. In a matter of seconds, we heard the unchaining of locks and saw the door fly open with Fran standing there with a big grin.

"Well hello there, ladies. Who is this pretty lady here with you, Summer?"

"Well, hello, Fran." Before I could answer, Amber took over. I stood there impressed with a surprised expression.

Amber extended a hand. "Hi, Fran, I'm Amber. How do you do? I have heard a lot of great things about you.

Accepting her hand, Fran raised her eyebrows, pleased with the news. "Well very good then. Amber, it's a pleasure. I'm well and you?"

"Very well, myself. You have a beautiful home, Fran."

Wow, this girl knew how to clean up for the right people. I had to give a nod to those parties with the rich. Fran gave Amber a very light but sincere hug and replied, "Thank you," as she capped Amber's hands with her own. Then she gave me a kiss on both cheeks and a hand brush on my shoulder.

"I'm so glad you could make it, Summer. It only seemed appropriate to have a small homecoming for Ruben."

"Oh? Other people are here?" Oh, no, I panicked but tried to look calm.

"Oh, no, no, noooo. I just invited you and your friend. Ruben is taking a shower." My mind couldn't help but produce an image of him naked in the shower and how I cared to join him. I would need one myself if I didn't control my thoughts. "He just got back in from Florida after vacationing with his parents. The pictures were nice. Maybe he will show them to you guys."

"He's not tired, Fran? Are you sure we shouldn't move this to another day?"

Fran's smile was a little forced. "Well, I'm sure I know my husband and he's okay. Don't you worry, Summer." She petted my arm. "You let me worry about him. You guys take a seat in the dining room down this hall and to the left, and I'll bring in the champagne. I'll be right back."

Shut up, Amber. I could already read her thoughts based on Fran's comment. I shot her a look with a lifted brow and placed a finger to my lips. Amber bit her lower lip and smiled.

I whispered, "Such a bad influence you are."

"But you love it this way," she shot back.

We arrived at a spacious dining room with ajar French doors. I could smell the food before noticing a variety of platters sprawled from one end of the table to the other. We entered and selected seats across from one another. A turkey waited in the middle with a ham and steak on either side. Side dishes complemented the meats as the desserts added the finishing touches.

I leaned forward to whisper a warning. "Amber, whatever you have to say, save it for later. Okay?"

I hope she didn't make me regret not choosing Brooke, but as fun punishment, I wanted to make Amber pay by enduring boredom. Still, I had to be honest and admit that I knew Amber's fun personality would help to take the edge off tonight. She served as a perfect choice for this moment. We could talk about this for months or even years to come.

"Relax, girl. I know how to roll with these people. Would you look at all this food in front of us? I'm starved."

"Well that's wonderful, Amber." Fran surprised us with her sudden presence.

Amber jerked her head to look behind her. "Well, yes, Fran. It was nice of you to go through all of this trouble just to have us here."

Fran waved a hand as she stood next to Amber, peering down on us. "Oh, my chef did all of this. I can't take the credit. I couldn't cook if I had to save my own neck." Her expression told me that she enjoyed the attention.

"Regardless," I added, "this is all so nice of you."

Fran smiled. "Well, ladies, I know we must all be ready to eat. Ruben will be down shortly."

My stomach flipped at the sound of his name.

That voice that always flipped my guts suddenly sang, "I'm here." It sounded more like a taunt than an announcement. Ruben had arrived, indeed. My eyes locked in on his. He had a subtle mischievous smile just for me. To Fran, it was probably just a smile that greeted visitors. To Amber, it was a half-hearted smile. To me, it was a message that said, "Tonight, you belong to me."

No. I wasn't going to let it happen. He had better savor that last fling we had because we wouldn't have a moment like that again. Yes. My mind was made up. Fran had almost become like a friend at this point, and she respected me. If not for the institution of marriage, then I would have to at least resist Ruben because of the friendliness of his wife.

I stood up and so did Amber. He shook her hand and they introduced themselves to one another. He walked around to meet me and grabbed my hand for a handshake. I felt the electricity like before. Oh. This was torture.

"Summer, you look well. It's nice to meet your friend here."

Ruben took a seat opposite from Fran at the other end of the table. I avoided his face, but didn't want to appear rude or weird in front of Fran, so I played it cool and turned to him.

"Ruben, it's nice seeing you again. How was your trip?" Yes, especially since he just "drove me home" that night, Fran would find it weird if he and I couldn't speak casually at this point. I had to feel confident in my acting abilities.

"My trip was exactly what the doctor ordered. I see my wife," he gestured toward her, "likes inviting you out, huh?"

"Shall we eat?" Fran asked with her charming grin.

About an hour into dinner, I had to use the bathroom. I needed a quick break away from Fran's piercing gaze of admiration and Ruben's odd vibe. I rose a timid hand and asked, "E-excuse me, Fran. Where's your bathroom?"

"Certainly. When you leave this room, turn to the right and head toward the foyer, but when you get to it, go left and down the other hall. The door is open and it will be the first one on the right."

"Thank you. I should also give my mom a quick ring to tell her I'll call her tomorrow."

Fran smiled at me. "Aww, how sweet."

"Yeah." I stood and headed toward the bathroom. A weight had lifted just from leaving the dining room. I heard Ruben say that he wanted to get some more wine. I could still hear Amber and Fran's talk and laughter as I moved closer to the foyer.

I made it to their generous-sized powder room. The room matched her taste. White wallpaper and gold flowers dressed the walls with a white toilet cover and rug. It certainly wasn't my taste. I grimaced before I checked myself out in the mirror. My appearance pretty much looked the same. My lipstick had faded, of course, but other than that, I opened my mouth to see that my teeth remained free of stuck food, and that my face didn't have any embarrassing surprises like eye or nose boogers. After I used the toilet, I washed my hands and dried them on one of her embroidered towels. I always felt guilty about using those types of towels, so I gently pressed my hands against them to remove the excess water. I picked up my clutch from the top of the wicker hamper, yanked the door open, and took a step out. A hand grabbed my right arm abruptly, causing my tiny body to jerk back. I saw Ruben, and he looked hungry. Not for food, but for me. This was not good. Did he really want to play with fire in this house with his wife just in the other room? It was bad enough I couldn't hear Fran or Amber and being gone too long together would certainly come across as suspicious.

"What are you doing?" I whispered through gritted teeth.

Ruben pressed me against the wall. "Summer. Why did you come here? What are you trying to do?" He tried to keep his voice low, but his emotions battled against his control.

"I couldn't reject your wife. She's my boss. Now let go so we can get back. Let me go first." I tried to retrieve my arm from his grasp, but he wouldn't let me. We stood there and argued back and forth through whispers. I couldn't believe that he attempted to push me around and confront me now. Did the Florida sun make him nuts?

"Summer, you being here is driving me wild. You're playing with fire being here." He pressed his body against mine, and I could tell that his ability to suppress his desire had fizzled. Somehow, his hand ended up under my dress and placed on my outer thigh, attempting to move higher, but I tousled with it. His hand had a mind of its own. What was he doing? I felt his hot breath on my nose, and I could smell the wine.

"Ruben, you have to back off. Back off now," I hissed.

"Regrets. I don't have any. Come on, baby, don't make me pleasure myself to you again. I can't take it." His accent thickened, and it made my stomach flip. Suddenly, my fight became weak. I tried. His hand invaded my inner thigh. I tried to hear the voices in the dining room. Nothing. I could only hear the rapid breathing from Ruben's mouth. Once again, I could see my belongings on the corner of the street. I could stay with Emily. She had a big home and she was lonely. We could split her mortgage. I could get a job at a fast-food chain since no one would hire me after being exposed for sleeping with my boss' husband.

Ruben kissed my neck and I tried to wiggle away. He wouldn't let me. There I stood, helpless . . . so helpless, and willing to be shamed if caught and fired from my job. I tried to push his face from my neck, but he proved to be too powerful and tenacious. He kept coming back for more. Ruben took a big hand and grabbed my face, and he forced me to face him. We paused and stared into each other's eyes.

"Go, leave me alone before it's too late, Ruben. We can't, we can't. You're crazy." My breath turned pathetic and shallow; I could barely hear my voice. I might as well have been a child at the bottom of a well.

He pressed his mouth against mine, enveloping my bottom lip. He sucked, caressed, and licked my mouth. I mustered enough force to break our kiss. He stared at me with needy dopey eyes.

"I can't do this to her." I had no more breath to give. My eyes felt crossed.

"Don't say this, Summer. Can't you feel what you do to me?"

And I could. I could feel his desire on my leg. It was all wrong, but I wanted to pretend it was right. "Go . . . go be with her before she gets suspicious. Please, Ruben, please."

"Okay, okay—just one more kiss."

I nodded quickly. One more couldn't hurt. His lips made love to mine. I decided to try to break away. But he betrayed his word. I pressed my little palms against his big, hard chest and tried to break. I wanted to be released from his spell, but he didn't budge. "Ruben . . . stop." When I moved my face left, his would go right, trying to follow me to land kisses on my lips. Our lips missed and then some kisses would land. Suddenly, the hem of my dress sat above my buttocks, and Ruben's hand ushered my thigh to cover his. Somehow, he ended up with pants unfastened while the crotch of my underwear had gotten pushed to the side. Amazingly, all of this happened without my knowledge.

"Ruben, no, no. We . . . we will be caught."

Ruben shoved his tongue inside my mouth. A wave of sexual desire flooded into my vagina. "It's okay, Summer, she won't know. I wanna take you. Shhh. Just let me put the tip in."

"Okay," I whispered. "But just the tip," I agreed foolishly. I could feel him and I couldn't stop it. I didn't want to stop it. It felt too good. He strolled in and almost out, and feeling his length was more than I could bear. Maybe Fran was watching, and if so, then she would have the best show of her life. The idea that she could catch us increased my chances of coming sooner than later. My arousal peaked and I couldn't stop it. It was time.

I gripped his neck with my arm, choking him, as I descended from my high. I saw unicorns in the fields, a rainbow in the pond, steam blow from a train and then my belongings in trash bags in the front lawn of my Delaware home. I grunted in his ear. "Summer." We collapsed and in one quick swoop, I reentered the bathroom with unreliable legs and shut the door quietly. I was a mess. My breathing grew frantic and shallow, my ponytail had been pushed out of place, and my body felt weak.

No, no, no, no. What had I done? Regret replaced my high. If Fran came around the corner, what would she say if she saw Ruben undone?

Suddenly, I heard a glass shatter. Minutes later, I heard Fran ask, "Ruben, what on Earth? You always have to make a mess, and on this night? Wh-where is Summer?" she asked in a weak but audible voice. She knocked.

"Come in."

I sat on the toilet lid, hunched over holding my stomach. "Oh, Summer, sweet dear. What happened to you? Amber and I were beginning to wonder what happened to you and Ruben. He dropped the bottle of wine and you're here sick. You look a mess."

"I think . . . I think something didn't agree with my stomach. Can you call me a cab?"

"I can take you—oh, Ruben can take you two home. Why wait for a cab and make things worse? How about a hospital, Summer? I feel awful. This was my dinner. Oh. My dear." Poor Fran turned hysterical and I felt like scum of the earth. I couldn't leave her husband alone.

"Okay, Fran, you or Ruben. No hospital. Just please, get me home."

Ruben appeared at the doorway. "Is she okay? What's wrong, honey?"

I wanted to say, "Nothing," but I realized that he was talking to his other honey. Close call. Fran came and helped me to my feet. She rubbed my back and helped me to the bathroom door.

"Summer is queasy and feeling horrible. You drive better at night than me. Ruben, take the ladies home."

He nodded frantically. What a good actor, too. Both of our characters were about as smelly as dog's poop.

I hugged Fran, trying to release my guilt and show my appreciation of her at the same time, which seemed impossible considering that I'd just received my backstabber certificate.

Amber talked the most in the car. I chose the back so I could avoid being in the hot seat. I sat up when Ruben said, "The coast is clear." Fran helped me into the backseat and I had lied down to seem more convincing. Obviously, I made the wrong career choice. I should've flown to Hollywood after college.

"I know," Amber told Ruben. "You guys are like a sexual Bonnie and Clyde, getting away with murder," she teased.

"Quiet, Amber."

She turned around and looked at me. "Hey, there's a party tonight. Wanna roll, Summer?"

I wasn't really in a party mood. Ruben kind of wiped that out of me. "Amber, home is good."

"Are you kidding me?" she started. "I've just endured a dinner party for you and all those last-minute shenanigans and this is it? This is the night?"

Ruben stole a quick peek at me as he turned around to tell me, "She—she's right. I think a cool person like her deserves a little party after putting up with small talk with my wife. I know that couldn't have been easy."

"One hour, Amber, please. I'm just ready to go home. You just don't understand." I couldn't believe that I relented, but Ruben was right. Amber was a trooper tonight to put up with Fran and my sexual escapade with Ruben. Things could have gotten ugly so fast and she would've been caught in the crossfire, so it was only right to take care of my girl.

"Thanks, Summer. Trust me, girl, you'll have fun."

"Anytime, Amber," I replied dully.

The party would've sounded so great if Ruben hadn't touched me. However, dancing with guilt was never fun.

"I really don't need much time guys. I really appreciate this."

The same class of people who attended the first party filled the Northwest DC mansion. Amber leaned into my ear and said in a low tone, "I have to find some work."

I think I knew a prostitute when Amber put it like that. I wanted to hang my head low, but I just nodded and continued looking straight. I held up one finger and mouthed, "One hour." She gave me thumbs up and disappeared around the corner.

Ruben warned me that he needed to take a casual stroll through the party to see if he happened to know anyone. When he returned and told me that so far the coast appeared clear, relief washed over me. Now, he casually dangled beside me, probably waiting for the perfect moment to whisk me away somewhere in a deep, dark corner.

I think I'd done the most taboo acts with him. We had sex outside on his car hood the first night we met, we had sex in my apartment when his wife expected a quick drop-off, and then we did it in his house with his wife right around the corner. Was the thrill gone?

Suddenly, I turned to him. "Ruben?"

He raised his eyebrows as he stood nonchalantly with his hands in his pockets.

Nervously, I bit my lower lip and shifted my weight from one heel to another. "I think we should mingle. I think you should see if you find something you like." Though unexpected, the words felt good to say. This thing between us started to feel like a relationship, and that thing I didn't do. Above all, he was my boss's husband, and the thrill slowly transitioned to the feel of a ball and chain.

Ruben's jaw tightened. "Summer, don't do this." He carefully controlled his tone as the violins competed with the sound of his voice. "Why don't we just take a break? Will that help?"

I wanted to roll my eyes to extend insight into my thoughts about that one. His words made me feel trapped, like I was in a relationship working it out with my boyfriend, when he was just a fling, an affair, hence, nothing serious in my book.

I wanted to sound stern, but the neighboring people would become nosey and suspicious if he and I became loud. I had to do my best with a controlled tone.

Through gritted teeth, I replied, "Ruben, I'm not asking now, I'm telling you. This," I pointed between him and me, "is becoming too much, too fast—and you're married—to my boss, no less."

"I think you're overreacting."

I could only stand there amazed and watch the man with whom I was having an affair stand there looking so cavalier. "I don't think you see this from my point of view at all, Ruben." I crossed my arms and glared into his unwavering eyes.

Suddenly, a large hand gripped my arm and tugged me toward a balcony. "Ouch," I said.

"Follow me." Ruben led me to the balcony and closed the sliding door behind him. We stood on a patio overlooking a vast lawn covered by a sheet of darkness. Instead of smelling random bouts of perfumes and colognes competing with wafts of food, I could inhale fresh, crisp air that not only cleared my nasal passage, but my head. He spun on his toes and peered into my eyes. "What are you talking about, Summer? You want to move on now?"

All I had to do was be direct. I didn't feel like softening anything. Tired and exhausted, I preferred to avoid a circuitous approach. I closed my eyes for a few seconds and opened them.

"Ruben, I didn't mean to sleep with my boss' husband, but when I found out, I should've left it at that and cut it loose, but I didn't. I kept allowing myself to go deeper until I didn't know what to do or how to handle myself. I'm not so upset that you are married, nor am I proud of that. But what I cannot do is pretend that you do not belong to someone with a very important role in my life. I want to have a career, Ruben, not a job. Your wife's company can do wonders for me for years to come." Silent, his eyes told me that he felt angry and that I had betrayed the rules to his game. "Goodbye, Ruben, and go home to Fran."

I headed toward the balcony door when he said, "Summer." I turned around, and he grabbed me closer by the waist. With ease, he spun my little body, pressing my back against the balcony railing before gripping both of my tiny arms. He shook me with each professed word. "Summer, I need you."

"Ruben." I tried to break free but I couldn't compete with his strength. I raised my voice. "What do you think can become of us, huh?"

Spiraling into desperation, he said, "Let's do something, Summer. Let's take it to the next step." He was handsome, tall, and physically in control, but it wasn't enough. I wanted to be free. "We have so much passion together, Summer. I don't remember feeling this way with any other woman. Are you going to stand there and lie about this connection?"

I'd become so emotional and angry that he couldn't see all that was at stake. Why wasn't his picture as clear as mine? "Because it's forbidden. It's forbidden, Ruben. The minute we can be together, we will fizzle. You will see that, Ruben."

Ruben wouldn't relent, and his grip remained tenacious. He tried to reach me fast, because he knew I was slipping away. "Baby, don't let my wife intimidate you. I can protect you. The night I first laid eyes on you, I was drawn to you. Your wild, wavy hair, your beautiful skin, your mysterious ways, it all drives me so wild, *mi amor*. When we touched each other, it felt like magic. You woke me up, baby. If you go, it will be like putting me back into a coma again. I was sleepwalking, and I didn't know just how much in a slumber I was in until you came around."

"Ruben?" I squinted at him as I prepared myself to study his eyes. "Then why haven't you left her yet?"

Ruben cleared his throat and peered at the ground as if the answers were legible against the concrete. "I told you. She can ruin me. My wife knows a lot of people in high places. She got me my job. Fran took me out of a dead-end job after we started dating, and placed me in a company with so much growth potential. I mean . . ." he shook his head. "This lady finds the best work for talented people. People in high places here trust her. If you live in this area and need a job, Fran can get you one. Needless to say, if you burn her, she can close your doors just as fast as she can open them. I would have to move away and start anew, and really, Summer, I love it here. And I would die before I let her run me out of here."

Listening to him talk made me feel nauseous by the second. I would really have to find myself getting used to slicing pizza at a parlor or dipping ice cream onto cones for a living. I sneered at him, feeling utterly confused. "Ruben, please humor me. Let's say that I did do what you wanted. How did you plan to protect me from Fran's repercussions?"

"I could ease out of the marriage and appear to be walking away single. When the divorce becomes finalized, I could be free to be with you, but it doesn't mean I'd have to drive by your job and see you. Or, you could also find another job while we divorce, so you wouldn't have to look at her once our divorce finalized. Hopefully by then, you'd be with another company. She and I don't have children, so she'd only see us by happenstance, and you'd be with another company, so . . . it wouldn't matter by then." He bit his lower lip as he looked at me. "Sweetheart, she doesn't have to rule our lives."

I couldn't seem to reply with the right words and could only say, "Well, you seem to have it all figured out, Ruben."

Ruben relaxed his expression and smiled as he stepped forward to grab my shoulders. "*Mi, cariña.* I haven't known you for long, but in this short amount of time, you have been the only one to remind me that passion is vital to life. It's like you've saved my life." Ruben came in suddenly on my lips and pressed hard with his. Caught off-guard, I didn't have a chance to close my eyes, nor did I pull away. Instead, I continued to stare at his closed eyes. He was really into me.

Amber

Amber found herself on the couch with a glass of champagne with her legs crossed and exposed, as she chatted with an older, White man. He was older than Eric but younger than George. Although this guy was taken by her disingenuous interaction, he failed to realize that her private time required payment.

"So, uhh, Alicia—"

Amber quickly raised a finger and said, "Amber," before she took another sip of champagne.

"Oh, of course, Amber." The overweight man chuckled nervously. "Well, I don't think I ever got to introduce myself. My name is Daniel Crosby. I'm the senior vice president of—"

Amber couldn't take it anymore. "Look, umm, David—"

"Oh, it's Daniel, actually." His struggle with confidence became clear as he repeatedly scratched the brown hairs on the sides of his semi-bald head. He'd adjusted his tie three times in the last sixty seconds. Daniel's bad breath kept Amber's nose in her champagne glass as she sipped frequently to avoid his halitosis.

Amber rolled her eyes. *What does this guy really want?* "Oh, right. Well listen, Daniel. I really don't need to know what you do. I'm more interested in what you want to do tonight."

Daniel's short, bushy eyebrows stood up at Amber's insinuating words. "Well, hot stuff, what did you have in mind?"

Jackpot. She graced him with a million-dollar smile and turned to face him. Her free hand traced up and down her thigh. Daniel's eyes darted between her eyes and her hand, causing him to find it difficult to keep up with her words.

"I wanna get out of here," she told him in a high whisper.

"Do you? Because there's a hotel next door I can book right now. I mean, I live in DC, but why drive to my house? A-and I don't really know you." Daniel surged with so much excitement, that he would've probably taken his clothes off right in front of the crowd if Amber asked.

"Hey, it's cool. Let's do it," Amber replied through her smile. Daniel extended a hand to help her up and she accepted.

Summer

My text notification sound went off, which broke up the kiss between Ruben and me. "I have to get this," I told Ruben suddenly as I fumbled for the buried phone in my clutch beneath my mirror. I opened it up to see a text from Amber. It read, *"Off with a client. Sorry, girl, please be safe. Call me tomorrow."*

I shook my head, not surprised at all. "This bitch," I mumbled.

Ruben's brows frowned at me. "Something wrong?"

"Ruben, I'm done here. Please take me home." And just like that, I dropped the mic on this relationship and walked off stage with two arms up like a Richard Prior comedy show coming to an end.

"Okay, but what about your friend?" he asked.

I pushed past him and reached for the lever on the sliding door. "She's fine. Let's just go." I started to move but hesitated. "Actually, can you just drop me off at a Metro, Ruben?" A sudden headache began to gain momentum, and I needed to get away immediately.

Ruben stood there, looking flabbergasted with his mouth open. "Yes, I can do that. But why don't you just let me take you home, Summer?"

"I need my space, Ruben." I turned around and let myself through the sliding door and located the front door to make a clean exit. I didn't check to see how far or close he walked, because my mental distance satisfied me for now. Then I had a thought and I found myself stopping in my tracks right outside the front porch of the house. I turned on my heels to see the tall, hot Cuban close on my trail. He stopped when I came face-to-face with him.

"What is it?" he asked.

"You know what?" I began. Then it occurred to me: *How am I ever going to see past this affair if I leave the boat of opportunity?* "Ruben, you can go. I want to stay. Please." I put up my palm as reassurance that I was okay and hadn't planned on backing down.

He didn't say anything for a few seconds. Then he said, "Okay." Ruben patted my shoulder gently as he walked past me. I stole a furtive glance before making my way back to the party. No Amber, no Ruben, just me.

Brooke

Brooke hugged Jackson from behind as he scattered spices from his hand into the pot of spaghetti. "You never take me out." She smiled into his sweater and squeezed him tight.

Jackson froze and then placed the wooden spoon down onto the counter. He pried her hands from around his waist as he turned to face her. He pretended to think.

"Shit. I forgot to tell you how embarrassed I am to be seen with you in public."

Brooke gently punched his chest and he pretended to gasp for air. "Oh, stop it, you. That didn't even hurt."

"Okay." Jackson straightened up and bowed. "Baby, you're right. Where should we go?"

"Clubbing." Brooke's eyes glistened with happiness as she clasped her hands together with a hop.

"Lady, what about my food?" Jackson pointed backward with a thumb.

"Turn it off and let's go. I'm okay so we can eat when we get back. Come on, it's Saturday night and besides, you should've cooked a long time ago."

Jackson peered down at Brooke below his eyelashes. "Tell the truth. You just wanna see my moves, don't you?"

"That, too." Brooke laughed. "Oh, come on, Jax. It'll be fun."

"Only you can call me that. Fine. You're right. We never go out, out. I guess it's been your place or mine and after a while, that does get pretty dry."

"Yup." Brooke tilted her head as she watched him head toward his bedroom. She'd never felt an attraction so deep before.

"Lucky for me," she called down the hallway as she waited for Jackson to emerge with something more club-ready to wear, "my black and white stripes can pass with flying colors at the club." Brooke twirled once in her Christian Dior short dress.

"You did it on purpose," he called back.

Brooke didn't say anything. She just laughed and pressed her back against the wall as she waited for her man to reappear, happy to be in a place of commitment. For the first time in life, everything felt together, despite the broken home element. Pride extended beyond just her career and looks. Lost in thought, in her peripheral, she turned to see a tall, lean figure come into view wearing a blue, buttoned-up shirt over black slacks. Brooke pushed off the wall with her back and turned to face him.

With outstretched arms, he asked, "How do I look?"

"Like I could eat you up." Brooke swayed her hips as she approached him. Placing a hand on his chest, she stared into his eyes as she allowed her hand to mindlessly skate downward. Her hand dropped at her side.

"Be good, girl. We don't have much time left."

"When we come back, you are all mine."

Amber

Daniel struggled to carry Amber through the threshold of his hotel room and barely maintained her normal body weight in time to settle her on the bed.

"Whoa, careful stranger. Don't strain your back," Amber warned with slight irritation. Amber couldn't believe she encountered so many losers with big wallets.

"Tell me about it. Maybe you should hit the gym with me." Daniel straightened up and held his back. "Whew."

Amber sat up on the bed abruptly and raised her eyebrows in disbelief. She could feel the blood boiling in her veins, sending a straight shot to her head. "Me? You gonna look at me? Are you jokin' right now?"

Daniel's attempt at conviction was all too transparent to Amber. "Well honey, I *have* picked up lighter."

Standing up to straighten her dress, Amber dismissed him with a flick of her hand and said, "Let's get this over with."

"Sure."

"You fat bastard," she muttered quietly.

"What's that, sweet cakes?" Daniel asked innocently.

"Maybe if you gave those up you could pick me up with ease next time." And that she meant to be heard.

"Hey, what do you want from me? So my strong point is money, not muscle. Big whoop." Daniel became defensive, and Amber didn't want that to ruin her moment or her payday.

"Right. So, let's just get this show on the road."

Daniel marched to close the gap between him and Amber. He placed both hands on her hips and revealed a naughty smile. "So." He smacked her buttocks with one big hand.

Amber jumped. "Ouch."

Daniel cocked his head back and laughed, only to reveal fillings and stained teeth. Amber cringed deep inside. Maybe the pole would be easier than this, she considered grimly.

"Where do we begin? I've been dying to kiss you all night."

What a nightmare. Amber panicked. She placed a hand on his chest to block him. "Daniel. There is something I need to tell you."

"Oh, really? You like S&M?"

"Noooooo," Amber replied casually as she descended to her knees. She began to unbuckle Daniel's belt. This moment always made her nervous. She didn't know what she should expect to find. Small ones, too big ones, droopy ones, very red ones . . . Amber held her breath as she pulled down his slacks and revealed white briefs. The man's choice of undergarments didn't surprise her. Amber released a gentle sigh. *No one's supposed to wear these anymore.* The moment of truth had arrived. What hid in prize box number one? Gripping his waistband, she dragged it down his thighs.

"Huh?"

Disbelief captured her as she couldn't believe her eyes.

Brooke

Brooke and Jackson ended up at Cloudless Nightclub in Northwest. The club offered five dance floors, but Jackson and Brooke escaped to the second floor, where the house music played. Brooke had no idea how to dance to it, so she bounced around like a college girl on her first night away from her parents.

With her arms flailing in the air, she called out to Jackson, "Do you listen to this kind of music?" Her laughter interrupted her dance moves. And despite being in a hot and crowded atmosphere that she'd usually avoid, nothing could erase her happiness as long as she had Jackson by her side.

Jackson created his own hysterical dance moves. It reminded Brooke of a mix between the arms of one dancing to hip hop and the legs of one dancing to dance hall. "I listen to whatever sounds good at the moment."

Brooke barely heard him, so she pulled him to the side as she leaned into his ear. "Let's get some drinks."

"I'm more of a champagne and wine kind of guy, but let's take one for the team tonight."

"Yeah." Brooke looked at him with a lingering smile. "We can do that." She grabbed his wrist and pulled him toward the bar. Jackson ordered two Piña Coladas and, in two minutes, they were served. Walking away from the bar once they retrieved and sipped their drinks, they both froze to analyze the taste.

"Good?" Brooke asked.

"Perfect. Let's get back to dancing."

Brooke shrugged and enjoyed the taste as she swayed her hips. "Let's sip and dance. I've always wanted to do that." Sipping their drinks, Jackson ushered her back to the dance floor with one big hand on the small of her back.

Brooke wanted to blame it on the alcohol when he started poking one finger in the air like a disco dancer. "Noooooooo," Brooke playfully protested.

"What's wrong? You don't like my moves?" he teased. He placed his empty plastic cup on a wall border and used his free hands to yank Brooke against his groin. He gyrated his hips as humor took over his expression.

"Stop it, boy." Brooke crinkled her nose with laughter as she tried to break free from his grip. "This is not how we dance to house music. I know you are not drunk from that one drink."

Relaxed, Jackson smiled warmly. "No, I'm not." He didn't yell anymore, but Brooke made out his words. "Come here."

He placed his fingers around her wrist and led her to a sofa in a dark corner. He wedged her between his body and the wall. They watched the crowd of young, wild dancers throw their arms and hands everywhere to the music. Long strands of hair whipped the air, girls bent over as they shook their butts against happy men who cheered with drinks raised to the ceiling. Brooke continued to sip as she observed the behavior of women her age and younger.

His head nodded toward the dancefloor. "You like this?"

"I do." She smiled and turned to him. "I like you . . . here with me."

Grinning, Jackson placed a hand on her bare leg and moved it inside the space between her legs. "Oh, yeah?" He moved in, blocking her view of the crowd, wanting to taste her piña colada-kissed lips.

A few seconds on her lips, Brooke felt doubtful and placed a gentle hand against his chest. "Jackson," she whispered.

"Shhh, baby." He located her ear with his lips. "I want you. And I'm gonna taste you, right here, right now." Easing back, he waited for her to say something as he admired her face.

Feeling nervous for the first time in a while with Jackson, Brooke nodded thoughtfully with parted lips. His thumb brushed her bottom lip, then eased down to her neck and between her breast, coasting along seductively over her stomach before landing under the hemline of her dress.

Brooke could see the nightclub and those around her fading away. No one cared about the bubble that screened them from the outsiders, but the two who were in it. Frankly, she didn't care. She cared about the friction of his thumb against her soft skin and how it made her feel. As Jackson's hand dared to explore higher, it found her smooth vagina.

Surprised, he told her, "You don't have any panties on." She grinned naughtily as her tongue played with the tip of the straw. Jackson moved the cup from her mouth with his other hand to caress her lips with his. His thumb rubbed her clitoris, and suddenly, she felt closed off from everything. She couldn't hear, nor could she feel the pulsating music against her heart. Instead, she could only see, and what she saw was a man with piercing eyes staring back at her. Brooke closed her eyes, and eased her head back without a care in the world, because she trusted Jackson. She never thought she would experience sexual satisfaction in public, let alone a club, but she was and she had no regrets.

Her teeth clutched down on her bottom lip, her knees saw more distance between one another, her heartbeat sped up, as if to chase the beating thump of the baseline in the room. Jackson switched to his pointer finger to explore the walls of her vagina. When she gripped his arm with a hand, he added his thumb to her pleasure point, and after 60 seconds of delectation, she couldn't take it anymore. His touch and the freedom of being among the crowd was all she needed to reach bliss. Crossing her legs to lock in his fingers while clutching his arm, she moaned from the depth of her throat, with her other hand, she searched for mercy against the fabric of the couch. Coming to from the high, her eyes fluttered open to find a narrowed-eyed Jackson tasting his fingers.

"Mm. Good." He kissed her shoulder and helped her to her wobbly feet. She relaxed in his arm that rested above her butt. He gave her a quick peck on her lips. Leading her away from the room, he took her outside into the crisp fall air, clear of the smoke, colognes and noise. Walking her down an alley, he found a dark corner outside, away from the street. Placing her against the wall, he told her, "No other woman, Brooke . . . no other woman . . ."

"What?" Brooke didn't mean to sound obtuse, but she had to hear his thoughts in full. Maybe that would make the moment feel more real.

"No other woman has gotten me this way. I can't stand to be around you without wanting you this badly."

Jackson leaned closer, and fit his lips gently into hers. Brooke's mouth responded slowly, as she tried to savor the moment. They were too lost in the moment to close their eyes. Brooke moaned, as she threw her arms around his neck and swung her legs around his waist. Her head rolled back as Jackson pressed into her body. Brooke hoped that the wall would cave in and envelope Jackson into her existence. He could never be close enough to her. She panted and moaned as she fumbled for his belt, but he helped her.

Jackson placed kisses all around her neck and back onto her lips as he transported gentle strokes into her body. He growled and struggled to breathe as passion choked his lungs while Brooke caressed his neck and back. Moments later, she looked up at the night sky and caught a glimpse of the stars. It'd all turned into a blur at this point. Her hand swung up and rested against the wall, and as she reached her climax, her arms collapsed over his shoulders. Brooke squeezed him tight with his chin resting over her shoulder as she called out his name in release.

As Jackson eased her down and eagerly spun her around with the side of her face pressed against the wall, he reentered her but from behind. With surrendering palms against the brick, she grunted at the aggression that emanated from Jackson's pumps into her backside. With one last harsh attempt, he released a muffled sound of satisfaction into her shoulder.

Jackson fastened up as Brooke slowly peeled herself from against the wall. When she turned to face him, he reached up to move her frizzy hair away from her full lips. Smiling at him, Brooke fought to subtly regain her balance and composure. "Well, what a night, Jax."

That moment signified a shift in feelings for Brooke. Immediately, she felt possessive of him. It made her want to give him the world. Something about her feelings told her that it wasn't just the high of an orgasm from her boyfriend. That moment put a new perspective in her heart. She loved him. What was she going to do with a man whom she loved, especially when she was unsure of his feelings?

Adjusting his shirt, he peered up at her and smiled. "One that I'll remember forever."

"Do you always do this in alleys?"

"No." He grabbed her hand as they leisurely ambled toward the street to find his red Challenger. They didn't say much. Their communication lay in the way he held her hand with a firm grip. His free hand caressed their intertwined hands. Any other man would've left her feeling like a two-dollar hooker desperate to make a quick twenty to buy drugs after that sexual escapade in the alley. But with Jackson, she would do just about anything he'd wanted. Anything. And that scared her, because she wasn't used to giving up so much control, especially to a man.

Brooke wanted to see what he was thinking. "What's next?"

"You control freak," he teased. "Do you always need to know the future?"

"Okay." Brooke had no idea that she came across pushy. "How about I let you take the lead?"

"Good."

She suspected that something about him seemed different. He quietly looked in the other direction. She figured that she wouldn't panic or press, but instead, just enjoy the moment and see where he and his Challenger took her.

S*ummer*

What a change of scenery to be in a house full of strangers. Although I loved my home, I wasn't quite ready to be confined in my own four walls of thought. My brain kept telling me that I needed a man, but I could never say that. And it couldn't be any man, but a new man.

Literally worn down emotionally and physically by Ruben, I almost found myself unrecognizable at this point. However, I should've learned my lesson from the last time about parties and men. I couldn't help but ask myself: *How's that working for you, Summer?*

Unlike the last time, I steered clear of the champagne . . . well, for now. I needed to keep my head clear this time and be on the lookout for single men. Not that searching for wedding bands served me any justice before.

I decided to follow the sounds of the notes coming from a piano in another room. About twenty people filled the room, which felt like heaven compared to the other rooms, so I nestled in with the crowd. They all seemed to have glasses of champagne or wine resting at their lips. I started to feel a little bare, so I decided to call out to the server who had his back turned as he served another woman. He got away from me as he stepped to the next person.

"Excuse me, sir?" He couldn't hear me and I didn't want to draw too much attention to myself. This time I didn't have a mask to hide behind. "Uhh, sir?" No avail. I felt like pouting. One very handsome man with a sun-kissed brown complexion and dark hair in closer proximity to the server took notice and tapped the server on the shoulder, while maintaining eye contact with me.

I heard him say, "Excuse me sir, but that pretty lady over there would like a glass, too." The solid-built man decided to take the glass and save the server a trip by delivering it to me personally, closing the gap between us. His eyes squinted as he smiled. What a handsome man.

"Here you go." He held the glass out for me to accept. I got a better sample of his deep voice and manly scent that tickled my nose. In awe, I slowly moved my hand to meet the glass.

"Thank you."

"Oliver." Every time he smiled, he flashed the whitest teeth known to man. This man was on point. He had cleaned up well in his three-piece suit with a subtle splash of cologne. His broad shoulders stretched above a chest surely defined by muscles. Already, I convinced myself in such a short amount of time that I had to be out of his league. With his other hand, he revealed a glass of champagne that he pressed against his lips before sipping.

"Thank you, Oliver," I managed to say.

"My pleasure." He licked his bottom lip to sweep up any excess champagne. "Are you here with somebody?"

"Alone. Well, I . . . I mean I was, but they left, so essentially, I'm here alone." My reckless nerves owned my ass.

He extended his hand. "Oliver Hunter."

"Summer Stevenson." When I placed my hand into his, he gripped it tightly. I saw that the left hand snaked around his champagne glass didn't have any rings. I learned my lesson that it didn't guarantee anything but a naked finger was a start. If I could get him in the bed tonight, then that would be added distance between Ruben and me.

"That's a pretty name."

I did a mock curtsy and he chuckled. "Thank you, sir." I would have to get over my nerves fast if I wanted to make some headway. "What about you? Who are you here with?" He started to answer, but I held up a hand to stop him. "Wait, don't tell me. Your awesome girlfriend made you come. But now she's off in another room chatting away and left you here to fight on your own?"

"Right." He just grinned. "Actually, I'm here alone. I'm good friends with the owner of this house."

I raised my eyebrows. "Ohhhh, so you left your woman at home?"

He pointed a finger at me as he flashed his pearly whites. "You're good, Summer, you're good. But you're quite bad at being subtle."

"Hmm." I pouted with a tilt of my head.

"I don't have an exclusive relationship. I'm quite busy with work."

"Oh, trust me, I understand," I lied. If there was one thing I was mastering, it was how to have a life beyond work. Maybe that explained why I didn't match Brooke's success. "My boss sure knows how to kill my social life."

He playfully grimaced as if he had a sour secret to share. "I'm not under anyone's thumb but my own."

I tilted my head again, but this time in confusion.

"I own my own business."

"Oh." Here we go again—just another person to make me feel sluggish in the career department.

"Yeah, see, I own a laundromat chain."

I felt taken aback. This man should meet Brooke. Together, they could be a financial force. *Stop that, Summer. You deserve to be happy, too.* "Wow. Which ones? Where?"

"Wash 'n' Fold." He stroked the top of his short, wavy hair.

"Oh, my, that's you?" I really couldn't recall seeing his chain of suds in my head, but I figured he didn't have to know. I took a quick swig of champagne to calm my nerves.

He nodded. "Well, what do you do?" Finishing his glass, he peeked at me from above the rim of his glass.

What was with these Washingtonians always having to know what people did for a living shortly after learning the other person's name? And why did I suddenly not feel good about my occupation? And why did I pick on Washingtonians like I hadn't been here long enough to probably qualify as one, or at least a transplant? I had to learn to get over my own insecurities. "I'm a job recruiter at an agency," I replied matter-of-factly.

"Oh, really?" Oliver sat the glass down on the closest end table. "Amazing. Do you like it?"

"I really enjoy it." That wasn't a lie. And why did I feel so happy about his positive reaction?

"How long have you been in the field?" He seemed genuinely intrigued.

"I just got promoted into this position, but prior to, I was their receptionist."

"What was your major in college?"

"Sociology." Err. This man wanted my resume? "It wasn't my thing though. I wanted something more upbeat. You?" Game on. Might as well find out more about Mr. Hunter since I planned to bed him.

He chuckled. "I studied business administration at Cornell University. Where did you go?"

"Wow." I shook my head. "I can't top that, but I went to American University right here in the city."

"Well I've heard great things about your college. Did you like it?"

"I had a blast. The best experience in my life." I had him pinned so I figured I should just go for it while my nerves were still up. "I'm done here. How about you?"

I noticed that I caught him off-guard. He placed a hand over his chest. "Oh, me? Sure, why not? What did you have in mind?"

My eyes rolled heavenward as I pondered his question. *Think, stupid. It was your idea.* "Okay, well, how about a diner?"

"Sounds like a plan." Oliver showed off his painted smile and offered his arm for me to link mine into. We walked out like we'd known each other before the party. We were too busy fighting through the crowd to create minor chit-chat as we made our way toward the front door.

It felt good to be with someone new, if only for this night. It felt even better not worrying about being in Ruben and Fran's tangled web, too.

Finally outside of the mansion, Oliver Hunter led us to his Corvette. A sports car seemed to fit him.

"Your car is sick," I told him as he eased me in with a hand.

"Thanks, Summer. Hard work, baby, hard work."

When he shut the door behind me, my nostrils immediately took in the smell of leather. "Must be nice," I mumbled.

The driver's door flew open as Oliver lowered himself into the car. "IHOP good for you?"

"Hey, free refills on coffee? I'm down."

Brooke

Jackson pulled up to Brooke's building, parallel parking out front. Silencing his motor, he turned his attention to Brooke. Along the way there, Brooke didn't know how to interpret Jackson's silence.

She turned to face him. "Why are you so quiet? You haven't said much during the whole drive." She couldn't help but worry that letting him have his way in the alley would kill his impression of her.

Jackson reached over and pinched Brooke's chin with his index finger and thumb. "You really made an imprint on my heart." Then her heart fell to her knees since she felt relieved that they weren't in trouble.

"Then why the silence, Jackson?"

"You always need answers, huh?" He briefly looked away as he chuckled quietly. His face turned serious when he faced her.

"It would help."

"I was thinking . . . that's all. You women shouldn't fear silence so much from a man, you know. Sometimes, it's a good thing. It keeps us from saying something stupid."

Brooke still wasn't satisfied. She'd already convinced herself that he was hiding something, and she didn't like feeling like someone's fool. "Look, Jackson, if you can't be straight with me, then we have nothing to discuss right now." Brooke reached for the door handle. "I'll see you."

"I love you."

She froze.

There they were. The three little words that changed everything. He said it with the upmost certainty and clarity. The words rolled out of his mouth with bravery. Brooke turned to face him with the same feelings. Her heart repeatedly clouted her chest like the Russian did Rocky Balboa's head in the boxing ring. Even still, she managed to say the words, even though she wanted to run outside and tell the city.

"And I love you too, Jackson."

"Oh, baby," he whispered. He leaned closer until their foreheads met. "I love you, Brooke. I know you want to ask, but I never said those words to another woman before."

She giggled as tears welled in her lower eyelids. "I don't believe you."

"Of course you wouldn't." With their foreheads still pressed, they snuck in quick kisses which quickly turned into expressions of passion. Brooke placed her palms against either cheek and broke away from his lips long enough to whisper, "Take me again, Jackson, in my room. Now."

Jackson managed to escape from the driver side to greet Brooke at her door. Normally, she would've waited for him to open her door, but not tonight. There was no time to waste.

Amber

Much to Amber's surprise, Daniel was the most well-endowed man she had ever laid eyes on in a long time. She hadn't seen such length since New York.

"You can't handle it?" he asked, peering down.

"Uhh . . . yeah. Yes, I can. It's just that . . ."

"Oh, yeah, you had something to tell me. My balls are flowing out and you have something to tell me?"

Still on her knees, Amber rested her buttocks against her heels. She looked up at him. "I charge. I'm not a prostitute though."

"You what?" Daniel stepped back and pointed down at her. "You charge? But you're not a prostitute?" Daniel's moment of hilarity took over. "Lady. That is the funniest thing ever." Mocking her, he added, "I deliver entrees to customers, but I'm not a server." Hysterical, he bent over into a bellow of laughter until his face turned red.

Amber felt low and silly. She immediately stood up and pointed a finger at him. "Shut up now or I'll strangle you with your own penis."

Daniel heard her and coughed his way back to sanity. He held up a palm. "Amber, if you need money, or a loan, just ask. But to present yourself like you want me for me and drop this bomb about money for sex without being a prostitute is just ludicrous. I've paid for it before. It's no big deal. Whew." He swiped his forehead with his hand. "That was rich though."

Amber squinted at him. "Are you through now?"

Daniel held up an index finger and looked at her from the corner of his eyes. "But can I get one more round in?"

Amber watched him with a hand on her hip. She wanted to stab her stiletto into his navel and make his belly pop. "Done?"

Daniel straightened one last time. "Whew, yes. Now, how much and what do you have to offer?" Amber thought he looked quite silly standing with his pants at his ankles and underwear at his knees.

"I do packages," Amber replied.

Slightly irritated, he asked, "What's that supposed to mean?"

Amber could see that his generous endowment made him a tougher sell, despite his extra girth, so she had to be careful. It wasn't like he was married and miserable, maybe just single and pathetic. Amber knew what she had to do. She had to convince him with a pleasure preview.

Ditching her crossed arms and making her way in front of him, she dropped to her knees and accepted him in her hands. She knew exactly where to move her hands and how to work him.

With his head cocked back, Daniel made noises. It appeared he'd drifted into another world. Amber stopped. Daniel looked down with surprise. "Hey, why'd you stop?"

Amber relaxed her posture and looked him right in the eye. "Pay me four thousand dollars for three days."

"Oh, I see: the package. Well what makes you so damn good, Amber? I can enjoy myself at a resort for that kind of money."

"Is that going to break you, sir?"

"Are you offering me a discount then?"

"Never had to. Besides, my other clients had no problem paying up and wouldn't dream of paying less. What they got was on point. But hey," Amber started to rise. "If I'm too much for you to handle then—"

"Get back down. I'll stroke you a check. Let me see what you got." Daniel was irritated but horny.

"Well you know I only take cash but I need your business card before we continue."

"Come again?"

Amber held out her hand. "Your business card. Cuz if you stop payment I need to know where to find you."

Daniel rolled his eyes and sighed. "I don't believe you," he mumbled as he reached inside his jacket to retrieve a card. "Take it and let's get moving. My balls are freezing and I'm losing tread with no action, you know."

Amber snatched it and smiled as she tucked it in her bra. "Thank you."

"Yeah, now show me what the fuss is all about."

Summer

Oliver and I arrived at IHOP and settled into a booth in the middle of the restaurant. Few diners surrounded us. We both fanned our hands to usher the smell of coffee and pancake batter into our nostrils as we placed an order for coffee.

Excited, I told him, "Well, this is random."

"Yes, it is." Oliver sat with his fingers laced into one another on top of the table as he leaned forward.

"What made you want to hang out with me instead of staying at that party?"

I didn't want to hold anything back. I needed to move quickly with money bags to forget about the cheating snake. I guess that would make me the whore. The thought made me feel out of touch with myself. Normally, when I slept with guys I let it happen organically. Instead, I felt like the woman who'd gone from the married man to the most available man. However, I didn't want tonight to go south because of my feelings. Things had to be moved along quickly, because Ruben would be in my head if I went home alone tonight.

"Well, one beautiful woman's attention versus a couple of verbal exchanges between me and some rich people ain't a real dilemma to choose from if you ask me." I smiled. "Besides, what do I really need from them? I don't need to network in hopes of being hired, and my customers are always going to be there as long as they have dirty clothes and no machines. I go to these events for sport. I'm just a bored, single workaholic." Oliver shrugged and smirked.

"I like the way you think, Oliver. You seem very simple and relaxed. You're like a breath of fresh air."

He nodded. "I'll take that. I like you, too. You're naturally charming."

We both didn't see the waitress pop up beside us with our coffee. "Can I get you two started with something to eat?"

"Summer?"

"Gee. Not sure. Let's see, how about one pancake and a side of eggs. Now you have to order something or I'm taking that back." My meal at Fran's house still satisfied my stomach, but I didn't want to recap my night to Oliver by bringing the event up. So, I ordered just to go along with the moment.

"Oh, well if that's the way it's going to be then I have no choice." He drummed his fingers as he thought. "Let me get a Belgium waffle and a side of hash browns then." Our server, whose name tag said "Natalie," removed our menus and we both thanked her with a smile.

"You have a very exotic look," I commented as he tasted his coffee.

"Mmm, just right." Oliver looked up. "I do?" He pretended to be unaware. "Nah, well, my mom is Black and my dad is Hawaiian."

"Wow, never met a Black Hawaiian before."

"Yup. My mom and dad divorced when I was four, so my mom raised me alone in California. Unfortunately, I don't know anything about my dad's culture. Dad flew the coop to Florida when I was two. He chose his career and my mom refused to move with him. Still though . . . he and I are pretty close."

"That's good. Sucks to have an absent parent, huh?" I twisted my mouth to one side.

"Yeah," he shrugged, "but you adjust. Life goes on. What about you?"

I held up a finger. "Hang tight. Let me get a sip of coffee first."

Oliver stared at me with eyes full of slight admiration as he waited for me to divulge any information. I could get used to this guy. I found Oliver to be very different than Ruben. This night just felt so right and it made me appreciate not accepting a ride home from Ruben. Lord knows how that ending would've turned out. This ending offered one less slash on the tally board against Fran, and that couldn't make me happier.

I swallowed and replied. "I was raised in Delaware and that's where I left my mom. My dad died when I was four, in a construction accident."

"I'm sorry to hear that, Summer."

"Thanks."

"Do you visit your mother frequently?"

"I should actually do it more. I need to go. I mean, there's really no excuse why I don't visit her at least bimonthly." The last time I spoke to her was when I last saw Max. I could do better. I'd been so petrified that my affair with a married man would come out and my mom would be disappointed. *No excuses, Summer, no excuses.*

Oliver's phone rang. He retrieved it from inside his jacket and put a finger up. "So sorry, Summer. This is my mom. Lemme grab this."

"Oh, sure." I waved a hand at him as I watched him slide between the tables and into the waiting area. I decided to give my mom a call, too.

"Hello?" Her hoarse voice told me she'd been sleeping.

"Mom, hey. I really wanted to talk to you. Did I wake you?"

"You know you did."

"I'm sorry, but I miss you. How have you been?"

"I'm okay, sweetie. I've left messages for you on your cell, but you don't call me back."

"Oh, I know there's no excuse, I'm sorry. I've been trying to adjust, that's all."

"Yeah, there is no excuse. I get a little lonely up here, and I try to talk to you to see how you're doing, but it's like you don't have time with your new position."

My heart broke. I never meant for her to feel this way. "No, Mom. Don't say that. Now you know I always have time for you, which is why I wanted to come up or invite you down."

"Well, it's about time. A girl was starting to feel unloved. Can you come up?"

"Yes, Mom, before the month is over, I'll pick a weekend and surprise you."

"That would be nice."

"How's work?"

"Ummm, crazy hours and sick people at the hospital. What else can I say?"

"But you love being a nurse."

"I do. Is everything okay with you? Did you find a man?"

I wanted to mock myself with amusement and tell her that that was the minimum bar that I'd hit. "Umm, I've been on dates for sure. Why don't I let you get some sleep and I'll tell you more when we see each other?"

"That'll work. I have to go in tomorrow anyway."

"Wait, Mom." I didn't want to let her go. I needed her. "Aren't you tired of being there alone in Delaware yet?"

"Well, funny that you ask. I don't want you to worry. But yeah, I guess I could go for a change, finally. You're the job recruiter. Find me a job and maybe I'll move."

"Oh, if I could get you down to DC or Virginia, I would be over-the-top happy, Mom. Would you really consider it?"

"Well, what if I told you I wasn't as poor as you think? I'm sitting on equity in this house you know. I'm in a booming field, so I suppose I could become a nurse anywhere, huh?"

"We have been separated for too long, Mom, and you're all I have. Maybe then you should visit me instead, and we can look at property together, including apartments."

"Well, you let me know when I can come, okay? I'm going back to bed."

Oliver slid back into the booth. "Okay, Mom, I love you tons."

"Tons back to you, I love you."

"Good night, Mom."

"Have a good night, baby."

"Bye." I hung up feeling a million times better. Obviously, Oliver could see me beaming because he said, "You miss her, huh?"

"Yes." Natalie slid our plates in front of us. Yes, food.

"What did she say?"

"Well what did your mom say?" I challenged.

"Someone broke into her car and stole her laptop. Now that fires me up, because I warned her about that. I told her to take it out but all she says is, 'I know, I know.'"

"I'm sorry to hear that, Oliver. Other than that, is she okay?"

"Ohh, it was a neighborhood punk. The twelve-year-old, Damon—son of one of her girlfriend's—snitched on another boy. The boy was bragging about it and Damon told his mom, and she told the thief's mom and she made her son give it back to my mom. They're going to pay for the glass and everything. It's really my fault. I should've bought her a newer car by now with more bells and whistles." Annoyed, he shook his head. "Now, how's your mom?" he asked as he placed the cloth napkin in his lap.

His consideration turned me on. "She's great, thank you," I replied as I ripped into my pancake with my knife and fork. "Talking to her really made my night. I needed that. She's going to come down for a visit, but I'm hoping to get her to move."

"Really. That'd be sweet. But what's really sweet is meeting a woman who wants to eat pancakes on the first night." He chewed on his waffle.

"I did ask you, huh?" I felt proud of myself. Did I hit the jackpot by accident?

"Do you date much or are you usually in a relationship?"

I wanted to choke on my food when he said 'relationship.' "To tell you the truth, I have never really been in one."

"A relationship?" He looked puzzled.

Reluctantly, I nodded. Oliver was the first person to really make me feel ashamed of my choice. I classified Max as a trial and for me, it just really didn't count. I tilted my head from left to right as I pondered how to gently tell him.

"Oliver, I like my freedom. I'm more like the see-what-happens kind of gal."

He shrugged, but he slightly failed at his attempt to hide his disappointment. "What about you?"

"I feel if something works, don't fight it. But if it doesn't, ball it up and put it in the trash where it belongs."

"I take it you've been in a relationship?"

"Oh, of course. I mean, I'm thirty-two. I think that's enough time to have something under my belt."

"How did they go?"

He chuckled. "Not good. I mean, I'm here on a date with you."

"Well, what's a guy like you single for?" I waited for an answer as I chewed up my egg.

"Where do I start? My last girlfriend was an aspiring model and didn't want to eat. You can't make fire in the bedroom with bones, now can you? The one before that was boring. She didn't have fight in her. She didn't like to leave the house. She just wanted to stay at home and read books all day and watch movies. It was like watching a woman live her dreams through characters in the fiction world."

"Wow. That's no good, Oliver."

"Summer, she didn't have any dreams. She was in a walking coma. Then she started picking up a little weight because she became so inactive. The weight was literally a physical sign that she was complacent, doing nothing in life."

"How long did you stay with each one?"

"I stayed with the starving model for a year and the nerd for four months. One got too fat and the other too skinny. Talk about options, huh?" I almost split my sides at his past dilemma. Finally, I composed myself. "Well, that's what they call good times."

Grinning, he agreed. "I suppose so."

I tapped my fingernails on the table. "Why is it so easy to talk to you? I feel like I've known you for years."

Oliver peered at me with a thoughtful smile as he thought about it. "Because we came honest and unashamed."

I felt like ducking. I lost my honestly points somewhere between DC and Alexandria. He had no clue that I used to be honest. But we all know what happened there.

All I could say was, "Well, I suppose so, Oliver. We're just us." I shrugged and Natalie came out of nowhere, once again.

"Can I get you two something else?"

"I can speak for myself when I say, that is all." I smiled at her before turning my attention to my date. "You?"

He smiled at Natalie. "We're good here, miss. Thank you."

"Okay, then it was my pleasure and here is your check. Thank you for coming, please come again." Natalie slid the check in the middle of the table and I swiftly picked it up.

"Hey, what are you doing there? Give me that," Oliver demanded playfully.

"Less than twenty but more than fifteen. Hey, I had to make sure I didn't break the piggy bank. Otherwise, you might not ask me out again."

"If you don't pass that to me and behave then, yes, you will miss your next time in my chariot."

I giggled as I slid it in his direction. "Well, I did invite you, you know."

He leaned forward and whispered with his wallet in his hand. "Let's make a deal."

"What?" I whispered back, turning on my coquettish charm.

"Tell no one that I paid for our first date at IHOP, because then I'll always be known as 'that cheap bastard.' So, maybe you can lie and tell people you treated me and then next time I can really treat you to the best seafood restaurants at the National Harbor.

My eyes widened. "That'll work." I extended my hand for him to shake to seal the deal. Oliver took it and placed a gentle kiss on top of my hand instead.

"Deal." He winked and guided my hand back toward me. I sat silently and blown away. Ruben wasn't the only one who could be suave.

I bit my lower lip. This man was clean and sexy. His sense of humor made him infectious, and so he reminded me of a used car with the rusted paint job and smashed hood.

What you see is what you get. I felt like I had the real deal, as they call it.

"Where do you live?" I asked.

"I live in Arlington, in the Ballston area. I just moved there from McLean."

"When I first moved here, I used to call it Mc Lean. Then my boss at my internship caught me saying it and told me that the 'c' and 'l' were joint and that 'lean' was pronounced 'lane' and that made it 'clane.' I was so embarrassed." I covered my face with both palms.

We laughed and he replied, "Don't feel bad. I think we all made that mistake until someone corrected us."

"Yeah? You're just saying that."

Oliver removed thirty dollars for the bill which included Natalie's tip. "No, I mean it. Ready to bounce?"

"Wow, you're a generous tipper." I eased out of the booth.

We linked arms again. "My mother always told me that if you can't tip, stay at home. I know she didn't have to do much, but she's here so late at night working for a buck."

I turned to face him as we walked. "Yeah. Hey," my linked arm quickly tugged his, "thanks for dinner."

"My pleasure." He winked and I smiled.

He helped me into my side of his car. It was nice to know that there were still men out there with traditional tendencies, but whether a man applied them didn't bother me one way or another. I suppose I should enjoy it, because Brooke would have my head if she suspected for a second that I was complaining.

Oliver jumped in on his side and asked as he pushed the start button to ignite the engine, "Do you like music of any particular kind?"

"I do, I do." I placed a finger on my lip and requested, "Anything upbeat."

"You got it." He snaked his neck and winked as he located a live Saturday club Go-Go mix. He warned me to inform him if the volume became too much. "Summer, where do you rest your head at night?"

"Well, that's a new one." I grinned. "The Waterfront."

"All right. When we get close, tell me where to go from there."

"Sure thing, boss." We enjoyed the sound of loud music, but I really wanted to know if he'd be in my bed by the end of the night or would I be giving him a curbside wave. If this man didn't touch me, I would be afraid that Ruben's touch would linger in my thoughts. The possibility made me frown. I needed to call someone, but I didn't have any privacy, so that left me on my own with this one. Maybe I should just go for it. *Fight your nerves Summer, fight your nerves.* I bit my lower lip and went in for the kill.

"You coming up?"

Oliver turned the music down so he could hear me. "What was that?"

Great. Now I had to repeat myself. "Are you coming up? You know, when we reach my place." I held my breath, wondering how he would take me. I wanted to hide, just because I was brave or stupid enough to ask.

"Su-re."

Oh, great. He sounded hesitant. He thought I was a slut. *Okay, Summer, who cares*? Maybe I could land a one-night stand and throw him to the wolves. But I kind of genuinely liked this charismatic and chilled guy. At the least, I could probably sleep with him once and keep him for friendship. Least of all he would turn out like Max and latch onto me like a baby to a mother's nipple. *Calm down, calm down*, I coached myself before we arrived at my place.

Oliver turned the music back up. "Remember this song?" He pointed to the radio as if a visual would manifest and it would all become so clear. I did remember this song but never the artist. The throwback jam of Go-Go beats rang with little words to the song.

I smiled. "I do, I do."

"Yeah, well, this was the jam." He seemed content to be in his own musical world, wired up. It amazed me how comfortable this guy felt after being with me for a few hours.

We arrived at my apartment building, and once I pointed out a visitor's space, he instructed me to stay put so he could come let me out. Once he helped me to my feet, we went on our way to my floor then to my door.

"Right here, homie." I fumbled around in my purse, looking for my keys, wondering why I didn't have it ready beforehand. Finally, my fingers gripped a key ring and I snatched it out to let us in.

"So, you're all alone here, huh?"

"Exactly." There you go, man, no excuse why you cannot ravish me tonight.

"I live alone, too," he informed me as we entered my apartment.

Knowing that he was a successful business owner, and assuming that he had a nice house, I felt like I had to justify my humble home. "This is the life of a recruiter in her late twenties."

"I like it. It's small and cozy." He stood with his hands in his pockets as he let his eyes do the scanning and not his head.

"Get comfortable." I motioned toward my couch. "I know we just ate, but can I get you anything?"

"You know, I'm good." He appeared reluctant to let his guard down, and I didn't know how to take things from here.

"Sooo," I bounced on my toes and heels, wondering why he didn't sit. "You just want to stand?"

"I just . . . want to know why you invited me up on the first night. I'm sure we're not trying to watch television this late."

I stood there, embarrassed and quiet. I peered down, hoping the right answer would be magically woven into my carpet. "I'm not sure," I lied.

He didn't believe me. That was a given by his very short, perfunctory chuckle with his hands still in is pants. "I don't buy that, Summer. No one invites a stranger into their home without a reason."

I decided to give him what he wanted, so I looked him square into his eyes. I bit my lower lip and raced a hand through my hair and gathered it to one side. I placed a hand on the back of my neck and let it slowly fall over my chest. Words were hard to express, so I decided to show what I wanted.

Placing one foot in front of the other, I eased toward him. It was as if something was taking over me. Nothing changed on his end. Damn. Why was he trying to make me work so hard for what I wanted?

When I came face to face with him, I placed each palm on his lapels and stared into his eyes. "No, no TV."

I stared at his ample lips and decided to taste them. I had to do what I had to do to rid my head of Ruben. If I didn't seal the deal tonight, I'd have Ruben and his touch in my bed the next week. I stood on my toes to extend my height and went in gently for his lips, resting mine on his. Slowly parting my mouth, my tongue slowly swiped his lower lip.

He released a very low groan before placing his hands on my tiny hips. *Yes. You can do it, Oliver.* As if he heard my mental permission, he gripped my long hair with one hand and used the other to caress my butt. It felt so good already. Maybe it didn't feel Ruben-good, but it felt good and it was a start. Our kiss had elevated to another level. My hands slid from his lapels to the sides of his neck. His arms embraced me harder as he moved them from my butt and hair to around my waist. Little moans escaped my throat, and it turned him on.

I couldn't believe that I was having sex two times in one night. Well, Ruben initiated it the first time around, but this time I did. So, technically, if Ruben had kept his hands to himself, then, either I would've left Oliver at the party, or our sexual encounter would've been the only one. That was my story, and I was sticking to it.

I had to remove my thin sweater and dress to let Oliver know that I meant business, so I pulled them over my head and to the side. He took a moment to appreciate me in my matching lace bra.

"Nice abs," he managed to say.

"Hard work, baby, hard work." I knew he'd like that.

Oliver mumbled a chipped laugh as he began to shed his suit jacket. "You're cute."

I helped him unbutton his shirt as he tore away his jacket. He took over his buttons at a speed greater than mine, and soon, he revealed his tight stomach below broad shoulders.

"Ahaaaa." I bit my lower lip in satisfaction and winked before partially bending at the knees to kiss his abs. Oliver suddenly gripped my arms to lift me and I locked in on him by wrapping my legs around his waist. We kissed torridly before I commanded, "To my room."

An extension of my index finger directed him to the door that awaited about four feet away. With my open bedroom door in my tiny apartment, I felt certain that the bed in plain view gave it away without the navigation of my finger.

Oliver lowered me to my bed and I watched as he removed his pants with haste. He bared black boxer briefs, which appeared to be hiding a generous endowment. My elbows propped me up, and I relaxed my feet on the bed with bent knees pointed at the ceiling. Oliver stared down at me over his heaving chest, tracing my eye contact to his manhood, so he reached for the band of his underwear to show me what he had to work with.

Immediately, my thoughts ran to Ruben. I had to compare; it was only right as well as natural. Not bad. Not as big as Ruben's but certainly not lagging either. With my turn to unleash my breasts, it felt like a game of give-and-take on the first night of going all the way. I unsnapped my bra, and Oliver reached out to place one of my breasts in his mouth as he eased between my legs. His teeth pulled at my nipple and it drove me wild. My hand cradled his neck as I continued to prop myself up with one hand.

He stayed intimate with my breast as I closed my eyes and released sounds of pleasure. His big hands pulled my underwear away from my hips and onto the carpet. We were now naked and intertwined.

He moaned words of pleasure.

Oliver felt so good. And thanks to this moment, I could return to work on Monday with a new edge, and one that didn't include Ruben and Miss Fran. Maybe I could put that wicked encounter between us behind me after all. It was safe to assume that Ruben was officially cancelled.

7: waterworks

Summer

Ⓢn Sunday afternoon, the girls and I met up at La Madeleine in Georgetown to grab lunch. As usual, diners crowded every square inch and noises of clacking dishes and voices filled the café, but the aroma of fresh food and pastries in the air made it all worth it every single time.

Weeks had passed, including Halloween, and everyone seemed to be in a good place. Brooke and Jackson had become stronger and more serious, Amber had more appointments with Daniel minimizing her need to book new clients for sex and piano lessons, and Emily and Eric took little steps toward rebuilding a new friendship. I, on the other hand, got to know Oliver as we'd decided to build on a friendship with benefits. Fran even traded her after-hour invites in favor of lunch dates. Ruben tried to call me from time to time, but I ignored his calls and it appeared he'd finally given up. Life was good. With the whole sexual mess behind me, Oliver and I had fun in our newfound friendship.

I felt the vibration of my phone coming through my purse and onto my thigh. The ladies looked at me as I fished for my phone. "Hang on, ladies."

They fell silent as I disclosed the name of the person calling. "Max?"

"A little too late, huh?" Brooke said.

"Tell me about it," I replied.

"Well you have to answer it," Emily suggested.

"No, she doesn't." Amber took a bite of bread. "He's a late loser. Ignore the toad."

I shot Amber my best motherly expression that read, 'Don't be mean.'

"What?" she asked.

My finger slid across the screen to answer my iPhone. "Max? H-hey, how are you?"

"Summer."

"What's going on, how have you been?" It was quite pleasant to hear from him given the legitimate break we had from one another. I felt relieved that he hadn't totally sworn me off and that I hadn't lost him as a friend.

"I'm okay. It's just been a while since I've heard from you, and I didn't want you to think we couldn't at least be friends, right?"

"That's right, Max. I'm in the middle of lunch with friends, so do you mind if I call you back later when I'm alone?"

"Yeah, it's no problem." He sounded a little disappointed but completely understanding.

"Wait, Max." I felt a little bad for his inopportune timing so I wanted to end this conversation on a good note.

"Yes?"

"It's good hearing from you, and I look forward to catching up with you later."

"Same here, Summer. Thanks, and uh, have a nice lunch with your crew."

"Okay, later." I hung up and felt happy that loose fences started to mended. He must've finally come to terms with our friendship being as far as we could go.

"Awkward?" Emily asked.

I shook my head before sipping my iced tea. "No, not at all. I'm actually happy he called, given the last bad run-in."

Brooke smiled and chuckled. "I remember that."

"Yes, you were the first face that I saw after he stormed off." Brooke nodded.

"His ole thirsty ass," Amber said with a grin.

I chuckled, shaking my head. "Be nice, Amber. So, what's been up lately?"

Brooke raised her hand mid-air. "I'll take the floor first, of course."

Amber playfully rolled her eyes. "Of course."

"And why shouldn't I, since I'm the only one in a legit relationship?"

Emily sighed. "Feel free to rub it in harder. Some of us are hopeless romantics here."

Brooke ignored her and jumped right into her news. "Jackson and I are strong and I'm so happy with him. He's a gentleman." Her eyes jumped when she remembered something. "Ooh. And I've never told you guys that weeks ago, after we went clubbing, he led me outside and we had sex in the alley against the building of the club.

My eyes enlarged. "So now you know what Ruben and I experienced, huh? Isn't it great outside?"

"The best," Brooke squealed. I saw Amber's eye's freeze in disbelief as she peered at Brooke, who sat beside her. "I blocked everything out and just enjoyed the moment. Don't tell anybody this." She placed a finger in front of her lips. Emily and I nodded frantically as we hungered for more.

"You little freak," Amber interjected.

Brooke turned to her. "Well if it's with the one you love, ahem, Amber, why not?"

Amber shook a finger at Brooke. "Oh, no. Don't even start with me and my clients. They expect me to get dirty. But I thought something like that would be beneath you."

"Oh, please," Brooke replied. "He's my man. Since he spanks me, I wanna try choking."

I almost choked on my drink. "You what?" I blinked uncontrollably.

Amber completely turned to face her. "Oh, snap." Her eyes were completely opened. "This man done turned you out."

Brooke cheesed with a look of accomplishment. "No. I will propose it to him just as I did the spanking on our first night."

Emily sat forward with a huge grin. "Way to go, Brooke. Eric used to spank me all the time on our honeymoon." She bit her lower lip as she coasted away with her private thoughts.

"Exactly. That's the minimum a couple should be doing," Brooke told us.

"I . . . I have never. Neither. No choking, no spanking."

"Then you should," Brooke advised casually.

"That sounds so dangerous," I said, still in a shocked trance.

"A little bit of choking ain't never hurt nobody," Brooke said.

Amber grinned. "She got that right. All right. Looks like Brooke and I may have more in common than I thought."

Brooke made it clear, "But only in this area."

Emily shifted in her chair. "Well, good for you." Then she pointed at Amber. "You." And finally, she pointed at me. "And you. At least all of you guys are getting laid. The hymen in my vagina probably regenerated by now. I'm such a virgin at this point. What is sex?"

We tried our best to hold in our laughter, so I rubbed her back. "Maybe you want to run clients with Amber."

We finally broke down. Emily joined in.

"Ha, ha," Amber said. "It's not like I'm a prostitute or something."

Brooke threw her hands up. "Oh, my, gosh. When are you going to own it Amber? You are a prostitute."

Amber threw her napkin onto her plate. "Shhhhh, you dirty wall whore. Keep your voice down. Look, if I were a prostitute, then I would just own it. I would be proud, but since I am not . . . there's nothing to claim."

Brooke shrugged nonchalantly. "Whatever, honey." Her high ponytail shook with her head as she placed a piece of chicken in her mouth. "Why not just make things official with Daniel and move in with him? You can hang up this side of your work, and you can be with a man with money. It's a win-win."

Emily added gently, "Yeah, you two are going strong as client . . . ummm . . . client-server, I mean Brooke has a point. Why not take it to the next level, Amber?" Emily tilted her head as she waited to hear from her. She was so genuine in her approach, as opposed to Brooke, who evoked irritation from Amber.

Amber grimaced. "Ew. Have you seen his teeth and belly? He doesn't have enough hair for me and his breath stinks. I can only lie down with him because of the money." Amber shook her head, clearly disgusted.

I laughed. "Attraction is key. I mean, that is one of the reasons why I couldn't leave Ruben alone. His whole thing was like a magnet. There was the accent, the height, his smell, his big hands, his clothes, and then there is Oliver."

Brooke's face lit up. "Ooh, tell us about him. How's that going?" She sipped anxiously on her water as she waited to hear new details.

"Umm, nothing." I felt shy about him as a grin took over my face. "We have fun together. We have lots of hot sex and we do things together. He's so cool and relaxed. It's like nothing bothers him, and he doesn't put any pressure on me, not like the kind Ruben and Max tried with me. It's like he doesn't want anything from me but my company, and if we have sex, we do, and if we don't, he doesn't trip."

"That must be nice," Amber said. "Lord knows I can't stand a man trying to pressure me."

"How does he compare to Ruben?" Brooke asked.

"Well, he may not be as tall, but he has these nice shoulders that are broad." I had a sudden flash of me gripping his shoulders every time he lowered his body onto mine.

"Ohhh, yeah," Brooke agreed. "Nice shoulders really define a man. You know, I love Jackson's height and his stomach. He's so cut, and mmm, so tasty."

"Dirty whore," Amber jested as she gave Brooke the stink eye.

"Don't hate, honey, don't hate." Brooke winked at Amber as she pushed her empty plate away from her and into the middle of the table.

Emily appeared void of humor as she remained slumped with crossed arms in her brown leather bomber jacket.

Amber asked her with an expression of concern, "What's wrong, babe?"

In a distant voice, she replied, "Oh, nothing." Her vacant eyes stared at the table. "I'm just listening to you guys specify your favorite part on your men's bodies, and it made me think of Eric, especially since I don't have a man to replace the memory of him."

I stroked her long ponytail. "Honey, why don't you do what I did? I got over Ruben with a new man."

Brooke said, "Because she was married to Eric, so that's different. That's harder."

Nodding understandably, it reinforced the fact that I hadn't a real clue about marriage and feelings. I couldn't even realize that her love for Eric could be so deep that replacing memories wasn't really an option.

"I mean, we're in a better place," she continued. "We have lunch together, we talk on the phone to ask about each other's day, but we don't speak of the past or anything romantic. It's like we have backtracked to friendship, but it's not what I want. It was never what I wanted. I wanted friendship and the commitment from Eric."

Curious and slightly confused I asked, "Wait. What happened to that chick named Kyele?" Turning to her abruptly I asked, "Did I say that right?"

Emily snickered. "Yeah. Oh, yeah I mentioned her and he told me that she was an office fling and that she'd been transferred to their New Jersey branch so that's that." Then, Emily became more animated with emotion. "I'm in love with him and I want him back." She finally looked at us.

"Have you thought of just telling him?" Amber asked with compassion and concern. It was nice to see this side of Amber, and hopefully we'd see more of it. It made her more attractive. I'd grown accustomed to her protecting herself with a shield. Given everything that she'd been through, I understood.

"I've been so hurt that I can't afford to do it to myself again. I'm still trying to heal."

Brooke suggested, "He should make the first move if you two try again."

"I agree," Emily said. A quick, somber laugh escaped her throat. "I remember parts of his body that drove me wild."

"Oooh, oh yeah?" Amber asked as she squirmed in her chair. "Like what?"

Emily bit her lip as her eyes looked from left to right as if she was about to share the biggest secret known to man. She sat up and leaned forward, dropping her voice to a whisper. "I love his salt and pepper hair."

"Oh, that's it? What else?" I asked with intrigue. It wasn't often that we heard details of Eric in this light.

"Hmmm, I would have to say his back. His back was sexy. It was well-defined."

"I can understand that one." Brooke's eyes widened as she leaned in. She rested her chin in her hand as a dreamy expression washed over her face.

"Oh, no," I warned. "A Jackson moment."

"Well . . ." Brooke replied as she laughed lightly. "I'm happy. What can I say?" she asked as she shrugged.

Amber beat the table with her palm. "Come on, Emily. Don't drop the ball. What else did you like about Eric?"

Emily thought about it for a second as she licked her upper lip. "Well, his back. The tattoo on his shoulder blade goes so well with the sinew on his back."

Amber tried to laugh, but it sounded more like she was choking. "What—what kind of tattoo?"

"Oh, it's an eagle."

My eyebrows raised. "Wow, awesome. That is hot."

Brooke held up her palms. "Crazy. I like it."

Amber, the anxious one, wanted to hear so badly what drove Emily wild about Eric, that it surprised me to see her eyebrows furrow. Suddenly, she rubbed her stomach.

"Are you okay?" I asked with worry.

Amber could barely speak or look at anyone. Instantly, her eyes had a glint of terror in them as she turned her knees from underneath the table.

Brooke placed a hand on Amber's arm. "Amber, even you are scaring me and I don't like you that much." With eyes contradicting her words, I could tell that beyond the joke, she cared.

Amber managed to stand with a hand over her stomach and with the appearance of wobbly legs. "I feel . . . sick. Suddenly, I feel sick."

"What did you eat again?" Emily asked.

"I had the potato galette and the chicken salad."

"Ooh," I said as I looked at Emily and Brooke. "Maybe the chicken was bad."

Brooke stood up so Emily and I followed suit. "Then we have to get you home. Let's hail you a cab. Do you want company?" Brooke asked.

"We should complain." Emily placed her hand on her hip and stared at the empty trays.

Amber insisted that we let it go and to let her go as well. I studied Amber as the girls made a fuss over the situation. Emily rubbed Amber's back while Brooke felt for a temperature on her forehead. The color on her face looked healthy. Something about this whole situation seemed off, and maybe because the other girls didn't know her quite like I knew her. I kept my query to myself as I pushed in my chair and snatched up my purse. We had all donned our jackets and coats with our purses in hand as we made our way through the crowded line and out the door. The crisp air hit us like a bus.

"Whewwwww," Amber cried. "This fresh air has really helped." She bent over to fan herself. If I could pop a cigarette and lean against a wall to study her through squinted eyes, I would've.

"Are you going home?" I asked her with cynicism.

Amber straightened and peered into my eyes. "Yes, I am," she answered matter-of-factly. The other girls were aloof to the vibe that had transpired between Amber and me.

She turned around to tell a fussy Brooke and Emily, who were deciding how to help her. I suggested that she and I could hitch a cab together since we lived closest to one another. I needed to get to the bottom of things.

"That does make sense," Brooke relented. "Summer, take great care of her. I think something in that food is going to have this poor girl throwing up any moment."

Amber gripped her stomach. I knew she wanted to throw up, just not for the reason Emily and Brooke suspected. Brooke, of course, managed to successfully hail a cab in the crowded streets of Georgetown.

Emily grabbed my arm. "From Georgetown to Southwest, this cab fare will cost a mint. Why don't you guys take the nearest Metro?"

Brooke reached into her wallet. "No worries Emily, it's on me. Summer will be lucky if Amber doesn't throw up on her BCBG boots." Brooke smirked at me and I poked my tongue out at her.

Emily helped ease Amber into the cab before reporting our destination to the cab driver. I turned to Brooke to say, "Oh, I'm sure your bucks won't be necessary. Amber should have a hefty roll in her bank account from Daniel. Please, keep your money Brooke, but thanks."

"Well are you sure?" Brooke asked with concern. "This ride won't be too cheap."

"We're working women and besides, I'm sure the two of us can cover a cab ride." I rubbed her arm with assurance and kissed her cheek, then Emily's. Once I lowered myself into the cab, Brooke shut our door then lowered her face to our window. I rolled it down as Emily peered through as well.

"Call us to let us know how she manages, okay, guys?" Brooke requested. "I gotta go meet Jackson."

"Will do. Talk to you ladies soon, okay?"

They waved and straightened as they linked arms to head down the sidewalk. I felt bad for them. There they were all worried over something that probably amounted to nothing.

I turned my attention to the leading lady of the morning. "Alright, girlfriend, what gives? Because I don't believe for a moment that you are sick."

Amber looked like she saw a ghost, and that made me question my skepticism. I placed my hand on her arm.

"Summer. You have no idea what I need to tell you, but you have to look me dead in my eyes and promise to keep this between us."

"I'm so afraid to ask, but go ahead, Amber. I swear you have my word."

Amber gripped my arm so tight that I thought she was going to read my blood pressure. She spoke slowly, with every trace of humor vacant in her expression. I wasn't used to seeing this Amber. It was very odd and kind of scary.

"You have to promise not to judge me, Summer. You cannot let this ruin what we have, because I really like you the most. Okay? Deal?"

"Deal, honey, deal. No judgment here. I swear on Ruben's package."

"That Eric, you know the one I met at the Charlestown casino—"

"Is Emily's?" I knew it before she confirmed it. Was it too late to die?

Amber nodded like it hurt. I felt awful for her.

"Oh, boy." I turned to look out of the window. That explained her sudden exit. I knew something was up, but I didn't know the connection.

"Do you hate me?" Amber's voice sounded desperate, but I didn't turn to look at her.

"No." My eyes never left the sights outside the window. I studied all the nice row houses, I saw the sign for George Washington University, saw—

"Then why won't you look at me?"

I turned to face her, not knowing what to say.

"Summer, think about how many Erics there are. I didn't mean to step on anyone's territory." Her eyes glistened with tears that fell slowly down her cheek.

I struggled with reeling in my emotions, because it affected Emily. Poor, fragile, Emily. I didn't want to appear judgmental, though hard not to, because I felt like she brought this on herself.

"Amber." I mustered the most gentle and sympathetic tone possible. "Honey, you step on territory all day long. You sleep with men who are married, and they are someone's territory, sweetie. You just don't know the victim. But it's all the same." Hearing me say the words made me think of my own situation. I was just as guilty as Amber. I may have stopped, but we mirrored one another. I placed my hands on hers. "Listen, I'm no saint. Look what I did with you-know-who." I didn't want to mention any names again, fearing that the cab driver had a secret connection to Ruben or Fran.

"Summer, I take money to do what I do, and I do it all the time. You just had a one-time incident."

"Honey, it doesn't matter. I don't get a pedestal in all of this either." I moved a piece of her hair from her face. My hand involuntarily rubbed her shoulder for encouragement. "But you should really consider telling Emily sooner than later."

"I . . . I can't." Despair choked her speech as she shed more tears. "I'm a slut. Everyone said it all along. I was so caught up in the money, needing more than my monthly expenses, trying to buy top-of-the-line clothes and just making up for the fact that I wasn't in Northwest or something. I was doing everything I could to erase the roughness that I became used to in New York. I wanted to be with the upper crust. I wanted to make up for the fact that my father didn't leave a penny when he died because he failed to get life insurance. I wanted to give my little sister whatever she needed so she could have just one hero in the family, but even she wouldn't want me to get my money like this. I just wanted to feel like I could make it on my own."

"But sometimes you can't, Amber. You just can't."

"But you do. Emily does and so does Brooke. I'm the only one sleeping around for money."

"You can stop, Amber. You have a gift and it's called that piano." I opened my purse and fortunately located a tissue to dab her face. I wiped away her tears. "You can become a private teacher, you can charge more, or take that energy you use to gain clients for sex and use it for gaining piano students. You can attend these parties and look for clients who have children and teach them. You can work for the Kennedy Center. Use your niche."

Amber shook her head and, for the first time since her fit of despair, she cracked a mild smile. "You're right."

"Besides," I slapped her arm. "I live in Southwest and life is a ladder. I learned from Brooke the first night we met that payoff from hard work takes time. We're putting in our time, girl, just make sure it's the right kind of time." I winked.

Amber rubbed my knee and said, "Thank you, Summer. You were just what I needed."

I leaned forward to hug her. When we pulled apart, I asked, "When do you think you will tell Emily?"

Emily

Emily turned the key to her front door as she crossed the threshold. Shutting and locking the door behind her, Emily realized that something about her home felt off. She saw rose petals on the stairs and smelled scented candles in the distance. What in the world . . . ?

"Surprise." Eric emerged from the distance in her living room. He waved a hand as he waited with a humble smile.

Surprised, Emily asked, "Eric?" She couldn't believe that he'd taken an extra step after their lunch together. After all the phone conversations, he'd finally made the extra step that Brooke suggested he should take first. Emily wanted to call a friend right away, but it'd have to wait.

"I see somebody hasn't changed her locks." He waited for her to join him.

Emily made her way to the transition point between the living room and kitchen where he stood. She raised herself on the tip of her toes to kiss him on the cheek. "You did this, huh?"

"I did indeed," he replied as he scratched his hair. "I think I grew a few more gray hairs trying to plan this mess."

"Hence, the last name 'Gray.'" Emily closed her eyes and inhaled. "I smell lavender?" She opened her eyes and smiled from ear to ear.

"You do. You like it? I also picked up some boardwalk chicken at Pop's Sea Bar for you, too. Remember? That was our favorite place in Adam's Morgan."

When she went through the kitchen and into the dining room, Emily spotted a layout of fries, potato salad and corn on the cob across her table. "Mmm, I do smell and remember it, Eric. Wow, you went all out didn't you?" She softly knocked him on his chest.

"I did. I got that delectable Jersey sauce, too." He grabbed both of her hands and she twisted her body to face him as he placed a kiss on each hand.

"I'm so surprised, Eric. I would have never guessed that you would have gone through all of this behind my back. I was just at lunch with the girls."

"Tell me, when am I going to meet these lovely ladies that you spend so much free time with? I have to learn their secret so I can get more free time myself."

Emily's eyes widened. "Soon. That's a great idea; we must do it soon."

"Can't wait." He leaned down to swiftly kiss her lips. Their fingers remained intertwined while they talked. "Emily, we lost so much time, and I want to get it back. I can't help but think we need a do over."

"What are you saying, Eric?" Emily had a surge of hope for the first time in months. She didn't want to be let down anymore.

"We headed for divorce after being married for a few months. That's a shame and it's embarrassing, and I want to punch my father and myself every morning before I do anything else. Let's take it day by day and see what happens. If marriage is in our hearts, then we can do it. If we need more time to grow, we will take it. No pressure, no plans, but I do want to be exclusive with you, at the least."

"Eric?" Emily heard what she wanted to hear for months. With a racing heart, she felt nervous and shy all at the same time. Though at a loss for words, she had to seize the moment and talk. He gazed at her curiously, waiting for her to continue. "All this time I thought it was me. You don't know how many nights I lie awake crying, feeling alone and rejected. I was so confused. I tried to pick up my self-esteem, but it was like it was hiding from me like a lost childhood garment, tucked away in the closet somewhere. I couldn't even think of dating."

"I'm sorry for that, Emily. You will never know how much unless I show you." He caressed her shoulders. Emily melted inside at each stroke. "We can start from square one." His blue eyes burned into hers.

Something deep inside made Emily hesitate. Something bothered her. "Remember when we ran into each other at that party a few months back?"

"Don't remind me. The only reason I went to that stupid party anyway was because of Kyele. Her father is good friends with uhh . . ." he twirled his finger around as he tried to think, "L-Leo. Yeah, Leo. All right, well, sorry. That's beside the point. Carry on."

"Something you said made me feel low." She took a few steps back to distance herself.

Eric crossed his arms as he waited. "Go on."

"You made a remark with such conviction about me using your name. Also, you intimated that I didn't have any friends. What was all of that about?"

"I told you, I wanted you to run from me, name and all. It was for the best. I knew you as kind of a loner, and you kind of liked it that way, so I played off that. I didn't know you had friends—well, close ones anyway." Eric stepped closer toward Emily. "I'm glad you're still a Gray, and don't you doubt that."

Emily reluctantly shifted her eyes onto his. Eric outstretched his arms.

"I need you to come back to me. I've laid everything out there for you to take hold of. I can take care of you, you know I can. I can pay off your student loans, I can—I can hire you a chef, take you shopping. Emily, I still love you, and I want you to have the world. Quit your job—well, I know you won't because teaching is your passion, but you *can.*"

With crossed arms, Emily managed a chuckle. She couldn't believe how passionate he was about her.

"I took these weeks of interacting with you to really assess everything. I paid attention to how I felt about you, and I had to process all of this. We can start as friends, but I want you back, Emily." He held her shoulders and squeezed them gently as he lightly shook her with passion. "What do you say, Ems?"

Emily stood there, lost in consternation. "Okay."

Reluctant to be overtaken by happiness, Eric took a moment to process Emily's response. "Okay, what?"

"Okay." Emily slapped her hands against her thighs. "We can give it another shot."

"Really, Emily, you're not playing?" Eric's jawbone relaxed as his mouth began to expand into a smile.

Emily beamed back at him as she realized what was unfolding in front of her: a relationship with Eric. "Yes. Yes, yes, yes, Eric! We can try again."

"That's what I want to hear, baby." Eric leaned forward to lift her up as their bodies pressed against each other's. Emily squeezed him before he released her back onto the floor. Eric and Emily simultaneously reached for each other's garments, ripping away any material that could separate their skin from making direct contact.

Down to his underwear, he held up an anxious finger as he headed back into the kitchen, "Ho—hold on, please." Eric came back to a naked Emily with a condiment cup in his hand. "We need this. No, wait. We can't waste no Jersey sauce, so lemme grab some leftover Peruvian chicken sauce." After making the switch, he placed it into her hands and with their old bedroom in mind, Eric picked her up, flinging her over his shoulder, where she could see the black eagle tattoo on his back that let her know he was her Eric. Arriving to their room, he placed her down gently onto her bed. Standing over her, he removed his underwear, and reaching for the sauce in her hand, he removed the top and said, "I guess that extra sauce for the chicken will be used on you." Emily grinned at him as she waited to be covered.

Eric tilted the container cup and watched the yellow sauce slowly drip onto her skin. He started on her breasts and stopped. Leaning over, he sucked the sauce from her nipples. "Mmmmmm. Emily's breast should be on the menu." Emily shook with laughter as she traced her fingers through his hair. Licking her clean again, he continued downward, letting the sauce drip over her stomach. Tracing the trail with his tongue, Emily watched her stomach quiver under his mouth. Pouring the sauce over her vagina, he raced to clean it up on the inside with his tongue, as Emily cried out, begging for mercy.

For every tongue tickle and stroke, Emily grabbed his hair with more intensity. Her legs fought with one another as Eric became lost in his own world of pleasure. She let him work it all out as he endeavored to clean up the sauce at the junction of her thighs. Kicking the air and drilling her feet into the sheets, her arms flung with hands grabbing desperately at the ends of her hair and the surrounding pillows. Months of absent touches added up all at once, sending her over the edge as the top and underside of Eric's tongue stroked up and down, coming and going like a car on a lonely two-lane street.

"Eric!" Emily made it to the mountain top and screamed in victory, that she didn't have to descend alone, and because she'd made it to the finish line.

Brooke

Brooke and Jackson decided on an afternoon walk at Meridian Hill Park, also known as Malcolm X Park by some residents. The holidays were coming in just a few short weeks, and they thought they should discuss Thanksgiving.

Jackson had an arm draped around Brooke's shoulders as he tightly held her close. They took in the scenery of the lower park with a plaza that framed the reflecting pool, and above it sat two identical stairways that stretched parallel to one another on either side of the cascading water. Jackson and Brooke stopped in front of the pool.

Nervous about bringing up topics that weighed heavy on her mind lately, Brooke knew that she should. They'd grown so close, they'd become inseparable. They spent many nights talking about the past, sharing childhood stories, sharing career ambitions, and philosophies of life. But something was missing: the topic of their future.

It wasn't like Brooke to pretend something was better than it was. She had no problem laying out all her cards, nor did she have a problem fighting for what she wanted and speaking up to make things happen. But Brooke wasn't one to waste time.

"Jackson. Jackson, Jackson, Jackson." Brooke rubbed his wool-coated chest. He smiled at her, a little confused at her reluctance to talk.

"Is there something on your mind, beauty?"

Holding back, she bit her lower lip and then released it. "Yes." She reminded herself that she never backed down from speaking her mind, and she couldn't start now.

"I'm here," he reminded her gently. "I'm listening, Brazile."

Brooke liked—no, she loved the random names they called each other. Yes. She could talk to him. "Okay." She clapped her leather-clad hands together. "Jackson, I know we're exclusive, and it's way too early to talk about the future. However, each day passed is an investment in each other."

"I understand that. I can see myself with you on another level."

Brooke felt highly accomplished inside to hear a man like Jackson speak that far first. Super. They were on the same page. "And that step requires time, right?"

"Right. Not forever, but time. Brooke, where is all of this going? Are you asking me about marriage?" His eyes squinted at her with one raised brow. That expression made her feel like she should hide behind a rock. Awkward.

Brooke bounced on her toes as she clasped her hands behind her back. "Well, yes."

"Okay. In the future, if I feel that that's where we should go, then, why not?" Jackson slightly raised his hands and flipped them palm side up. "But I can't ask today." He smirked and came to hug her close.

As relieved as Brooke felt, she shook her hands at him. "Wait, wait, wait." She pressed her hands against him to prevent him from coming closer. "I'm not done."

"What?" Jackson appeared irritated.

"I'm sorry, but there's more." She had to cover children. All her life she knew she wanted at least two, but no more than three. Although her mother screwed up her childhood, she didn't want to use that as an excuse to steer away from motherhood.

Jackson sighed, completely irritated with her. "What Brooke, what? I don't understand why you're trying to cover so much ground when we haven't even exchanged keys to our homes yet? We don't even know if we'll work out. Do you want to know how I feel about you? Fine. I love you. I'm crazy about you. I haven't felt this way for another woman ever. Good enough?"

He angered her, but she suppressed it long enough to keep from becoming emotional. How dare he explode at her?

But on the other hand, he just vocalized how he really felt for her. Some men don't do that. If she could do a victory dance, she would. But until they discussed children, then there was no way she could celebrate yet. Her face must've said it all, because his expression softened.

"I'm sorry, Brooke. I'm sorry. I didn't mean to explode, but I'm feeling a little pressured."

"From what? I'm not asking for a ring. I'm a lady and that's not how I'm going down in the romance game."

Jackson snickered. He cupped her face. "Yes, you are a lady indeed. My bad, baby. I know you're not trying to pressure me for a ring. I just like enjoying the moments in life, and if that means giving you a ring, then that's what I would do. But a series of events would need to take place first."

Brooke looked perplexed. "Like what?"

"Well, for starters," he caressed her hair, "we don't know each other's families. We haven't met each other's friends, nothing. It's time to do some of these things, Brooke."

Brooke snickered. "That's for sure." She knew a good man like Jackson would want children. She'd wait to ask him about that. They were both educated with money, had great heads on their shoulders, and they wanted the same things in life. Of course, he would want children, and now she realized that discussing marriage and children all at the same time would be an overload for any man. That kind of pressure could send him for the hills, even if it related to years down the road. She relaxed and reveled in knowing how he felt about her. Besides, he said it all first.

Brooke removed her panic, placed it in a container and stored it back on the shelf. She didn't want to ruin a moment like this. Instead, she cupped his face, too, and placed her lips on his and enjoyed the moment.

Summer

"Sixteen thirty-five." The cab driver rested his arm on the back of the passenger seat as he turned his neck to look at us.

"Well, obviously, Brooke didn't know her fare rate as well as she thought."

Amber cracked a brief, nervous laugh. "When would she ever come to our neck of the woods unless she wanted fried fish?"

"Brooke doesn't like seafood," I reminded her as I shuffled in my purse for a twenty.

"Of course," she mumbled to herself. "I got it baby, I got it," Amber assured me dryly. She whipped a twenty over the driver's shoulder. "Keep the change, sir." He thanked us as we crawled out.

Outside the cab, I realized that I'd never been inside her or Emily's home before. As we sauntered toward Amber's building, my phone rang. We stopped walking as I answered it.

Amber joked with forced humor, "You're hot today."

"Hello, Brooke." I plugged my other ear from the noise of car horns and loud engines.

"We need to set a date for all of our men to meet. Amber can even bring Daniel."

I wanted to jump all over the opportunity, but I froze as I remembered the nasty secret that Amber swore me to. I didn't know what to say.

"Summer?"

"Uh, hang on." I whispered the news to Amber. Her eyes got big.

"Do it," she whispered. "You have to. I can stay away or something but do it."

"Oh, okay Brooke. When?" It was a shame that Amber's secret had become mine.

"I'm not sure of the details right now but how about this Friday? Will that work?"

"Absolutely."

"That's great. How is Amber? Is she doing better?"

I wanted to admit that she was far from it. But I lied. "Y-yeah, she's improving."

"Okay, glad to hear it. Listen, I'll check with Emily at some point, too, to ask her about our date with our dates." She chuckled at her choice of words. "So, tell Amber to get well, okay? Gotta go."

"I will, Brooke. Talk to you later." I hung up anxiously and looked at Amber as we continued our stroll. "She says 'feel better.'"

Amber cursed beneath her breath and nodded with a grimace.

I made mention of my disbelief when I told her, "I really can't believe that you literally live behind me and across the street and we haven't been to each other's house before. Bizarre."

"That is kinda' stupid though. I guess we be busy." She shrugged. "But you're welcome to come anytime."

"Same here."

We stayed silent as I followed her to the second floor of her building. I struggled to think of something to say and I probably didn't want to talk. I couldn't lie to myself. A part of me became upset that I was burdened with her secret and, the longer she took to reveal it to Emily, the longer I suffered, too.

Amber rummaged for her keys as she struggled to keep her wits. When she managed to unlock her door, we walked through. My pointy-heeled boots clanked across her scratched wooden floor. The slight smell of paint mixed with cigarette smoke skated through my nostrils. I noticed that even though her apartment had more square footage than mine, it lacked any kind of appeal. It was modest at best. A small kitchen filled with outdated white appliances sat to the left of the foyer, and to the right of us, a lacquer dining set sat alone in the middle of a small dining room. Straight ahead, the Steinway piano highlighted the small living room.

"Your home is cozy." That was the nicest thing I could say. I felt bad that she didn't have carpet to cover her old wooden floor.

Amber shot me a look of disbelief. "No, this is a dump. I want something better. One day you should show me your home. But keep Oliver away. I may ruin that for you, too," she said bitterly. I marched over to hug her.

"Amber, you have to stop. You didn't know. But now you do and this you can control. Tell her. You have to tell Emily." I stared into her eyes. Amber never wore fear so strongly before.

"What will she say?" she asked as she wiped away a tear and sat on her couch.

"She will," I flapped my arms in the air as I struggled to think of Emily's reaction. I plopped down beside her. "I don't know. Be understanding, and think of this from your point of view." Even my own advice didn't sound right to me. What a mess.

Amber looked at me like I was a clown trying to cheer her up by juggling balls. "Really, Summer? No one ever, I mean *ever*, understands someone sleeping with the love of their life, not even by accident."

You got that right. But out loud, I replied, "How she takes it is how she takes it, honey, and there is nothing you can do about that. So, just tell her." Would I have taken my own advice if it were Fran and me but with her as a friend versus my boss? I had to stop doling out advice.

"I really like Emily. I really do. She's kind, but so delicate. The girl is a hopeless romantic trying to mend fences with her ex-husband. If only she showed me a picture of her husband prior to me meeting him."

"I know, Amber, I know."

"I mean, really, Summer. Many men have that name and what are the odds that I would meet the same one and in West Virginia?" She shrugged slowly and absently. "I just thought that he was just another Eric. I even asked if he was married, and he said that he ain't never been married."

My eyebrows furrowed as I received the information. "Really? He said that?"

"Yes. He said that. You know, I don't care about wives, but a part of me knew I had to ask since his name was Eric, just like Emily's ex."

I placed my hand on her leg. "Well, see, there you go. Go with that. Tell Emily about that conversation and go from there. She'll understand. I mean, she may not like it, but at least she will understand."

"Summer." Amber hesitated to collect her thoughts. "Look, I have to tell you how appreciative I am of your help and sworn secrecy. Sometime this week, I'll deal with Emily. Just—just promise to let me do it my way in my own time. Please?"

I agreed. "Fine, but make it this week, Amber, because I cannot wake up every morning with this on the brain."

"It will be." Amber gave me a smile, but the look in her eyes made her expression sorrowful.

I jumped up. "I gotta run. Oliver is home today, and I planned to see him."

"Go. Have fun, and thanks again." Amber stood up to hug me and to show me out. Once outside, I walked to the Waterfront Metrorail Station and caught a train to the Clarendon Metro, to be greeted by a man standing outside of his Corvette.

"I live just right here in these condos." He made a right into a parking garage of a new development among other residential and business buildings. I knew from the new structural brick that his home would more than likely be at least on the same caliber as Brooke's. I was ready to reach for a barf bag.

"Hm. You live here, huh?" I stared straight ahead uncomfortably, knowing that my place must've looked like a refurbished closet to him. And earlier I gave Amber's home the side eye. I scolded myself.

"I do. Haven't been here long though."

"I see." I didn't feel like saying more. When the elevator reached his floor, we marched to his door. I didn't even want to see him place his million-dollar hand on his knob to reveal something that I was sure should be in MTV's Cribs. Holding my breath, I reminded myself not to forget that it was just a building.

Oliver turned the knob after dancing his key through the lock, and when he opened his home, warm air hit us. At least I felt like a million bucks in my dark skinny jeans and beige cashmere sweater, topped off by my black BCBG boots. Nothing compared to showing up in someone's lofty home looking raggedy. I gave myself a fist pump.

I stood in the foyer as I took it all in. Brooke's home was just a warm-up compared to this, but I would never tell her that. Somehow, my eyes noticed everything all at once. The white contemporary furniture highlighted his barrel-colored oak floor. The only walls in place sectioned off bedrooms hidden behind big wooden doors. A spiral staircase led to a loft. I noticed a huge flat screen that fit perfectly into one of the sectioned squares of a built-in bookcase. All the other squares displayed vases, books, candles, or paintings. Artwork sprinkled the walls here and there.

"Here, I'll take you to my guest bedroom. You never know when you may be spending the night." I just nodded with my mouth open and followed with no success in snapping out of wonderment.

In a few steps, we arrived to a door that led to a beautiful, bright room that had its own bathroom. Simplistic, it shined in its own beauty with a bed covered in all-white linen and a matching chair beside it. The French balcony doors that led to a personal patio really caught my eye. I opened it and took a breath of fresh cold air. I pressed my tiny stomach against the railing as I beheld the sight of a twin building. Oliver appeared beside me and placed an arm around my waist.

"You like?"

I snapped my head toward him. "No wonder you live alone. I'd be afraid of someone messing up my home, too."

"No." He smiled and shook his head as he walked toward the glass doors. "I just haven't found the right person yet."

I stood there, looking into the distance as his words rang in my head.

He turned to me and asked, "Ready?"

I nodded and followed him in, placing my arms around his neck. "And the bedroom?" I asked.

"Umm," he moaned. "If you want to see that then you have to remove a piece of clothing."

"You dirty dog," I teased as my sweater came over my neck. "There goes one, as requested."

"Hmm, not quite good enough. Remove your bra, and I may be inclined." He stood there with his hands on his hips as he waited to see my next move.

Instead, I decided to turn my back to him and threatened to show the neighbors my breasts. "Do you want them to see these things or what?"

"Well, I'd hate for my neighbors to key my car on account of you."

I turned my head to face him as I placed my fingers around my bra clasps. "Then you take off something, too, mister, because the last time I checked, you had a nice body to offer."

"Okay, you may have a point." I heard his belt unbuckle and his legs sliding from inside his jeans. He threw them to the side. "There."

I turned and saw him completely naked from the waist down. "Oh, wow. I really gotta pick things up." I unsnapped by bra, setting my twins free. Then I placed my fingers inside my waistline to unsnap by button. "Here you go, buddy." I swayed my little hips from side to side to accommodate the process of simultaneous jean and underwear removal. "Come get it, tiger."

Oliver quickly removed his shirt and charged at me, taking us down together on the fluffy, white bed. We shared a laugh as he tickled me with his mouth while making animal growls. He came up for air to search my eyes for something more than I could explain.

"You make me silly, you know that?" The corners of his lips curled up as his eyes did the same. I liked that part.

"I do now." I returned the expression.

"It's . . . Summertiiiiiiiiiime." He pinned my hands above my head and quietly kissed me.

I managed to break away from his lips long enough to say, "Well, since we're having fun with words, why don't you extend me your olive branch?"

He nodded and literally got down to business. I may've had passion with Ruben, but we definitely didn't have any fun.

Amber

Amber removed a cigarette from her purse as she watched television in her bedroom. The biggest room in her apartment only had a nightstand on either side of her bed, a dresser, and a television. A simple space to collect her thoughts and fall asleep at night. She didn't spend as much time in it as she preferred, especially since when she was home, she had piano students, and when she didn't, she found herself at the houses of those filthy clients.

Yes, she had determined that they were filthy clients. To her surprise, Daniel would be her only exception at this point. He made her laugh, bought her anything she wanted in addition to giving her money, and they did things couples do, such as catch a meal together or do things like two unattached lovers and just have meaningless sex. Amber didn't find it necessary to stray from him. They never bothered with labels; they just existed in the company of one another.

Regretfully, she hadn't been able to do much about his breath, even when offering the gum and mints from her purse. Sometimes he'd reject them, and it made Amber wonder why people with the worst breath seemed to reject breath fresheners. She just couldn't make heads or tails of it. On the other hand, beyond blow jobs and hand jobs, she had magnificent sex with Daniel. Not only did he have one remarkable endowment, but he knew how to use it. Sometimes Amber thought she should offer it up for free.

Puffing on her cigarette with her feet crossed at the ankles, a short-lived, warm smile spread across her face when her mind suddenly thought of Emily. She stroked her cheek with her palm as she considered how to handle that dilemma. The whole day had been shot. She couldn't forget what she'd done to her friend. The girls were the best friends she never had. In New York, she barely bonded with females, because she mostly surrounded herself with male friends. Amber just didn't have as much fun with women, and they never amused her quite like the men. Thinking of New York made her think of her sister, Mara, and how she wished her sister would hurry up and use her plane fare to arrive in DC sooner than later. She needed an old familiar face.

Her cell phone rang suddenly, jarring her out of her thoughts. Her hand tried to follow the sound, but she couldn't find the phone. Then she realized it was under her left buttock. Daniel's name marked the screen, so she answered it.

"Hello, there. How are you?" Amber tried to put on her best casual voice to deflect suspicion that something was wrong. There was no possibility of sharing the Emily and Eric nightmare with him. She didn't need to feel more tarnished than she already had. Amber located the cigarette dish on the nightstand to kill her smoke.

"It was approaching nine o' clock and I figured a call was in order since I haven't heard from you all day." She found his voice obnoxious over the phone since he naturally had a loud tone and everything out of his mouth almost sounded hyper.

Amber didn't have a history of reporting to anyone and she surely would stay true to form. "I just had a busy day with my girls, that's all. Now I'm just chilling with the TV."

"Well, you know . . ." She could hear him trying to breathe. It irritated her. *Why won't he just lose the weight?* "I just ate some pasta take-out for dinner, and now my belly is full, and nothing good is on television, so a call to you sounded good."

"Oh, I was a second thought?" she teased.

"However, you want to look at it. So," he cleared his congested throat and Amber winced. "What day should I pencil you in? I'm not used to regular sex and it feels good to know I got somewhere to get it. You know?"

Amber rolled her eyes and chuckled with shame under her breath. She found herself asking if she really wanted to play this game anymore despite the nice gifts and money, but when she cogitated on what she did to Emily, she realized that now could be a moment for redemption. "Listen, I have to tell you something." Then she realized that she should tell him in person and that she would surprise him Monday at noon at his job. It would be great to surprise him anyway. "I'm busy so I'll have to get back to you tomorrow. I have to check my piano schedule for lessons, and then we can go from there. Will that work?" she asked even though she knew tomorrow would be their day.

"I can't say that I'm not bummed about the delay in penciling, but sure. I can wait, but don't keep me waiting for too long. Talk to you tomorrow." As usual, he clicked before she could respond.

Amber rested her phone on her bosom as she cocked her head back against her headboard. She didn't know if she should think positive, fall into self-pity, or cry.

Summer

Oliver woke me up at 5:00 in the morning, as discussed the night before. The plan was to drive me back to DC, but I insisted he drive me to a Metro station to catch a train. He didn't like the idea, but I hated the idea of him missing his seven o' clock flight to California to meet his mom.

He'd booked it last Friday since his mom called crying about another break-in. This time it happened in her home, and Oliver refused to risk her safety. He vowed to take her house-hunting in a nicer neighborhood. She sounded stubborn, just like my mother. However, between the break-ins and his generous budget, his mom relented quite easily to the idea of moving.

I had to hustle, because it was 5:50, and I needed to be at work by eight. Crossing the street, I mulled over all that I had to do within the next two hours: breakfast, showering, picking an outfit, and then my Metro commute. I expected I would have to pay for staying the night with Oliver, especially on a Sunday when working people generally needed that night to mentally recoup for the next day. Instead, I chose sex and then pillow talk with Oliver, but I didn't regret it. Stepping onto the curb of my neighborhood,

I smiled to myself, as I thought about the intimate moment in bed between us.

I'd collapsed on top of his body and rolled over next to him. We'd struggled to compose ourselves by reestablishing a normal breathing pattern as we lay together, gazing at the ceiling. Wiping the beads of sweat from my forehead, I turned my body to face him, as I slid my thigh on top of his leg. My hand propped my head up as my wild and wavy hair surrounded my face. I placed my other hand on top of his sweat-kissed chest. To become more comfortable, he placed a forearm behind his head before turning it to face me.

"That ride is going to make me sleep like a baby tonight."

"Are you flirting again? I can't let you steal all my energy. Jet leg and awesome sex will comatose me in California."

I could only shake my head at him with a smirk as I placed my head on my pillow. My eyes went to the foot of the bed as I reflected on the hard day I had with Amber in the taxi. I worried how that whole scenario would play out. Even a great orgasm couldn't have kept my mind off my friends for too long.

"Something wrong?" he asked as he propped his head up with a hand and twisted his body toward mine. My eyes must've grown distant, giving my emotions away.

"I . . . can't really talk about it, but I guess you can say that I know someone who is going to be hurt by some information once it's revealed to her. She's a good person, so I feel sad that it may destroy her."

"Well," he started to rub my bare shoulder. "Do you have to deliver the news?"

"It doesn't quite involve me. I just know the bad news while she remains oblivious."

"Sometimes, Summer, we get so caught up in how the other person will or may take bad news that we let that deter us from just letting them in. As friends, our job is to be fair enough to tell them, but supportive enough to help them handle it." He kissed my forehead. "You'll be fine, and so will everyone else involved."

That advice sounded sane and reasonable. It instantly made me feel better. I understood that no one could control Emily's reaction but Emily. She would just have to be mindful that Amber told her within a decent time frame instead of hiding it indefinitely.

That moment had me thinking. I'd never had pillow talk before, because to me it was something that couples did. While I remained against relationships, I could see how people became sucked into them. It felt good to know that someone had your back. If Oliver were mine to call my own, I would have someone else on my team aside from my mom and friends, and knowing that felt nice. On the other hand, the other fold of the relationship involved the expectation of answering to the other half. To me, that's what bosses were for, and to come home to that beyond the clock sounded too much like work. Besides, it was enough worrying about myself, let alone another person.

"Thank you. Thank you, Oliver," I replied as I allowed his advice to marinate.

Shaking off the sugary moment so I could get my brain into high gear, I took the backdoor into my building, hearing multiple sirens at a distance. Too early for drama. I pushed the elevator button to go up, but it didn't illuminate. Hearing some shuffling, I turned to my right to see three people exit from the stairwell. Without breaking stride, the man said, "You'll have to take the stairs."

I thanked him with a sigh as I mentally griped with the idea of climbing five stories and in heels no less. I decided to focus on all the good going on in my life. Though slightly panting for breath and hot from the workout, I let on a faint smile as I readied my key for the door. Life felt good and calmer since I left Ruben. Too bad I didn't meet Oliver right after I ended things with Max. Max—oh, no. I forgot to call him back yesterday. Well, later today, maybe during my walk from the subway station to my home I can return his phone call. At the least, I can text him after nine to let him know my intentions.

Strangely, resistance met my efforts to push my door open as I turned the knob to my apartment door. With the deep submersion into my thoughts, I didn't realize the dampness beneath my boots outside of my door until now. "Huh?"

Pushing harder, I barely eased in my apartment. I found my feet swallowed in water. "What happened? Oh, no! Oh, no, no, no, no, no, noooooooooooooooo." Now I knew why I'd just climbed five stories.

I wanted to cry but first I had to take in the horrible sight. My eyes didn't know where to start. There was water everywhere. The low water level would've soaked my feet if they hadn't been protected in my boots. I didn't even want to walk past my foyer.

Suddenly, I heard voices in the hallway, but with facing devastation, I just couldn't hear them. Instead, I focused on all the damage done to all my possessions and valuables. The water soaked my new couch at the hem, the sorted laundry clothes piled on my bedroom floor, and my carpet of course.

I jumped at the sudden touch on my shoulder. Before I could turn, the voice said, "Ma'am, excuse me, but you cannot be here. You need to evacuate with the rest of the residents."

I spun around to see a young, blue-eyed fireman. "Oh. I'm—I'm sorry." I rested my fingers across my lips. I had to be at work, I had to grab some clothes, I had to make a call but to whom? "Wait," I cried in a hoarse, emotional voice.

I ran to my room to snatch random clothes off hangers and one pair of pajamas and threw them in my laundry bag. I heard the fireman repeat his order. "Okay," I called back. In a hurry, I took one last look at my room and lifted my heavy laundry bag over my tiny shoulder while my purse swung on my forearm. And where did I think I was going without a car and no home? "Shit."

Just like the other residents, I took the stairs. Luckily, a man helped me carry my laundry bag as I clanked down in boots with heels. After crossing the stairway door, I stood outside with other devastated residents. We gathered in front of the building looking for answers. There were cop cars, two ambulances, and three fire trucks. Multiple families stood outside, freezing and wet, rubbing each other's shoulders, sobbing, communicating with other families, and approaching authorities with questions. I reviewed my phone contacts. For now, I knew who I could lean on. With a desperate hand, I dialed Oliver's number, who picked up on the second ring.

"Hello?"

"Hello, Oliver? You won't believe what just happened to me." I knew I sounded whiney, but I really didn't care. My heart escaped into my throat as sheer panic rushed over my body.

"Oh, snap. What happened, Summer?"

"I'm not really sure. People are outside and we all had to evacuate. I came home and my apartment was soaked. Well, water was all over my floor, and now I'm standing outside homeless without a car with a laundry bag in tow."

"Tell me you're kidding." A hint of masked pity existed in his voice.

"No, I'm not." Tears rushed to the rim of my eyes as I swallowed hard to fight the ocean of knots rising in my throat again.

"I'm so sorry, sweetie. I don't have a way of turning around. I'm at the airport now. Do you need money? I can wire you money tonight for a hotel and other expenses."

Argh. I couldn't possibly take this man's money. I didn't want to be one of those women who depended on rich men. My mom would find her own way out, and I needed to do the same. "Ohhh," I moaned. "I guess I'll be okay."

"Summer, don't be ridiculous. Why did you call me then if you won't accept any of my help? I like you and I have the means to help, so let me."

I pushed the hair on top of my head away from my face, bunching it into a balled fist. I couldn't. No, I just couldn't. He already had to finance his mom's troubles. Two women in despair wouldn't be fair to no man. "No, no, I do appreciate it but please, I can't. Just let me call you back. I guess I can crash on the couch of a friend's."

"Your choice." He sounded slightly offended. "Just let me know what you decide to do, or if you want to change your mind. I'm here."

"Honey, you are a lifesaver that I'm going to put in my back pocket and take out when I need something sweet."

"Obviously." I could just see him rolling his eyes.

"You know, I cannot burden you with my madness. It's too soon for all of that, don't you think?"

"Let me know how things pan out. I should get checked in and what not. Take care, sweetie."

"Thank you for listening. Let me know when you land." He hung up as I surprised myself by requesting an update of his whereabouts and safety. Who was I with this man? I shook my head rapidly to clear my head and focus on the now. I bit my lip as I thought of people to call. This would be a challenge, but I needed a shower. First, I needed to find out what happened.

I located a Hispanic family and approached the mother of the family. She raked her hand through her wavy, wet hair as she placed her hands on her youngest child's shoulders. Her older child, a daughter, stood beside her with a worrisome look on her face as they hugged themselves through wet clothes and damp skin.

"Excuse me, ma'am?" I waved a quick nervous hand at the mother to divert her attention from the building. She raised her eyebrows at me. "Hi. Do you know what happened here?"

With a prominent accent, she answered, "I don't know, something about a pipe burst."

"Wow. How badly was your apartment damaged?"

"*Ay, Dios mio*, there was water all over the floor. We were sleeping when it happened. I'm a deep sleeper. My daughter," she pointed a thumb at her child, "came to wake me up and she say, 'Mama, mama. Get up. Look.' So, I get up and as soon as my foot hits the floor, it's water all over."

"Goodness. Where can we go?" Speaking with the authorities seemed out of the question, as they busily communicated with one another. Everyone probably felt lost in the shuffle.

"Well, I call my brother and tell him to come get us because look," she gestured around her, "we have nowhere to go if they don't fix this now. We cannot go back in. I don't see how."

Her son looked up at her. "Mommy, I'm cold." He rubbed his arms frantically and she pulled him closer.

I felt so bad for the lady and her family. They didn't have on any jackets, just pajamas. I sighed loudly. "My name is, Summer. You?" I held out my hand for her to shake and she did.

"Guadalupe. Nice to meet you. It's bad that neighbors only talk during these times, you know?"

"That is very true and unfortunate."

"Well, maybe when things get smooth again, you can come over for cookies or something. We make dinner for you. I'm on the fourth floor, letter G."

"Great. I'm in 5F if you ever want to stop by for anything. I need to call for help, so take care, Guadalupe."

My weak smile matched my heavy heart. Though forced, Guadalupe's smile was as genuine as possible given the awful circumstance. I moved away from the family and pulled out my phone to call Amber. Not only did she live the closest, but her schedule was more forgiving than Emily's and Brooke's. God forbid I wake up Brooke before a morning meeting with a client or ruin her routine. Emily, on the other hand, I couldn't even face. Even the idea of being around her would tempt me to spill the beans. Therefore, those two were definitely off-limits. I really needed my space from Amber, especially until she made Emily aware of the fact that she slept with Eric. Unfortunately, when you find yourself standing outside homeless without a car, with limited funds in the bank and feeling like a beggar, being choosey becomes counterproductive.

I exhaled as I swung the phone to my ear to dial Amber. Finally, after the fifth ring, a very husky but familiar voice answered the phone.

Feisty and irritated, she answered with, "Who the hell is this right now?"

Dry and defeated I replied, "This is, Summer, Amber. I apologize."

"Girl. Do you know what the time is right now? I said I'll tell Emily this week."

"No, Amber, please. This is not about that. My apartment was drenched in water. We had a pipe burst. I have nowhere to go."

"Oh, no. I'm so sorry, sweetie. Wait a minute." There was a pause. "Okay, sorry. I needed to find my pack of cigarettes." I rolled my eyes and exhaled again. "Come, come over. I can offer you my couch."

"I have to use your shower for now. I gotta get to work."

A voice struggled to sound alert. "Yeah, yeah. Do whatever you need to do, you know?"

"Thanks, Amber, I don't have much, but I'll be there soon."

"All right, hon. See you when you get here."

Once Amber hung up, I thought about Fran. I needed to tell her, but she was probably catching her last Zs. I decided that I would tell her about this in person. I planned to drop my clothes off at Amber's, then catch the train and get going. I could call the rental office at noon. What was done was done and my stuff should be okay, although, the leasing office had better pay for something.

In a short time, I found myself at Amber's doorstep, waiting for her to let me in. She came to the door with a scarf around her head and a silk flower-print robe covering her matching short gown with slippers on her feet.

"Come in, sugar." Her eyes were barely open as I slid past her.

"Thanks, Amber—really appreciate it."

"It's really no problem. I do what I can for a good friend." A sleepy smile crossed her face as she locked the door behind me. I watched her tighten the belt of her robe around her waist as she peered at my pathetic laundry bag. "Cigarette?" she asked, even though she was empty-handed.

"No thanks, Amber. I actually have to bounce, like now. I'll be back after my shift. You know I get off at five and then there's the train ride, so say about, 6:15?"

"I'll be here then to let you in. I'm going to see Daniel today, but I won't let you down."

My expression turned worrisome. "Please don't since I have no other place to go."

"I wouldn't dream of it, sweetie. Now if you want to take a shower, follow the hallway toward my room and it's the door to the right. I have a towel laid all out for you." She patted her hair through her scarf. I guess to scratch an itch.

"You're so sweet. Thanks, Amber. I'll boogie with this shower thing and pick my clothes from this bag."

Amber suggested, "How about this? I can lay out your clothes as you shower so when you get back your selection will be a smoother process? You gotta lot of shit on your plate right now, so let me do what I can."

I marched over to embrace her as I lightly rubbed her back. I withdrew, and looking into her eyes, I told her, "You're a doll."

"Well, scat." Her fingers snapped in the direction of the hall. I raced off in my clanking heels toward the bathroom and enjoyed the steamy water as I applied Amber's coconut-flavored shampoo through my hair. I followed up with the matching conditioner and lathered my body with her apple-fragranced body wash.

I finished up and headed to the living room in a towel. Amber stood over her couch with a coffee cup in one hand and a cigarette in the other, checking out the display of my clothes she had straightened.

"Girl, you got some nice clothes."

I smirked. "The things you can do with a bonus check."

"I see."

"By the way, I love your coconut collection in the bathroom." I placed a chunk of hair under my nostrils to take in the scent.

"Oh, please, I hate it. Please, take it with you. Don't forget to grab the lotion that came with it. It's on the countertop."

"Not kidding?" I'd only feel guilty if she really wanted it. Besides, in addition to having no place to go, that sounded like a nice survival kit. The look she shot dared me to question her again. "Awesome."

"What are you going to wear?"

"This towel if I don't hurry up." The clock on her wall displayed 6:50. In a hurry, I chose the skinny red jeans and a white, button-down blouse with bell sleeves. A cracked laugh of disbelief escaped my throat. "Gee, I guess these boots again. And I had the perfect red shoes for this outfit. Oh, well."

Amber twisted her mouth in thought. "Too bad our feet are different sizes. You have tiny feet." She took a puff and exhaled from one corner of her mouth as she sized me up.

"It's okay," I replied quickly as I snatched up the clothes and made my way back to the bathroom to change. My eyes gave my reflection one last look-over, and given what I went through this morning, my appearance impressed me if I did say so myself. I grabbed all the coconut products in a hurry. Back in the living room, I placed the bath products in my laundry bag. Chuckling within, I almost felt pathetic. Earlier, my life felt like paradise and now, I was throwing bathroom products from a melancholy friend into my laundry bag.

I did a quick scan of the living room for my purse and boots. I donned the boots and my coat and slung my purse on my arm before heading for the door. "Thanks again for everything, angel. See you later," I called behind me.

"Have a good day, love," Amber called back.

Emily

Emily woke up with Eric by her side. Seeing him there in her bed, or maybe their bed, was the best sight for her eyes. She rolled over to glance at her clock. When she saw seven o' clock, she smacked a hand on her head at the realization that she was really pushing it. Even though her school wasn't more than ten miles away, it was imperative that teachers made it to work early for many reasons.

She climbed out of bed and stretched while standing. Normally she wore actual pajamas to bed, but after her endless sex with Eric, she'd slipped on a t-shirt that she found flung over her chair next to her bed. Standing barefoot in her t-shirt and underwear, she made her way to the bathroom to get dressed. Time didn't permit a shower. Besides, smelling Eric on her all day wasn't the worst trade-off.

"Where do you think you're going, beautiful?" Eric's groggy voice surprised her.

She spun quickly on her toes and pretended to be caught with an open mouth. "Some place called work." With a tilted head, her brunette hair lowered as it swung with her movement.

Eric patted the bed. "Get over here. I told you to quit," he teased with an arm relaxed behind his head. He knew how much she loved teaching, so she couldn't figure out why he would suggest such a thing.

Emily smiled with her lips pressed together. "Can't do that, and you know it. Tell me you're putting up a pococurante front regarding my career." She absently played with her fingernails.

Setting aside that topic, he told her, "All right then, we can make plans tonight. There's a lot of time to make up for." His other hand caressed his chest.

"That works." Emily's thumb pointed behind her toward the bathroom door. "But I have to get going. If I'm late, my record could become tarnished."

He waved an understanding hand at her. "Gotcha. Get going, sexy, and we'll catch up tonight." Eric remained in bed and stared at the ceiling as Emily nodded and made a quick dash to the bathroom.

With the door closed behind her, she spotted a cloth headband on the countertop and slid it over her head to push her hair back. Emily splashed cold water on her face and applied her cleanser. Examining her oval face, she removed the foam and patted her clean face dry with her favorite terry cloth.

Thinking about Eric's compliments, she studied her face. *Am I really beautiful?* She felt like it. The man of her dreams, her original husband, treated her like the queen she wanted to be for him. Even she could see the new glow in her face. Perhaps the frustration of pent-up sex had absconded through her pores overnight. She reached for her toothbrush and toothpaste as she shrugged, because it really didn't matter. Emily felt certain that last night Eric made her the happiest woman in the world, as cliché as that sounded. After gargling and checking out her sleek teeth, she patted her mouth dry and replaced her brush.

Emily located her watch and bra in the bathroom, and after catching the time, she donned both before opening the door. "If I don't—"

The bed was empty. "Eric?" she called. "Eric?" she repeated in a louder tone with furrowed eyebrows. Would he really leave just because she didn't want to quit her job? Emily snatched her shirt over her head and swapped her panties for a fresh pair. At her closet, she chose the first thing she saw—a cardigan and black slacks. She snatched up a thin, gold belt and slid it through the pants loops. Her size nine-and-a-half feet slipped into her Dolce Vita boots before grabbing her purse off the floor. *Oh, great.* She realized her hairbrush was upstairs as soon as she landed on the last step. It was just going to be one of those days. *Now, where did Eric go?*

The scent of turkey bacon and eggs drifted to her nose. When she reached the kitchen, Eric was removing a Panini sandwich from her griddle—one of their wedding presents. Eric let her keep all the wedding gifts when he moved out. At the time, distance from her and the whole situation seemed to be the only gift he'd yearned for. She closed her eyes briefly in regret. When she opened them, he spun around with the sandwich in a Ziploc bag. She caught a glimpse of the black eagle that she loved so much.

"Sweetheart, you need to take this. I know you said you were late and I'm a bad cook, but I know how being out of routine drives you nuts. Didn't want you to go without food."

Emily flashed a wholesome smile. "You know me well." She trudged toward him as she spread her arms for a hug.

He pointed past her with his chin before he accepted her embrace. "Don't forget your briefcase there." Emily felt a quick tight squeeze before he relinquished his grip. "Here." He passed her the sandwich. "Get out, goodbye."

"What, no coffee?" she teased with a mock pout.

"I couldn't find your traveler's mug." His big shoulders shrugged as he mimicked her pout.

"No worries. I know it's in the car cup holder."

"Bye. Don't be late, Ems," Eric warned firmly. He hated tardiness as much as Emily hated a hit to her routine.

"Okay, okay, okay," she replied as she shuffled away in a hurry. Emily quickly seized her coat from the coat rack and headed out the door. As she strutted toward her four-by-four in the street, she smiled for the first time in months for no reason. It felt damn good to have a loving man back in her life that thought enough of her to make breakfast. Emily disarmed her truck and threw her belongings into the passenger seat. After she cranked the motor, she retrieved her cell phone from her purse and dialed Eric's cell number on speakerphone, so the police couldn't catch her on the phone while driving in DC. Emily didn't expect him to pick up since he was downstairs, but he did.

"Aren't you driving?"

"I just wanted to thank you for breakfast. I have you on speakerphone, and I'm going to make this quick."
"Next time, tell me when you're stable and not behind the wheel, Ems. However, it was my pleasure, especially after last night."

Emily blushed as she bit her lower lip. A brief memory of him ravishing her, licking her from head to toe, and in a private place, made her stomach flip. "Maybe we can do it again tonight."

"Emily, get off the phone. Call me during lunch. This isn't a good time to talk."

"Okay, okay, okay. You killjoy." Emily rolled her eyes. Eric clicked on her before responding. He was exactly how she remembered: protective, slightly controlling and bossy, but she loved it. That was her Eric.

Brooke

Brooke sipped her coffee as she waited to meet her client at the Georgetown Waterfront Park. Sighing, her breath turned into a white puff as it left her lips. Nothing made her more irritable than waiting for late people. After spending almost a grand on her trench coat which failed to repel the cold, Brooke resisted cussing. It didn't make a lot of sense to blame the coat, since she failed to check the weather to find out the exact temperature. She expected it to be cold, but not this cold.

A frown crossed her face when the last drop of coffee sat at the bottom of her cup. Depositing it into the nearest trash bin and returning to her place on the bench, she crossed her legs and sandwiched her gloved hands between them. At least she could take in the scenery until her French client, Jacqueline Laurent, arrived.

Brooke was happy that the park had reopened after years of construction and couldn't wait to bring Jackson the next time she visited. It stretched for many miles along the Potomac River from Maryland to Virginia. Looking to the right, Brooke could view the Key Bridge as cars rushed by to enter or leave Georgetown. In front of her, people jogged past, owners leisurely walked their dogs, and some couples sat on the grass-covered terrain, smiling, talking, and cuddling. Brooke used to roll her eyes at happy couples in their own world. Now, she realized she was just like them, and that it was okay to take pride in a relationship. A little girl's sudden presence jarred her out of her thoughts.

"I like your shoes." The redhead girl giggled and skipped back to her mom before Brooke could thank her. At least the little girl saw Brooke smile at her. The mom reached for her daughter's hand and used the other to wave to Brooke before walking away. Brooke grinned as she waved with wiggled fingers. She peeked at her silver snakeskin Manolo pumps and shrugged. *The little girl has good taste.* A humored smirk spread across Brooke's face. The girl also had a mom who took her to parks, which made her think of her own mom

Brooke recalled back to when she was a little girl. Her mother never took her to parks. The best parks she went to in her life were arranged, school field trips. There were so many things her mom failed to do with her as a little girl. As a grown woman, Brooke found it easier to hold it in than to confront her mother about her rotten upbringing. That's what work was for, she reasoned. As good as exercise, it relieved her stress. The process of attending her clients' weddings to ensure quality and order rewarded her. Her pat on the back came in the form of seeing all her hard work come together, which validated all her choices. One choice she knew she had to make today involved leaving the park.

Brooke picked up her hobo bag and day planner case and headed toward the street. Even though Jacqueline had called to warn her that she was running late, Brooke didn't care. That call came thirty minutes ago, and Jacqueline didn't follow up. Even as a newbie desperate for clients, she didn't wait for late people. It came across as a jab to her character, an insult to think that her time meant nothing. As a professional, Brooke refused to tolerate it, even from a client.

"Ms. Brazile. Ms. Brazile. Wait! I'm coming." Brooke turned and recognized the woman running toward her. Brooke's eyebrows dropped as she squinted in disbelief. A mink coat-clad Jacqueline Laurent—who never seemed to apply her makeup correctly and typically wore her shoulder-length brunette hair half-up and half-down—reached Brooke. The fiftyish-year-old client struggled to catch her breath despite her extremely small frame. Ms. Laurent held her side as she bent over to recuperate. Even though Brooke considered that maybe something bad really did happen, she couldn't help but peg Ms. Laurent as the dramatic type.

"Are you okay, Ms. Laurent?" Brooke almost placed a hand of comfort on Ms. Laurent's back, but her client straightened.

"Oh, honey," she began in between gasps, "my Jaguar overheated and I had to hail a taxi after the tow truck came. It was so hard making it through this awful Georgetown traffic." Recognized as a well-known fundraiser with extensive connections in the DC area, Ms. Laurent was a very wealthy woman from Paris who moved to Bethesda, Maryland, for a new experience years back. They met about a year ago, and Ms. Laurent usually appeared at some of the same events as Brooke.

"You didn't call, so I assumed you weren't coming after all," Brooke stated. "I waited thirty minutes after your initial warning." She reminded herself to camouflage her inner attitude due to her client's status. Brooke reminded herself that she could take out her anger in kickboxing classes.

"I certainly didn't anticipate a thirty-minute delay. My apologies, but my cell phone didn't charge last night like I had thought. My battery just died." She did appear apologetic, so Brooke decided to move on.

"I'm very sorry about your morning, Ms. Laurent. I do hope you feel better, and if there's anything I can do . . ." she offered, rubbing Ms. Laurent's shoulder.

"Thank you, Ms. Brazile. How sweet." Ms. Laurent appeared touched by Brooke's words.

"It's just that I'm cold now, so can we take this into a restaurant or coffee shop now?" Brooke gestured toward the nearby buildings.

"Absolutely, I'm famished."

Brooke and Ms. Laurent settled on La Madeleine's, of course, since they served French food—something Ms. Laurent couldn't resist. "I adore this restaurant," she marveled once they entered. Brooke nodded as she silently rejoiced at the slow pace of customers.

"I eat here on the weekends with my girlfriends."

"Oh really? Then we have the same taste."

Brooke silently disagreed with that comment, especially when she peered at Ms. Laurent's leopard-print pants and oversized mink coat. "Yes, in food, that's a great thing."

"Spinach pochette and quiche please. Oh, and a cup for coffee," she told the food attendants as she placed a finger on her lip.

Brooke's eyes widened when she considered the calories while noting Ms. Laurent's frame. *Such a big appetite on a small stomach.* Brooke only ordered a chicken Caesar salad and a cup-sized tomato basil soup. They moved along the line with their trays in hand. Ms. Laurent spoke to the cashier in French as they shared a giggle.

Turning to Brooke she asked, "Something to drink, Ms. Brazile?" as she held her debit card between two fingers before handing it over to make an official payment.

"Water is fine. Thank you." Brooke didn't like someone else paying for her meal. "I can pay, Ms. Laurent." It was too late. Ms. Laurent just smirked at her as she relinquished her debit card to the cashier. "I don't think so dear. The least I can do is pay for your meal, considering your patience."

Brooke just smiled and took one for the team. "Then, thank you, Ms. Laurent. Next time it's on me, though."

They settled on a table next to the unlit fireplace.

"So, Ms. Laurent, I was thinking—"

She placed an aged hand on Brooke's. "Please, I think you can call me Jacqueline now."

"Okay, Brooke is fine for me, too. Well, Jacqueline, I was thinking of the perfect place to have your wedding." She placed a manicured finger in the air. "Brooke, something needs to be clarified. I'm not getting married."

With a wrinkled forehead, Brooke's shoulders slumped in surprise. "What? I . . . I don't understand. Then why are we here?"

"My daughter. I'm planning her wedding." Jacqueline Laurent crossed her legs and tapped her finger on the table.

"Jacqueline." Taken aback, Brooke composed herself. "How—I mean . . . I was under the impression that this wedding was for you." Her eyes took a furtive glance at a naked wedding finger.

"Oh, please my darling. I'm not sharing my wealth with any man with funds unmatched. And since he doesn't seem to exist, for now, I'll take my daughter's wedding into my own hands. My money, my decisions, and I know what's best. What do these young women know about taste?"

"Okay, so, umm, since it's your taste and not your daughters then you're telling me that everything I have in mind should stay the same?"

"Oh, absolutely Brooke." Ms. Laurent placed a hand on her chest. "It's my money. Now, go on." Ms. Laurent started to sample her spinach pochette.

"I think the wedding should be at the Georgetown University Dahlgren Chapel and the reception should take place at *Las Maison Française* at the Embassy of France."

Wearing a pleased expression, Ms. Laurent shifted in her chair. She leaned in slightly. "Ooh, how I love your French pronunciation, Brooke. Did you take French?"

Brooke chuckled. "One class in high school, Jacqueline. It was hard."

She waved a hand at her. "Oh, nonsense. Planning a wedding is hard, but you make it all so simple."

"Well, these places are less than a mile from one another and they are both classy selections." Brooke sipped some soup.

"You get me, Brooke. Many people say you get them when they put their trust in you."

Brooke loved hearing those words. It was nice to hear a compliment, no matter how many times they mirrored one another. "That means a lot, Jacqueline. But you never quite told me your budget, you know."

"Money, let's talk money indeed." Jaqueline patted her mouth with a napkin. "Do you know how much a high-end, fully loaded Mercedes costs Brooke?" she asked casually as she placed a piece of quiche in her mouth.

"I have an idea." Brooke almost choked. This was her highest-paying client yet!

"Well I suppose you'd better find out, because I'm not paying you thirty percent for nothing." The casual gloves came off as they went back to business, Brooke noticed, which proved why she should never abandon her professional demeanor with clients. "She's my daughter. I'm very proud of my only child, Veronique, who also happens to be a Yale graduate. She's my only child, and I won't be able to do something like this again. I cannot tell you how to do your job, but unless you're prepared to take on this massive responsibility alone, you may want to hire a team. They will be paid a fee separate from yours. I don't care if you direct them and do nothing hands-on, as long as it all comes together under your direction and care. I want the Brooke Brazile experience."

Brooke nodded. "I hear you completely, Jacqueline."

Ms. Laurent hesitated. "Good, because I want the best for my daughter. Her dad lives in France. He and I couldn't make it work. The bastard promised me life in the United States since I did France for many years. But when it came time for him to come here, he backed down. So needless to say, she barely sees her dad. She's also quite pissed at him as well."

"I'm sorry to hear that, Jacqueline." Brooke stopped eating. Both of her legs rested straight under the table as she listened with her hands crossed on the table.

"That's okay. I'm fine now." Her eyes drifted to the floor as she told her story. "Not having enough time to make memories with your father, especially as a daughter, hurts." Her eyes swung back to Brooke's, whose eyes were lost in Ms. Laurent's. "Now you see why my daughter must have the best by the best."

"I'm flattered." Brooke placed her hand over her heart with her hand.

"Don't be. Flattery is for people who doubt that they deserve the praise. You deserve it and you know you do. I looked around and no one else can do it the way you do it."

"I handle my profession with passion."

"And that is why you impressed me when you headed for the hills at thirty minutes past my call. You knew what you had to offer and feared not about losing my money. True professionals always know how to weed the serious from the clowns. I'm sold. Just please don't let my daughter down. Now let's hit some details on time frame and guest capacity."

She had this in the bag. It literally came down to the future bride and groom keeping their engagement on. "Thank you for sharing your story with me. I'm honored to have learned more about you. So now, let's get started."

Summer

I had a headache. No breakfast, no coffee, what a disaster. Literally late, Fran had yet to come in. After butting heads with the other junior recruiters and dealing with two angry clients who didn't have our candidates show up to work, it really made me want to quit for the day and go home. When I remembered the unlivable condition of my home, I picked up the phone to call the leasing office. I told the leasing agent, Sandi, my name and inquired about the dilemma.

"Ms. Stevenson, we're so sorry about your home and everyone else's. We're doing what we can to assess the damage and to see what happened. We did have a pipe burst, but it's too early to release any other specifics now. All we ask is that residents make sure that we have a reliable number and email address on file so that we may follow up as things progress."

"What do I do next? How long will I be homeless?"

"Okay, Ms. Stevenson, maybe Wednesday you can collect some essentials after the crew has had sufficient time to clean up. Now, obviously, no two apartments were affected the same, but we don't know the extent of damage done to your particular unit. Please keep in mind that the damage may be worse than what you saw. Once that information is known, we can email you or call when we can let you pick up some essentials. But safety is our first priority."

"I understand. What about my coverage?"

"So, do you have renter's insurance and one that covers water damage in particular?"

My heart paused a beat. It picked back up but rapidly. What was I hearing? My hand met my chest. "Do I have what? R-renter's insurance? Hmmmm, why do I need that when you guys are responsible?"

Sandi replied with a slight sound of pity, like a chuckle. "Well, we're one hundred percent responsible for the pipe damage and will be replacing the walls, carpets and the like—basically, the foundation of your home. But as the renter, the contents of the home will be your responsibility."

I was officially done for the day. One disaster after the other overwhelmed me. Tempted to feel sorry for myself, I refused, because I figured that this was my debt to pay for messing up Fran's home, and now my one-person home suffered, too.

Void of sufficient oxygen, in a flat tone I asked, "So, what are you saying Sandi?" She probably didn't hear me too well. I could barely keep my hand on my chest as I gripped the collar of my blouse.

"Ms. Stevenson, unfortunately, you will be one hundred percent responsible for the contents of your home, whether it's fixing or replacing. I'm so, so sorry. If you need to reread the section of your lease outlining this, you can find it on page—"

Feeling as hot as a tamale, I responded with, "No, I'm good. I'm good. I don't even have time nor do I want to see what you're saying right now. I have to find some place to live indefinitely." The walls were closing in on me, and I needed to get out of here. But where could I go? Home? That wasn't exactly an option right now.

"It really shouldn't be too, too long. I totally understand the dilemma you are in right now."

"Do you?" I whined into the phone. "Because I know it's not your fault, but I'm sure you will be going home to a comfy sofa and a bag of microwaved popcorn tonight." Why did I project my fantasy off onto this poor woman and with attitude? "Just please, keep Summer Stevenson 5F in the loop using the email in my file. Thank you, goodbye."

I could feel the tears welling in my eyes as I hung up. Standing up, I felt the need to pace in front of my desk. *You don't get to cry, you don't get to cry, you homewrecker.* I hissed at that nasty but truthful voice to shut up. I didn't mean to be so mean to Sandi; I felt awful.

"Knock, knock." A playful knock sounded at my office door. I knew it was Fran before looking up, but seeing her confirmed it. Gee, could she ever just knock?

"Oh, dear. Hey, hey, hey. What's going on, Summer?" Great. She could see the tears in my eyes. "Oh, Fran, this morning has been terrible." I bit my thumbnail and stopped fighting my tears. Letting them flow, I knew I sounded hysterical, but considering my messy morning, I didn't care. Fran closed the door and surprisingly, I was happy to be in her presence.

Her familiar floral fragrance comforted my senses. Fran felt as good as the mother I couldn't hug right now. But I didn't deserve her compassion or concern, not even her touch. When she finds herself needing comfort because of what I did to her, she will look back and think of this ironic moment.

Call it selfishness, I suppose, because I accepted her hug regardless of my realization that she may need one when her marriage falls apart. She rubbed my back the way elementary teachers and mothers did when something went wrong. It felt good, but I pulled away from the moment.

My fingers frantically swiped away my tears. "I have no place to go and my stuff is ruined. I don't have any insurance and I'm afraid that I won't have anything now."

"Summer, slow down. Sweetie, what on Earth are you talking about? Why are you without a home, dear?" Fran's genuine expression of concern scared me.

"I came home this morning, and my place was flooded." It felt odd telling her that I hadn't been home, but she didn't have to know why. I couldn't even think about that now. She gripped my hands into hers. "The apartment people said that we have to wait to see what happens and that rental insurance will cover our contents, but I don't have insurance. Now I'm scared I'll be wiped out of everything or anything special."

"Go, Summer. No work for you today. The day will be paid but you cannot work like this, and I don't want you to try. Where are you staying, dear?"

I shrugged as I gathered what little strength I had so I could speak more clearly. "On my friend's couch." Fran gripped me by the shoulders and gave me a gentle shake. "Come stay with me."

I just heard the nicest and worst offer she could ever make. My eyes widened with horror as I imagined looking at Ruben across the dinner table while eating, walking past me in the hall, or even watching me pour my morning cup of coffee. No, absolutely not. This wouldn't work. "Fran, I'm touched but this would be an imposition." *Oh, come on, Summer. Was that the best you could come up with? How trite.*

"No, don't be silly. Are bosses not allowed to be there for their employees outside of work?"

I nodded. "It's not your problem, Fran, so thanks but no thanks."

"It will be perfect, Summer. You're like my friend anyway, right?" She looked around despite the closed door and leaned forward to whisper, "Besides, I hate everyone else and only like you."

I giggled for the first time today while my guilty meter rose. "Well, Fran, don't do me any favors, I don't deserve it." Her compassion made me want to spill the beans, but I couldn't be homeless and jobless at the same time.

"Summer, we cannot worry about what we do and don't deserve. How far back do we go back in life to measure that determination? The here and now is all that matters, and what matters is that you need someone right now. So, you will be with me until your home is ready or unless you find some place, but you are welcomed to stay with me as long as you like. I'll let you drive our spare car to work, because I go in later." She patted the back of her hair gently and smiled. "Besides, a gal my age needs a few extra hours of sleep."

We shared a laugh, mine filled with nervousness but somehow refreshing at the same time. I realized just how much I liked her. However, I knew that if I rejected her, she would take it personal or become suspicious. My plan had to include avoiding Ruben and staying in my guest room. But to keep Fran from experiencing either reaction, reluctantly, I relented.

"What time do we leave tonight, Fran?"

8: visitors

Amber

Amber marched on the cork flooring of the T.P. Cowell building located in Tyson's Corner, in her red pumps wearing a skirt suit. She didn't know what the company did, but she liked the seven-story building already. Pretending like she fit right in, she had to admit to herself that it felt fun to feel important or at least polished and guessed that Daniel would be surprised to see her new look. It wasn't so bad dressing for success instead of sex.

Located in the middle of the lobby and manned by a very young blonde, Amber stopped at the receptionist desk and said, "Amber Hamilton. I'm here to see Daniel Cosby."

The receptionist's eyebrows crinkled as she typed into her computer. "Ma'am, we don't have a Daniel Cosby here, just a Crosby. Is that what you meant?" Her blue eyes redirected back to Amber.

"Oh, yes, that's him. Daniel Crosby." Amber berated herself to be more detail-oriented to successfully pull off the professional demeanor.

The receptionist reached for the sign-in log. "Did you have an appointment with him?" She peered at the screen while she scrolled with the mouse.

"Umm, yes." Amber lied to avoid being rejected. She hoped that a call to Daniel Crosby wouldn't take place because that would spoil the surprise. They had become almost like friends, a rarity for Amber. She felt like a visit on the job for the first time would be a nice treat for him. Besides, she didn't want him to think that she came for wild sex under the desk instead of treating him to lunch.

"I don't see you here."

Amber fell silent, scrambling for something to say. She quietly stomped her foot for not thinking ahead on the subway, but she was not used to corporate offices. "It should be there."

"Let me call." The receptionist seemed a tad annoyed as she tried to disguise it with professionalism. Suddenly, a man in a security uniform approached the desk.

"Never mind, I'll come back another day." Amber wanted to see if she could stall and blend in with the random business people who shuffled in and out. In a sparse crowd, she decided to take a chance.

The receptionist didn't bother to try to deter Amber from changing her mind. "Okay."

Amber pulled out her phone to appear busy as she listened to what the security guard wanted to say.

"We have a problem, Mandy. We need to get in touch with someone to fix the back door."

Amber peeked up to see what Mandy was doing and in what direction. Perfect. Turned away from Amber, Mandy spoke intensely with the guard. Amber walked to the side of Mandy's desk as the plants hid her. She scurried to the set of elevators and pulled out the business card with Daniel's information to see his specific office location. Seventh floor. She smiled with delight as she hopped in a summoned elevator and pressed the necessary button to take her there.

Showtime. Ready to surprise him with her presence, Amber knew he would be happy to see her. She reasoned that even sort of friends did last-minute things together. Amber checked her hair and makeup in the elevator mirror and prepared to step out when the chime signaled her floor. The time had come to tell Daniel that their sexual escapades had to stop, but that they could actually be friends. Considering what she did to Emily, this felt like the best choice she'd made in a long time aside from becoming a piano teacher. Before that, her resume of right choices showed up blank.

Stepping out, Amber didn't expect to be faced with an ocean of cubicles surrounded by a perimeter of closed-door offices. A few faces looked up at her, but then they turned away to continue working. Apparently, her face reflected confusion, because a man in a suit asked, "May I help you, ma'am?"

Amber became a little nervous, like she'd been found out. Gripping her purse for silent support, she almost found herself twisting it. "Daniel Crosby. I need to see him."

Somehow, standing amid those office workers made her feel like an imposter. The lady on the inside contradicted the lady everyone saw in the suit. Ironically, standing among business workers of various social classes brought out feelings of insecurity, but she felt just fine in a room full of rich people at parties. Perhaps it was because she didn't pretend to be anyone but herself at parties.

The man replied without smiling, "Daniel Crosby? Sure, right this way. Umm, I'm sorry. What's your name?"

"Amber Hamilton. We had an appointment. I'm his friend." As a direct person, she didn't feel too good about lying. Also, it didn't feel good to lie after her decision to clean up her act.

The man led her down a hall beside the elevators. Behind him, she studied his wavy brunette hair and broad shoulders. *Stop it, Amber, stop it. Pleasure is trouble.* She decided to direct her eyes at the names posted next to the office doors that scrolled by on the right: Linda Lacey, Heath Corner, Barry Young . . . and then the names stopped coming. Turning back to the man facing her with an extended hand, he presented her to a familiar face, Daniel Crosby.

"Here you are ma'am."

"Oh." She was so caught up on reading names, she forgot to look out for the one that counted.

The man stood beside Amber as he verified her presence to Daniel, who had already been standing while hanging up his phone. Her eyes met a surprised Daniel.

"Excuse me, Mr. Crosby, but Amber Hamilton is here to see you sir."

Amber briefly caught a glimpse of his name header outside of his door. It read: Daniel Crosby Senior Vice President. Awesome. Seeing his title posted outside of an office impressed her more than hearing it. At least she could say that she slept with a senior vice president of a big company—or maybe it was mid-sized. Amber didn't know which, but it looked big to her. When her eyes met with Daniel's again, she saw him quickly hide his surprise with a casual expression.

"Amber Hamilton?" Daniel asked as he picked up a few sheets of paper and placed a pair of glasses over his eyes. His eyes pretended to gaze over the text.

Amber was totally flummoxed as to why he didn't seem happy to see her. Why didn't he greet her? The man stole a glance at Amber before turning his face back to Daniel's.

"Yes, Mr. Crosby, Amber . . . Hamilton." The man spoke as a wave of ambiguity washed over him. "You were expecting her, right."

Amber felt weak with the drop of her stomach to her knees as she realized what might be going on. She was not welcomed in his world. He wanted to tell her to come back later; she had imposed.

Daniel peered from above the rim of his glasses. He shook his head almost vehemently as he replied, "No, I don't know her."

What? Was he serious? Amber's mouth fell open as the man looked back at her with lines of frustration creasing his forehead. The hallway spun. Maybe just in her head, but it spun. Her hand clung to Daniel's door frame while the other held her stomach. His words rang through her head as she saw the brown carpet spin. *I don't know her, I don't know her, I don't know her.* When she managed to briefly steady herself, her eyes flicked up toward Daniel.

Daniel wouldn't even look at her. Instead, he looked at the irritated and embarrassed man standing next to her. By now, the man probably took her as a joke. She began to feel like a one, too.

"Now, if you'll excuse me, Scott, I have a meeting for which I need to prepare. Now shut the door on your way out."

"Of course."

Before Scott grabbed the door, Daniel added, "And Scott, find out what happened to Mandy. She knows we don't just let anyone into our building."

"Will do, sir." On the other side of Daniel's door stood an embarrassed Scott and a humiliated Amber. She wanted to tell the man who peered at her with suspicious eyes that Daniel lied. In fact, the old Amber would've made a scene and shouted that he paid to sleep with her. But this Amber wanted to know what some sense of class felt like. She wanted to have a slice of the same pride pie from which her friends ate. The closing of Daniel's office door also shut the portal to her past.

Amber didn't want to wait for Scott's condescending words. She found herself running past random unknown faces in business suits as she approached the set of elevators. She couldn't punch the down button fast enough. "Come on, come on, come on," she chanted inaudibly. The tears welled up in her eyes, her stomach twisted in a knot of uncertainty.

Amber didn't want to turn to see any eyes of scrutiny, and she certainly didn't want to see Scott turn the corner. Luckily, the elevators chimed before opening and Amber hopped in. With her head at her knees, she desperately gasped for breath. In twenty-four hours or less, she went from a somewhat prideful woman to one of despair.

The chiming of the elevator was one that she wouldn't soon miss. The doors flung open to reveal Mandy standing there with the security guard.

"There she is." The young blonde with angered eyes pointed at Amber.

Amber's eyes widened as she threw her hands up and promised, "I'm leaving. Please."

The tall African security guard didn't wait. He firmly grabbed her by the arm. "You will not be allowed back into this building, and you're lucky I don't call the cops," he lectured as he steered her toward the revolving doors. "If you come back you will be arrested. Do you understand?"

"Please, sir, this is unnecessary. I can find my way out." Amber's pleas fell on deaf ears as she struggled to maintain her balance in pumps while nearly being dragged. It was so humiliating seeing the business people stare back at her with expressions of irritation and sheer disgust. Amber felt like Monday's trash being removed from the neighborhood of the affluent.

"You have compromised my position as well as that of the receptionist's." The security guard and Amber reached the revolving doors. He waited for one of the cylindrical enclosures to align before throwing Amber into one of them. "Go."

Amber barely managed to maintain her footing as the enclosure scurried her along until it yielded her the opportunity to step outdoors.

Amber pressed her back against the building as she struggled to catch her breath. Outside never felt so refreshing. She felt sicker than a gambler who had gone all in too soon at a poker table. She had no way of suppressing the disgust that made its way from her stomach to her throat. The saliva built up along the insides of her jaws. Soon, the vomit would be on the concrete. A shaky hand fished desperately for a tissue in her purse. Given her fragile state of mind, a quick moment of gratuity was almost lost on her for being prepared as she never left home without them. Succumbing to the victory of the vomit, she could only let it happen, and she mentally cussed every which way known to man due to the inopportune timing. She opened her mouth to accommodate the foul liquid as it poured and pooled on the sidewalk. Gross. Her legs managed to support her attempt to walk away from the building as she wiped her mouth. Amber Hamilton vomited away many nights of sleeping with rich, miserable men for cash, she vomited away the humiliation of Daniel's betrayal, and she vomited away her betrayal to Emily.

Away from a busy street full of people, Amber felt grateful for the building's location. She didn't need the extra attention. Instead, she needed a Metro bus stop, so she made her way to the main street outside of the building and took a seat on the bench under the shelter. Amber checked her purse for a cigarette. "Shoot."

She didn't bring the box because of limited space, and she certainly hated having loose sticks floating around in her purses. Daniel hated her smoking, so she used a smaller purse so she wouldn't have space to buy a pack if she craved one. That would be the last time she did anything for a man.

A part of her told herself that she couldn't smoke around a paying client because money called the shots. The other part of her knew better. She kind of found herself being mindful of a man who made her laugh. At times, he made her forget that he paid for her company and sexual services. The strictly-business approach made her feel somewhat confined after having more than one encounter with a man. It was easy for her to let her hair down, because it felt more humane. Unfortunately, the strictly-business approach was better. It wasn't like she endeavored to find love, and if she needed friends, she had three dependable women on her team already. Shouldn't that have been enough?

A sigh leaked between her trembly lips as she crossed her legs and rested her hands on the purse in her lap. It felt impossible to cry anymore as she reflected on her own realization. People perceived accepting money for sex as one of the ultimate lows a woman could experience in her life. However, being thrown out on your ass by someone who denied your existence out of sheer embarrassment seemed unparalleled to that. Room for her kind didn't exist in Daniel's kind of world. Men like that didn't want to be seen with the same woman who traded sex for cash. She could be overweight, she could be unattractive, she could be unintelligent, but she couldn't be a prostitute of any kind. She may not have been looking for love, but on that Metro bus bench, Amber vowed to one day be that woman, that a man could feel proud to call his.

As a vacant smile absently appeared on her face, she heard the squealing brakes as the bus came to a stop. Amber's eyes wearily lifted with reluctance to read the screen on the front of the bus displaying her destination. Despite the small crowd of people she'd have to face, the Metro bus was the highlight of her day. Rising with little strength, Amber willed her body toward the bus steps. She left the ghost of a whore on the bench as she carried a lady to an empty blue seat.

Emily

Emily parallel parked her truck after arriving home from work, wishing that she had her own driveway. With a quick snatch of her purse and sling bag from the passenger side, she climbed out of the truck and armed it before heading toward her row house. Earlier, she'd spoken with Eric to confirm his presence this evening. For the first time in months, she headed home with a smile. Her cell phone chimes sang, and she stopped on her porch to read her screen. Brooke's name appeared. She didn't want her time with Eric to be interrupted, so she answered it despite the cold.

"Hey, Brooke."

"Emily, how was your day?" Brooke sounded chipper.

"Great, thanks."

"Hey, listen. Before I forget, did you get my voicemail?"

"Oh. I'm sorry. I forgot to listen to it. Why, what's up?"

"Wanted to know if you could come over for a date this Friday night. We're bringing our men. It's time for everyone to meet."

It sounded like music to Emily's ears. "Yes, I agree. This is a great idea, Brooke. How about my house?"

Without hesitation Brooke replied, "You know what? I like that idea, Emily. It's intimate and casual. We can have a great time. Are you going to cover the food and stuff? My new wedding-planning gig is humongous, and I'm swamped."

Emily's eyes brightened as she felt that life couldn't be more perfect now. "I can do that. I can certainly handle that. You relax, Brooke, and bring the champagne or something, and I'll take care of the food. Keep a look out for a text message verifying the time. Okay?"

"Absolutely. Thank you, girl."

"Brooke, what about Amber? Isn't she single? Who can she bring?" Emily placed a concerned hand over her heart. "I would hate for her to feel left out."

Brooke laughed. "Amber is very resourceful, trust me. Either she will bring a random guy, if not Daniel, or she'll be more than happy to come alone. If anyone knows how to handle her own, it'd be Amber. We never have to worry about that woman."

Reluctant, Emily acquiesced. "Okay. I suppose so. I'll call her anyway."

"Okay, well, thanks again and talk to you soon."

"Bye now."

Emily hung up and pulled out the house key to let herself in. The aroma of rotisserie chicken pleased her senses when she opened the door. Yummy.

"Babe, is that you?" Eric called from a distance.

"Yes," she called back as she hung her coat on the rack. She realized just how nice it felt to come home to a man whom she loved. The aroma led her to the kitchen to see an apron-clad Eric. Emily laughed with glee when she saw him. She pointed a finger at him as he stood there with outstretched arms and a grin.

"What? Something funny?" he asked.

"You didn't cook anything, mister. You can't cook like this and you hate trying. Go ahead and take it off." Emily held onto the counter as months of pent up stress vacated her body with each laugh.

"That funny, huh?" His house shoes scuffed across the wooden floor as he approached her for a hug. They embraced, and to calm her reaction she pressed her mouth into his shoulder. "How was your day?" he asked.

"It was great, baby. It was great because I knew I was coming home to you."

Eric's hand eased down toward her ample bottom. "With a body like this, did you expect me to stay away?"

She tightened her grip around his neck. "Eric?"

"Hmm?"

"Thank you for providing me with breakfast and dinner, but I know you can't do this every night." She scanned the table full of food from over his shoulder before he eased her away from his embrace. His eyes glimmered.

"Who says, Ems?"

"Well, it's not really plausible, given your schedule. How did you manage this tonight?"

"I took off and just enjoyed the beauty of being back in a real home."

Emily smiled as she bit her lower lip in thought. Her hands caressed his shoulders. "I love you, Eric Gray."

"I love you, too, Emily Gray." He leaned forward to place a prolonged kiss on her lips.

Leading her by the wrist to the food, he said, "Let's go eat." He smacked her butt and she cried out playfully in pain as she placed a hand over the stricken area. They took their places across from one another at the table and placed the cloth napkins on their laps. He placed a few carved pieces of chicken onto her plate and then Emily added small portions of green beans, mashed potatoes, and roasted baby carrots to complete her serving.

"Our meal was made possible by . . ." she started to say as she placed mashed potatoes into her mouth.

"Hey, a man deserves a secret or two, don't you think?" He winked as he chewed his chicken. "Have a roll." His hand gestured at the plate of rolls that Emily avoided.

"Why, so it can land on my midsection? No thank you, mister." She winked back at him.

"You'll be fine. I don't know why some women think they will grow girth overnight before having the chance to work it off at the gym."

The dinner party had almost slipped her mind. Now was the perfect time to bring that up. "Hey, speaking of women, remember my newfound pack of friends?" He shrugged and nodded loosely. "Well, the two in addition to Brooke—anyway, I would like to have a get-together here at our house on Friday night. We're bringing the men in our lives. You interested?" Her expression proved that she couldn't contain her excitement.

"If it makes you this happy, then why not?" Obviously, he was genuinely okay with the idea of meeting her friends. "It will actually be great meeting the two ladies for the first time."

S*ummer*

I sat in the passenger side of Fran's car as we rode the last mile to her home. The ride wasn't as awkward as I'd anticipated, but I did wish that I didn't have to endure it. Fran allowed me to leave work early to collect my few belongings from Amber's. When I arrived at Amber's apartment, she had been worn out. I made sure to keep the visit swift, since I had to take the Metro back to work and meet Fran on time, or at least before the close of business. Despite my time crunch, I did happen to notice the puffy appearance of Amber's eyes. Her quiet demeanor made it apparent that she didn't want to talk about it. I deeply expressed my gratitude to her as we parted domestic ways.

Quiet and deep in thought, I was appreciative of the fact that somehow, we managed to dodge any uncomfortable subjects while we focused on work-related topics. Fran carried on about Lora, my former roommate.

"That Lora is doing such a fantastic job. I tell you, if it weren't for you and her, I would be ripping my hair out every night."

"Thank you, Fran."

"Now, before I forget, I would like to remind you of a few things. Ruben will be away until tomorrow night so it will be just me and you tonight. Secondly, I'll give you a spare key to my house so you can come and go as you like just as long as you get to work on time and don't disturb my beauty rest. Thirdly, you will have the key to our spare car, as stated earlier. Once you leave we will need all keys back. Is that all understood?"

I faced Fran as we pulled into her driveway and then waited for the garage door to lift. "Fran, your generosity is above and beyond. Thank you. You will barely notice me." This woman took my guilt to new heights with every word. How was I going to stand this?

"Just follow the rules, and you'll be okay," she replied in a singing tone. I smirked.

We parked and climbed out of the car. She popped the trunk to her Volvo so I could retrieve my laundry bag. How embarrassing, living out of a laundry bag. Well I guess this was why people say be careful how you treat others, because you never know when you may need them. Gee, not only had I learned that lesson, but it really sucked to live with it. I didn't even know how this would all play out. It worried me that I could move up in my career at DuBois Staffing just to have it all taken away if the truth escaped somehow. Shaking my head, I decided not to worry about it for now.

I couldn't help but think back to Fran's words. *"Just follow the rules, and you'll be okay."* Boy, she had no idea that I'd already broken a major one. We reached her kitchen via the door from the garage. Her home smelled of a peach-floral scent. Fran placed her keys on the key rack and said, "Follow me."

Parts of her home rang familiar, and that included the kitchen, of course. As we passed through, pictures of the night that Ruben ravished my body in less than five minutes relentlessly flashed in my head. My cheeks burned with embarrassment. When we passed the kitchen, I spotted the powder room adjacent to it. We had sex against that wall. So, the kitchen and the wall would be sweet and sore spots.

Fran led me up the stairs that curved to the right and when she hit the landing, she turned and pointed to the first door facing the staircase. "This is Ruben's and my bedroom."

"Oh, okay."

She continued to walk as she led me down a narrow hallway to a door on the opposite side of her bedroom. Fran turned to face me as she placed an aged hand on the doorknob. Smiling, she said, "And this will be your bedroom, dear."

The door opened to reveal a queen-sized bed in the middle of the room with a floral comforter on top and a boring wooden headboard. Yuck. Oh, no. Nightstands sat on either side of the bed, and a brown armoire rested against a wall. Oh, God, please let my home be ready soon. Home. It sounded so bittersweet. I kept my sigh in my head as I berated myself for not being grateful for escaping Amber's couch.

Fran turned around abruptly, catching me off-guard. "So, what do you think?" she asked with clasped hands.

"Fran, this is a very pretty room. Who decorated this?" I asked with disingenuous interest.

"Well—me." Fran felt so proud to claim this wreck. Poor Ruben, I lamented. These two were like night and day.

"Well," my head nodded, "you did a great job."

"That pleases me, Summer. Are you hungry?"

"Yes." My stomach started to feel like stretching insides.

"Do you like pizza? If you don't, you are welcome to raid my fridge for something palatable."

"No, pizza sounds great."

"Good. Get settled in. Take a shower, if you like. Your bathroom is that door right there." Her bony finger pointed at the door in the corner next to the armoire.

"Awesome." I really meant that. Not going out into the hallway allowed for more privacy and a chance to avoid Ruben.

"Toppings?"

"Huh?" It took me a second to remember the pizza. "Oh, yes, the toppings. I really like anything Fran. There is not one pizza out there that I don't think I dislike. Seriously," I held a palm in the air. "You can feed me rabbit stew tonight. I'm just so grateful to have a nice home to place my tired little head. So, thanks again, Fran."

Fran approached me with open arms. Her skinny arms embraced me with the strength of a bodybuilder. When we pulled apart, she ran a hand over my hair as she looked at me with shining eyes. Fran disappeared from my room, and I locked the door behind me and peeled out of my clothes.

I entered my small, naked frame one foot at a time into the tub once the faucet released warm water. The smell of coconut in my hair sang through my nostrils as the steam relinquished its scent. Good shampoo choice, Amber. Immediately, I remembered that calling her should be my next priority before the pizza arrived.

Luckily, I brought my sweat pants and a t-shirt, so I donned them once I dried off. Crisscrossed on the bed, I pulled out my cell phone as a cry of horror escaped my lips. "My cell phone charger," I growled in a loud whisper. I threw my head back in disbelief and squeezed my temples. Dropping my head back to its normal position and examining my cell phone, my eyes darted quickly to the battery. Apparently, I had a seventy-five percent charge left, so that relieved me a bit. It would be better news if Fran told me she had a compatible charger.

I had to decide who to call first: Oliver or Amber. Amber won, because Oliver wasn't my man. Besides, I knew she needed me more than him. After locating her name in the call log, I pressed her name and waited for her to pick up.

"Summer, how are you?" she asked. Her voice sounded rough—not at all pleasant like usual.

"Fran is taking great care of me. I don't have my battery charger, so this has to be quick. Did you have a better day today, sweetie?"

"No, the worst." Remembering the coconut lotion and finding it in the laundry bag, I decided to moisturize my arms as I balanced the phone on my shoulder.

"Wanna quickly chat about it?" I felt so awful. It was so hard to hear Amber in a defeated state of mind.

"Daniel denied me when I went to see him. He pretended like we never happened."

"Oh, no."

"I simply wanted to tell him that we could be friends, you know—without the money aspect. He better not call here or else I'm going off on him."

"That puss has no clue what he's missing out on. Don't worry, Amber, really. If he acted like this now, just imagine what would be in store down the line. You really are better off without him."

"I keep telling myself that." Amber's voice sounded lifeless. "But I thought we were legit friends. Who does that? I'm done. I am so done."

"Hate to bail, boo, but I'll check back on you tomorrow? I'm sorry." I knew that my battery would be threatened by this conversation if I didn't end it right away.

"I understand. All right, girl."

"Feel better, hon. Good night." We hung up. It was time to check in on Oliver to see how he made out during his trip. I quickly tapped his name on my screen to dial his number.

"Hello?" he answered in his semi-deep voice. I loved it.

"So, you arrived in California on time?" I attempted a low and sexy tone. It just sounded obvious, so I jettisoned the idea of acting like a sex kitten. "How's California and your mother?"

"My mom is great and California is always a pleasure. What about you, Summer Stevenson? Did things work out?" His phone voice teased my senses. I could only lick my lips in response.

I told him, "I've got some bad news for you."

"Nothing sounds bad when it comes from your lips."

A chuckle squeezed from my throat as my mouth curled. "I forgot to grab my cell phone charger, so I'm on borrowed time here.

"Ah, come on, Summer. You're breaking my heart," he joked. "No. That's really a bummer."

"Now, I have some good news," I sang.

"Give it to me."

"My boss took me in until another option opens up or my place is livable. The choice is up to me, but she has been amazing."

"Yeah, that sounds good, baby."

"I have my own bathroom inside my bedroom."

"I'm glad your boss is great enough to take you under her wing until I get back. Give me your work number."

After repeating the numbers, he replied, "Now I know where to rescue my princess."

I was taken aback. Now while most girls would go crazy upon receiving such a reference, hearing him call me his princess scared me. I wasn't ready to be anyone's something. So, I panicked.

"Oliver, I have to go."

"Already?" His voice gave way to disappointment.

"My boss ordered us pizza and with the battery, too, and all . . . I should."

"Right, right." Relief swept over his tone and it eased my worry that perhaps I sounded mean.

"You can call me tomorrow at work, though. Is that good?" I tried to bargain.

"I can manage till then," he joked.

"Good night, Oliver." As if on cue, I heard the doorbell ring.

"Take care, Summer, and hopefully, tomorrow brings nothing but greatness."

"You, too." We hung up and I checked my battery signal. It had decreased mildly, which made me cringe. Anyone would die these days without a cell phone. I bit down on my nail, wondering why men had to get so attached so quickly. Society portrayed women as the needy ones. Well who were these so-called needy women? Because between Max, Oliver and Ruben, they made me want to challenge that theory. I felt just fine on my own, and I'd like to keep it that way.

Fran called my name, so I hopped out of the bed to meet her downstairs. It felt great not to worry about Ruben. Dealing with him on top of today's events would just be too much. As I inched closer to the kitchen, the smell of pepperoni drifted into my olfactory canals. Things would really be great if Fran had ordered deep-dish. My arms hugged my body as I entered the kitchen to see Fran hovering over the open pizza box. She passed me a flower-patterned plate.

"Thanks again, Fran. It smells yummy."

"One's got to eat." When I accepted the plate, Fran stopped in her tracks to inhale sharply. "Is that you smelling so good?"

Pleased that she could smell it, I replied, "It's coconut. Smells good, huh?"

Fran grabbed my wrist and inhaled. "Body mist?" she asked.

"Lotion."

She relinquished my wrist. "I could get used to that scent."

Fran and I headed to her living room to watch a DVR'd episode of an eighties gameshow. Pizza and a gameshow— what a night. I had hopes of watching a great *HBO* movie or something, but not anything like a dreadful game show. The whole setting reminded me of being trapped in a retirement home. Older woman, check. Flower-patterned dishes, check. Game show on DVR, check. Game show period, check. Nothing justified watching a game show from the eighties. But, instead of griping to myself, I decided to remind myself of the cold outside and to focus on the fact that I still had a job and a home, though it wasn't livable.

"How's that pizza?" Fran sat on her floral-patterned sofa and I on the mauve recliner. I threw her a bonus point for having a flat screen, which appeared to be over fifty-five inches versus my thirty-seven inches. No doubt Ruben chose to get that monster screen.

"Delicious." I returned her warm smile.

"Oh." Fran jumped up. She placed her plate on the end table beside the sofa. "We need something to drink." She placed a hand over her heart. "My dear, we need wine." Her eyes sparkled as I chuckled.

"Sounds good." That was the truth. Wine would be the best treat of the night. I guess I could spare Fran another point. Well, the pizza would make it the third.

Fran returned with two glasses of red wine. Passing me one, she placed her glass down and picked up her plate while positioning herself comfortably back into place. "So, is there anyone special in your life?"

Chewing, I stopped as I absorbed her spoken words. Was she serious? I bit my lower lip as the wheels in my head turned. My surprise must've been apparent, because she added, "Oh, dear, I'm sorry. Am I being nosy?"

I had to gather my thoughts. Shaking my head frantically, I replied, "No, Fran, no. It's okay." A choked laugh fled from my throat. I wiped my hand up and down my thigh nervously. I turned my eyes to hers. A look of slight horror almost consumed her face as she took note of all the nuances of my nonverbal responses.

"Yes. Well, kind of. I met him weeks ago. He's umm," I tried to think of vague information regarding Oliver that was far from Ruben's description. "He's not too tall, he's half-Hawaiian and he's gorgeous." There. That didn't give away much.

Fran tilted her head as she studied my words. "Huh. I see, Summer. Well," she lifted her glass and tilted it at me, "he sounds lovely." Her thin lips squeezed the top of the glass as she drank her wine while peering at me from above the rim.

Once she finished her swig, she placed the glass on the end table again. "Do you think it's going to go somewhere?"

Fran made me feel uncomfortable. The contestants' voices sounded like music to my ears at this point. "I don't know. I don't really—" Should I tell her my opinion of marriage or would that be overstepping? Ever since I met her husband, I'd become dishonest, so redemption had to begin at some point. "I don't really need anything more right now."

"No?" Her eyes challenged mine, or at least it felt that way. "I wouldn't want to live a life without my husband. You may wake up one day to find that you are missing something."

The problem was that I hadn't downed my wine. I grabbed the glass and tilted my head back to catch up with Fran. The wine must've been making her bold, so it was my turn to enjoy the juice.

"Okay, so you're becoming uncomfortable. We don't have to talk about it, Summer. Forget I asked."
I slightly turned to face her with a raised eyebrow. "Fran, my mother raised me on her own, and I don't have a problem with women going at it alone." I wiped the wine from my lips with my sleeve. "I care for companionship at times, because no one wants to be alone all the time."

"Just because you're alone doesn't mean you're lonely." She smiled and raised one eyebrow as she held the glass of wine on the arm of the sofa.

I shrugged. I had an empty plate and the two slices filled me, but somehow, I didn't remember eating them so fast. Without knowing what else to say, I finished my wine.

"More pizza?" she asked.

Standing, I replied, "Oh, no thank you. I'm good, Fran." I stretched. "But I think I should turn in. I can honestly say I'm exhausted."

"More wine?"

Was this lady trying to find some truth or something by drugging me up with wine? "I think my stomach will explode if I do that." I grinned and added, "Good night and thanks for everything, Fran." She started to scare me with her calm and quiet intrusion, but that's how it starts. I deposited my dishes into her sink and gave her a final wave.

"Okay, Summer. Sleep well." Fran returned my grin with a cozy and withdrawn smile as the wine took over. I, too, felt calmer, but sleep sounded like the best medicine. After climbing the staircase and reaching my room, I peeled back the layers of sheets that dressed the bed and hopped in. My head hit the fluffy pillow as I settled on my side. I rested against my pressed hands sandwiched between my pillow and face. My wild and wavy hair sprawled carelessly about my head and face. I remembered sighing before drifting fast asleep.

Brooke

The sun beam angled into Jackson's room. Brooke's hand rested on his bare chest as it lifted and fell gingerly with each breath he took. Her eyes studied his mahogany furnished bedroom before landing on his alarm clock—nine o' clock, past Jackson's wake up time.

She shook him gently as she whispered, "Jackson. Jackson? Wake up."

He grunted but didn't move. A naughty grin spread across her face. Wearing nothing but the sheets, Brooke saddled him carefully as she leaned forward with her face hovering over his. She kissed his full lips, and eased back to see a smile crack through his groggily face.

"What are you up to now, girl?" His eyes remained shut.

"At first nothing, but now your punishment for being late is to punish me." Brooke rocked rapidly on his groin to wake him up. "Come on, mister, move it. I'm horny now."

Jackson's eyes eased open. "When I first met you, you were a freaky lady. Now you're a freakier lady." He grabbed her by the hips and aligned his manhood with her womanhood. "What a way to wake me up."

"It's this freakiness that will keep you coming back."

"No, it's everything about you that will keep me with you."

Brooke smiled as she caught onto the fact that he implied that he didn't have any plans of leaving her. She decided that sometimes you have to stop thinking and just enjoy the ride.

Half an hour later, they rolled off one another and onto their backs as they struggled to catch their breath.

"You are so late, Jackson."

"I'd really like to see you lecture me while you're gasping for air."

"I'm not gasping. On a serious note, why aren't you at work today?"

Jackson turned his neck to face her. "Are you worried I'm unemployed or something?"

Brooke didn't know how to take his slight change of tone. "Umm, no." She turned on her side to face him. "You're a prompt person, that's all. I wasn't implying or worried about anything."

"Well, since you always have to know the answers to everything, I took the day off to spend some time with you. I missed you."

"Jackson." Touched, Brooke flung her hand over her heart. With normalized breathing, she told him, "That was sick leave that could've gone to something else."

"I have so much sick leave it's making me sick." He chuckled. "And I'm sorry I got pitchy with you. I just don't like being questioned."

"I'm sorry, too." Brooke was also sorry that she had to tell him that, "I have a massive wedding to plan and missing one day may throw me in the rear." She closed her eyes to avoid his stare. When he didn't say anything, she lifted one eyelid slowly to see his expression.

Jackson smiled as he stroked her shoulder-length hair. "It's okay. I didn't run it by you first. I shoulda' known, from one workaholic to another, to never surprise one." He rolled out of bed with nothing on, revealing tight buttocks. "I can just chill for the first time in a year. Let's go brush our teeth."

He started to walk but froze when Brooke said, "Hey." His eyebrows jumped in response. "I'm going to be here until noon. You took off for me, and I don't have any appointments today, just planning and phone calls. So, I should let my hair down, too, even if it's just for half a day."

Pleased, he replied with, "Mmm. Woman, do I have plans for you then."

Grinning, Brooke jumped out of the bed and grabbed her silk robe from the floor. She donned it as she followed him to his chocolate-tiled bathroom. Jackson stood in front of Brooke, tying a towel around his waist before using one of the large porcelain sinks, leaving the other one for her. Lusting after his abs, Brooke grinned to herself, happy that he belonged to her.

"What are you all smiles about over there?" he asked before poking his toothbrush into his mouth.

"Gee, I can never have a secret if you're hanging around."

Jackson winked, and Brooke decided to delay her effort to brush her teeth in exchange for hugging him from behind. Her face rested against his shoulder blades as she caressed his chest.

"Girl, stop before you make me walk away with toothpaste falling from my mouth."

She relented and headed toward the other porcelain sink. "Okay, you win."

Minutes later and almost done with brushing her teeth, Jackson snuck up from behind and released the belt to her robe, exposing her breasts and taut stomach. One big hand caressed her stomach as the other one ran between her thighs. Brooke didn't know what to do while his lips came down on her neck, massaging her skin as he kissed every nook.

"I'm brushing my teeth, silly."

"Just bend over while I take care of business back here," he instructed with a deeper voice. Jackson's hands rubbed her back, her stomach, her thighs, her neck, and her butt. Brooke capitulated and bent over as she reached for a paper cup to rinse out her mouth. She could feel Jackson, feel his motion, feel each thrust, and feel his hands run freely and wildly over any part of her body that he could reach. She turned around to face him with glistening water dripping from her lower lip and onto her chest. They stood and stared into each other's eyes, not wanting to blink for fear of missing the beauty shared between them.

Her feminine hands fell on each broad shoulder, and Jackson took her by the hips to lift her to the left side of the sink, placing her bare bottom on the cold countertop. He closed the small gap between them and reminded her why he took the day off.

Summer

I couldn't believe that Fran let me drive a red 2009 Mercedes hatchback as a spare car. Fran called it, "that raggedy thing." She preferred the Volvo because it was newer but refused to sell the Mercedes that no one drove because Ruben gave it as a gift. She insisted that he wouldn't mind me driving it, because he'd even tried to persuade her to sell it. The car drove perfectly, but because of the fall weather, I debated whether to enjoy the sunroof. I decided to peel back the roof anyway, to at least enjoy the extra light.

The make of the car, the sunroof, and a pop song on the radio, made me feel like a million bucks. The song ended, and the deejays of some station, The Kane Show, started talking about catching cheaters. Even though my heart jumped in a quick panic, I had to admit that I downright enjoyed the show that I hadn't heard of before. Wow, the things I missed out on from not having a car.

Having a break from the Metro morning rush relieved me. I warned myself not to get used to this, because managing rent and a car note would be too difficult on my salary, and if Fran were to find out about Ruben and me, then there wouldn't be a salary anyway. As quick as I became somber, I became happy again when Oliver called my cell phone, so I lowered the radio volume. Remembering the time zone difference between California and Virginia, I couldn't believe that he called me this early.

"Mr. Hollywood, isn't it quite early for you to call me? I'm flattered though."

Oliver chuckled. "Actually, I never fell asleep yet. I decided to stay up to finish this horror movie." Oliver sounded alert for someone hanging up way past midnight.

"You're bold for watching that mess so late and alone."

"It's not that bad. I don't get all scared over this Hollywood makeup mess. So, how's it going?"

"It's going quite well considering the situation. And you?"

"I'm enjoying the break from work and the cold weather. It's nice not having to bundle up for a change."

"Oh. Well, okay then. Lucky, you. Hey, Fran is letting me drive her hatchback Mercedes. It's old to her, but new to me."

"Oh, yeah? I like that. You must be happy avoiding the rush of the train ride."

"Oh, definitely. How's your mom?"

"Ma's better. We're going to go look for a house today, this evening, in fact."

"How sweet of you, Oliver, really." I could get used to hearing his voice first thing in the morning. But I wouldn't dare tell him so. I had to stop letting this man pull me in little by little. I had to.

"But I do miss you, I must say."

I let out a skittish giggle, not knowing what to say. Though okay with our space, to a certain degree, I guess I missed him. "Me, too, Oliver. I miss you, too." There, I said the words—words that I never said to a man before. It wasn't that bad, but I could live without all the mushy talk.

"I know that was a hard one for you, Summer. Hey, look. Do you need anything? I mean anything?"

"Look," I said gently. "I know what you mean by anything, but I'm okay, Oliver, I really am. I think Fran and I'll work out until the leasing office calls me with good news." I pushed wild strands of hair behind my ear.

"Summer, if you ever need me, I'm right here, though I'm really in California. Please. Don't hesitate." The humorless sound in his voice crunched down on my heart. This man cared. I wasn't used to a man who cared. Max tried to be that man, but I didn't have confidence that he could do more than for himself even after failed attempts to convince me. Speaking of Max, I still owed him a phone call.

"Oliver, I promise to holler loudly for you. Again, thanks for being there for me, buddy."

He chuckled. "Buddy, huh?"

"I think you know better. More than a buddy, but not quite there yet."

"Don't worry. No labels, I know. Okay, sweetheart, check in with me later."

"Remember, my cell phone must charge in Fran's car. Luckily, she let me use her car charger for this one. She has really been my Wonder Woman this week."

"But I can be your Superman."

With no words left to say among the awkward silence, I could only reply with an, "Okay," before we disconnected.

Emily drove to Ballston to meet me for a late lunch at Subway. She had just come from the dentist and had the whole day off and wanted to talk just because. Unbeknownst to Emily, I texted Amber so she could have a chance to join us, but she didn't respond. Guess she didn't want to be bothered yet.

My steak and cheese foot long sat in front of me as I waited for Emily. She approached me with her tray and situated herself across from me with her tuna sandwich and potato chips. She looked nice in her red pencil skirt and black-and-white-striped blouse. Looking unintentionally sexy, I surmised that Eric had a lot to do with her new glow and appeal.

Emily and I took our first bites into our sandwiches. "I'm so excited to be with my man. It was like we were never apart." For once, life finally filled her hazel eyes, but I felt a sucker punch to my stomach as I held back the information I had that could devastate her fantasy. *Why, Amber, why?*

"That's good, Emily. It's great to finally see you genuinely happy." I made sure to take a bite.

"Tell me about it." Emily picked at her food. She clearly preferred to stare off and chat about Eric. Eat, Emily, eat. Spare me.

Maybe I should change the subject. "So, you know the day when I first met you?" She nodded. "You already knew Brooke. How did you guys meet?"

Flipping her hair off her breasts, she asked, "Oh, I didn't tell you?" She took a sip of her iced tea.

I shook my head. "No."

Placing her drink down, she replied, "She planned my wedding."

Never considering that, I sat back in my chair with my hands resting on top of my crossed legs as I played with a balled-up napkin. "I never knew that."

"Well, yeah," she explained as her hands moved to pick up her sandwich. "Brooke did an excellent job. Someone referred her to me, and, boy, was she expensive but worth it. Too bad she put in all that effort for such a short wedding. Brooke and I became friends just because we connected during the whole process."

"Tell me about your wedding experience." My eyes peered into hers as I inexplicably found myself thirsty for a first-hand account of the Brooke experience.

Emily's tongue quickly fished around her mouth as she swallowed before talking. "Brooke is all about the customer service. She works to make sure the bride and groom aren't stressed during it all. She really invests in the whole experience."

"Yeah, but isn't that a wedding planner's job?" Leaning forward, I rested my elbow on the table and placed a hand under my wild hair on the nape of my neck. "What wedding planner wouldn't ensure that they are on top of everything?" Did I sound like a hater?

"Yes, it's her job. But this lady sent us out for a couple's massage the night before our reception. She spoke of how tense couples can appear on their big day. So, she treats her clients with those and a gift basket full of relaxing treats to take home." Emily's eyes rolled up as she counted on her fingers. "It came with wine, chocolate, a relaxation CD, hmm, what else? Oh, yeah. Oils. You know," she winded her hand, "stuff like that."

"Gee. That is great." My eyebrows bounced as I leaned back into my chair. "Basically, she pampers the bride and groom?"

"Man. She knows that couples may struggle to balance their time between work, sometimes kids and then meeting with her. The escape to the spa allows her clients to clear their minds and to take a break from the pressure and all. She started that because she said her clients tend to get snappy at her. And it's her way of thanking them for picking her."

Wide eyed, I said, "She sounds like a rock star." I sipped my soda.

"Not to mention all of the connections this lady has. She knows babysitters for couples who want to use her coupons but have children, she also has great relationships with vendors. They do last-minute jobs for her, she has deejays who may be super booked but will take on one more gig for her." Emily's hand sliced the air. "You name it. She can make it happen."

"I get it, I get it," I giggled. "She is the queen bee of wedding planning."

Emily shrugged. "I guess you could say that."

"Wow. If I ever get married in another lifetime, I would go to her."

"I mean it, Summer, if Brooke cannot marry you, you might as well elope." Emily giggled. Turning serious she said, "Hey, I understand that you are homeless now, as you put it. Why didn't you come stay with Eric and me? We have four other rooms, *chica*."

"You can't do that to a couple who's missed out on so much." A partial lie? Yes. But only because of the secret I held onto. Damn that whore. Although I loved her, she really did make my friendship uncomfortable right now.

Emily shrugged as she sipped. "You may have a point, but a friend in need—"

"Is a pest," I interrupted.

Emily's shoulders collapsed, her head tilted at me in disappointment. "No. You guys put up with all my sulking all this time, so, if you need money, space, time, help, whatever, just call me, and I'll be happy to oblige."

I pouted at her. "Awww. I love you, Emily." I could say these things to my friends, but not to men. Either that was safe and smart, or wrong of me when I knew that the man who expressed interest in me wanted to test the waters of professing feelings.

"I love you too, girl." She gazed at me with a smile and we resumed wolfing down our sandwiches. I was glad to have had private time with Emily.

Amber

A knock at the door made Amber jump. Struggling to her feet and wiping her face with a hand, she woke from the nap she'd taken after teaching her last piano lesson. Wearing nothing but underwear, Amber searched her living room to locate her favorite silk robe draped over the arm of the sofa. Amber picked it up, donned it, and tightened it as she approached the door. The person at the door knocked again.

"Coming, I'm coming." Her heels dragged in the bunny slippers she'd fallen asleep in. "Gee," she complained under her breath. Thanks to her height, she didn't have to peek through the hole on her toes. The person she saw on the other side of the door startled her. She couldn't believe her eyes. Amber's mouth fell open; she couldn't unchain the door fast enough because of her elation to see the outstretched arms of a curvy woman with luggage in tow waiting to embrace her.

"Mara, get in here." Amber embraced her sister as they wobbled through the door together. The heavyset woman with curly hair stepped back to take in Amber's appearance.

"You look so good, Amber."

Amber look downward to check herself out as if she needed reminding of her looks. She lifted her sister's luggage and placed them into the foyer before shutting the door.

"I don't feel so good, but you look so pretty and great, Mara." Amber grabbed her sister's hands. Their hands swung as they exchanged comments.

"And you look so thin and beautiful as always."

"Well weren't you always the smart one who never failed to make Mom and Dad proud? And now me." Amber brushed her sister's light-colored skin with the back of her hand. "Your timing couldn't be better. Really stoked, you know? Come sit."

Leading her sister by the hand, they sat down with their knees pointing toward one another. "I'm glad that you're proud of me and that you think Mommy and Daddy were, too."

"Well they were," Amber replied with all certainty.

"How are you, Sis? I've been so worried about you." Amber noticed the crinkles in her sister's forehead.

Amber hesitated and exhaled, "Pshh, I mean I'm good. I got into a little trouble but nothing that I can't handle." Amber rubbed her knees. "Do you want something to drink sweetie?"

Ignoring her offer, Mara hastily inquired, "What kind of trouble, Amber?" Her eyes locked onto Amber's.

Reluctant to spill the truth, she knew that honesty came with turning a new leaf. No one else's opinion counted. Only Mara's opinion mattered. "You know how I slept with men for cash?" Mara nodded with an open mouth. "Well one of them—a one-night stand—was the ex-husband of one of my closest friends. I hadn't seen him before, so I couldn't of known who he was. How do you recognize a man that you never met before?"

Mara's perfect posture collapsed when she plopped her forehead into the palm of her hand. "Amber," she called with irritation. "I warned you to stop and you thought you had it all under control, just like in New York. Remember when that hood rat caught you on your knees with her man?"

It embarrassed Amber that Mara knew that. How did she know? When Amber's mouth opened, Mara could tell that Amber was oblivious to her knowledge. "Your snitch buddy, Jasmine, told me the things that you couldn't always tell me. All I had to do was ask Jasmine Josef what I needed to know and she would break."

It annoyed Amber that Jasmine shared more things than she'd realized. "Okay, first of all, Dontess, told me he was not seeing Alexis. But it's all water under the bridge at this point. I'm done with that stuff."

Mara peered at her through suspicious eyes. "Oh, come on, Amber. Why should I believe you?"

"Because I have a heart and doing that to my friend hurt me. I'm devastated."

"What did she say to you?"

"Nothing," Amber shook her head. "Because she doesn't know yet, and I'm telling her this week."

"She doesn't know? Well, what are you waiting for?"

"I had to digest this myself." Amber positioned her elbow on her leg to rest her chin in the palm of her hand. "But she's not the only reason why I'm changing, Mara."

She shrugged. "Well what else is there?"

"I was humiliated beyond belief, Sis." Amber's tone had turned dry.

"Oh, no," Mara pouted. She reached out to rub Amber's back. "What happened now?"

Amber caught Mara up to speed regarding Daniel without all the convoluted details. "He never even called me to check up on me, apologize, or even yell at me."

"I'm so sorry, Sis. I'm so, so sorry. That's too bad. People can be very fake and cruel."

"Because I snuck past security to get in, the guard met me at the lobby elevator to throw me out on my ass."

"Ouch." Mara grimaced as she folded her hands in her lap.

"I threw up outside then caught the bus. End of the story. I need to change and I'm changing. No more easy money, Mara. I'm going to be like you and make something of myself, like my friends."

"That sounds like a plan. Remember the past to avoid looking back, look to the future to see what it holds."

Amber giggled as she straightened to cross her legs. "You were always like my little fortune cookie." Mara laughed with her. "I try."

Amber placed a hand on her sister's knee. "I'm really glad that you're here, Sis. How long are you going to be here? Your presence is desperately needed."

"Until Saturday morning. I got all my assignments for the week, because I really needed to see my family. You're all that I have left. I was lonely, too." They reached to embrace each other simultaneously. "I love you, Amber. Thank God for you, no matter what you've done."

"I thank God for you, too, but not enough. I love you, Mara."

9: the price of admission

Summer

Ruben came home last night, but luckily, I didn't see him. Fran and I were already asleep, and, this morning, he was still in bed. I called the leasing office during my lunch break, and they told me that they didn't have any new information just yet, but to look out for an email or listen for a phone call.

I ate a salad before returning to my temporary home. Eating in front of a game show with my boss for a third night in the row was more than any woman in her twenties should endure. Fran seemed surprised when I told her that I'd eaten. I told her I was tired before escaping to my room to be alone. Seeing her at work and then beyond the clock had become harder than I'd imagined. I needed space, that little piece of heaven that I had when I had my apartment. Sitting on my bed with my legs crossed and back against the headboard, I could feel the tears rise to my eyelids.

I could no longer endure living out of a bag and staring at the limited amount of clothes and undergarments. I had the same pair of shoes on since Sunday. Even though I tinkered with the idea of going shopping for new clothes, I had to be careful not to waste money, especially before seeing the damage done in the apartment without renter's insurance. Why didn't I know better? I bet Brooke knew that she needed renter's insurance when she first moved out on her own. But somehow, I wasn't smart enough to know to protect my possessions.

It occurred to me that I also wasn't smart enough to protect my future. Who sleeps with their own boss' spouse? If Fran found out, my possibility of a career in DC would be over, according to Ruben. She owned a staffing firm, so I could believe it.

It also occurred to me that I really needed to return Max's phone call, and on half a battery, I could do that. While the car charger didn't generate the same power as a house charge, it still did a great job keeping my phone alive. Picking up my phone from the nightstand, I selected his name and listened to the rings.

He picked up on the third one. "Summer?"

"Max. How's it going with you? I've been meaning to call you back. Things have just been so crazy."

"Yeah? How so?"

I offered a quick brief of my situation to which he replied, "Shit, Summer. Wow. I'm sorry to hear that. Where you living?"

"At my boss' house. She's been wonderful in all ways. Enough about me, how are you doing?"

"You won't believe it, but I'm engaged. I was calling to tell you that since we've been in each other's lives for some time now. It seemed like the right thing to do."

Slapped with astonishment, I didn't know how to respond. Engaged? Hmm. Engaged? I wasn't surprised, given his neediness. But who on Earth could he have found so quickly to settle down with? I pretended to be happy for him, even though marriage couldn't compare to the single life.

"That's awesome, Max. Who's the lucky lady?" I ran a hand through my hair as I lied.

He laughed and replied, "Don't even bother trying to fake like you're happy for me. Remember when we had our last date?"

"Yeah."

"You practically choked on your broccoli when I confessed my feelings to you. You wanted to bolt right then and there."

Wincing at his words, I said, "Sorry. I mean, congratulations and all, but yeah, you know that commitment stuff is for the birds."

"Well, I'll take that, Summer, so thank you. I've known Jayne since high school."

"I know a fantastic wedding planner. She's my friend. You guys can go over fees and stuff."

"Umm, I can always take her information, but we won't have too much money. I'm not too loaded, Summer." Max laughed.

Shrugging, I replied, "You won't know unless you try. She's the best in this business." It felt weird recommending a wedding planner since I didn't have any experience with one, but at least I could help Brooke.

"Okay, I appreciate that. Do you, uh, need anything, Summer?"

I shook my head. "No, no thank you, Max. So, what does Jayne do for a living?"

"She's a librarian." I could sense his smile through the phone.

"Oh, okay, Max." I tried to sound animated. "That's great. You found a librarian, huh? Every man's fantasy," I teased.

He chuckled, "You could say that."

Clearing my throat and rising to my feet to pull the sheets down, I said, "Hey listen, Max, it was wonderful catching up, but make sure I know about the wedding date and all, you got that?"

"Definitely, Summer, definitely." As soon as we hung up, my phone rang. With Emily's name spread across the screen, I answered it.

"Emily. You miss me already?" I joked.

Laughing, she replied, "Yeah, I guess I do. No, I'm calling to ask if we can move the dinner date to Thursday night. Eric's job needs him in Las Vegas by Friday, so we're leaving Friday morning and we'll return Monday. Do you mind?"

"Oh, gee, you lucky girl, you. Yeah. We can definitely have a blast on Thursday night instead. What did the others say?"

"Yes, you are the last to know and the others are cool with that."

"Well I guess it's see you Thursday then."

"*Gracias, mujer. Hasta luego.*" I chuckled at my ability to only translate one word. I decided to give Oliver a call to tell him about the changes. He picked up.

"Dinner is Thursday night now."

He chuckled. "Hello to you, too, Summer."

Smiling from ear-to-ear, I replied, "Sorry. Hello, Oliver. Can you make that night instead of Friday?" I inhaled, waiting for his confirmation.

"I can, though I'll be returning that afternoon," he laughed. "I can. Let me call you back, Summer. My mom and I are talking with the realtor. When should I give you a ring?"

"It's way too early to talk proposals, don't you think?" I teased. I wormed my body underneath the covers to get cozy.

Oliver found my remark hilarious. "Summer, Summer, Summer, you are a mess indeed. You keep me feeling young. Yes, it's too early."

"Okay, so since we agree on something, call me anytime. But for now, I'm going to sleep. I had a tiresome day, so happy house hunting and good luck with that, sir."

"Good early night, Summer."

I placed my phone on the nightstand and closed my eyes. Oliver didn't know that aside from tiredness, I needed to avoid Ruben. Yes, I was very tired indeed, and sad to be without my belongings, and afraid of being homeless indefinitely, but I feared what seeing Ruben may do to me, and what it would do to Fran in the long run.

Brooke

Staring out of the window to take in the scenic view of the National Harbor Marina, Brooke hugged herself as she tried to ignore the questions of her future with Jackson echoing in her head. She loved him, and most importantly, he loved her back. On the other hand, the more she thought about him, the more it made her think of her mother and childhood. In some odd way, even though his love for her was romantic, it made her realize just how starved for motherly love she'd been her whole life. Brooke's thoughts were interrupted when she felt his body slam behind hers. She smiled as he wrapped his arms around her waist.

"What are you thinking about, baby?" She loved his manly voice. It was the most comforting sound she'd ever heard. His lowered face brushed against her cheeks.

"I should buy a car," she lied, although a car had been on her mind.

Jackson's head jerked back. "Oh, yeah? What made you think of that?"

"I'm a little tired of flagging down taxis. You dropped me off this afternoon just to come back to pick me up. Besides, if I were in New York, that would be okay, but a wedding planner of my caliber should be stepping out of a car, right?"

"I think a car would be nice for you. Why haven't you made that move before now?" He kissed her cheek, squeezed her tight and nibbled her neck.

Brooke placed her hands over his as they rocked from left to right. "I didn't want to spend more money than necessary. I wanted to leave my budget open for my mortgage and clothes and other necessities like health insurance and whatever else. It would just be easy to take one check and buy a car than to keep paying for it month after month."

"If you can afford to, do it." His hands went underneath her oversized angora sweater.

"The problem is I don't know what kind to get. Maybe you should help me."

Jackson removed his hands and turned her around by her shoulders. He stroked her strands as they talked. "What's your style: trucks, cars, sports car, vans, or motorcycles?"

"No." Brooke's eyes enlarged. "No vans or motorcycles. One is for families with children and the other freaks me out."

"One day you may need that minivan, but for now, you need something that goes with your look. You need feminine and eloquence."

Brooke didn't want to tell him that when they were married with children, that a van would still be unforgivable, not to mention unfashionable. "Cars feel like a waste of money. I'm not a big car chick. I like keeping my money for more important things. Maybe I should move to New York," she suggested as she pouted. "Then I wouldn't need a stupid vehicle."

"Oh, come on now. You should be driving yourself by now. Do you even have a license?"

Brooke gave him the side eye before smacking his chest playfully. "Of course, I do." She pointed a finger at him. "But I hope it hasn't expired by now though."

He rolled his eyes heavenward. "Good Lord, Brooke. Tell you what. Look at some crossovers and go from there."

"What, what are those?"

"Goodness . . ." He placed his fingers next to his eyes and stared at his floor. Looking back up at her with a grin, he shook his head and answered, "A hybrid of a car and an SUV."

Stepping back, she snapped a finger and pointed it in his direction. "Pfft. That's silly. Why not get a car or an SUV?" She turned to the side as she lent consideration to the idea.

"Brooke?" he cried with a smile.

"Right. Forget that I asked. Well, I can start from there. A car or an SUV." Brooke pivoted to face him. "But will you help me go car shopping?"

He nodded once. "I will."

"Good." Brooke closed the gap between them and leapt on him, wrapping both legs around his waist with her ankles tied behind his back. He smacked her bottom with both hands. "Let's have sex, sexy and give choking a shot."

"Excuse me?" His mouth didn't spread with satisfaction, so Brooke considered that a rejection.

"No?"

He eased her down. "Why?" He shook his head, walking away to the kitchen with a hand cutting the air. "No. No, no, no, no, no."

"Oh, come on. It'll be—fun," she replied, following him.

Spinning to face her, he asked, "What . . . where do you get these ideas from? Do you think I would wanna put my hands around your neck like that?"

Appearing upset, Brooke tried to conceal her regret and embarrassment. "Fine. I mean, I didn't really mean it. Forget it."

Biting down on his tucked in lips, it was clear that Jackson didn't believe her. "Hey. We can do things but I ain't tryna hurt my queen. That's my limit. No choking, Brooke. Nah."

There was no way that Brooke would compromise her relationship for a sexual experience. Instead, she relented with, "No, baby. I don't wanna do anything that will make you uncomfortable. It's just that, I trust you and I like having bedroom fun with you. I wanna try everything with you."

With a firm expression, he told her, "No choking, no threesomes."

"Well, hold up. I hadn't planned on sharing you. No way. Not my style."

His face loosened up with a smile. "Glad we got that cleared up. But bedroom fun? We can do that."

"Do you know why I trust you?"

"Tell me."

Brooke looked upward and then back to him. It was time to be completely honest with him. Hesitating she told him, "Because I gave my virginity to you."

Flabbergasted, his widened eyes froze. "You what?"

Silenced, Brooke bit her lower lip, realizing that she may've made him upset. "You were the only one to make it that far with me. That's how special you are to me."

"Are you freakin' for real? And you didn't bother to tell me?"

"Number one," she picked up her stare, "I didn't want you to make a big deal of it or freak out about it. I was sick of being one. Number two, at my age it's embarrassing. Why do you think I wanted to be spanked? I didn't wanna feel like a scared woman during her first time. When you spanked me, I felt like a woman in charge, someone with experience."

"Whoa," he scoffed. He shot a thumb over his shoulder. "Do your friends know?"

"No. Only you know."

"Good. At least I'm first to know." Closing in on the space between them, he said, "Brooke, virginity is beautiful. Not everyone can hang on to that." Reaching to lift her up, he situated her onto his concrete countertop, stripping her of her sweater and removing her boots. "I'm honored that you chose me to get the job done." His grin widened. "Hey. Only Jackson's been up in there."

"Yup. All yours, baby." She unfastened her bra, and he wiggled her out of her leggings and underwear. With Brooke on the countertop naked, he removed his shirt, never breaking eye contact with her. He closed in on Brooke and she walled him in with her arms. Jackson grabbed her face with his hands, peering into her eyes, licking her lips and moving toward her breasts. As he took one into his mouth, Brooke called out in pleasure with each nipple bite.

Jackson picked her up, allowing her to straddle him once more while supporting her weight and walking toward his dining room table. He extended one long arm to blindly remove one chair from the table as he ravished Brooke's mouth with his. He placed her on the end of his contemporary mahogany table and stood in the place of the chair. Brooke looked up at him, waiting anxiously for him to carry on. He leaned forward as he placed both fisted hands on either side of Brooke.

He stared directly into her brown eyes. Speaking intently in a factual tone, Jackson said, "I'm going to eat you for dinner." Dropping to his knees, he rested each of Brooke's legs on his shoulders. That night, Brooke was on the menu.

Summer

Thursday evening, I found myself in my temporary bedroom, heavily excited and feeling beautiful. I decided to splurge on a dress for tonight, because I really didn't have much choice, nor did I want Oliver to offer me any financial assistance. I never had financial help outside of student loans for school, and since I had a job, I refused to start now.

I had successfully managed to avoid Ruben this whole week, and that really made me want to celebrate tonight. He usual came home very late and supposedly, because of heavy office work, according to Fran. I really didn't care if he ran around town poking random women, as long as he stayed away from me.

It felt like the prom night that I'd missed. I kept turning to study my reflection from different angles in the full-length mirror. I swept my hair to the side into a loose braid, which happened to look good with my white, ruffled-bottom cocktail dress. It stopped inches above my knees, and I felt flirty. Splurging on shoes as well, I slipped my foot into my red satin, peep-toe pump and shook it in front of me. I grabbed my new white purse that had to come home with me when I saw it on the purse rack on sale. Regardless of the last-minute splurge, spending two hundred fifty dollars for three key pieces made me feel like I'd gotten away with a crime. I heard the doorbell ring.

Oliver.

Giving myself the once-over in the mirror, I second-guessed every fashion decision made down to my red lipstick until I heard Fran call, "Summer, you have company."

I emerged from the bedroom to see Ruben standing in the hallway. I froze outside of the bedroom doorway as our eyes locked. He stood with his hands in his pockets as he clenched his jaw. Uneasily, I murmured a quick, "Hi," noticing that he didn't say anything in return. Brushing past him, I eased down the stairs as my eyes studied Oliver's grin and attire. He wore a slim-fit suit and from here, I noticed his defined physique. Was this enough to make Ruben realize that I had moved on?

Fran watched me descend her curved staircase as I took the last few steps before hitting the foyer. She reacted with a pleased and surprised expression to my outfit. The moment made me feel like Cinderella, and Ruben could play one of the jealous stepsisters.

"My, oh, my." Fran held a hand against her mouth as she stared at me with raised eyebrows. "Where are you going, pretty lady?"

"You look so beautiful, Summer," Oliver added, slipping his hand into mine.

"Thank you, sir. You look very handsome yourself," I replied before turning my attention to Fran. "We have a dinner party." My uncontrollable smile struggled to hide the fact that I wanted to have my way with Oliver. "Fran, this is my friend and date tonight, Oliver Hunter." My hand gestured toward Fran. "And Oliver, this is Fran DuBois-Sotolongo."

Saying her last name made me think of Ruben, so to keep from being rude, I decided to gesture toward Ruben to say, "And—" However, when I peered back up toward the stair rails overlooking the steps and foyer, he'd disappeared. Oliver and Fran didn't even notice my attempt to introduce Ruben. They'd moved on to discussing Oliver's suit.

"Burberry," he told her.

"A man with great fashion." She eyed me with all teeth exposed. "An important factor." Fran clapped her hands in front of her and rested them against her thighs. "Well, kids, you two have fun, and I'll leave the top lock off for you if you just put it on upon your return."

"I'll do that Fran," I replied as I kissed her goodbye on the cheek. We headed out toward the street as she called out for us to have fun.

We waved back before Oliver helped me into his car. Oh, how I'd missed the Corvette. I watched the driver's side, waiting for him to slip in. When he did, I leaned toward him to take his face into my palm. We kissed passionately.

When we withdrew, he told me, "I really missed those lips, Summer Stevenson."

"Oliver Hunter, I missed your car and your lips."

Grinning, he readjusted his rearview mirror. "Why did you miss my car?" His engine purred and growled at the same time upon starting it. I tittered before I could reply.

My finger rested on my bottom lip as I struggled to tell him. Peeking his way, I admitted, "Because being in your car reminds me of how great it feels to be around you."

"I'm touched, baby, I really am." He squeezed my hand. "Was that so hard to say?" He narrowed his eyes at me and then quickly added, "No, no, baby, don't worry. I know it was." We chuckled at his words, because he knew me so well already.

"I'm trying, I'm trying." I reached into my purse to hand him Emily's address. "This is where we need to go." He took it and punched the information into his GPS and then placed the car into gear before shooting off.

"Why is that so hard for you? You're so different from the average woman, you know that, right?" He ripped through his gears without breaking his focus on the road.

"I don't know. I mean, I told you I've never really been in a relationship. I feel claustrophobic; I don't think I'll like them."

"Have you ever tried one?"

"Kind of, but as me and the guy got close, I panicked, as I always do. And our schedules . . . You know, I can't do affectionate nicknames and all of those communicating things like checking in and whatnot."

Chuckling, he replied, "You called me with no problem the minute your apartment flooded. You tell me how your day goes. I don't see the harm or stuffiness in that. And I didn't ask you to do those things."

"Well, with the right guy, I could possibly change."

"I'll keep that in mind."

I found it more soothing to face the window to take in the sights instead of engaging in the same topic. It all almost began to feel like a therapist's office. I didn't know what he expected me to say. He may not prefer to know that my personality and idiosyncrasies were fine with me. At the risk of opening that topic up again, I decided to keep that tidbit to myself.

"How was your trip? You never told me."

"Oh, right, the trip. Thank you for asking. It was great. We found a house in Ventura, actually, and made an offer we're waiting on."

"That's great, Oliver. How happy did you make your mom?"

"She went through the roof. She loved the kitchen, and it's got three bedrooms and two-and-a-half baths. We agreed that I'll pay the monthly note and she can pay me whatever she can per month, no biggie. She just felt better knowing that I would accept something from her. I didn't care though."

Turning to face him, I replied, "You really are amazing for doing that for your mother, you know." He squeezed my knee in reply.

We arrived in Northeast as the GPS guided us toward the final street. "Take a left on Sixth Street. Your destination will be on your left," the computer informed us.

"I see she lives on Capitol Hill."

"I guess so. This is my first time coming here. We never really made it to each other's houses. Strange, huh?"

"Mmm, I guess not," he replied as he parallel parked. "People get busy with work and all."

"I've been to Brooke's and Amber's, and now Emily's, but I'm the only one who has seen each friend's home. I guess I'm special," I teased.

"Either that or your friends may be lazy after all," he replied as he focused through his rearview mirror. "Wait."

After he came to my side to assist me out of his car, we headed toward the narrow, brick house. Though I counted four stories, it appeared tiny.

"This house is small. Don't you think?" I asked.

With his hand on my lower back, he just turned at me and replied, "Are you kidding me?"

"What?"

Oliver shook his head. "Goodness, Summer, you think row houses are small? I bet once you see the inside of that sucker, you'll be shocked."

"Well, I mean the outside looks tiny, that's all."

"Watch your step," he cautioned as we inched closer to her home. Our parking space wasn't exactly in front of her house, but we were lucky enough to find one about six houses down. He gripped his hand gingerly around my elbow since I wore heels on the cracked and uneven concrete.

"Well, how much do you think it costs?"

"This home?" Once I nodded, he replied, "Easily over a million. A lot of these start at two. And I bet you the inside is gorgeous. Summer, we have to teach you about real estate."

"What?" I replied more from innocence than as a question. He was right. Not having a lot of money shielded me from the finer things in life. I lived in DC and didn't know a thing about rental insurance or row houses. I shook my head at my own ignorance. We arrived at the door and barely after the first ring of the bell, it flung open.

Emily greeted us in her chiffon lace cocktail dress. She had her usual high ponytail pinned down into a fancy design. Full of humor, Emily placed a hand on my arm and said, "Uh-oh. Two new hairstyles in one week, girl? You're killing me," before kissing my cheek. "Glad you made it, come on in. You look so freaking gorgeous, Summer."

With my head tilted, I replied, "Aww, thank you. You, too, Emily." I introduced her to Oliver and him to her. She welcomed us and guided us back to the dining room.

Taking mental notes of her home as we followed her, Oliver nudged me and leaned in to ask quietly, "Wasn't I right?"

Grinning, I nodded and decided that maybe I should order a side of crow with rolls tonight inside my friend's elegant home. The home elevated by crown molding along the unblemished ceilings stood opposite to the dark and narrow wood-plank flooring that encouraged visitors to think twice about proceeding with shoes. I got it. Emily graded her papers at night in a structure that easily cost more than any Ivy League law student's tuition. So, when people say don't judge a book by its cover, houses were included.

I took a quick inventory of everyone in the room—everyone but the missing Amber—while Emily linked arms with a handsome man in a suit with a chiseled jawbone and salt and pepper hair. Her hand motioned toward him. "Summer and Oliver, meet Eric Gray." Eric came forward from the other side of the table to shake our hands. I fought my flinch as his overpowering grip squeezed my hand effortlessly like wringing a washcloth of excess water. His real estate smile and baby blues assured me that he meant no harm.

"Welcome, Summer, it's a pleasure to finally meet you after hearing so many wonderful things about you."

"Emily speaks so highly of you." Our introduction balanced on a fine rope of trite and polite, humored by the visual of the rehearsed little school child meeting her teacher for the first time, initiated by Mommy.

"Oh, great." He turned to Oliver and greeted him as well. Brooke and Jackson stood up from their places at the table to do the same.

As usual, Brooke looked stunning, showing off her legs in a champagne-colored, sequined cocktail dress with hair that fell in waves. We exchanged compliments and kisses on the cheek before we introduced our men to one another. Jackson wore a suit jacket that failed to hide his muscles. Wow. Brooke had a very good-looking man indeed with long lashes and a well-trimmed goatee. People often say that no one is born lucky, but Brooke made me want to challenge that theory. He shook my hand and then Oliver's, but at least he didn't try to break it like Eric.

The doorbell rang.

An already standing Emily jumped with excitement. "That must be Amber." My eyes carefully gazed over a table placed against the wall, taking in the feast that lay before us. The catered Thai food smelled heavenly. Different dishes stretched from one end to the other. The perfectly set dining room table included three different bottles of wine. A champagne ice bucket balanced on a stand next to the table. So far, I'd seen three different men come in and out of the kitchen to add, adjust, and remove things from the feast table and the dining room.

"Amberrrrrrr," Brooke called upon seeing her.

I turned to see a shy-looking Amber on the outside, but on the inside I knew she had to be uncomfortable given her secret. Amber looked contrary to her norm—classy and conservative in her blue cocktail dress. Regardless of how classy she looked, my stomach dropped, even though I knew that she'd probably come. How were we supposed to eat with Eric in the room with the knowledge that we had? I knew Eric would be thrown for a loop. Perhaps though, she had the wrong Eric, and she'd met another Eric with an eagle tattoo on his back. I may have been kidding myself, but I needed one last moment of hope. Eric's expression and reaction would tell me all that I needed to know.

Amber stood there with another woman. The other woman wore a big, inviting smile and appeared more alive than Amber. They moved in closer to us after Brooke embraced Amber with a hug and the other woman with a handshake. Amber could barely crack a smile as she dully introduced them. I made my way toward my friend to hug her. When I pulled back, I gave her a look that communicated what we secretly knew. It hurt me that Amber would rather sit down and dine with Emily and Eric first, before telling them the truth. I just hoped that she had the right place and time in mind at the time of confession. The woman accepted my handshake, and she introduced herself as Mara, her sister.

When Amber stepped forward, Emily took it upon herself to introduce all the men. She introduced Eric last. When they had a better view of one another, her eyes nervously ping-ponged between his eyes and the floor while Eric's jaw clenched tight and his stare hardened like a hunter fixated on a deer in the woods. Coming across as distant, he slid his hands in his pants. When he realized that his distance was coming across as rude, he reluctantly stepped forward to greet her with a handshake. No one else appeared to have picked up on the abrasive vibe, and certainly not Emily. She was just so happy to have everyone under the same roof.

I watched as Eric barely gripped her hand. Others were busy chatting, but not me. My eyes studied their encounter. He grinned at Mara insincerely. When he walked away, they walked over to join Oliver and me. Emily announced our time to sit as she and Eric took to the ends of the table while the rest of us sat in the surrounding chairs.

Oliver and I sat across from Brooke and Jackson, Mara sat next to me and Amber sat next to Brooke. With Emily and Amber joined at the corner, perhaps that would be best to keep her far away from Eric. I stole multiple furtive glances at him. He seemed so nervous and uneasy, but as a business man, surely, he had practice wearing poker faces. I had the feeling that if she hadn't shown up, he would be very talkative. Barely looking up, he kept his mouth consumed with food. Emily spearheaded the conversations.

"So, what's everyone got planned for Thanksgiving?"

Brooke responded first. "I would love for us to get together again. I mean, you guys know I don't have any family."

Emily sounded so eager, but the skin on Eric's stoic face went from peach to white. "That sounds so good," she agreed excitedly. "Eric, honey, what do you think?"

His eyes flickered between his spring roll and Emily's face. "Honey, I may have some special plans for us on that holiday. Maybe Christmas, huh?" Eric did his best to appear natural with a wan smile.

Liar. Christmas bought him time. Emily probably wouldn't back off, so I decided to jump in.

"I have no clue what I'm doing. Maybe Oliver and I could fly our mothers here—or mine can at least drive since she's only about two hours away."

"That sounds good, Summer," Oliver agreed. I squeezed his thigh with a grin. I realized how solid that sounded, like we were a couple. No wonder he went along with it so pleasingly. I, on the other hand, froze for a second with scared telling eyes that hit my plate. Whoa. I just did that. *Get yourself together, we have a real crisis at hand.*

Jackson cleared his throat. "Usually I go to Chicago since my family is there. Maybe I'll take Brooke." He winked at her and she flashed her teeth at him.

Mara added, "Well, I know I'll be at school, but I would love to be with my sister."

Amber smiled at her and took a bite of food to avoid talking. Emily placed a hand on Amber's. "Are you okay?" she whispered.

Amber nodded, "I'm just so tired that's all."

"What? You, tired?" Emily chuckled and pointed at her friend. "This girl says she's tired. I know no one else with energy like hers. She keeps going and going and going . . ." Emily laughed. "This is my human Energizer Bunny." Brooke joined her in laughter. Amber bit her lip, so I overcompensated in an effort to steal the spotlight from her.

I joined Emily and Brooke with a slap on the table, gaping with forced laughter. Suddenly, my chuckling friends calmed and everyone threw quick, casual glances at me, trying to hide their uneasiness. I quickly turned to Oliver and with pinched brows. I goofily asked, "A bit much?"

With no hesitation and slight embarrassment, he answered, "Yeah," as he shuffled food with his fork.

Awkwardly, I said, "Ah, 'kay." I sighed.

Mara snickered.

Desperately hoping to move on from my weird moment, I decided to change the subject. "So, Brooke," I started. She looked up at me. "Emily just confessed to me that you were her wedding planner. You guys never said anything about that before." Should I have brought up any marital talk of Emily and Eric knowing what went down between our friend and him? Grr. I was bombing badly here.

She placed a hand over her heart as she tilted her head. "I didn't, did I? I apologize, but, yes, I did plan her wedding. I'll always remember how serious and almost quiet Eric was." He jerked his head up at the mention of his name. "He just sat back and let Emily do what made her happy."

Eric said, "You know you are right. I was so busy with work that I let Emily do everything. I had to wrap up so many projects before our honeymoon. Emily was glad but brokenhearted while I was pushed to the background." His face eased up a little from the tension of Amber's presence. "Brides like being in charge for that special day, but then there were moments that she felt like she was marrying herself. I felt bad, you know. It was stressful but Brooke gave us those massages and boy did I love her for that." We all laughed with him. Amber looked at Brooke and smiled. I could see that she was pushing herself to let go some.

"I could see how that would be exciting for a bride to plan with almost total free reign but lonely at the same time," Mara commented.

Emily said, "You're right about that. But it wasn't as bad as Eric says. He actually showed up more than I thought he would."

Oliver asked, "How long have you guys had this beautiful house?"

"It was mine, but I gave it to her in the divorce. I didn't think she should move back out again after uprooting from her place. But together, we've had it for under a year. I'm going to be officially moving back in since we're going to take another stab at a relationship."

Brooke said, "I was so happy when Emily told us you had reconnected. I'm very happy for you two."

Emily just smiled as Eric nodded. "Thank you, Brooke. I never got to tell you just how impressed I was with our wedding. I'm not into all of those details and things, but you really earned that check." Eric tugged at his lapels as a huge grin spread across his face. "And let me tell you that it was a huge check." Everyone laughed.

Batting her lashes dramatically with pride, she told him, "Thank yooooooou. Told cha' I was worth it." Jackson gave her a one-armed side squeeze. I peeked at Amber to see her squirm.

Eric suddenly asked, "So, Brooke, will you be planning your own wedding soon or would you rather let someone else do it?"

She took a swig of wine. Obviously, she didn't feel comfortable with his question. "Oh, no. Whenever it happens, no one will be planning my wedding but me. I'm way too controlling to trust anyone for my big day."

The room grew silent. Since the corner of the table separated Eric and Oliver, Eric asked, "So, what do you do for a living?"

Oliver mentioned his business, but I tuned out the chatting voices at the table. Eric then turned to Jackson to ask him the same thing. I heard voices but couldn't focus on the words as I grew increasingly concerned for Amber. Emily, Brooke, and Mara tried to engage her in a conversation, but she just stabbed at her food, took bites, and then sipped a lot of wine. And I noticed that the more wine everyone had, the more talkative they became, except for Amber. Every sip pulled Amber into a quiet black hole.

Laughter spread around the table through the night. Conversations went from jobs, promotions, handling responsibility upon graduating from college, to love. Suddenly, Eric asked Brooke and Jackson, "So, do you two want to have children if you get married?"

They both became silent, but Brooke smiled and said, "Having children doesn't bother me none." She poked around at her food as she looked to Jackson to reply.

He shrugged and replied, "Brooke and I'll have to discuss everything when we get a chance to sit down. I know that I love her very much." He laced his fingers into each other above his plate.

Oliver said, "Awww, that's cute."

Eric nodded and then he peered at me and Oliver. "You guys?"

With a blushing grin, Emily warned, "*Eric*?"

"What? I just want to get to know them," he told her innocently with shrugged shoulders.

Words failed to come out of my mouth. I felt like stabbing him with my fork. My heart started to race like a track star at the Olympics. I couldn't stop shifting in my chair. Luckily, Oliver knew my reluctance to dwell on such subjects, so I left the opportunity for him to reply on our behalf. Besides, I had already shoved wine and rice in my mouth to avoid speaking right away.

A suave Oliver handled it like a champ. "Who knows what the future holds, but you know circumstances determine a lot of decisions at the time that they must be made."

Eric held a glass of wine in his hand as he listened. "True. I guess saying yay or nay is not always so cut and dried until one is faced with that possibility." He paused. "But I would love to have children with Emily one day." His wink broke the stare between the two.

Oh, my, gosh, could they just kill the topic or at least leave Oliver and me out of it? Watching poor Amber listen to everything as she pretended to be too focused on her food had reached a point of inhumanity. I still couldn't figure out why she didn't decide to tell Emily before this night.

As the minutes passed, Oliver decided to ask Jackson about his residence. "So, do you like living at the National Harbor?"

Jackson's face lit up. "Yeah, bruh. Brooke loves coming to my house, just so she can stare out at the marina. It's so quiet over there, and the scenery at night makes waking up early every morning to make the money to keep paying for it worth it."

Eric replied, "But that MGM that they're building is about to create a lot of noise and traffic."

"Oh, I can't wait man. I'm gonna have so much fun over there with Brooke." Her eyes glowed.

Eric suggested, "Well, maybe we can go hit up a table game. I love those."

Jackson agreed. "Yeah, man. I'm down."

I couldn't believe his nerve to bring up a casino when he met Amber there. As he chatted with Jackson about it, I watched Amber rub the back of her neck as Emily and Mara chatted away. Brooke was too caught up in the conversation between Eric and Jackson to notice her, but I sipped and studied above the rim of my flute.

Eric rubbed his hands together. "Yes, working is a must if you want to live the good life. You know that well, huh, Oliver and Brooke? I mean, you two are very reliant on your personal efforts, and I find that beyond remarkable."

They agreed vehemently. Brooke sighed, "A vacation becomes a dream." Oliver cackled at her comment.

"Tell me about it. Your dreams of escaping become a vacation. It's a mess and a big sacrifice. But you know . . ."

he stared blankly at his glass before looking up at Brooke. "I couldn't have it any other way."

"That's right," Brooke agreed.

"Being self-sufficient is the biggest gift you can give yourself."

Brooke reached across the table to high-five him. Jackson pointed his head at Brooke. "Why do you think I love her? I don't have to pay for her sense of fashion." Everyone laughed, and Brooke delivered a punch to his arm. Amber managed a giggle as she quickly glanced in Brooke and Jackson's direction. She carefully avoided Eric's eyes. I could see that Hester Prynne must've been dying to rip the secret off that she wore on her chest, given the fact that her nerves overtook any ability to maintain a decent amount of composure. I really didn't envy her at all.

Emily added, "You know my dad became a real estate king from property investments and all that stuff. So, yes, Brooke and Oliver, you two are really doing the right thing, you know, with going at this career thing with your own independence and motivation."

Amber said, "I didn't know that, Emily."

"Yeah," she said, nodding. "He even owns some houses here in DC and in Virginia."

"That's what I'm talking about," Oliver said. "I love real estate."

"Do you?" Emily asked. "You should call my dad for advice, Oliver. He really made a killing over the years."

Oliver raised a glass at her before taking a sip. "So, it appears I know where to turn if I need something."

Amber managed to ask, "Speaking of property, Summer," I turned to look at her. "How's your apartment?"

With a nervous grin, I replied, "Well, I get to go there this weekend to get some valuables, but they gave me an unfortunate heads-up that my apartment suffered some significant damage. Without renter's insurance, I'm really in a rut."

Eric winced as he faced me. "Oooh, no renter's insurance?"

I gave him an expression that read, "Yeah, I know," but said nothing.

He reached over to pat my hand that rested on the table. "Let me or Emily know if you need anything."

Emily chimed, "Yes, please do, Summer. We're here for whatever that help may be."

"You guys are sweet. Thank you." My eyes danced between Emily's and Eric's. Though I appreciated Eric's offer, I knew that he'd be the last person I'd accept help from.

Oliver added, "But Summer knows that if she needs anything, then she better come to me." He cracked a grin, although I knew he would be hurt or even upset if I turned elsewhere first.

"Now that's what's up," Jackson said.

An hour later we laughed, talked, and of course, as Washingtonians, we debated politics, and sipped more wine while nibbling at extra servings of food. Eric was quite animated for someone who knew he'd slept with his girlfriend's friend, and Amber remained subdued but managed a few strained laughs and comments here and there. Her sister, Mara, turned out to be a pleasure; she offered humor and entertaining stories of dorm life in the Big Apple. Despite all the fun, we had grown a bit tired and generously infused with wine and champagne. The time to depart had come, especially since we had to go to work and the Grays needed to wake up for Las Vegas the next morning.

Brooke and Jackson stood first. Brooke told us, "Well, we should be on our way. This was really nice, and I had a ball meeting you." She pointed her head at Oliver and Mara. She shook Eric's hand. "It was nice seeing you again."

Jackson spoke the same sentiments as he and Brooke made their rounds to each person to say goodnight.

"I'm sorry, where's your bathroom?" Jackson asked Emily. She pointed down the narrow hallway of her open floor plan toward the front door. He thanked her before heading toward it. Brooke decided to check out the artwork in the living room adjacent to the dining room. She studied each painting with both hands tied behind her back as she clutched her purse.

Standing, Emily asked Eric, "Honey, can you handle the caterers and the tip?"

"Absolutely. I just need to go upstairs to get my wallet and checkbook." Eric looked at everyone. "If I don't get back down here on time, then please, drive safely and thank you all for coming. I hope to do this again." We thanked him almost in unison with a wave and shook hands before he took off to head upstairs.

I happened to catch a glance at Amber nervously adjusting her dress at the hem as she stood behind her chair. It was about to happen.

Turning to Oliver, I asked with fake nonchalance, "I hate cold cars. Do—do you mind warming up the car while I wait for the bathroom?"

Without question or suspicion, Oliver nodded. "Sure, baby. I can do that." Oliver shook everyone's hands before leaving.

"I'm going to go bring my rental around, so I'll walk out with Oliver, I suppose." Mara had to have known what was to come. Sadly, not Emily. She just stood there sipping on her wine as she watched her guests and caterers shuffle around in her home.

Amber nodded at Mara, like a silent cue that everything would be okay and to stick to the plan. Amber's eyes whipped at me for a second before she turned to Emily to ask, "M-may I talk to you for a moment?"

Emily placed her glass of wine down and with a wide smile, she replied, "Of course, sweetheart. What's going on? You seemed so out of it tonight."

Such bad timing. I took a subtle glance over my shoulder to check out what appeared to be an oblivious Brooke still looking at the artwork. One never knew with her. She probably knew how to listen without using her ears. My heart knocked around in my chest like a fierce African drumbeat, because I knew I had to stay to defend my knowledge of the "one-night stand" and to play the mediator. Not knowing how Brooke would react, my nerves stood on edge like two first-time tourists standing high on the Grand Canyon cliff. I could totally see her lighting into Amber about her life choices and making the situation one hundred times worse.

Amber sighed as she nervously knocked her fingertips together. "There is something that you need to know. Something bad happened and it involves you, too." Emily's eyes widened. She froze with her arms crossed. I heard footsteps and turned to see Eric's long legs fast approaching. What was Jackson doing in that bathroom, and why did Brooke have to be here to hear all of this? Eric apparently lost his pep as he realized what he walked into. To his consternation, his eyebrows jumped high into his forehead with the understanding that he'd have to do damage control. His eyes froze, and his legs reluctantly moved to close the gap between him and his girlfriend. Absently, the hand holding the check lowered to his side as he tried to assess the situation.

"What's going on?" he asked.

"Shhhh," Emily replied as she waved in his direction without taking her eyes off Amber. "Amber and I are in the middle of something, Eric. Go pay the caterers so they can get home, please."

Emily never turned around to discover that Eric never moved. I didn't realize that Jackson had come out of the bathroom until I heard his voice as he and Brooke discussed an intriguing painting. My eyes couldn't leave the sight of the talking triangle. In my peripheral, I could see the uniformed men walking in and out of the kitchen and the dining room. I could hear everything.

Eric cried, "No, please, honey." Panicked had already settled in, but Emily wouldn't turn to face him.

"Eric, please."

Pressing on, Amber continued. "Recently, I found out something. When we were eating lunch this past Sunday, you mentioned something that made me sick. That's why I went home, out of the blue."

"What? What did I say?" Nervousness suddenly washed over Emily as if she were guilty of something. Poor thing. Her hand suddenly fell to the table to steady her weight. Her mouth opened and her chest heaved almost aggressively. I had to turn around; I had to do it. I had to see Brooke slowly ease her way toward us with her eyes zoomed in on Emily and Amber. Jackson stood in the distance with his hands in his pockets curiously looking at everyone.

Clearly, Amber didn't want to wait and had reached the point of no return. It had to be that freaking wine. With her mind made up, her eyes were more awake now than during the entire evening. I could see the invisible ball of courage that she'd swallowed resting in her throat.

"One time, Summer and I went to the casino." Amber hesitated.

Emily nodded desperately. "Okay, go on."

"I met a man. He paid me for sex, and during lunch, you said Eric had a black eagle on his shoulder."

"Okay." Emily took a quick look back at Eric, who stood with his head cocked back and his nose squeezed between two long hands. She turned her attention back to Amber. "So, what about his tattoo?" she asked defensively.

Amber inhaled sharply with a hand on her stomach. "The man who paid me for sex . . . his name was Eric. I didn't think it was your Eric, but when you mentioned the tattoo, I knew it was your Eric."

Emily's eyes became glassy. Her mouth fell open. Her eyes darted madly about—everywhere but on Amber and Eric. She a hand on her stomach then steadied herself with two balled fists on the table. Her head tucked downward as she swept one heel back and forth over the wooden floor.

Brooke whispered, "I don't believe this." Then she repeated herself so they could all hear. She pointed her clutch at her. "I don't believe this, Amber. I knew this lifestyle of yours was going to backfire. Why couldn't you just be a secretary? You know, do something normal?" Tears fell over her cheeks. She swiped them frantically. "Emily was finally happy." Jackson marched over to Brooke. He placed his large hands on her tiny shoulders.

In his deep voice, he told her, "We need to go. Come on." He tried to turn her stubborn shoulders. "This is not our business, and we need to go now, Brooke." Jackson spoke firmly as she allowed him to turn her away.

Pointing her clutch one last time at Amber she called out through gritted teeth, "This is wrong. Wrong, Amber!" Amber sighed as Eric tried to placate Emily by placing his hands on her shoulders. My eyes glistened, and my vision blurred. I could only see them through a wavy bubble as my tears clouded my vision.

Emily shook him off vehemently. "Get off me." She took a few steps away from him, giving her back to the two of them with her face in my direction. I looked at her but she didn't look at me. Her arms folded against her chest with eyes that absently searched the floor.

With a voice of angst and regret, Amber explained to her friend, "Emily, I had no clue who he was. He definitely didn't know who I was."

Emily spun around, showing both palms at them. "So, wait a minute." She closed her eyes and exhaled before opening them again. "Eric paid for your company or service, or whatever it is you call yourself doing?"

Eric's head hung low as he raced an anxious hand through his salon hair. Looking up at Emily, he added, "Emily, we didn't belong to each other. I was just being a man. I had money to spend and I was lonely. That's it."

"Really?" Emily peered at them through crossed eyes. "Really?" She inched closer to them. "So-so-so, I should move on with a man who paid for sex and continue to eat croissants with the woman who saddled my ex-husband in the bed for money? Who does that? And don't blame this on being a man."

Eric tried to remain calm, but he didn't have a firm grip on the situation at all. "Emily, I haven't thought about her since that night. I only want and think about you." His tone had begun to crumble. "Can we please not let this destroy all of our progress? I never thought you and I would have this much headway so soon. We seemed so final when I met her."

"How much Eric, huh? How much did you pay for that?" Emily's balled fists flopped at her side. Eric's jaw clenched. "How much?" she demanded.

"A grand." Eric looked as pissed as he did ashamed for having to reveal his personal affairs.

"*What*?" she exclaimed sharply. "A grand? You really spent a thousand dollars for a piece of booty that you didn't even know? Did you know that this is what she does?" Emily's face contorted with humiliation and anger. She tossed a finger toward his groin. "You better check that dick for STDs! And if I caught something, too, I'm gonna kill you both!"

"I don't do it anymore, Emily." Emotionless, Amber looked defeated in a losing battle.

Emily shrugged. "And that reverses what you did?" Hurt washed over her voice. "How many times can you sock it to me, Eric? How many times do I have to get burned by your wild flames?"

Emotion gripped Eric like a tenacious pit bull. He really appeared to be distraught by the prospect of losing Emily. He held his hands together as he pleaded. "Emily. Yes, I know I messed up with my parents and then with her." He pointed in Amber's direction before he took steps toward Emily. One of his hands gripped her chin as he stared intensely into her hazel eyes. "I. Love. You." Eric's breathing intensified. "I love you. And if you think I would do anything to hurt you intentionally after what my family and I did to you, you must be crazy. You are dead wrong to think I want to get back out there in the dating scene and find another Emily. You are not walking away from all of this." Emily yanked her chin from his grip. She walked away a few steps with her arms folded.

Amber added, "Emily, I even asked him if he was married when he told me his name. He said he hadn't been married before."

Emily spun around so quickly I thought she was going to fall. "Excuse me? What did you say? *Never been married*? Is that what you've been telling all the ladies, man?"

Eric threw his hands in the air. "No! I only said that to *her*, because she didn't need to know a thing about me. I didn't want to reveal personal information about me." His hand cut the air. "Not a thing. So don't even go there."

Emily shook her head with folded arms as she turned her back to them once more.

I wiped the tears from my eyes; I didn't know what to say or do. My heart stopped when she looked at me with sudden realization.

"Why are you still here?" She pointed at me with a quick lift of her chin. "Why are you so quiet over there?"

"Emily," I started with a weak voice. My mouth shivered as I struggled to talk. "Amber told me in the cab. I knew."

Her arms dropped suddenly. "What?" she exclaimed. "Am I the only dummy in this room?"

I knew I had to fight for Amber. "Amber is really sorry. This whole week she's been soul-searching. I wanted to tell you." I shook my head as I struggled to keep my distraught tone even. "It just wasn't my place."

Emily nodded. "*Summer*? We ate lunch together. You really covered it well. You let me down."

I stood there speechless, ready to run and cry. Instead, I stood there and took it for Amber's sake.

She squeezed her eyes at me before pivoting to face Eric and Amber. "Eric! You sat here through the night, like everything was all right. At least I could tell something was off with Amber. But don't you dare think you are off the hook any," she warned her. "Eric, tell me, when would you have told me if Amber went home without saying anything? Because you tried to shut her up after dinner, didn't you?" Emily appeared too angry to cry and let down by the people she trusted most.

Eric sighed as he placed his hands in his pockets, his eyes cast down on his shoes. He gazed back up at Emily. "Knowing who she is now, of course I was going to tell you. I just don't appreciate her timing. I didn't want to embarrass you."

Sarcastically, Emily replied, "Oh, how magnanimous." She turned her back to them again as she ran a hand through her pinned-up hair. Stray hairs escaped from her gathered hair. She sighed before facing them again. "There is never a best time to break someone's heart." Her voice cracked as her sentence barely made it through her lips. Tears fell from her eyes and landed on the floor.

"Baby, please, don't cry. Please don't, please don't." Eric pleaded and tried to lay hands on her but she wedged away.

"Stop! Stop it, Eric. Knowing you has brought nothing but pain. You sat there the whole night putting on the greatest show of your life." In distress, Eric placed both hands on top of his head. "You are so good at deception that you don't even see it. And you know what, had you just told me when you found out who she was, I would have hated it, and I would have hated you for paying for sex, but you paid for it and it was my friend and then you tried to cover it up. This is sick and weird. You are so good-looking Eric, why did you pay her?" Emily held her head before speaking. "I mean, really. All you have to do is look at a woman and she'll fall in the bed with you, so what was it about Amber that made you pay?"

Eric dropped his hands at his sides. He gasped as his gaze fell into Emily's. I could tell that he dreaded answering her. "I was curious, bored and lonely with money to burn." He undid his tie. It draped around his neck.

"About what?"

"She was Black; it was a new experience."

Emily grimaced. "Nice." She walked away from him and headed into the dark living room. I turned around to face her back. "I'm Puerto Rican, so what? You trying to taste the rainbow?"

Amber met her in the living room. "Emily, it's a little too late." A drained Amber placed a hand over her chest. "But I'm no longer leading that lifestyle. When I realized what I did, I decided to become a better person. I would love to know what it's like to be loved. It hurt me terribly to know that I hurt you."

She turned to face her. Her vacant expression and cold voice told her, "No, Amber. You wish you hurt me but you didn't. To hurt me means that I expected more from you."

She snarled. "You disgust me." She walked back over toward Eric as Amber leaned forward, on the verge of a collapse. She held her stomach as she struggled to repress her angst. Eric clasped both hands behind his neck.

"And as for you. You and I will not be going to Vegas tomorrow. You and I will not be living together. You and I will not be trying for any type of relationship. And thank God we have no children, because I would throw up if I had to see you on my lawn."

Emily pointed upstairs and in a calm voice she said, "Get your shit and get out. Don't call me, because I can't trust another word that comes out of your mouth. I don't know who you are, but it's time I get past you. What we had was a lie, our marriage was a joke, and your family sucks anyway. I'll do this all on my own. And when I was sad I loved the color gray, but now that I see the light, it doesn't look so good on me after all. I'm going back to Rosado." She spun to me and came close. My heart dropped in fear. I had no clue Emily could lay down the law so fiercely. "I don't like what you did, but you did the right thing. You shouldn't have to clean up the mess of these idiots. So, thank you." I responded with a perfunctory nod.

Her hazel eyes darted between Amber and Eric. "I never want to see you two again." With that Emily strutted with the most confidence that she'd ever exhibited as she approached the front of her house and walked up the stairs.

We stood there alone. Eric plopped in the chair that Emily sat in for dinner with the tie still dangling around his neck and hands resting on each thigh. With an open mouth, his absent stare fixated on the wall opposite of him. I bet that if he could find the right words, he would've spoken them. He probably wanted to fight, but Emily's words knocked him out. Already defeated, no referee could help him up.

Amber cried in the dark. Even though my legs felt like spaghetti, they managed to take me to rescue my friend.

Helpless on the floor, she sat on her calves with her face buried in her hands. I didn't know how to help her to her feet, but I grabbed her arm and struggled to ease her up. I slid my arm around her waist and guided her toward the door and out of the house of heartbreak.

Oliver drove to Fran's home in silence. He didn't push, but I warned him upon settling into his car that I didn't want to talk. We arrived in front of Fran's house.

"Summer, you should go grab some clothes and come stay with me tonight." He rubbed my hair.

I knew my mascara had run and that I looked a mess. "I need to be alone," I whispered. "You understand?"

Disappointed, he nodded. "I do."

"Okay, this weekend you can pick me up."

"Will you move in? You know, until something works out?"

"Oliver," I pleaded. "Can we just let me deal with tonight?" I had a headache after watching two women lose each other.

"I'm sorry. Of course. I won't push."

Somehow, I managed a forced smile. "No, sweetie, please don't look at it like that. Tonight has been something I want to forget but it won't happen that way. I need to sleep on everything. My possessions may be gone, my friends are in shattered places, and we're no longer tight." I sighed. "It's just all a mess."

"Get some sleep, Summer, and call me tomorrow when you're ready." Oliver offered me an assuring smile.

"Thank you, Oliver." I gripped the door latch.

"Hey, I was promoted to sweetie tonight, so there's my bright spot."

"Well, where's mine?" I must've looked hopeless and solemn to Oliver, but it matched my feelings. "I'm sorry. I do need some sleep." My face leaned in so we could kiss. Oliver's lips were very comforting.

"You're so beautiful," he mumbled. His hand flipped my braid. I smiled as I climbed out.

"Thanks for the ride, sir. Good night."

"Good night, baby."

When I landed on the porch and turned the key, Oliver waited for me to be inside safely before he drove away. The sexy sound of his car pipes quieted into the night. As tired as I felt, I managed to climb the stairs. A shower had a place on my agenda tonight. I had no clue that I would be so happy to be rid of tonight's outfit. Dinner had turned into such a disaster. Why did I act so shocked? Tears threatened my eyes again as I turned on the water faucet. When I hopped in the shower, I let it all out.

Memories of a pissed-off Emily flashed in my head. Brooke pointing at Amber with her clutch pushed out the prior memory. Seeing Emily sashay away from us made me sad. Hearing those words of dismissal to Eric placed a black cloud over my head. That sealed her fate of a happy ending with Eric. My wet head shook. Being with Eric made Emily so happy. She really didn't deserve to be hurt.

At least I had the smell of coconuts in my hair, although I'd welcome another fragrance to bask in, but I was happy to be enveloped in the familiar scent. Hell. That smell had been there for me this whole week amid chaos. It had almost become my therapy session in a shower.

Out of the shower, I returned to my room wearing a towel around the top of my chest as I headed back to the bed. I lathered in the matching lotion before donning my new ankle-length nightgown. Fran seemed to be a little cheap with the heat so I decided to grab the capped-sleeved nightgown from the sale rack to add to my splurge. Not my usual style but it was nice to have something that reminded me of my childhood days. My mom used to tuck me into bed wearing something similar to this. It didn't matter anyway. I probably wouldn't wear it once I moved out of here, which would be soon if I were to accept Oliver's offer.

A lot weighed on my mind like an elephant on a scale. A wave of sadness washed over me again as I crawled under the sheets and onto my side. I had a slim chance of falling asleep, but I had to try; sometimes just lying still with thoughts running through my mind provided the best medicine for sleep. Usually, before I knew it, slumber would take hold of me and I'd end up waking with nothing solved. Take Oliver, for instance.

Whenever I was around him, the world felt safe and sweet. He made me feel like I could learn things from him, and around him, anything felt possible. He was a very handsome man to whom I was attracted. He wasn't the kind of guy that would walk in the room and make every woman want to drop their panties. That would be Ruben. He was the suave one. On the other hand, Oliver could walk into the kitchen and a sudden wave of desire would take me away from cooking, and I would just ravish him. A hot man on the outside with a substance on the inside, that made him desirable. To me, that would last a long time. Somehow, I got the feeling that whatever sizzle Ruben had would fizzle in time after becoming used to his shenanigans. I guess he'd be what they would call a fine distraction.

Moments later, I could feel myself drifting off to sleep. Even in my second stage of sleep, I could tell something seemed different. I heard a faint noise. Something felt off, as if I were no longer alone and being watched. My heart started to beat rapidly as I forced myself to stay calm while pulling myself out of sleep's grasp. My muscles wanted to relax, but I had to gear them for movement. Still on my side, I reluctantly decided to shift on my bed as I needed to identify the odd presence that I could feel. I sent a quick mental prayer to God that Fran didn't have any weird activity in her house. Finally, on my back and arched on my elbows, I could see that something was in my room and it shook me to the core with rapid shallow breaths.

Brooke

Jackson parked his car and took Brooke to one of his favorite romantic locations. In Georgetown, he surprised her with a place Brooke had always heard of, but had never been: the Chesapeake and Ohio Canal. He walked her to the pedestrian bridge that overlooked the towpath that ran along the canal. The Potomac River—the canal's body of water—raced from Georgetown to Cumberland, Maryland, for many, many miles. The idea was to allow them to enjoy the scenery. He wanted to help relieve her of the angst from the disastrous dinner party.

His hand rested on the lower half of her back as her breasts pressed against the railing of the bridge. Joy flashed in her eyes as she peered from the water to him.

"You just don't know. I've always wanted to come here, but I didn't have anyone to enjoy it with. Have you been here with a woman before?" She sniffled, still recovering from being upset.

Jackson playfully tried to hide a grin by pursing his lips to the side. "Well, yes. A few years back, but she and I didn't work out. She became too pushy, too fast."

Brooke rolled her eyes. "Of course." The slight wind pushed through, whipping Brooke's hair against her cheek. "Look, I'm sorry that tonight turned out to be a mess." She shook her head to move her hair from her face. "I had no clue that Amber had a sick confession to make."

"Maybe you should wait a few days before you determine who's right and who's wrong, you know? Let it blow over first."

She turned her eyes from the water to him. "I know who's wrong: her."

Jackson let out a quick laugh of disbelief. "Brooke . . ." He looked away and then back to her. "I think you should stay out of it and let them work it out. And you should remain neutral."

"Okay, maybe you're right, but anyway, I have something to ask you."

"Okay."

"We may not be sitting down, but we're alone." Brooke decided that she had to get something off her chest. It was one thing to know how they felt about each other, but it was another to know what they each expected in the future. In regards to love, there was never the right moment to discuss future expectations. Couples just had to wait for a tasteful moment and throw it out there with fingers crossed. With the night and the romantic scenery, it seemed appropriate to discuss their future.

"I realize that." Jackson stood with his hands in the pockets of his wool coat, waiting for her to proceed.

"Tonight, at the dinner table, you said that we would have to sit down to discuss our future."

"I did."

"Well, some things have been on my mind. And one of those things is knowing if we have a common ground or not."

"Common in what way?"

She bit her lower lip. "Well, one of the things I would like to know is how you feel about children. I know that if we work out, you would be open to marriage, and we will work that out if it's meant for us. I agree." She exhaled. "If we find that down the line we're compatible, then, yes, why not talk about the next step involving you and me."

"I think we should worry about enjoying each other before factoring in children, don't you think?"

"Yes, but I need to know how you feel about parenthood, even if it happens ten years from now. Who knows what the future holds, but certainly we should know each other's attitudes."

His jaw became firm. "Brooke, would you also like to know if we will be living in a foreign country five years from now? I mean, come on, girl, you're jumping the gun here."

Irritation swept over Brooke. "And you're dodging my question."

"What is with this bridge? Is it so romantic that women become entranced with the future? Man." He pinched the inner points of his eyes. "You want to clear it all out, then let's go for it, Brooke."

The quick increase of her heartbeat mimicked the tempo of a dance track in a club. *Why was he suddenly being so harsh?*

"Let's get down, dirty, and honest Brooke. You know I have a sister, right?"

Brooke didn't feel like talking anymore, but she indulged him. "Yes," she replied through gritted teeth.

"She already had a child." His tone turned hostile and louder.

"What does that have to do with us, Jackson? What, only one of you guys can have a child?" she asked facetiously. Brooke held onto the railing with one hand for support. Suddenly, the cold air didn't bother her anymore. The coldest wind couldn't compare to Jackson's sudden shift in attitude.

"She *had* a daughter, Kristina, who fell ill and died." Jackson immediately became flushed with angst, and Brooke felt like a jerk.

She placed a hand on his back. "I'm so sorry, sweetheart. I really didn't mean to—"

"I know." He nodded as he reluctantly met her eyes.

"But, Jackson, what does that have to do with *you* not having children?"

He smacked his hand against his wool-covered chest. "I took really good care of her as an uncle. Her dad didn't want to have anything to do with them. He wasn't ready to be no one's father. Kristina and I had a very strong bond. When she died a year ago, it felt like I had lost my own child. Do you know how devastated my sister was? I felt her pain on top of mine." Tears welled up in his eyes, and Brooke considered that perhaps she had pushed too hard, too soon. But she couldn't have known, she assured herself.

"No, no. I cannot imagine that, Jackson. It sounds horrific, and I feel terrible that your sister had to go through that and that you had to endure that type of pain as well." Brooke shook her head as she imagined seeing Jackson bear that type of pain day in and day out. "So, how did you move past it?"

"I haven't. I moved on with life, but I still miss that girl. Imagine a little four-year-old girl being wiped off the face of this earth. It hurts, Brooke, it hurts."

Brooke still didn't understand one important factor. At the risk of sounding selfish or inconsiderate, she confessed, "And you'll never know how sad I am about this, and I hate that you had to go through that. I am so, so sorry, sweetheart. But, Jackson, I'm still confused. I know that you had to deal with more than you ever thought possible, but I don't understand how that affects us."

Jackson just stared into her eyes. The frown lines that developed around his mouth hinted that he might be disgusted at her. "You don't see it, do you? I don't want to go through that again. I love you so much, Brooke, I do. But you are asking me to have a child one day in the future and risk losing him or her. That pain is not worth revisiting."

Her hands waved frantically. "Wait, wait, wait, wait, wait," she rapidly begged. "So, you think that if we have a child, he or she will die? Are you living in fear?"

"Fear? Fear? It's reality, Brooke. It's a nasty feeling that anyone is better off not experiencing. I don't know how my sister lived through that. Kristina wasn't even my daughter, and it destroyed me."

"Jackson, no, Jackson, no." She fought to be heard. "You were not destroyed because you are still here. You can love me to pieces, more tomorrow than today, and lose me. Then what? Should you not fall in love out of fear?"

He frowned. "Don't be a smart aleck. You can't help it if you fall in love with someone. You can help having a child. You take birth control, and to really be in control, I can wear a condom."

Brooke felt a sucker punch to her gut. "Listen to yourself. Listen. You are not God. How many people do all that they can and still have babies? So, you may want to consider abstinence? Jackson, wake up. I don't believe that you would throw your genes away out of fear. She wasn't your child. Kristina was your sister's." Brooke panted as anger stole her breath. People in the distance were looking back and Jackson stared at her like he could light her head on fire with his eyes. "What?" she yelled.

Emotion ruled Jackson's eyes as he fought back tears. He exhaled as he appeared to be searching for answers in the canal. His eyes rolled to the sky and back down to the ground. Struggling to stay warm, his hands were buried deep into the pockets of his coat as he slightly bounced on his toes. He shook his head, placed one heel on the bridge rail and stared out into the Potomac River. Finally, he took one look at her and whispered, "Damn."

Scared of what he would say, Brooke couldn't look at him. Her hands covered her cheeks as she desperately wiped tears from her eyes. In that moment, she questioned if women really did need children. What if she and Jackson could just be happy alone? Wouldn't it work? What about those moms who have difficulty conceiving? They have to learn to live without children. However, she realized that husbands usually supported the idea of adoption. The realization occurred that some women do not want children, but that didn't include her. Many men wanted children, too. Her mom stole her happiness during childhood, and letting Jackson win would be allowing a man to steal her happiness during adulthood. She would be known as the woman who had a stellar career and nothing else. Over time, resentment towards Jackson would build up, and she never wanted to hate him.

Her voice quivered in despair. "When were you going to tell me?"

"What, that I didn't want children?" He shrugged as he continued to rest on the bridge rail. "I guess I assumed that a heavily career-oriented woman could do without them. I didn't know the right time to talk about this children stuff. Actually, I was hoping it would never come up. But I knew that was naïve of me, perhaps stupid."

Instead of speaking, they glowered with turned heads.

"Jackson?" Brooke turned to him with her hands in the pockets of her coat. He turned to look at her with a raised eyebrow. It was safe to assume that her romantic world was crumbling and that she would be back in the dating market. Brooke didn't expect to be at that place anytime soon, but playing the fool for anyone didn't fall under one of her strongpoints.

"I want to hear you say it." Her head nodded once, as if to give him permission to break her heart. Silence. Brooke sensed that Jackson knew exactly what she wanted to hear. He already knew her well enough and playing games was something that straight shooters didn't do. His body straightened as he turned to face her. His eyes softened. Heart-wrenching words were in the works. Inside, she braced herself for the collision of aspirations. Too bad life didn't come with emotional safety belts, she realized miserably.

Closing her eyes while biting her bottom lip, she prepared herself to hear his words. He cleared his throat, but it didn't help his cracked voice.

"I'm not having any children with you or any other woman."

Somehow, she heard him loud and clear.

And it was a done deal.

The idea of living without him went down as easy as a porcupine in her throat. She could feel her head become lighter, as if it were made of air. Could feel the burn in her chest, as her heart smashed to pieces. Could feel his eyes studying her reaction, though she couldn't see him. Could only see memories of him rubbing her feet on the first date at her house; memories of him introducing himself while she sipped her coffee. Memories of him waking her out of her deep sleep while he pretended to be working on the other end of the phone. Memories of him driving them through the pedestrian-filled streets of DC in his red Challenger. Memories of them clubbing and having raw, hot sex outside against the brick wall. She could feel each fiber of her being slowly peel away as she relived it.

Brooke opened her eyes to see his cheeks coated in tears. With a barely audible voice, she asked, "Are you sure?" Her eyes searched his, with pointless hope of finding a possible different truth.

His eyes dropped as he nodded absently.

"Okay." She wiped her tears. "Goodbye then, Jackson." She began to walk around him to head toward the street.

"Brooke?" They both spun around simultaneously to face one another. "I should take you home."

She shook her head vehemently. "No. I'm going to be on my own again, so a cab ride is what I need." Saying those words didn't feel natural. She turned around to leave.

"Brooke?"

Certainly, he was going to change his mind because seeing her literally walk out of his life would make him think straight, she reasoned. She turned around, but refused to show hope on her face.

"I love you with all of my heart. That will never change," he professed.

"Why?" She shrugged with irritation. "Where will that ever take us?"

Brooke turned and marched away from him on a mission. A mission to look forward, and never back, just like she'd done with her mom. Jackson fell into her past now, as much as that slashed her soul to admit it. Her mom taught her one inadvertent lesson: when people let you down, shut them down.

It worked for her in regards to her mother, so she figured it should certainly work in regards to Jackson. It may not be easy, but she would try.

Her arm stretched out in the cold air to flag a cab. And as usual, she didn't have to wait long for whatever she beckoned, including cabs. Brooke hopped in and told the driver where to take her. Her heart told her to steal one last look at Jackson, but her head told her to search for what lies ahead rather than behind. And even though she cried like a baby that night and shuffled restlessly in her sheets, Brooke held onto hope that one day, she would be the wedding planner of her own "big day" with a baby bump to show.

Amber

Across town, Amber kissed her sister good night on the cheek before heading toward the sofa. Mara sat up in her sister's bed before Amber cut off the light.

"Hey."

Amber froze with her hand on the switch before cutting the lights off. "Hmm?"

"Why'd you do it?" Mara plopped her hands on top of the comforter. "Why'd you confront your friend after dinner as opposed to before?"

Amber bit her lower lip in thought before releasing a sigh. "I . . . I didn't have the balls to do it sooner. I was a coward."

"But you said you did all that in front of your friends. Why?" Mara's perplexed expression couldn't hide the disappointment underneath the furrowed brows.

"I couldn't let her go to Vegas and make another memory with that man without giving her the truth. And I didn't mean to embarrass her by confessing around our friends, but I had sunk into a hole so dark that I wasn't thinking straight. I knew I had to speak up with the little bit of courage I had mustered." Amber shrugged. "I mean, there's never a perfect time or place to confess stuff like that."

"But, Amber, there's always a better time and place—I . . . I don't know, Sis. Emily made a memory with Eric at the table with friends tonight anyway. It just sounds dirty the way you did it."

"You—you're right. You're right." Amber nodded repeatedly, now lost in her own thoughts. "Looking back, I should've done it better, but I was the biggest pussy, because I was scared, Mara." She stared at the floor with wide eyes. Speaking almost more to herself than to her sister, she added, "I was just so scared."

Mara said, "You guys will figure it all out someday." She offered Amber a listless smile. With a chuckle, she added, "I still love you, even if Emily doesn't."

Amber stuck her tongue out at her before turning off the lights. "Good night, butthead. I love you, too."

Mara replied with a muffled, "Yeah, yeah."

She wanted her sister to have her bed the entire stay so she moved to the living room. Taking out a cigarette, she lit it up as she cuddled into the cushion with the heels of her feet pressed against her bottom. Locating her cell phone on the coffee table with her eyes, she picked up her phone and stared at Emily's name. She exhaled a puff of smoke before dialing Emily's number. If she tried her luck on slot machines, then she might as well try her luck with rejection. Amber figured she had nothing to lose. At least it'd be worth the gamble.

With the phone pressed against her ear, she waited for the dialing to stop and for the click to take over to reveal Emily's voice. Some may suggest that she give it time before calling, or even call her selfish for reaching out on the same night, but Amber felt desperate for Emily's forgiveness. Feeling the pain of losing their friendship ate away at her core.

The call went to voicemail.

Amber knew that she had to either prepare to be without Emily's friendship, or believe that one day it would repair itself. She wiped a tear from her eye and smoked the pain away. If she couldn't have another chance with Emily to show her how much of a good friend she could be, then she would have to prove it to her other friends. That is, if she still had them.

Amber pressed a thumb against her head, balancing her cigarette through two fingers. "You win some, you lose some," she whispered. "But I've lost more than some." Amber stared ahead resting her eyes absently on her piano bench, looking at the black Steinway piano that she'd purchased from Emily. A piece of Emily stayed with her, and for now, that would have to be good enough for her.

Emily

"Are you just going to throw everything away?" Eric pleaded more than asked. Not allowing herself to look at him, her eyes chased the cars that raced through her street. "Emily. I need you. Amber meant nothing—nothing. Please, please let me take you away from here so we can be alone to think. Come on, Emily, look at me." Eric spoke with a scratchy voice, burdened with emotion.

With folded arms, she turned at the neck to look at him out the corner of her eye. A stoic expression took over her face, her eyes void of expression. "What am I looking at?" she scoffed. When Eric had her attention, he struggled to find words to an unmovable woman.

"Is this how you want it, Emily? I paid for sex on a lonely night, she happened to be a skanky friend of yours, which I just found out tonight, and I didn't want to ruin your night with friends. You know I wouldn't have lived with that knowledge without telling you." He became breathless with shaky hands raking through his hair. "Baby, you were having a good time. I couldn't embarrass you like that. I'm not even into her. What are you doing hanging out with a woman like her anyway? Come on."

Emily spun hastily, just long enough to scream, "Well she's not in my life anymore. And neither are you!"

When Emily turned back to the window to study the cars, Eric became frustrated and gave up.

"Fine! Fine, Emily." Eric pointed a finger at her. "You're gonna wake up one day and realize that you threw away a committed man for an encounter that meant absolutely nothing to me." He stormed out of the bedroom and raced down the stairs. A few minutes later, Emily heard the door slam.

With her hands balled into fists at her sides, Emily didn't move in her cocktail dress. She watched Eric pack his trunk with his belongings. She was either back at square one, or in a new chapter in her life. Either way, Eric managed to make her feel like the dumbest teacher in the world. This time, Emily knew she had a lesson to teach, and it extended beyond the confines of her class.

When he finally drove off, Emily turned away from the window, void of all emotion except desire for revenge. Many thoughts ran through her head as she peeled off the clothes of the night that ruined her life. She froze for a moment, when she suddenly remembered Eric's comment the night that he had food prepared for her after work.

"Hey, a man deserves a secret or two, don't you think?"

Was this what the bastard meant? She didn't think she could become angrier than before. Old pieces of Emily disappeared with each layer of clothing removed. All her life, family and friends had accused her of being passive. She decided that that was no longer her. Whether she got scorched on purpose or by accident, the scars of her third-degree burns ran deep. Unfortunately, someone played with matches and she'd gotten burned. No amount of skin grafts or ointment could fix the damage. For the first time in her life, she felt justified in thinking that revenge was the answer. Do unto others as you would have others do unto you, she remembered. Someone was going to burn.

Summer

A tall, dark outline stood at my bedroom door. It entered and closed the door behind it. As it approached me, I almost started to scream, but the familiar voice quietly called out, "Summer."

"Ruben?" I gathered the sheets around my chin as I waited for confirmation.

"Summer. Yes, it's me. I need to talk to you." He stood at the foot of my bed. Startled, I jumped out of my bed and greeted him anxiously.

"What are you doing? Are you trying to get us caught? I mean there's no more us, but you know what I mean." I whispered firmly to mask my nerves. With legs as wobbly as jellyfish, I struggled to recover my nerves.

Ruben placed his big hands on my shoulders. He gripped me tightly, almost desperately. With his face just inches from mine, he said, "Summer." His accent did things to me that couldn't be ignored, like make my stomach flip.

"Summer." His breathing intensified. "Are you crazy for tempting me like this? You know I would fail." Ruben's hands stroked my arms up and down as he questioned me. "What do you think you are doing staying in my house?" he whispered loudly.

My whisper almost gave way to a louder tone. "Take your hands off me. We can't, so deal with it." I knew the perils of having him in my room behind a closed door and in the dark. As we stood in her house and down the hall, I realized that Fran was no longer the single factor. More importantly, I had Oliver in my life. Though we didn't share a commitment, doing anything with Ruben no longer felt right.

But he didn't listen. Instead, his forearm cradled my buttocks as he lifted me up. When I resisted by pounding his shoulders and back, my breasts flopped against his face.

"Put me down. Put me down," I demanded in a loud whisper. Ruben didn't listen. He rebelled by grabbing my thighs and hugging me against him. After locating the nearest wall, he moved toward it and steadied my back against its surface.

"Shhhhh, don't wake up the crow. You will love it. Trust me."

I knew I was in trouble when he didn't take me seriously. How could I get him to when we writhed together in the dark and becoming too loud would wake up my boss?

"Ruben, if you don't let me down, I'll scream."

"Go ahead." Those familiar full lips pressed along my neck and chest. The bulge in his pants grew as I felt his groin pressed into mine.

My arms fell lifelessly on top of his shoulders. Tears greeted my eyeballs as I struggled to choose consideration over pleasure. No amount of Oliver could rid my attraction to Ruben. This Cuban ruled my lustful ways and possessed my willpower before Oliver came into my life. On the other hand, I didn't count on feeling anything more than sexual attraction for Oliver. But the truth remained: he had been so good to me.

I closed my eyes, taking it all in. As he ravished my skin with kisses, I realized that Ruben reminded me of the buffet that a dieter always reacted to. Grappling with the temptation of a buffet meant avoiding the restaurants that had one. I played the dieter who felt the need to indulge in the buffet when faced with one. His lips connected with mine. As I tasted him, I couldn't say no. My legs hugged him from behind like they always do. His hands had somehow already snuck under my long nightgown, bunching the material at the top of my thighs. I could feel his hands cupping my bottom and caressing my cheeks. Ruben was right. Of course, I would love it. The only thing missing was the intercourse. And when I realized that that hadn't taken place, I knew there was a chance for self-redemption. Besides, considering what happened between Amber and Emily, did I really need to be thrown out on my ass?

Deep down, I really couldn't do this to Oliver. Even though I wasn't necessarily exclusive with Oliver, was that any excuse not to practice loyalty? Besides, if we did what we wanted until the actual confirmation of exclusivity, then how would we keep out intruders like Ruben if we kept planting seeds of temptation?

I had to disengage.

It wasn't the easiest or hardest thing to do. Without much effort, I managed to wiggle out of Ruben's grasp for the first time that night, because he probably thought I wanted to move to the bed. Finally free, I used all my little might to push him off me. In the dark, I could see his dreary eyes. Together we panted out of breath.

"What?" Ruben launched forward to continue, but I slapped him with full force. He stood there and held his cheek. "So, you like it rough now?" Even though he sounded confused, I didn't care. It became my job to make sure that Ruben got the picture.

I pointed an angry finger at him and through clamped teeth I warned, "Get back now, or I'll press charges if you touch me again. You do not have permission to touch me, now back off." I didn't whisper, but I didn't yell either.

Ruben realized that I'd definitively folded the boards to all the games, so he held up both hands in capitulation. Walking backward, he didn't say anything as he headed toward my door, showing himself out. I released one loud sigh of relief, because it felt like I had fought a monster from underneath my bed. At least his visit made everything clearer.

Kneeling over, I caught my breath. After straightening, I situated my nightgown and dived onto the bed to call Oliver. He picked up on the third ring.

He sounded casual but pleased to hear from me. "Well, hello there, baby. What's good?"

Desperation and anxiety choked my vocal cords. "Come get me, please. I've made up my mind. I want to be there with you."

"Then I'll be right over."

I left Fran a note with a brief explanation regarding my departure with assurance that I was fine and would see her at work. Luckily, Fran didn't hear any of my light commotion as I swiftly collected my belongings and locked the front door behind me. I left the room in the same condition as my first night there. The odd cloud hanging over my head all week had begun to fade. It never felt one hundred percent right living temporarily in her home with or without Ruben's presence.

I stood outside, shivering in the cold as I waited impatiently for Oliver to make it to Alexandria from Arlington. Ten minutes later, I heard the sexy familiar purr of his motor from a distance before his fog lights came into view. Resisting the urge to jump in excitement, I prepared to swing my laundry bag over my shoulder as Oliver hopped out of his car. He ran across the lawn, looking concerned until he reached me.

"Hey, baby, I got this." Oliver took the bag from my grip and easily carried it with one hand as we approached his car via her driveway. He placed his other hand on the small of my back.

"Thank you so much, Oliver, for coming to get me. You have no idea." Emotion gathered in my chest and congested my lungs. I could barely speak without difficulty. We reached his car and Oliver still managed to help me in first even with full hands.

Oliver tossed my bag into his trunk and joined me in his car. His eyes exposed concern as he eased up on the clutch to take off. "Sweetheart, what in the hell happened? You were just okay—well I mean that lightly considering our dinner fiasco."

"This whole thing." I placed a hand over my heart before continuing. "This was nothing short of a mistake. I knew this was going to happen."

"What?" He tried to steer while inspecting me.

"Can we talk when we get settled in?" I wiped a tear, saw him nod, and turned to the window.

We arrived fifteen minutes later at his parking garage. Once inside his refreshing apartment, he guided me toward his fireplace and turned it on, then headed to the kitchen to make us something hot. I sat at the base of the fireplace mantle as I dwelled on my living conditions and friendship matters. Now, the ironic constant continued to be this man named Oliver. Lost in my thoughts, I didn't even see him coming. Instead, the sight of his pointy dress shoes came into view along with a brown hand holding a mug of something hot.

"Hot chocolate for a hot woman."

I tittered. "Very corny but cute."

Oliver lowered himself beside me as we slumped over our drinks. "If you like whipped cream—"

"No. Thanks, Oliver. This is perfect." My hand ran through the top of my hair, moving it away from my face.

"Now, what happened?"

I exhaled, my eyes focused on his wooden floors. "You don't know what I have to tell you. It will possibly change the way you see me." He wanted to speak, but I held up a hand to cut him off. My eyes reluctantly greeted his. "Oliver, what I did was more than wrong as well as immoral. You will see me differently."

His expression became serious with undivided attention. "You should let me decide that."

We never broke eye contact. Once I decided that I could trust him enough to expose the truth, I relented. "Okay. You want to know, huh?" I smirked in shame before taking a sip of hot chocolate. It needed to cool off so I placed it beside me. "While my drink cools, I can tell you what I have to say." Oliver nodded in agreement.

"I grew up, as you know, with a single mother." I straightened my legs and knocked my toes together for a few seconds. I placed my hands flat on the mantle base with eyes focused forward.

"I'm listening." He sipped as he studied my profile.

"I didn't see marriage so I couldn't respect it. I mean, I know it's seen as something sacred, but that meant nothing to me, because I never witnessed it growing up. I had few friends, and most of them had broken homes. My mom rarely allowed me to visit other friends' homes, so I almost lived in a bubble. Went to college and, you know, all your friends are in dorms. So, what I'm really trying to say is, that is why I'm this way today. I don't see relationships as anything desirable, and I've been a loner all my life. I do independent just fine." I mustered enough courage to look him in the eyes.

"So, that's why you're so incredulous concerning the idea of becoming a couple?"

I nodded faintly. "I went to a party one night, a few months back with the friends you met tonight. Amber had an invitation and we escorted her." I reeled my legs back in and placed my forehead on my knees. My hair fell all over. I flung my head back up, revealing my face once more. "I met a man that same night."

"Oh." Oliver inhaled deeply and stared into his mug.

"We left the party together and had pretty hot sex outside. It was an unforgettable night." I turned my head in Oliver's direction. He placed his hot chocolate down and turned toward me. With a hand on his knee, he nodded once for me to continue. "My boss invited me out for dinner one night. Her husband was running late and it happened to be Ruben, the same guy I had met at the party. Now, you would think that would end any shot of seeing him again."

Oliver cleared his throat. "Forbidden fruit, huh?"

I rubbed my hands up and down my thighs nervously. "Guess so, because I warned him that we had to stop, but between the sex and red tape around our flings, it was enticing more so than repulsive. Everything was at stake and it kept me up at night, but only because he belonged to my boss, not so much because he was married. I became so ensnarled in his web of charm that I couldn't make rational decisions. When I tried, he didn't, and I couldn't pull away until . . . until I met you."

He reacted with a faint smile, but I saw the visible stress in the creases at the ends of his eyes. "I see."

"But, Oliver, there's more." I licked my dry lips. "I decided to forget him the night I met you. I told him that we were over, and I purposely looked for a man to help me move on."

"Me?" Uneasiness brushed across his face. I nodded with shame.

"Yup. I can say that I experienced an immediate and genuine attraction toward you. I really didn't think we would make it past that night, but we did and I don't regret it. Everything I did with you after that night was because I wanted it to happen, not because of an agenda."

"So, the first night we slept together, what was that?"

"I was trying to forget him. But I was drawn to you. After that first night, you did take away my thoughts toward him."

"So, I did my job, huh?" He seemed irritated and upset.

"Yes. You served a purpose, but after that, I associated with you because I found something within you. You were chilled, relaxed and genuinely nice. But there is more."

He exhaled. "Go ahead, Summer."

"Look, if you're going to hate me, I'd rather you hate me with all the facts so you can hate me right. Tonight, he came into my room."

Oliver's hands balled up. "That stupid bastard. I should go back there and rip his neck off." His eyes burned with anger as he gnashed his teeth with an immediate change in his breathing pattern. I placed my tiny hands around his shoulders.

"Please, Oliver. Calm down. He doesn't know about you. He just saw us tonight."

He peered at me. "Well, he knows about his wife."

Seeing him angered for the first time felt odd. While I found it sexy, it upset me to know that I had everything to do with it. My causing him pain made him angry.

"Yes, Oliver. But, please, let me finish." I took my hands back. As I continued, his pupils dilated and his lips snarled.

"Hurry."

"Even though I was falling back into his web, the more we kissed, the more I realized that it wasn't what I wanted anymore. Kissing him actually led me to you." I turned my knees toward him and placed a hand on his leg. "Oliver. It was at that moment with Ruben that I realized being with you was not so scary. I coulda' gone all the way with that creep all over again. Instead I sent him away. But, Oliver," a smile of relief replaced my stressed expression, "I felt like I was betraying not only Fran, but you, too."

"Wow. Another man has been in play." He swallowed hard and his eyes locked on mine.

"Well, just tonight after meeting you. I swear it." I couldn't lose him.

"Not happy that you were kissing some other man. Not one bit. I've always felt like you were mine." His rage dulled and then faded. "But I know you weren't."

"But at that moment," I grabbed and squeezed his hand, "I felt like I belonged to someone." Realizing how much I needed to be with this man, I couldn't stop the words from coming out if I wanted to. The bird that often flew the endless blue skies had found a resting point. Tired of flying and feeling withered with almost broken wings, the bird had a desire to seek shelter into a cage that wasn't so restraining after all. "It felt great, because I knew where I wanted to be. And that's with you."

One of Oliver's big hands covered my jawline with a palm. His thumb stroked my skin. "Only me, huh?"

With a smile, I nodded. "Yes. I only want to be with you, baby."

He cracked a huge smile, revealing one dimple. "I can't believe it. I finally have a promotion or two. You called me something other than by my name and you want to be with me."

"I do." I shrugged before Oliver grabbed me and hugged me close. "You may not want an unemployed woman though if Fran finds out about out the affair."

He gripped the back of my head by holding a handful of hair as we rocked side to side in each other's arms. "If she fires you, you won't be without. You'll have me." His words melted my heart. I wanted to cry, but managed to hold back. He pointed a firm finger at me. "But no more Ruben. You got it?"

I shook my head and whispered, "No. No more anyone."

"Fine. Then I'll take care of you," he smirked.

"Thank you."

He pulled back to read my face, closing in with a small kiss before progressing with passion. It grew deeper with need as it ignited a pang of lust. He eased me up by the arms, and I lifted them to let him know that I wanted to move on to the next step. He removed his shirt, too. I wasn't sure where my sweater landed, but I knew where his hand did. His hand squeezed between my thighs and up to my point of pleasure; I cried out with satisfaction.

"Summer," he whispered against my ear. "Tomorrow after work, you will take my card and go buy some new clothes. And if we find out Saturday that your valuable stuff is ruined, then we'll upgrade that, too. Okay?"

"No," I managed between heavy breaths. With my eyes closed and my head turned heavenward, I rebelled with a, "Don't."

"If you say no," he said as he nibbled my earlobe, "then we got problems."

Oliver ceased all movement as he waited for my decision. I thought he was playing until I second-guessed my assessment.

"I won't try to change your independence, but let me be your hero." He continued to whisper, "If you reject me, then you don't trust what we have. Do you trust me, Summer?" His hand gripped the back of my neck as my chin fell to his shoulder. With faces hidden from one another, our bodies did all the talking.

I didn't waste any time responding, because my realization had become clear. "Yes."

"You bring me sunshine, Summer. You live up to your name. Move in with me."

"You're so corny," I whispered.

"Is that a yes?"

"Okay. I don't want to lose you or break your heart. So, yes to both." I pushed away with my palms against his forearms. We stared at one another with smiling eyes and lips. I'd found happiness when I didn't know it could exist with a man. All my need for independence still resided within me, but I didn't wear it as a repellant, nor did Oliver try to take it away.

He stroked my face. "The most self-sufficient people accept help, but the dumbest people struggle unnecessarily, hiding behind pride. I'm glad you're one of the smart ones."

Oliver's lips covered mine as I reciprocated the affection. As we kissed, I realized that I wouldn't want it any other way.

As our hands moved wildly about on one another, I imagined him lying in bed with me at night, watching a movie with a bowl of popcorn. I imagined me massaging his shoulders after a long day of work. I imagined having a romantic dinner with him on Valentine's Day. The more I imagined, the more I felt happy to call him my own. If another woman did to me what I did to Fran, I wouldn't know how to handle it. They say you should put yourself in someone else's shoes to understand what he or she's going through. Now that my feet were in the shoes of one with a significant other, I could understand the devastation a betrayal could spark.

"You smell like coconuts and it's driving me crazy." He pushed his body into mine, and I could tell that he wanted me. I felt his hands on my shoulder, and he spun me around, pulling my jeans past my knees and down to my ankles. "Get over here." For once, I experienced all the pleasure without any kind of pain.

Feeling like a new woman, I marched down the hallway with purpose after greeting Jessica. Despite the tiresome events that transpired yesterday, the late evening moments with Oliver last night rejuvenated me. Obviously, I'd have to carry the usual morning weight with the other recruiters until Fran arrived, so I'd mentally prepared myself on the short ride here on the Metro bus. I'd rejected a ride from Oliver to avoid becoming too dependent overnight.

My closed office door came into view as I steadily approached it. Before I could reach the handle, a gentle poke on my back startled me as the familiar voice said, "I need to talk to you. Now."

When I turned to my right, I didn't see anyone until I turned to my left. Fran. She walked toward the head office at the end of the hall. I didn't bother to open my door or place my bag and purse down. Instead, I did as instructed and followed her.

Not knowing what to expect, I entered her office. I found Fran behind her desk with fists resting on top as if to hold herself steady. A stiff jawbone and tightly pressed lips replaced her normal smile that I'd grown accustomed to. I stood as scared as a child who heard something go bump in the night.

She ordered, "Close my door." Firm and direct.

I obeyed, savoring each moment that offered her my back. Knowing that the moment couldn't last forever, I willed my shaky feet to turn me so I could face her. When I did, her grim eyes scrutinized me like two laser beams that could burn through my soul. Chills needled my skin with discomfort and worry.

Was it normal for women in relationships to want to call their boyfriends in a time of fear? If my mom knew the truth about my affair with Ruben, I would want to call her for help, too. Even though I didn't know the exact reason as to why she summoned me to her office, I bet my latest clothing collection that it involved Ruben.

"Y-yes?" My voice trembled, my hands pressed together. I stood closer to the door than to her desk as I tried to hide my fear, but to no avail.

"You moved out. Why?"

Her demeanor wasn't as harsh as I'd thought. Exhaling before responding, I told her, "Oh. It was just time. Oliver wouldn't let up and I knew you two needed your peace. That's all, Fran." She nodded. I threw my hand out at her. "But I thank you. This past week would've been so impossible without you."

She crossed her arms and smiled. "Well you're welcome, Summer. And I'm sorry if I surprised you back there. I just wanted to honor your privacy."

"I appreciate that, Fran. You're fantastic."

She kicked her hand out. "Key. I mean as much as I love you . . ."

I giggled as I approached her desk. "No problem." I swung my purse over my stomach as I fished around for her keys. "All this junk, sorry." She nodded as I placed my cell phone on her desk. "These smartphones take up so much space."

"Tell me about it. I find it easier to just carry it by hand."

I chuckled. "True." When my fingers looped around a ring, I held up her keys like a fish reeled from the ocean, as I stared at them to make sure I had the right set. "Yup. Here you go." When I started to deposit the keys in her hand, my phone chimed.

"Thank you, dear. Whoo, early phone call."

Combing my hair away from my face before answering the phone, I said, "Yeah, probably, Oliver."

"Or probably not."

My eyes fell downward to see why she said that, and at that moment, I wanted to hide and die. Ruben's name appeared on my screen as my phone rang away. My eyes moved to her face, watching her face stiffen and turn as hard as stone. Her arms slipped back into a folded position. I no longer had control when my arms slid downward as my hands slowly moved out of my hair. My mouth parted and the only sound that came out was a cracked, "Uh—" Without a clue as to what I thought I was attempting to say, I felt a putrid burn of fear hit the back of my throat.

"I'm getting straight to the point, and I expect you to as well." Her firm voice choked with anger. "What is my husband doing calling you? And I know it's him, because I see the initial of our last name."

There. She did it. She asked. The room began to spin and my stomach dropped to my vagina, or so it felt. My heartbeat became rapid and my eyes widened with fear. My throat went as dry as the overcooked chicken breast I attempted to cook as an adult when I had my first roommate. I had visions of her calling the cops so they could escort me to the paddy wagon for sleeping with Ruben more than once; my wavy hair would conceal my shameful face. I had a quick flash of coworkers glaring at me with disappointment as the cops gripped me tight by the arms. They would want to throw paperclips, staplers, pens, mouse pads—anything they could get their angry little hands on. Both eyelids felt heavier than the mysterious fat kid who loved cake, and my eyes almost wiped out the unfortunate circumstances around me before I could hear the question in a sharp and demanding tone ask, "Is something going on between you two?"

Panic rushed over me with no sense of relief that the cat had finally come running out of the bag. The ax came down on my head in one quick whoosh. A quick vision of me in the unemployment line flashed before my eyes. I couldn't muster the strength to answer her for fear of what would happen. I closed my eyes, wishing it were a dream, willing her and this stuffy office to disappear. But when I opened my eyes to blurry details, nothing had changed. There she stood, my boss, with fists on the desk, as she waited for her answer.

Fran may have been waiting for my answer, but she wasted no time skirting around her desk to meet me up close. Solid anger bodied her eyes. As she demanded her answer, fury replaced the familiar smile that I had grown to love.

"Well? Is there something going on with you two? Why is he calling you?" The enunciation of each word was less of a question, and more of a need for confirmation. At this point, she had to have known. My overwhelmed expression was her nonverbal answer.

"Summer!" She stomped her foot at me. I jumped, hurled from my random thoughts of fear.

"F-Fran, come on," I implored. I didn't want to do it here, or anywhere for that matter. It was nearly impossible to push back the tears that were beginning to feel like a waterfall coating my eyes. The embarrassment was rushing into my system like an attack of bad bacteria on my immune system.

Fran spun around, huffing with her hand on her hip as she stared at the floor. Her shoulders rose and fell with every inhale and exhale. Now was my time to confirm her suspicions. With her back turned, I felt better because I was a coward. However, I was ready for all this to be out in the open. My intention wasn't to become the office whore, but I knew others were listening, or that they could at least hear our dirty laundry. She had already screamed my name, so people had to have known that it was me.

My fingers wiped at my runny nose. Reluctantly, I shifted my hazy gaze at her back, praying that she would never turn around. It was time to blurt out, "Yes, Fran. I slept with him. But I didn't know who he was though."

Instantly, Fran's little body swung around to meet my gawk. She placed a thoughtful hand underneath her nose. For a minute, she didn't say anything. "What do you mean?"

"Fran." My voice cracked and gave way to the stress of my emotions as tears ambushed my cheeks. "Fran, I met him at a party a few nights before you invited me to that first dinner." I shook my head vehemently. "I didn't know he was your husband. He didn't have a ring on. I swear."

She released a tight, bitter chuckle as she folded her blazer-clad arms over her chest. I wanted to believe that she was softening a bit, since she wasn't yelling at me.

"Summer, that may be the truth but you do realize that you slept with my husband, and smiled across the table from me as if you two had never met?"

I wanted to defend myself, but the truth was irrefutable. Fran would never understand nor care. She would see me as a slut just as much as I saw myself as a poltroon. I was Amber; I had wrecked a union. Fran was Emily, the victim.

"You fell for a man who had nothing until I made him somebody." She stabbed her chest with an angry thumb. I flinched. "He had nothing before I set him up with the job he has. And now, he would love nothing more than a divorce."

I tried to make sense of her story. "But if he married you, he must've loved you."

"Loved me?" We stared at each other. She titled her head back and threw her hands up in disgust. "My goodness, Summer, are all you little girls made so stupid these days? Marriage is not always about love. It's about opportunity. He wanted to be with someone who could take him places," another angry thumb stabbed her chest, "and I didn't want to be the typical successful woman without a husband? And by the way if no one has ever told you, it gets a little harder to compete with the younger ones." Her tongue fished around the inside of her mouth as she fell silent with a thoughtful look. "You think I don't know that he could land a young, hot bimbo?" She shook her head. "Who's dumber, you or him? I'm not sure at this point. But you know what? We took vows, and he will need to honor that." Her speech confirmed why I believed marriage wasn't any good. Her speech also revealed a woman with floating insecurities.

I'd calmed down some during her explanation of the madness between her and Ruben. "If he's not practicing them, then what's the point, Fran?" Perhaps I was overstepping, but I believed that paled in comparison to my transgression.

"So, you want to give me marital advice, huh? You," she twirled a hand at me as she snarled, "who has no husband. How can you tell me what to do with something that you don't even have?" I savored the brief respite of her broken gaze when she walked toward her desk, but I was back in hell again once she turned to face me again to rest her bottom against it.

I folded my arms and averted my eyes. "Touché, Fran. Touché." I didn't want to get ahead of myself, but I believed my normal breathing patterned had almost returned.

"How close did you let him get to you, Summer, for him to come back smelling like coconuts? Hmm?" She tilted her head, challenging me to defend my innocence, but she knew it was impossible.

Excuse me? Did she just mention my coconuts? "Y-you smelled coconuts?"

"A very faint smell of it. It was brief. But, I, the trusting one, believed that maybe he passed you in the hall or something and just brought the smell back in. I didn't think you'd rubbed it into his skin."

We were back to that again. My chest caved in a second time. "No. I didn't let anything happen, Fran."

Sarcastically, she replied through squinted eyes, "Oh, how considerate of you, Summer." Crossing her arms, she informed me, "You know something? The first time he cheated on me, it devastated me. I knew one day he would become a slave to his wandering eye and want to chase the geese. In fact, he can stab the dartboard until his little arrow falls off. But I wasn't going to move over so fast. Making him miserable has been the best revenge."

"That sounds . . ." I exhaled, not knowing that I had placed myself in such a huge crossfire between two twisted people.

"Horrible?" She waved an irritated hand at me. "Oh, please. We have so much hope as young women." She pointed a finger at me and tapped it in the air. "But life teaches you, little girl, that you can't go screwing with people." With crossed arms, Fran briefly studied me with softer eyes. "Had you approached me the first night with the truth, I would have been very disappointed. But I believe the creep partied without a wedding ring on. All of this is a shame, Summer, honestly. Because I really liked you. Instead, I found out like this—a stupid cellphone."

My heart sank, and she could see it. She pushed herself from against the desk and took her place in the chair behind it. This was not the Fran I knew. This one was intimidating in a way I would've never imagined. If her employees found her scary now, then they should try sleeping with her husband. As my brain computed the damages of this whole situation, suddenly, my purse and bag became too heavy. I wasn't sure if I let them drop or if my body gave out.

"But you lied to me, dear. You did it over and over, knowing you were wrecking a marriage." Her eyes dropped to my belongings on the floor. "Pick those up, you won't be here long."

I nodded nervously as I swept down quickly to pick up my belongings with the realization that my days of unemployment would start today. "Sorry."

"So, how many times, Summer? Because I think it is quite sick that you let him drive you home twice after you knew he was my husband. I opened my home to you, gave you my car, fed you, supported you." She released a perfunctory chuckle of disbelief.

"I know. You've been so won—"

"Did anything happen on those nights?"

"I broke it off after the dinner date at your house. I never wanted to continue, Fran, after I found out the night of our first dinner." The hard tears were back.

"How many times?" She didn't give up as she tapped a fingernail on the wood.

Fran appeared too calm. I knew that she would explode any moment. She didn't have to know that we did it twice on the night he drove me home after the first dinner date with her. So, I lied. "Three, Fran. Three times. Twice after I knew you were his wife. And for what it's worth, I'm so, so incredibly sorry." The confession was refreshing, but I felt so dirty at the same time.

Fran rested her elbows on top of the desk and pressed her hands together. With a nod, she stared everywhere else but at me. "Oh. Okay. Okay."

I stood there and watched her boldly, as long as her eyes didn't fall on me. It felt like an eternity before she spoke again. Fran placed her reading glasses on her face. She didn't look at me as she picked up a pen to write something that I couldn't discern from a distance. It appeared a flare-up wasn't imminent after all.

"Well, dear, I hope it was all worth it." She continued to write as she spoke with her eyes on her paper. "I hope you enjoyed recruiting, because you killed a career that would have been stellar with my assistance." She spoke very calmly, as if she were discussing the weather with little interest.

My chest burned, my skin was on fire. My body shook as I grasped the collapse of my own future from my own wrongdoing. A crack of horror eased from my throat, one I'm sure she heard.

"You will have to live with the fact that you shattered your career at the hands of your own foolishness while contributing to the destruction of a marriage. Someone will pack and mail your belongings."

With a burdened chest, I could only muster a slight, "'Kay."

"Oh, wait, darling." It was almost like a taunt. She removed her reading glasses to tell me one more thing with a smile on her face with a tone no higher than a whisper. "Don't even exhaust yourself with trying to get a job with the big dogs. I will take care of that, and you can continue to take care of Ruben, if it pleases you. I hope Oliver knows who he's dealing with."

I shook my head at her, angered by the mentioning of Oliver's name. When I turned to leave, she called my name, stopping me in my tracks.

When she had my attention, she said, "But, you know, I hear fast food is always hiring."

She shrugged with one shoulder and winked at me. From irate to calm, she took me by surprise and shook me to my core. I couldn't stop looking at her, but now hatred replaced my fear, and she could see it. Her smile never faded, but she broke our duel of the eyes by replacing her glasses on her face as she resumed writing with her pen.

Angry and humiliated, I spun around and flung open her door and took off past bewildered coworkers, bumping random shoulders, squeezing past familiar and unfamiliar faces. Tears tracked my face, my eyebrows furrowed. I heard my name called with confusion. I heard someone asking another person if I was okay. In my peripheral, I saw Jessica in the reception area sitting behind her desk. I heard her concerned voice call my name before my hands pushed the glass doors open with all my might. I marched down the carpeted hallway and approached the elevators, but ended up choosing the stairwell.

In my heels, I flew down seven flights of stairs, landing at the foyer with the security guard behind the desk taking the identification of people who wished to have access to the secured elevators. Reaching the main doors to the building, I rushed out into the crowd of people and into the busy streets of Ballston.

Brooke had admitted to Jackson what she wanted in life, and lost what she'd found. Amber had decided to be truthful to her friend, and had lost that friendship, too. Eric had confirmed Amber's story as true, and Emily decided to cut her ties with him. Now, backed into a corner, I was forced to admit to my boss that I'd slept with her husband more than once, and it cost me my career. We're advised in our lives to tell the truth no matter what, but no one could ever tell you the exact price of admission.

Without a destination in mind, I marched down the sidewalk, mindlessly dodging strangers as I raked random windblown strands of hair from my face and mouth. I didn't know where my pointy heels were taking me, but I knew a serious chapter of my life had closed all too soon.

Please remember to leave a review on Amazon. I appreciate your feedback!

Follow me @ . . .
Facebook: www.facebook.com/dawn.wright.54738
Instagram: dawnwright_author
Twitter: Dawn Wright@_dawn_wright
Email me at: authordawnwright@gmail.com
Sign up for my newsletters to find out what's new at
www.dawnwrightbooks.com/newsletter/
To learn more about Dawn Wright visit
www.dawnwrightbooks.com/interview/

acknowledgements

Proofreader: Dianne McCann
Editor: Richard "Tony" Held
Cover design by C. Winey
Cover Model Photography by Evan Christopher Photography
Cover Model: Starleigh Caldwell

<u>*The Capital Trilogy*</u>
Capital Encounters (books one)
Capital Consequences (book two)
Capital Resolutions (book three)

Next Release: Capital Consequences, spring 2017

About the Author

Before committing to writing novels, Dawn Wright, spent a decent amount of time teaching and studying business, while having a fascination for the corporate environment.

Determined to someday make the workforce a place where employees would want to work without dread, she made it her mission to obtain her masters in human resource management. However, in her last semester, two classes away from graduation in fact, she pulled out her laptop for other than studying or Internet surfing, and decided to give life to Capital Encounters. Unaware that this book would lead to a trilogy, she set it to the side to keep from compromising her GPA. After years of countless and persistent prayers, she realized that her book didn't have to be second to a traditional career, but that by stepping out on faith, it was just time to say goodbye to what was expected and hello to passion.

Dawn Wright currently lives in Alexandria, VA as a full-time writer. She frequents DC when she and her boyfriend feel like crossing the bridge. Ever since writing her first book, there's never been a time that she doesn't visit DC without feeling like her characters are right down the street.